The Tiger Hunter

by

Captain Mayne Reid

Double9
BOOKS

The Tiger Hunter
by Captain Mayne Reid

ISBN: 978-93-61156-46-5

Published by

DOUBLE 9 BOOKS

2/13-B, Ansari Road
Daryaganj, New Delhi – 110002
info@double9books.com
www.double9books.com
Tel. 011-40042856

This book is under public domain

ABOUT THE AUTHOR

Thomas Mayne Reid, an Irish-American novelist, participated in the Mexican–American War. His numerous books on American life discuss colonial policy in the American colonies, the horrors of slave labor, and the lifestyles of American Indians. "Captain" Reid created adventure stories similar to those of Frederick Marryat and Robert Louis Stevenson. They were primarily situated in the American West, Mexico, South Africa, the Himalayas, and Jamaica. He admired Lord Byron. Dion Boucicault turned his anti-slavery novel Quadroon (1856) into a drama called The Octoroon (1859), which was staged in New York. Reid was born in Ballyroney, a hamlet near Katesbridge in County Down, Northern Ireland, as the son of Rev. Thomas Mayne Reid Sr., a senior clerk of the General Assembly of the Presbyterian Church in Ireland, and his wife. Reid's father intended him to become a Presbyterian pastor, so he enrolled at the Royal Belfast Academical Institution in September 1834. He stayed for four years, but lacked the ambition to finish his studies and graduate. He returned to Ballyroney to teach at a school.

CONTENTS

Prologue

During one of many journeyings through the remote provinces of the Mexican republic, it was my fortune to encounter an old revolutionary officer, in the person of Captain Castaños. From time to time as we travelled together, he was good enough to give me an account of some of the more noted actions of the prolonged and sanguinary war of the Independence; and, among other narratives, one which especially interested me was the famed battle of the *Puente de Calderon*, where the Captain himself had fought during the whole length of a summer's day!

Of all the leaders of the Mexican revolution, there was none in whose history I felt so much interest as in the *priest-soldier*, Morelos—or, as he is familiarly styled in Mexican annals, the "illustrious Morelos"—and yet there was none of whose private life I could obtain so few details. His public career having become historic, was, of course, known to every one who chose to read of him. But what I desired was a more personal and intimate knowledge of this remarkable man, who from being the humble curate of an obscure village in Oajaca, became in a few short months the victorious leader of a well-appointed army, and master of all the southern provinces of New Spain.

"Can you give me any information regarding Morelos?" I asked of Captain Castaños, as we were journeying along the route between Tepic and Guadalaxara.

"Ah! Morelos? he was a great soldier," replied the ex-captain of guerilleros. "In the single year of 1811, he fought no less than twenty-six battles with the Spaniards. Of these he won twenty-two; and though he lost the other four, each time he retreated with honour—"

"Hum! I know all that already," said I, interrupting my fellow-traveller. "You are narrating history to me, while I want only chronicles. In other words, I want to hear those more private and particular details of Morelos' life which the historians have not given."

"Ah! I understand you," said the captain, "and I am sorry that I cannot satisfy your desires: since, during the war I was mostly engaged in the northern provinces, and had no opportunity of knowing much of Morelos personally. But if my good friend, Don Cornelio Lantejas, is still living at Tepic, when we arrive there, I shall put you in communication with him. He can tell you more about Morelos than any other living man: since he was *aide-de-camp* to the General through all his campaigns, and served him faithfully up to the hour of his death."

Our conversation here ended, for we had arrived at the inn where we intended to pass the night—the *Venta de la Sierra Madre*.

Early on the following morning, before any one had yet arisen, I left my chamber—in a corner of which, rolled in his ample *manga*, Captain Castaños was still soundly asleep. Without making any noise to disturb him, I converted my coverlet into a cloak—that is, I folded my serape around my shoulders, and walked forth from the inn. Other travellers, along with the people of the hostelry inside, with the domestics and muleteers out of doors, were still slumbering profoundly, and an imposing silence reigned over the mountain platform on which the venta stood.

Nothing appeared awake around me save the voices of the *sierras*, that never sleep—with the sound of distant waterfalls, as they rushed through vast ravines, keeping up, as it were, an eternal dialogue between the highest summits of the mountains and the deepest gulfs that yawned around their bases.

I walked forward to the edge of the table-like platform on which the venta was built; and halting there stood listening to these mysterious conversations of nature. And at once it appeared to me that other sounds were mingling with them—sounds that suggested the presence of human beings. At first they appeared like the intonations of a hunter's horn—but of so harsh and hoarse a character, that I could scarcely believe them to be produced by such an instrument. As a profound silence succeeded, I began to think my senses had been deceiving me; but once more the same rude melody broke upon my ears, in a tone that, taken in connexion with the place where I listened to it, impressed me with an idea of the supernatural. It had something of the character of those horns used by the shepherds of the Swiss valleys; and it seemed to ascend out of the bottom of a deep ravine that yawned far beneath my feet.

I stepped forward to the extreme edge of the rock, and looked downwards. Again the hoarse cornet resounded in my ears; and this time so near, that I no longer doubted as to its proceeding from some human agency. In fact, the moment after, a man's form appeared ascending from below, along the narrow pathway that zigzagged up the face of the cliff.

I had scarce time to make this observation, when the man, suddenly turning the angle of the rock, stood close by my side, where he halted apparently to recover his breath.

His costume at once revealed to me that he was an Indian; though his garments, his tall stature, and haughty mien, lent to him an aspect altogether different from that of most of the Indians I had hitherto encountered in Mexico. The proud air with which he bore himself, the fiery expression of his eye, his athletic limbs, and odd apparel, were none of them in keeping with the abject mien which now characterises the descendants of the ancient masters of Anahuac. In the grey light of the morning, I could see suspended from his shoulders the instrument that had made the mysterious music—a large sea-shell—a long, slender, curved conch, that hung glistening under his arm.

Struck with the singular appearance of this man, I could not help entering into conversation with him; though he appeared as if he would have passed me without speaking a word.

"You are early abroad, friend?" I remarked.

"Yes, master," he replied; "early for a man as old as I am."

I could not help regarding this as a jest; for over the shoulders of the Indian fell immense masses of jet black hair, which seemed to give contradiction to the statement of his being an old man.

I looked more narrowly into his countenance. His bronzed skin appeared to cling closely to his angular features, but there were none of those deep furrows that betray the presence of advanced age.

"How old are you?" I asked at length.

"That I cannot tell, cavallero," replied he. "I tried from the time I was able to distinguish the dry season from that of the rains to keep an account of my age; and I succeeded in doing so up till I was fifty. After that, for particular reasons, I did not care to know it, and so I left off counting."

"You say you are more than fifty years old?" and as I put this inquiry I glanced at the long purple black tresses that hung over his shoulders.

"Nearly half as much more," was the reply. "You are looking at the colour of my hair. There are ravens who have seen a hundred seasons of rain without having a feather whitened. Ah! what matters the course of years to me? A raven croaked upon the roof of my father's cabin when I was born, at the same instant that my father had traced upon the floor the figure of one of these birds. Well, then! of course I shall live as long as that raven lives. What use then to keep a reckoning of years that cannot be numbered?"

"You think, then, that your life is in some way attached to that of the raven that perched on the paternal roof when you came into the world?"

"It is the belief of my ancestors, the Zapoteques, and it is also mine," seriously responded the Indian.

It was not my desire to combat the superstitions of the Zapoteques; and, dropping the subject, I inquired from him his purpose in carrying the conch—whether it was for whiling away his time upon the journey, or whether there was not also connected with it some other belief of his ancestors?

The Indian hesitated a moment before making reply.

"It is only a remembrance of my country," he said, after a short silence. "When I hear the echoes of the Sierra repeat the sounds of my shell, I can fancy myself among the mountains of Tehuantepec, where I used to hunt the tiger—in pursuing my profession of *tigrero*. Or at other times I may fancy it to be the signals of the pearl-seekers in the Gulf, when I followed the calling of a *buzo* (diver); for I have hunted the sea tigers who guard the banks of pearls under the water, as I have those that ravage the herds of cattle upon the great savannas. But time passes, cavallero; I must say good day to you. I have to reach the hacienda of Portezuelo by noon, and it's a long journey to make in the time. *Puez, adios, cavallero!*"

So saying, the Indian strode off with that measured step peculiar to his race; and was soon lost to my sight, as he descended into the ravine on the opposite side of the plateau.

As I returned towards the inn I could hear the prolonged notes of his marine trumpet rising up out of the chasm, and reverberating afar off against the precipitous sides of the Sierra Madre.

"What the devil is all this row about?" inquired Captain Ruperto Castaños, as he issued forth from the venta.

I recounted to him the interview I had just had; and the singular communications I had received from the Indian.

"It don't astonish me," said he; "the Zapoteques are still more pagan than Christian, and given to superstitious practices to a greater degree than any other Indians in Mexico. Our Catholic *curas* in their villages are there only for the name of the thing, and as a matter of formality. The business of the worthy padres among them must be a perfect sinecure. I fancy I understand what the fellow meant, well enough. Whenever a Zapoteque woman is about to add one to the number of their community, the expectant father of the child assembles all his relations in his cabin; and, having traced out the figures of certain animals on the floor, he rubs them out one after another in their turn. That which is being blotted out, at the precise moment when the child is born, is called its *tona*. They believe that, ever after, the life of the newborn is connected in some mysterious manner with that of the animal which is its *tona*; and that when the latter dies so will the former! The child thus consecrated to the tona, while growing up, seeks out some animal of the kind, takes care of it, and pays respect to it, as the negroes of Africa do to their *fetish*."

"It is to be presumed, then, that the Indian father will make choice only of such animals as may be gifted with longevity?"

The captain made no reply to my suggestion, farther than to say that the Zapoteque Indians were a brave race, easily disciplined, and out of whom excellent soldiers had been made during the war of the Revolution.

After a hasty *desayuno* at the venta, my travelling companion and I resumed our journey; and, crossing the second great chain of the Mexican Andes, at the end of six days of fatiguing travel we reached the ancient town of Tepic.

Here it was necessary for me to remain some time, awaiting the arrival of important letters which I expected to receive from the capital of Mexico.

During the first week of my stay at Tepic, I saw but very little of my fellow-voyager—who was all the time busy with his own affairs, and most part of it absent from the little *fonda* where we had taken up our abode. What these affairs might be, God only knows; but I could not help thinking that the worthy ex-captain of guerilleros carried on his commercial transactions, as in past times he had his military ones—a little after the partisan fashion, and not altogether in accordance with legal rules.

After all, it was no affair of mine. What most concerned me, was that with all his running about he had not yet been able to meet with his friend, Don Cornelio Lantejas—whom no one in Tepic seemed to know anything of—and I was beginning to suspect that the existence of this individual was as problematical as the business of the captain himself, when a lucky chance led to the discovery of the ex-aide-de-camp of Morelos.

"Don Ruperto appears to have gone crazy," said Doña Faustina, our hostess of the fonda, one morning as I seated myself to breakfast.

"Why, Doña Faustina?" I inquired.

"Because, Cavallero," replied she, evidently piqued at the captain's disregard of her hospitable board, "he is hardly ever here at meal times, and when he does show himself, it is so late that the *tortillas enchiladas* are quite cold, and scarce fit to eat."

"Ah, señora!" replied I, by way of excusing the irregularity of the captain's habits, "that is not astonishing. An old soldier of the Revolution is not likely to be very punctual about his time of eating."

"That is no reason at all," rejoined the hostess. "We have here, for instance, the good *presbitero*, Don Lucas de Alacuesta, who was an insurgent officer through the whole campaign of the illustrious Morelos, and yet he is to-day a very model of regularity in his habits."

"What! an officer of Morelos, was he?"

"Certainly; all the world knows that."

"Do you chance to know another old officer of Morelos, who is said to live here in Tepic, Don Cornelio Lantejas?"

"Never heard of him, Señor."

At this moment Don Ruperto's voice sounded outside, announcing his return from one of his matutinal expeditions.

"To the devil with your tortillas and black beans!" cried he, rushing into the room, and making answer to the reproaches of his hostess. "No, Doña Faustina—I have breakfasted already; and what is more, I shall dine to-day as a man should dine—with viands at discretion, and wine, as much as I can drink, of the best vintage of Xeres! I have breakfasted to-day, good clerical fashion. Who with, do you think?" asked he, turning to me.

"Don Lucas de Alacuesta, perhaps?"

"Precisely; otherwise Don Cornelio Lantejas, who, on changing his profession, has made a slight alteration in his name; and who, but for a lucky chance, I should never have found till the day of judgment, since the worthy *presbitero* hardly ever stirs out from his house. Who would have believed that an old soldier of the Independence should so change his habits? In fact, however, we have had so many priests turned officers during the Revolution, that it is only natural one officer should become a priest, by way of compensation."

In continuation, Don Ruperto announced to me, that we were both invited to dine with his old acquaintance; and further, that the latter had promised to place at my disposition such souvenirs of the illustrious Morelos as I desired to be made acquainted with.

I eagerly accepted the invitation; and in three hours after under the conduct of the captain, I entered the domicile of the worthy padre, Don

Lucas de Alacuesta. It was a large house, situated near the outskirts of the town, with an extensive garden, enclosed by a high wall, rendered still higher by a stockade of the organ cactus that grew along its top.

We found our host awaiting us—a thin little man, of some fifty years of age, nimble in his movements, and extremely courteous and affable. He appeared to be one who occupied himself, much less with the affairs of his parish, than with the cultivation of his garden, and the preservation of entomological specimens—of which he possessed a bountiful collection.

Nothing either in his speech or features, as in those of Captain Castaños, recalled the *ex-militario*, who had borne a conspicuous part in the long and bloody campaigns of the revolutionary war.

It is not necessary to give any details of the dinner—which was after the fashion of the Mexican *cuisine*, and excellent of its kind. Neither shall I repeat the conversation upon general topics; but enter at once upon those scenes described by the ex-aide-de-camp of Morelos, and that of which our drama has been constructed.

Chapter One
The Grito of Hidalgo

The great revolutionary war of 1790 was not confined to France, nor yet to Europe. Crossing the Atlantic, it equally affected the nations of the New World—especially those who for three centuries had submitted to the yoke of Spain. These, profiting by the example set them by the English colonies in the north, had taken advantage of the confusion of affairs in Europe, and declared their independence of the mother country.

Of the Spanish-American vice-kingdoms, New Spain—or Mexico more properly called—was the last to raise the standard of independence; and perhaps had the wise measures of her viceroy, Iturrigaray, been endorsed by the court of Madrid, the revolution might have been still further delayed, if not altogether prevented.

Don José Iturrigaray, then vice-king of New Spain, on the eve of the insurrection had deemed it wise policy to grant large political concessions to the Creoles, or native white population of the country, and confer upon them certain rights of citizenship hitherto withheld from them.

These concessions might have satisfied the Creoles with the government of the mother country, and perhaps rendered their loyalty permanent. Mexico, like Cuba, might still have been a "precious jewel" in the Spanish crown, had it not been that the decrees of Iturrigaray produced dissatisfaction in another quarter—that is, among the pure Spaniards themselves—the *Gachupinos*, or colonists from Old Spain, established in Mexico; and who had up to this time managed the government of the country, to the complete exclusion of the Creoles from every office of honour or emolument.

These egoists, considering the acts of the viceroy ruinous to their selfish interests, and the privileges they had hitherto enjoyed, seized upon his person, and sent him to Spain to give an account of his conduct.

Tyrannous counsels prevailed; the prudent plans of Iturrigaray were rejected, and Mexico fell back into the same political bondage under which she had groaned since the conquest of Cortez.

The dismissal of Iturrigaray took place in 1808. The Gachupinos were not without apprehensions of an outbreak; but as two years passed over in tranquillity, their doubts became dissipated, and they ceased to believe in the possibility of such an event.

Theirs was but fancied security, and lasted only two years. In 1810 it was abruptly terminated by the rising of Hidalgo in one of the northern provinces, the news of which event descended upon the Gachupinos like a thunderbolt.

Strange enough that a priest should be the leader of this movement in favour of liberty: since it was through priestly influence that Mexico had all along been governed and oppressed! But in truth Hidalgo, and the other priests who figured in this insurrection, were a very different class of men from the great metropolitan ecclesiastics of the capital and the larger cities, who conducted the affairs of state. Hidalgo was but a simple village *cura*—a child of the people—and so, too, were most of the other patriot priests who espoused the popular cause.

In October 1810, Hidalgo had nearly one hundred thousand men in the ranks of his army. They were badly armed and equipped, but still formidable from their very numbers. This immense host, which consisted principally of native Indians, overspreading the country like a torrent, could not fail to produce consternation in the minds of the Gachupinos.

Even among the Creoles themselves it created a certain confusion of ideas. All these were the sons or descendants of Spaniards, and of course connected with the latter by ties of consanguinity. It was but natural, therefore, that some of them should believe it to be their duty to take the part of the government against the insurrection, while others should sacrifice the ties of family relationship to the more noble idea of liberating their country from a foreign yoke.

This difference of opinion among the Creoles existed only in families of the higher and wealthier classes. Among the poorer Mexicans—the people— whether white or half caste, there existed only one sentiment, and that was in favour of independence from Spain. The Indians of pure blood had their own ideas. They had been more enslaved than the Creoles, and of course readily united with them for the expulsion of the Spaniard—their common oppressor. Some of them also indulged in the idle dream that circumstances might restore the ancient splendour of the Aztec race.

Chapter Two
An Irksome Journey

In a morning of the month of October, a solitary traveller was pursuing his route across the vast plains which extend from the limits of the state of Vera Cruz through that of Oajaca. It is scarcely necessary to say that the traveller was on horseback—in a country where no one ever thinks of journeying on foot. He was armed also, as well as mounted; but both horse and weapon were of such an indifferent character as to be ill suited for an encounter with an enemy of any kind. This, too, in a country just then in a state of revolution, where the traveller might expect to meet with an enemy at any moment—either a political adversary, or one of those professional bandits with whom Mexico at this time abounded, and who robbed all alike, irrespective of party.

The only weapon our traveller possessed was an old curved sabre; but it was doubtful whether it could be drawn from its iron scabbard, which appeared as rusty as if it had lain for years at the bottom of a river. It was carried obliquely along the flap of the saddle, and under the thigh of the horseman—the common mode in Mexico—thus transferring the weight of the weapon from the hip of the rider to the ribs of his horse.

The steed of our traveller showed evident signs of having been at one time the property of some *picador de toros*: as was manifested by the numerous scars that traversed his flanks and counter; but whatever good qualities he may have once possessed, he was evidently now one of the sorriest of jades—worth no more than the value of his own skin. Notwithstanding the repeated strokes of the spur, which his rider administered without stint, it was impossible to force him into anything more rapid than a shambling walk, and at this slow pace was he proceeding, evidently to the great chagrin of the impatient traveller.

The costume of the horseman thus ill mounted consisted of a sort of jacket of white cotton stuff, with open *calzoneros* of olive-coloured velveteen. On his feet were short boots of goat-skin—dressed in imitation of cordovar leather—and covering his head was a broad-brimmed hat of common palmetto plait. Though not positively shabby, his garments had the appearance of having been a long time in wear, out of regard to economy. There was something, however, in their cut and texture that bespoke the wearer to belong to a class above that of the mere peasant.

He was a young man—apparently two or three and twenty—of slender figure and rather thin in flesh. His countenance bespoke gentleness of disposition, amounting almost to simplicity; and this would have been the impression produced upon an observer, but for a pair of lively spiritual eyes that sparkled in sockets somewhat sunken. These, combined with a well-formed mouth, and lips of a sarcastic cut, relieved the otherwise too ingenuous expression of his features, and proved that the young man was capable, when occasion required, of exhibiting a considerable power of repartee and acute observation. Just then the predominant expression upon his features was that of chagrin, mixed with a certain degree of uneasiness.

The scenes through which he was passing were of a character to cause apprehension—especially to one journeying alone. On all sides extended a vast plain of sterile soil—the brown earth but thinly covered with a growth of cactus and wild aloes, under the shadow of which appeared a sparse herbage, wild, and of yellowish hue. The aspect was monotonous and dreary beyond expression; while here and there vast clouds of dust rose in whirlwinds, and moved like spectres over the plain. The straggling huts encountered at long intervals on the way were all empty—apparently abandoned by their owners! This strange circumstance combined with the heat of a tropic sun, the absence of all signs of water, the profound silence that reigned over these solitary steppes, had created a sense of discouragement in the mind of the young traveller, amounting almost to fear.

Notwithstanding a liberal use of the spur, his horse could not be induced to depart from a walk. If by a desperate effort he was once or twice forced into a trot it was only to return again to his old gait as soon as the spur was taken from his flanks. The painful exertions of the rider had no other result than to cause the perspiration to flow profusely over his face, rendering it necessary for him every now and then to make use of his pocket-kerchief.

"*Maldito cavallo!*" (Good-for-nothing beast!) he exclaimed at intervals as his patience became exhausted; but the horse, fatigued with a long journey, was as insensible to the insults of his rider's speech as he had been to the strokes of his spur, and moved not a whit the faster.

Wearied with these idle efforts to increase the speed of the animal, the young traveller turned in his saddle and looked back. His object was to compare the route he had come with that which lay before him—in order to form some calculation as to the distance yet to be travelled before he could reach the other side of the desert plain.

The observation did not appear to gratify him. On the contrary, his countenance became clouded with a still deeper shade of chagrin; and, abandoning himself to a complete despair, he made no further attempt to urge forward his unwilling roadster, but left the sorry brute to his creeping pace.

For several hours the traveller kept on his slow course—his spirit alternately exasperated and depressed.

Mid-day had arrived, and the tropic sun, glaring down vertically from a cloudless sky, was causing a degree of heat almost intolerable. The breeze had ceased to cool the atmosphere; and even the dry leaves of the trees hung motionless from the boughs. At every moment the horse, crawling painfully forward, threatened to become motionless as they.

Suffering from thirst, and wearied with the journey he had already made, the young traveller at length dismounted, and threw his bridle-rein over the neck of his horse. He had no fear that the animal would take advantage of the freedom thus given him. There was not the slightest danger of its running away.

Leaving the steed to himself, therefore, the rider walked towards a clump of *nopals*—in hopes of finding some fruit upon them, by which he might relieve his thirst.

As good luck would have it, he was not deceived in his expectation. The *nopals* were in fruit; and having plucked a number of these "Indian figs," and stripped them of their spinous skins, he was enabled, by swallowing a quantity of the sweetish pulp, to allay in some measure the excessive thirst that had been hitherto torturing him. Thus satisfied, he once more mounted into his saddle, and continued his interrupted journey.

Chapter Three
An Enigma

After riding several miles farther, he arrived at a small village, situated in the same plain through which he had been journeying. There, as all along the route, he found the houses deserted and abandoned by their owners! Not a soul was to be seen—no one to offer him hospitality; and as nothing could be found in the empty houses—neither food to satisfy his hunger, nor water to quench his thirst—the traveller was compelled to ride on without halting. "*Cosa estrana*!" muttered he to himself, "what on earth can be the meaning of this complete depopulation?"

In addition to the desertion of the houses, another odd circumstance had struck his attention. Almost at every hut which he passed, he saw canoes and *periaguas* suspended from the branches of the trees, and raised many feet above the ground! In a part of the country where there is neither lake nor river—not so much as the tiniest stream—no wonder the sight astonished our traveller, considering that he was a stranger to the district, and had not yet encountered a single individual who might explain the ludicrous phenomenon.

Just as he was pondering over an explanation of these singularities, a sound fell upon his ear, that produced within him a feeling of joy. It was the hoof-stroke of a horse, breaking upon the profound solitude. It came from behind him; and betokened that some horseman was approaching in his rear, though still invisible on account of a turning in the road, which the young traveller had just doubled.

In a few seconds' time the horseman appeared in sight; and galloping freely forward, soon came side by side with our traveller.

"*Santos Dios*!" saluted the new-comer, at the same time raising his hand to his hat.

"*Santos Dios*!" responded the young man, with a similar gesture.

The meeting of two travellers in the midst of a profound solitude is always an event, which leads to their regarding one another with a certain degree of curiosity; and such occurred in the present instance.

He who had just arrived was also a young man—apparently of twenty-four or twenty-five years; and this conformity of age was the only point in which the two travellers resembled each other. The new-comer was somewhat above medium stature, with a figure combining both elegance and strength. His features were regular and well defined; his eyes black and brilliant; his moustache thick and curving, and his complexion deeply embrowned with the sun. All these circumstances tended to show that he was a man of action; while a certain air of energy and command bespoke fiery passions, and the hot Arabian blood, which flows in the veins of many Spanish-Mexican families.

His horse was a bay-brown, whose slender limbs and sinewy form declared him also to be descended from an oriental race. The ease with which his rider managed him, and his firm graceful seat in the saddle, betokened a horseman of the first quality.

His costume was both costly and elegant. A vest of unbleached cambric suited well the heat of the climate. His limbs were covered with *calzoneros* of silk velvet of a bright purple colour; while boots of buff leather, armed with long glancing spurs, encased his feet. A hat of *vicuña* cloth, with its trimming of gold lace, completed a costume half-military, half-civilian. To strengthen its military character a rapier in a leathern sheath hung from his waist-belt, and a carbine, suspended in front, rested against the pommel of his saddle.

"*Puez, amigo!*" said the newly-arrived horseman, after a pause, and glancing significantly at the back of the traveller. "May I ask if you have far to go upon that horse?"

"No, thank goodness!" replied the other; "only to the hacienda of San Salvador; which, if I'm not mistaken, is scarce six leagues distant."

"San Salvador? I think I've heard the name. Is it not near to an estate called hacienda of Las Palmas?"

"Within two leagues of it, I believe."

"Ah! then we are following the same route," said he in the laced cap; "I fear, however," he continued, checking the ardour of his steed, "that there will soon be some distance between us. Your horse does not appear to be in any particular hurry?"

The last speech was accompanied by a significant smile.

"It is quite true," rejoined the other, also smiling, as he spoke; "and more than once upon my journey I have had reason to blame the mistaken economy of my good father, who, instead of letting me have a proper roadster, has munificently furnished me with a steed that has escaped from the horns of all the bulls of the Valladolid Circus; the consequence of which is, that the poor beast cannot see even a cow on the distant horizon without taking to his heels in the opposite direction."

"*Carrambo*! and do you mean to say you have come all the way from Valladolid on that sorry hack?"

"Indeed, yes, Señor—only I have been two months on the way."

Just then the Rosinante of the circus, roused by the presence of the other horse, appeared to pique himself on a point of honour, and made an effort to keep up with his new companion. Thanks to the courtesy of the moustached cavalier, who continued to restrain the ardour of his fine steed, the two horses kept abreast, and the travellers were left free to continue the conversation.

"You have been courteous enough," said the stranger, "to inform me that you are from Valladolid. In return, let me tell you that I am from Mexico, and that my name is Rafael Tres-Villas, captain in the Queen's dragoons."

"And mine," rejoined the young traveller, "is Cornelio Lantejas, student in the University of Valladolid."

"Well, Señor Don Cornelio, can you give me the solution of an enigma which has puzzled me for two days, and which I have been unable to ask any one else, for the reason that I have not met with a soul since I entered this accursed country. How do you explain this complete solitude—the houses, and villages without inhabitant, and skiffs and canoes suspended from the trees in a district where you may go ten leagues without finding a drop of water?"

"I cannot explain it at all, Señor Don Rafael," replied the student; "it has equally astonished myself; and more than that—has caused me most horrible fear."

"Fear!" echoed the captain of dragoons; "of what?"

"The truth is, Señor Capitan, I have a bad habit of being more afraid of dangers which I cannot comprehend, than those which I know. I fear that the insurrection has gained this province—though I was told to the contrary—and that the State of Oajaca was perfectly tranquil. Like enough the people have abandoned their dwellings to avoid falling into the hands of some party of insurgents that may be scouring the country?"

"Bah!" exclaimed the dragoon, with a contemptuous toss of his head. "Poor devils like them are not in the habit of fleeing from marauders. Besides, the country-people have nothing to fear from those who follow the banner of the insurrection. In any case, it was not for sailing through these sandy plains that the canoes and *periaguas* have been hung up to the trees? There's some other cause, than the panic of the insurrection, that has breathed a spirit of vertigo into the people here; though, for the life of me, I can't guess what it is."

For a while the two travellers continued their journey in silence—each absorbed in speculating upon the singular mystery that surrounded them, and of which neither could give an explanation.

Chapter Four
The Hungry Travellers

The dragoon was the first to resume the conversation.

"You, Señor Don Cornelio," said he, "you who have come from Valladolid, perhaps you can give me some later news, than I have received about the march of Hidalgo and his army?"

"Not any, I fear," replied the student; "you forget, Señor, that, thanks to the slow pace of my old horse, I have been two months on the route? When I left Valladolid, nobody had any more thought of an insurrection than of a new deluge. All I know of it is what I have heard from public rumour—that is, so much as could be divulged without fear of the Holy Inquisition. If, moreover, we are to believe the mandate of the Lord Bishop of Oajaca, the insurrection will not find many supporters in his diocese."

"And for what reason?" asked the captain of dragoons, with a certain hauteur, which proved, without committing himself to any disclosure of his political opinions, that the insurgent cause would not find an enemy in him. "What reason does the bishop assign?"

"What reason?" replied the student. "Simply because my Lord Bishop Bergosa y Jordan will excommunicate them. He affirms, moreover, that every insurgent will be recognisable by his horns and cloven hoofs, which before long they will all have from the hands of the devil!"

Instead of smiling at the childish credulity of the young student, the dragoon shook his head with an air of discontent, while the hairs of his black moustachios curled with indignation.

"Yes," said he, as if speaking to himself, "thus is it that our priests fight with the weapons of calumny and falsehood, perverting the minds of the Creoles with fanatical superstition! So, Señor Lantejas," he continued in a louder tone, addressing himself to the student, "you are afraid to enrol yourself in the ranks of the insurgents, lest you might obtain these diabolical ornaments promised by the bishop?"

"Heaven preserve me from doing such a thing!" replied the student. "Is it not an article of faith? And who should know better than the respectable

Lord Bishop of Oajaca? Besides," continued he, hastening his explanation, as he saw the angry flash of his companion's eye, "I am altogether of a peaceable disposition, and about to enter into holy orders. Whatever party I might take, it would be with prayer alone I should seek to make it triumph. The Church has a horror of blood."

While the student was thus delivering himself, the dragoon regarded him with a side glance; which seemed to say: that it mattered little which side he might take, as neither would be much benefited by such a sorry champion.

"Is it for the purpose of passing your thesis that you have come to Oajaca?"

"No," replied Lantejas, "my errand into this country is altogether different. I am here in obedience to the commands of my father, whose brother is the proprietor of the rich estate of San Salvador. I am to remind my uncle that he is a widower—rich—and without children; and that he has half-a-dozen nephews to provide for. That is my business at San Salvador. What can I do? My honoured father is more attached to the good things of this life than is perhaps right; and I have been obliged to make this journey of two hundred leagues, for the purpose of sounding our relative's disposition in regard to us."

"And ascertaining the value of his property as well?"

"Oh! as to that, we know exactly how much it is worth; though none of us has ever been on the estate."

This answer of the young student did more honour to his heart than to his discretion.

"Well," continued he, after a pause, "I may safely say, that never did nephew present himself before an uncle in a more famished condition than I shall do. Thanks to the inexplicable desertion of all the houses and villages through which I have passed—and the care which their owners have taken to carry with them even the leanest chicken—there is not a jackal in the country hungrier than I at this minute."

The dragoon was in pretty much the same case. For two days he had been travelling without seeing a soul, and though his horse had picked up a little forage along the road, he had been unable to obtain food for himself— other than such wild fruits and berries as he could gather by the way.

The sympathy for a like suffering at once dissipated any ill-blood which the difference in their political sentiments might have stirred up; and harmony was restored between them.

The captain in his turn informed his new *compagnon du voyage*, that, since the imprisonment of the Viceroy, Iturrigaray, his own father, a Spanish gentleman, had retired to his estate of Del Valle, where he was now proceeding to join him. He was not acquainted with this estate, having never been upon it since he was a mere child; but he knew that it was not far from the hacienda of Las Palmas, already mentioned. Less communicative than Don Cornelio, he did not inform the student of another motive for his journey, though there was one that interested him far more than revisiting the scenes of his childhood.

As the travellers rode on, the evanescent ardour of Don Cornelio's roadster insensibly cooled down; while the student himself, fatigued by the incessant application of whip and spur, gradually allowed to languish a conversation, that had enabled them to kill a long hour of their monotonous journey.

The sun was now declining towards the western horizon, and the shadows of the two horsemen were beaming elongated upon the dusty road, while from the tops of the palm-trees the red cardinals and parroquets had commenced to chaunt their evening song.

Thirst—from which both the travellers suffered even more than from hunger—was still increasing upon them; and at intervals the dragoon captain cast a look of impatience toward the horse of his companion. He could not help observing that the poor brute, for the want of water, was every moment slackening his pace.

On his side, Don Cornelio perceived, that, from a generous motive, his travelling companion was resisting the temptation to ride forward. By putting his fine horse into a gallop, the latter could in a short time reach the hacienda—now less than three leagues distant. Under the apprehension of losing his company, therefore, the student redoubled his efforts to keep his old circus hack abreast with the bay-brown of the dragoon.

The journey thus continued for half an hour longer; when it became evident to both travellers that the *escapado* of the bull-ring was every moment growing more unable to proceed.

"Señor student," said the dragoon, after a long spell of silence, "have you ever read of those shipwrecks, where the poor devils, to avoid starvation, cast lots to see which shall be eaten by the others?"

"Alas! yes, I have," answered Lantejas, with a slight trembling in his speech; "but I hope with us it will not come to that deplorable extremity."

"*Carrambo!*" rejoined the dragoon with a grave air, "I feel at this moment hungry enough to eat a relative—even if he were rich and I his heir, as you of your uncle, the *haciendado* of San Salvador!"

"But we are not at sea, Señor captain, and in a boat from which there is no chance of escape?"

The dragoon fancied that he might amuse himself a little at the expense of the young student of divinity—of whose excessive credulity he had already had proofs. Perhaps he meant also to revenge himself on this foolish credulity, upon which the fulmination of the Bishop Bergosa—already celebrated throughout Mexico—had made such an impression. His chief motive, however, was to demonstrate to his travelling companion the necessity for their parting company; in order, that, by riding forward himself, he might be able to send back succour to his fellow-traveller. He was no little surprised, therefore, to perceive that his pleasantry was taken in actually a serious light; and therefore had determined to desist from making any further innuendos.

"I hope, Señor captain," said Don Cornelio, "I hope neither of us will ever be in such extremities."

Then casting a glance over the arid waste that stretched before them, a new idea seemed to strike the student; and with a haste that bespoke his agitation he continued—

"As for me, if I were mounted on a horse equal in strength and vigour to yours, I should gallop either to the hacienda of Las Palmas or San Salvador, without drawing bridle; and from there send assistance to the fellow-traveller I had left behind."

"Ah! is that your advice?"

"I could not think of giving any other."

"Good, then!" cried the dragoon; "I shall follow it; for to be candid, I felt a delicacy in parting company with you."

As Don Rafael spoke, he held out his hand to the student.

"Señor Lantejas," said he, "we part friends. Let us hope we may never meet as enemies! Who can foresee the future? You appear disposed to look with an evil eye on those attempts at emancipation of a country, that has been enslaved for three hundred years. As for myself, it is possible I may offer my arm—and, if need be, my life—to aid her in conquering her liberty. *Hasta luego!* I shall not forget to send you assistance."

Saying this, the officer clasped warmly the chill attenuated fingers of the student of theology, gave the reign to his horse, that needed no spur, and disappeared the moment after amidst a cloud of dust.

"God be praised!" said Lantejas, breathing freely; "I do believe the famished Lestrygon would have been quite capable of devouring me! As for my being found on a field of battle in front of this Goliath, or any other, there's not much danger. I defy the devil with all his horns to make a soldier of me, either *for* the insurrection or *against* it."

The student proceeded on his solitary route—congratulating himself on having escaped, from what his credulous fancy had believed to be a danger.

Some time had passed, and the red clouds of sunset were tinting the horizon, when he saw before him the form of a man, whose gait and complexion proved him to be an Indian. In hopes of obtaining some provisions from this man, or, at all events, an explanation of the singular circumstances already mentioned, the student urged his horse into a more rapid pace, heading him towards the Indian.

He saw that the latter was driving two cows before him, whose distended udders proved them to be milch cattle. This increased the desire of the horseman, hungry and thirsty as he was, to join company with the cowherd.

"*Hola*! José!" cried he, at the top of his voice.

An Indian will always respond to the name *José*, as an Irishman to that of *Pat* or *Paddy*. On hearing it, the cow-driver looked round in alarm. At that moment the *escapado* of the bull-ring caught sight of the two cows, and suddenly broke off into a gallop—unfortunately, however, in a direction the very opposite to that which his rider desired him to take!

Notwithstanding this, the student still continued to shout to the cowherd, in hopes of bringing him to comprehend his dilemma. But the odd spectacle of a horseman calling to him to approach, while he himself kept riding off in the opposite direction, so astounded the Indian that, uttering a cry of affright, he also took to his heels, followed in a long shambling trot by the two cows!

It was not until all three were out of sight, that the student could prevail on his affrighted steed to return into the proper path.

"In the name of the Holy Virgin!" soliloquised he, "what has got into the people of this country? Every one of them appears to have gone mad!"

And once more setting his horse to the road, he proceeded onward—now, however, hungrier and more disconsolate than ever.

Just as night was coming down, he arrived at a place where two or three small huts stood by the side of the road. These, like all the others, he found deserted. At sight of them, however, the old horse came to a dead stop, and refused to proceed. His rider, equally fatigued, resolved upon remaining by the huts, until the assistance promised by the dragoon captain should arrive.

In front of one of the huts stood two tall tamarind trees—between which a hammock was suspended, at the height of seven or eight feet from the ground. It was a capacious one, made of the strong plaited thread of the *maguey*. It seemed to invite the wearied traveller to repose—as if placed there on purpose for him.

As the heat was still suffocating, instead of entering one of the huts, he unsaddled his horse, permitted the animal to go at will, and by the trunk of one of the tamarinds climbed up into the hammock. There, stretching himself, he lay a good while listening attentively, in hopes of hearing some sound that might announce the approach of the promised succour.

It was now dark night. All nature had gone to sleep; and the profound silence was unbroken by any sound that resembled the tramp of a horse. Nothing was heard to indicate the approach of the expected relief.

As the student continued to listen, however, he became sensible of sounds, of a singular and mysterious character. There was a continuous noise, like the rumbling of distant thunder, or the roaring of the ocean during a storm. Although the air was calm around him, he fancied he could hear a strong wind blowing at a distance, mingled with hoarse bellowings of unearthly voices!

Affrighted by these inexplicable noises—which seemed the warning voices of an approaching tempest—he lay for a while awake; but fatigue overcoming him, he sunk at length into a profound sleep.

Chapter Five
Black and Red

On that same evening, and about an hour before sunset, two men made their appearance on the banks of a small river that traversed the country not far from the group of huts where the traveller had halted—at a point about halfway between them and the hacienda Las Palmas.

At the place where the two men appeared upon its banks, the river in question ran through the middle of a narrow valley; flowing so gently along, that its unrippled surface mirrored the blue sky. At this place the water filled its channel up to the level of the banks, that were treeless, and covered with a sward of grass. Farther down trees grew along the edge of the stream—tall oaks and cotton woods, whose branches were interlaced by flowering llianas. Still farther down, the river entered between high banks of wilder appearance, and covered with yet more luxuriant vegetation. From the grassy meadow, in which the two men were standing, the noise of a cataract, like the breaking of the sea upon a rocky beach, was distinctly audible.

The complexion and costume of one of the men pronounced him an Indian. The former was a copper-brown, the well-known colour of the American aboriginal. His dress consisted of a coarse shirt of greyish woollen stuff, rayed with black stripes. Its short sleeves, scarce reaching to the elbows, permitted to be seen a pair of strong, sinewy arms of deepest bronze. It was confined round the waist with a thick leathern belt, while its skirt hung down to mid-thigh. Below this appeared the legs of a pair of trowsers, wide, but reaching only to the knee. These were of tanned sheep-skin, and of a reddish brown hue. From the bottoms of the trowsers, the legs and ankles of the Indian were naked; while the *chaussure* consisted of leathern buskins, also of a brownish red colour. A hat of rush plaiting covered his head, from under which hung two long tresses of black hair— one over each cheek—and reaching down to his elbows.

He was a man of tall stature, and with a physiognomy remarkable for one of his race. Instead of the servile aspect so characteristic of the *Indios mangos* (subdued Indians) of Mexico, he had more the air of the true savage, or *Indio bravo*. This appearance was strengthened by the fact of his having a slight moustache and beard—a rare distinction among the aborigines of Mexico.

Over his shoulder he carried a short, thick carbine, somewhat rusty; while a long *macheté* (half sword, half knife), was stuck behind his belt.

His companion was a negro, whose clothing consisted of little else than rags. Otherwise there was nothing remarkable about him—if we except the air of stupified credulity with which he appeared to be listening to the discourse of the Indian. From time to time his features assumed an expression of ill-concealed fear.

The red man, closely followed by the black, was advancing along the bank at a place destitute of timber and where the ground was smooth and soft. He was going slowly, his body bent slightly forwards, and his eyes turned upon the earth as if in search of some object, or tracking an animal. Suddenly he came to a top—

"Now!" he exclaimed, turning to the negro, and pointing to the ground, "I told you I should find their traces in less than half an hour. Look there!"

The Indian spoke in a tone of triumph; but the feeling was far from being shared by his companion, who bent his eyes upon the earth rather with a look of dismay. The sight was sufficient to have caused uneasiness to any one other than a hunter of wild beasts. In the soft mud was exhibited a number of tracks—twenty of them in all. They were of different sizes, too; and appeared to have been recently made. The marks of sharp claws, distinctly outlined in the clayey soil, told what kind of animal had made the tracks. It was the fierce jaguar—the tiger (*tigré*) of the Spanish-Americans.

"It's not half an hour since they have been here," continued the Indian. "*Mira!*" exclaimed he, pointing to a little eddy on the edge of the stream, "they have been drinking there not ten minutes ago: the water is yet muddy!"

"Let us get away," suggested the negro, whose black face was now pale with fear. "I see no use in our remaining here. See! there are many tracks, and of different sizes, too. Lord bless me! a whole procession of tigers must have passed here."

"Oh! you are exaggerating," rejoined the Indian, with a sneering laugh. "Let us count them," he continued, bending down over the foot-prints, "one—two—three—four: a male, a female, and her two *cachorros* (cubs). That is all. *Carrambo!* what a sight for a *tigrero* (tiger-hunter)."

"Ah! indeed!" assented the negro, in a hesitating way.

"Yes," rejoined the other; "but we shan't go after them to-day. We have more important business on our hands."

"Would it not be better to defer the business you were speaking of till to-morrow, and now return to the hacienda? However curious I am to see the wonderful things you promised, still—"

"What!" exclaimed the Indian, interrupting his companion's speech, "defer that business till another day? Impossible. The opportunity would not come round for another month, and then we shall be far from this place. No, no, Clara," continued he, addressing the black by this *very* odd cognomen, "no, no; we must about it to-day and at this very moment. Sit down, then."

Suiting the action to the word, the Indian squatted himself on the grass; and the negro, willing or unwilling, was forced to follow his example.

Chapter Six
The Tiger-Hunter

Notwithstanding the change of attitude, the negro still continued the victim of his fears. Instead of paying proper attention to what his companion was saying, his eyes wandered abroad, searching the horizon on every side of him, as if at every moment he expected to see the jaguars returning to attack them.

Noticing his uneasiness, the Indian made an attempt to reassure him.

"You have nothing to fear, comrade," said he. "The tigers have the whole river to drink out of; and it is not likely they will come back here."

"They may be hungry," rejoined Clara, "and I have heard say that they prefer a black man, like me, to either a white or an Indian."

"Ha, ha!" laughed his companion. "You need not flatter yourself on that score. Bah, man! there's not a tiger in all the State that would be fool enough to prefer a carcass tough and black as yours, to the flesh of a young colt or heifer, either of which they can have at any time. Ha, ha! If the jaguars only heard what you've said, they would shake their sides with laughter."

The fearlessness exhibited by the Indian himself in regard to the jaguars is easily explained, since it was by the destruction of these fierce animals that he got his living. His calling was a peculiar one, though common enough throughout the tropical regions of America. He was, in fact, a *tigrero*, or tiger-hunter, a class of men whose sole occupation consists in pursuing, *à l'outrance*, the different beasts of prey that ravage the flocks and herds of the great *haciendas de ganado*, or grazing estates. Among these predatory creatures the jaguar is the most destructive; and the hunting and slaying of these animals is followed by many men—usually Indians or half-breeds—as a regular profession.

As the jaguar (*Felis onca*) in all parts of Spanish-America is erroneously called the tiger (*tigré*), so the hunter of this animal is termed a tiger-hunter (*tigrero*). Many of the more extensive estates keep one or more of these hunters in their pay; and the Indian we have introduced to the reader was the *tigrero* of the hacienda Del Valle. His name and nation were declared by himself in the speech that followed—

"Ah!" he exclaimed with an air of savage exultation, "neither tigers nor men may laugh with impunity at Costal, the Zapoteque. As for these jaguars," he continued after a pause, "let them go for this night. There will be nothing lost by waiting till to-morrow. I can soon get upon their trail again; and a jaguar whose haunt is once known to me, is a dead animal. To-night we have other business. There will be a new moon; and that is the time when, in the foam of the cascade, and the surface of the solitary lake, the Siren shows herself—the Siren of the dishevelled hair."

"The Siren of the dishevelled hair?"

"Yes; she who points out to the gold-seeker the rich *placers* of gold—to the diver the pearls that lie sparkling within their shells at the bottom of the great ocean."

"But who has told you this?" inquired Clara, with a look of incredulity.

"My fathers—the Zapoteques," replied Costal, in a solemn tone of voice; "and why should *they* not know? They have learnt these things from Tlaloc and Matlacuezc—gods they were, as powerful as the Christ of the pale faces. Why—"

"Don't speak so loud!" interrupted Clara, in a voice that betokened alarm. "The priests of the Christians have their ears everywhere. They might call it blasphemy; and *carrambo*! the Inquisition has its dangers for blacks as well as whites!"

On hearing the word Inquisition the Indian involuntarily lowered his voice; but continued speaking in a tone that his companion could still hear him.

"My fathers," said he, "have told me that the Siren never appears to any one who is alone. It is necessary that two be present—two men of tried courage they must be—for the divinity is often wrathful at being invoked, and at such times her anger is terrible. As two men are required, I need another besides myself. Will you then be my companion?"

"Hum!" said Clara. "I may boast that I am not afraid of a man; though I confess I cannot say the same about a tiger. As to your Siren, that appears to be the very devil—"

"Man, tiger, or devil," cried Costal, "why fear any of the three? What need one care for them—one who has a stout heart—especially when the reward of his courage is gold, and enough of it to make a grand lord out of a poor Indian?"

"And of a negro as well?"

"Without doubt."

"Say, rather," rejoined Clara, with an air of discouragement, "that gold could serve neither one nor the other. Black and Indian, both are slaves, and our masters would soon take it from us."

"True enough what you say; but let me tell you, Clara, that the bondage of the Indian is approaching its end. Have you not heard that up in the north—in the *tierra adentro*—a priest has proclaimed the emancipation of all races, and equal liberty for all?"

"No," replied the negro, betraying his total ignorance of the political affairs of the country, "I have heard nothing about it."

"Know, then, that the day is at hand when the Indian will be on an equality with the white, the Creole with the Spaniard; and when an Indian, such as I, will be the master of both!"

The descendant of the Zapoteques delivered this speech with an air of proud exultation.

"Yes!" continued he, "the day of our ancient splendour will soon return. That is why I am desirous at present of acquiring gold. Hitherto I have not troubled myself about finding it; since, as you say, it would soon be wrested from the hands of a poor slave. Now that I am to be free, the circumstances are changed; and I want gold, by which I may revive the glories of my ancestors."

Clara could not help casting a look of astonishment at his companion. The air of savage grandeur, visible in the countenance of the tiger-hunter—vassal of the hacienda Las Palmas—surprised him, as did also the pretentious manner in which he spoke about reviving the ancient splendours of his race.

The look and its meaning did not escape the observation of the Indian.

"Friend Clara!" said he, in a confidential tone, "listen to me, while I reveal to you a secret which I have kept for many long years—long enough for me to have seen fifty dry seasons, and fifty seasons of rain; and this fact can be confirmed to you by all of my colour and race."

"You have seen fifty seasons of rain?" cried the negro, in a tone of astonishment, at the same time regarding his companion attentively, who in truth did not appear to be over thirty years of age. "Fifty seasons of rain?"

"Well, not quite fifty," replied Costal, with a smile, "but very near it."

"Ah! I shall see fifty more," continued he. "Omens have told me that I shall live as long as the ravens."

The negro remained silent, still held in surprise by the wild declarations which his companion was volunteering to make to him.

"Listen, friend Clara!" continued the tiger-hunter, extending his arm in a circle, and designating the four points of the compass; "in all the space that a horseman could traverse between sunrise and sunset—from north to south, from east to west—there is not a spot of ground that was not once possessed by my ancestors—the ancient lords of Zapoteca. Before the vessels of the white men touched upon our coasts, they were sovereign masters of all this land—from ocean to ocean. The sea alone was their boundary. Thousands of warriors followed their banners, and crowded around their plume-bedecked standards of war. In the ocean the pearl-banks, and on the land the *placers* of gold belonged to them. The yellow metal glanced upon their dresses and armour, or ornamented the very sandals upon their feet. They possessed it in such abundance, they scarce knew what to do with it.

"Where now are the once powerful Caciques of Tehuantepec? Most of their subjects have been slaughtered by the thunder of the white men, or buried in the dark mines—while the conquerors have divided among them and made slaves of the survivors! An hundred needy adventurers have been transformed into grand magnates—each endowed with a portion of the conquered territory; and at this moment the last descendant of the Caciques is forced to earn his subsistence almost as a slave—to submit to the tyranny of a white master—to expose his life daily for the destruction of fierce beasts, lest they should ravage the flocks and herds of his thankless employer; while, of the vast plains over which he is compelled to pursue his perilous calling, there remains to him not a spot he can call his own—not even the ground occupied by his miserable hut."

The speaker might have gone on much longer without fear of his hearer interrupting him. The latter was held mute with astonishment, as well as by a kind of involuntary respect with which the words of his companion had inspired him. In all probability the negro had never before heard that a powerful and civilised people existed in that country previous to the arrival of the Spaniards. At all events he had never suspected that the man who was thus enlightening him—the half-Pagan, half-Christian tiger-hunter—was the descendant of the ancient masters of Tehuantepec.

As for Costal himself, after making these statements of the former splendours of his family—in which, notwithstanding his pompous mode of declaring them, there was much truth—he lapsed into a profound silence; and, his face turned with a melancholy expression upon the ground, he took no notice of the effect produced on the mind of his black companion.

Chapter Seven
The Chase of the Jaguar

The sun was gradually inclining towards the horizon, when a prolonged howl, shrill at first, but ending in a hoarse roar, fell upon the ears of the two adventurers. It appeared to come from a brake some distance down the river; but, near or distant, it at once changed the expression upon the countenance of the negro. Fear took the place of astonishment; and, on hearing the sound, he sprang suddenly to his feet.

"*Jesus Maria!*" exclaimed he, "it is the jaguar again!"

"Well, what if it be?" said Costal, who had neither risen, nor made the slightest gesture.

"The jaguar!" repeated the negro in his terror.

"The jaguar? You are mistaken," said Costal.

"God grant that I may be," rejoined the black, beginning to hope that the sounds had deceived him.

"You are mistaken as to the number," coolly proceeded Costal. "There is not one jaguar, but four—if you include the *cachorros*!"

Perceiving the sense in which Costal meant he was mistaken, the negro, with terror gleaming in his eyes, appeared as if about to start off towards the hacienda.

"Take care what you do!" said the Indian, apparently inclined to amuse himself with the fears of his companion. "It is quite true, I believe, that these animals are very fond of black men's flesh."

"*Carrambo!* just now you told me the contrary?"

"Well, perhaps I am mistaken upon that point; but one thing I know well—for I have proved it a hundred times—that is, that a brace of tigers, when the male and female are together, seldom roar in that fashion—especially if they suspect the presence of a human being. It is more likely, therefore, that at this moment they are separated; and by going towards the hacienda, you might risk getting between the two."

"Heaven preserve me from getting into such a scrap," muttered the negro.

"Well, then; the best thing you can do is to stay where you are—beside a man who don't care a *claco* for the jaguars."

The negro hesitated, not quite certain that it would be the best thing for him. At that moment, however, a second howl, coming in a direction entirely opposite to the first, decided his uncertainty, and convinced him that the *tigrero* had spoken the truth.

"You see," said Costal, "the brutes are in search of something to eat. That's why they are calling to one another. Well, now! if you're still in the mind, off with you to the hacienda!"

This was of course meant as a taunt; for the negro, who now perceived that there was a jaguar howling in the way that led to the hacienda, had given up all notion of proceeding in that direction. On the contrary, while his black face turned of an ashen-grey colour, he drew closer to his imperturbable companion—who had not even attempted to take hold of the carbine which lay on the grass by his side!

"Bah!" muttered Costal, speaking to himself, "this comrade of mine is scarce brave enough for my purpose. I must defer it, till I meet with one possessed of more courage." Then resuming the current of his thoughts, which had been interrupted by the howling of the jaguars, he said aloud— "Where is the red man, where the black, who would not lift his arm to aid this brave priest?—he who has risen against the oppressor—the oppressor of all Zapoteques, Creoles, and Aztecs. Have these Spaniards not been more ferocious than even the tigers themselves?"

"I should not fear *them*, at any rate," interposed Clara.

"Good! I am glad you talk that way, comrade. To-morrow let us give warning to our master, Don Mariano de Silva. He must find another tigrero; and we shall go and join the insurgents in the west."

The Indian had scarce finished his speech, when another howl came from the jaguars, as if to put the patience of the tiger-hunter to the test. It was even more spitefully prolonged, coming in the direction in which the first had been heard—that is, from a point upon the river a little above where the two men were seated.

On hearing it, thus uttered as a signal of defiance, the eyes of the tigrero began to sparkle with an irresistible desire for the chase.

"By the souls of the Caciques of Tehuantepec!" exclaimed he, "this is too much for human patience. I shall teach those two braggarts not to talk so loud of their affairs. Now, Clara!" continued he, springing to his feet, "you shall have the opportunity of becoming acquainted with a jaguar at closer quarters than you have hitherto been."

"*Carrambo!*" exclaimed the black, "why should I go near them? I have no weapon, and would be of no use to you?"

"Hear me, Clara!" said the Indian, without replying to the speech of his comrade. "The one that howled last is the male. He was calling to the female, his mate. He is a good distance from here, up stream. We must go up to him; and as there's not a stream on all the estate, where I haven't either a canoe or *periagua*, for the purposes of my calling—"

"You have one here, then?" interrupted Clara.

"Certainly I have. We can go up the river; and in the canoe you will not be in the slightest danger. I have my own notions as to how we may best approach this noisy brute."

"But the jaguars can swim like seals, I have heard?"

"I don't deny it. Never mind that; come on!"

Without deigning further speech, the tigrero started forward; and going cautiously, approached that part of the bank where his canoe was moored.

Clara seeing that it would be perhaps less dangerous to accompany him than remain where he was alone, reluctantly followed.

In a few minutes they arrived at the place where the canoe was fastened to the bank; a rude craft, just large enough to carry two men. A paddle lay at the bottom; along with a piece of matting of plaited palm-leaf, which on occasions was called into requisition as a sail. But Costal threw out the matting, as there was no likelihood of its being required upon the present occasion.

Having loosed the cord by which the canoe was attached to the branch of a willow, the Indian leaped aboard, and seated himself near the stem. The negro took his place abaft. A vigorous push was given against the bank, the little craft shot out into the middle of the stream, and, impelled by the paddle, commenced ascending the current.

The sun was still shining on the river, but with his last rays; and the willows and *alamos* that grew along the bank threw their trembling shadows far over the water. The breeze of the desert sighed among their leaves, bearing upon its wings sweet perfumes stolen from a thousand flowers. It seemed the intoxicating incense of liberty.

Costal, an Indian and a hunter, inhaled it with an instinctive delight. Clara was altogether insensible to the sweetness of the scene; and his anxious countenance offered as great a contrast to the calm unmoved features of his companion, as the black shadows of the trees thrown upon the water with the brilliant hues of the sky.

The canoe for a time kept close along the bank, and followed the windings of the stream. Here and there the bushes hung over; and in passing such places Clara kept a sharp look out, in dread of seeing a pair of fiery orbs glancing upon him through the leaves.

"*Por Dios*!" cried he, every time the canoe approached too closely to the bank, "keep her farther off, friend Costal. Who knows but that the jaguars may be up there, ready to spring down upon us?"

"Possible enough," rejoined Costal, vigorously plying his paddle; and without giving any farther thought to the appeals of his companion. "Possible enough; but I have my idea—"

"What is it?" asked Clara, interrupting him.

"A very simple one, and one which I have no doubt you will approve of."

"Let us hear it first."

"Well, then; there are two jaguars, without speaking of the brace of *cachorros*. These I shall leave to you, since you have no weapon. Your plan will be this: take up one of the whelps in each hand, and break in their skulls, by striking them one against the rather. Nothing can be more simple."

"On the contrary, friend Costal, it appears to me very complicated. Besides, how can I lay hold upon them if they should run away?"

"Very likely, they will save you that trouble by laying hold on you. Never fear your getting close enough. If I'm not mistaken, we shall have all four of them within arm's length in less than a quarter of an hour."

"All four!" exclaimed the negro, with a start that caused the canoe to oscillate as if it would upset.

"Beyond doubt," rejoined Costal, making an effort to counterbalance the shock which the frail bark had received. "It is the only plan by which we can bring the chase to a speedy termination; and when one is pressed for time, one must do his best. I was going to tell you, when you interrupted me, that there are two jaguars—one on the right bank, the other on the left—the male and female, beyond doubt. Now by their cries I can tell that these animals are desirous of rejoining one another; and if we place ourselves between the two, it is evident they will both come upon us at once. What say you? I defy you to prove the contrary?"

Clara made no reply to the challenge. His profound belief in the infallibility of his companion's perceptions kept him silent.

"Look out now, Clara!" continued the hunter, "we are going to double that bend in the river where the bushes hide the plain from our view. Your face will be turned the right way. Tell me, then, what you see."

From his position in the canoe, Costal, who plied the paddle, was seated with his back to the open ground towards which they were advancing; and he could only see in front by turning his head, which from time to time he had been doing. But he needed not to look around very often. The countenance of the negro, who was face to face with him, resembled a faithful mirror, in which he could read whatever might be passing behind him.

Chapter Eight
A Grand Spectacle

Hitherto the features of Clara had expressed nothing more than a kind of vague fear; but at the moment when the canoe rounded the last turn in the river, a sudden terror became depicted upon them. The hunter thus warned quickly faced round. An immense plain came before his eye, that seemed to stretch to the verge of the horizon. Through this ran the river, its waters almost on a level with the banks—which were covered with a grassy sward, and without a single tree. At some distance from the curve the stream almost doubled back on itself—forming a verdant delta, around the apex of which ran the road that led to the hacienda Las Palmas.

The rays of the setting sun were flooding the plain with a transparent golden haze, which hung over the empurpled bosom of the water on which the canoe was floating. Just above, in the middle of the current, and scarce two shots distant from where the two men were, a sight appeared to the ravished eyes of the tiger-hunter that caused him at once to change his position in the boat.

"*Mira!*" exclaimed he in a half-whisper. "Look, Clara! Did you ever behold a more beautiful sight?"

With his claws stuck into the floating carcass of a colt upon which he was feeding, an enormous jaguar was suffering himself to float gently down the stream. It was the male one, the same from which the last howlings had proceeded.

With his head outstretched and curving over his fore paws, his hind legs drawn up under his belly, his back highly arched, and his flanks quivering with a supple undulation that betokened activity and power, was seen the royal beast of the American jungle. The dying rays of the sun falling upon his glossy skin displayed his splendid coat of bright yellow ocellated with spots of deepest black.

It was one of those beautiful savage spectacles often exhibited to the eyes of the Indian hunter—a magnificent episode in that eternal poem which the wilderness is constantly repeating.

Scarce taking time to gaze upon it, Costal passed the paddle to his companion; and, gun in hand, crouched down in the bottom of the canoe.

Clara accepted the oar, and half mechanically commenced rowing. He had made no reply to the enthusiastic interrogatory of the hunter. Fear held him speechless.

At that moment a growl, resembling the deepest tones of an ophicleide, resounded from the throat of the jaguar, rolling over the surface of the water to the ears of the men seated in the canoe. He had seen his enemies, and this was his signal of defiance.

The Indian replied by a cry somewhat similar, as the bloodhound utters his wild bay on seeing his victim before him.

"It's the male!" said Costal, apparently pleased that it was so.

"Fire, then!" cried Clara, at last finding his tongue.

"Fire, *Carrambo*! no. My gun does not carry so far. Besides, I shoot best when my game is nearer the muzzle. I wonder," continued he, looking up to the bank, "that the female has not found him! No doubt, if we wait a little, we'll see her coming bounding up with the *cachorros* at her heels."

"*Dios nos ampare*!" (God preserve us!) muttered the negro in a melancholy tone; for he feared that Costal would still insist upon his carrying out the plan he had proposed. "God preserve us! I hope not: one at a time is sufficient."

The words were scarce out of the negro's mouth, when a sharp screech, heard at some distance, proclaimed the coming of the other jaguar; and the moment after she was seen bounding over the savanna, with a rapidity and gracefulness superb beyond admiration.

At the distance of about two hundred yards from the bank, as also from the canoe, she came to a sudden stop; and with muzzle raised aloft, scenting the air, and flanks quivering like an arrow after striking its mark, she remained for some moments fixed to the spot. Meanwhile the two whelps, that had been left in the covert of the bushes, were seen hastening to join her. The canoe, no longer propelled by the paddle, began to spin round with the ripple, keeping about the same distance between it and the tiger crouched on the floating carcass.

"For Heaven's sake, Clara," said Costal impatiently, "keep the boat's head to the current, or I shall never get close enough to fire. There now— that is right—keep a steady hand—mine never shakes. It is important I should kill this jaguar at the first shot. If not, one of us is lost, to a certainty. Perhaps both; for if I miss we shall have both the brutes to contend with, to say nothing of the brace of whelps."

All this while the jaguar was quietly descending the stream upon his floating pedestal, and the distance between him and the canoe was gradually diminishing. Already could be seen his fiery eyeballs rolling in their sockets, and the quick oscillations of his tail, expressive of his gathering rage.

The hunter had taken aim, and was about to pull trigger, when the canoe commenced rocking about, as if tossed upon a stormy sea!

"What the devil are you about, Clara?" inquired the Indian in an angry tone. "If you move in that way I could not hit one in a whole crowd of tigers."

Whether it was through design, or that fear was troubling his senses, and causing him to shift about, Clara, instead of keeping quiet, only seemed to shake all the more.

"A thousand devils take you!" cried Costal, with increased rage. "Just then I had him between the eyes."

Laying down his gun, the hunter snatched the paddle from the hands of the black, and set about turning the canoe into its proper position.

This proved a work of some little time; and before Costal could succeed in accomplishing his purpose, the tiger had taken to flight. Giving utterance to a loud scream, the animal buried his sharp teeth in the carcass, tore from it a large mouthful, and then making a desperate bound passed from the floating body to the bank. In another moment he had rejoined his mate with her young ones, and all were soon beyond the range of the hunter's carbine. The two terrible creatures appeared to hesitate as to whether they should return to the attack, or retreat. Then giving a simultaneous scream, both stretched off at full gallop across the plain, followed by their *cachorros*.

The disappointed hunter looked after them, giving utterance to a fierce exclamation expressive of his disappointment. Then seating himself in the stern of the canoe, he turned its head down stream, and put forth all his strength to regain the point from which they had set out.

Chapter Nine
The Cascade

The canoe carrying the two men continued slowly to descend the course of the river—the negro felicitating himself on his escape from the claws of the jaguars; while the thoughts of the Indian were dwelling with regret upon his want of success.

Clara, however, did not enjoy an unalloyed satisfaction. The jaguars had fled, it was true, but in what direction? It was evident they had gone down stream, and might be encountered below.

This thought troubling Clara, he inquired of his companion if there was any probability of their again falling in with this dangerous enemy.

"Probable enough," responded Costal, "and more than probable. If we descend below the cascade, we shall be almost certain of seeing the jaguars there. The carcass of a fine young colt is not to be met with every day; and these brutes can reason like a man. They know well though that the current will carry the floating body over the fall, and that, below, it will be rendered up to them again. I do not say it will then be whole; for I have seen the trunks of great trees broken into fragments from being carried over that very cascade."

"Then you really think the jaguars may be waiting below?"

"No doubt but they will be there. If I don't mistake, you shall hear their roar before ten minutes have passed, and it will come from the bottom of the cascade, just where our business is now taking us."

"But they may feel inclined to take revenge on us for having driven them from the carcass?"

"And if they should, what care I? Not a straw. *Vamos!* friend Clara, we've given too much thought to these animals. Fortunately we have not lost much; and now to our affair. The young moon will be up in a trice, and I must invoke Tlaloc, the god of the waters, to bestow some gold on the Caciques of Tehuantepec."

The two men had by this time arrived at the place from which the canoe had been taken; and here both disembarked, Costal carefully refastening the craft to the trunk of the willow. Then leaving his companion, he walked off down the bank alone.

"Do not go far away!" said Clara, entreatingly, still troubled with the fear of the jaguars.

"Bah!" exclaimed Costal, "I leave my gun with you!"

"Oh, indeed!" murmured the negro; "what signifies that? one bullet for four tigers!"

Without vouchsafing any reply to this last speech, the Indian advanced a little farther along the bank, and then came to a pause. A large tree grew upon the edge of the stream, its branches extending outwards. Into this he climbed; and then stretching out his arms over the water, he commenced chaunting a lugubrious measure—a species of Indian invocation, of which Clara could hear the words, but without in the least comprehending their signification.

There was something in the wild melody of the Indian's voice to cause his companion a certain mysterious dread; and this was increased by additional notes of an equally mournful character that came pealing up the ravine, mingling with the hoarse roaring of the cascade. It was the scream of the jaguar; though it actually appeared as if some demon was answering to the invocations of the Indian. The lugubrious chaunt of the pagan, and the coincident scream of the tiger, formed a kind of infernal accompaniment, well calculated to strike awe into the mind of one of Clara's superstitious race; and as he stood upon the bank he fancied he saw fiery eyes glaring upon him through the leaves, and the Siren with the dishevelled hair rising above the surface of the water.

A double chill passed through his black skin, from the soles of his feet to the roots of his kinky hair.

At this moment Costal returned to him.

"Are you ready?" inquired the Indian.

"For what?"

"To accompany me to the cascade—there to invoke the Siren, and ask if she may be seen."

"What! down there, where the tigers are roaring?"

"Oh, a fig for them! Remember, Clara, it is gold *we* seek; and, believe me, if fortunate in our application, the Siren will tell us where it is to be found. Gold in masses!"

"Enough!" cried Clara, overcome by the rich prospect. "I am with you," continued he—"lead on! From this hour I am the slave of the Siren who can show us the *placers* of gold!"

The Indian took up his hat and carbine, both of which he had laid aside while chaunting his invocation; and, throwing the gun over his shoulder, started down stream. Clara followed close at his heels—his spirit alternately possessed with cupidity and fear.

As they advanced, the banks rose higher above the surface of the stream, and the channel became the bottom of a deep, narrow ravine, where the water rushed foaming among rocks. The great trees growing on each side stretched towards one another, until their branches interlocked, forming a dark sombre tunnel underneath. At the lower end of this, the stream, once more bursting forth into light, leaped vertically at one bound through a space of two hundred feet sheer, falling into the bottom of a deep gorge, with a noise louder than the roar of the mighty ocean.

Just where the foaming flood broke over the crest of the rocks, grew two enormous cypresses of the kind known to the Mexicans as *ahuehuetes,* or "lords of the water." They stood on opposite sides of the stream, with their long arms extended towards each other. Thickly loaded with lianas, and profusely festooned with the silvery Spanish moss, which, drooping downwards, every now and then dipped into the foaming arch of the cascade, these two great trees looked like the ancient genii of the waters.

At this point the two men made a halt. Although they were now very near to the place where the jaguars were supposed to be, Clara had become more regardless of the danger. His fear, both of wild beasts and evil spirits, had yielded to his thirst for gold, which had been gradually growing stronger.

"Now, Clara!" said Costal, turning a severe look upon his comrade; "listen attentively to the instructions I am about to give you. If the Siren should appear to you, and you should exhibit, either by look or gesture, the slightest symptoms of fear, you are a lost man!"

"All right!" replied the negro. "The hope of being shown a mine of gold gives me courage to risk even my neck in a halter, if need be. Never fear, Costal. Speak on—I am ready to listen."

As the negro pronounced these words, his countenance to all appearance expressed as much firmness as that of Costal himself. The Indian, thus assured, seated himself upon the very edge of the precipice, overlooking the gorge into which the waters were precipitated, while Clara, without invitation, sat down by his side.

Chapter Ten
Strayed from the Track

The ravine, below the spot where the Indian and negro had seated themselves, was covered with a luxuriant vegetation—plants and trees of tropical growth so thickly standing over the ground that the rays of the sun could not have penetrated through the umbrageous foliage. Notwithstanding this abundance of vegetation, if the two gold-seekers had not been so absorbed in their designs, they might have seen below them the figure of a man, who was standing at the bottom of the cascade, directly under their feet.

This man, who had just arrived on the spot, and who appeared to be regarding the waterfall with looks of curiosity and admiration, was no other than Rafael Tres-Villas, Captain of the Queen's Dragoons.

It is necessary to explain how Don Rafael had come to be found in this wild spot, altogether away from the path which he should have followed to the hacienda Las Palmas. Accident, not design, had conducted him to the bottom of the cascade.

On parting from the student of theology, who, recalling the classic scenes of his Odyssey, had mistaken him for a man-eater—a Lestrygon—the dragoon captain, without searching any longer for an explanation of the odd circumstances observed along the way, at once stretched his horse into a gallop. The animal required no propulsion of the spur. His instinct enabled him to scent the proximity of a stable; and he responded to the wishes of his rider by galloping swiftly forward.

Unfortunately the Captain, though a Creole or native Mexican, was entirely unacquainted with this part of the country. He had been born in it, as already hinted; but at a very early age had been taken to reside in the capital; and since then had never revisited the place of his nativity. He was consequently ignorant of the road leading to the paternal hacienda Del Valle—as also to that of Las Palmas—for both were one.

He had not ridden many miles when he arrived at a point where the road forked into two separate paths. Both however continued on, running at no great distance from each other.

Not knowing which he should take, and having met no human being that could direct him, the Captain left the choice to his horse.

The animal, that was no doubt suffering more from thirst than hunger, spread his nostrils to the air, and scenting the fresh exhalations of water, struck off in the direction whence it came. This was to the right.

The choice was fortunate for the student of theology, but rather unlucky for the dragoon captain, as will presently appear.

In fact, the path leading to the left was that which conducted to the hacienda of Las Palmas—which the Captain, for a certain reason, was desirous of reaching, and on that very evening.

After following the right-hand branch for some minutes, the horseman arrived at a spot where the path suddenly gave out. In front appeared only a thick tangle of trees and bushes, behind which could be heard the roaring of a torrent.

Don Rafael was now completely at fault. To return on his track would not only be disagreeable, but there would still exist the same uncertainty as to his route. Even the right-hand branch of the road might not be the right one!

After a minute or two spent in considering what was best to be done, the Captain dismounted, and tying his steed to a tree, commenced making his way through the thicket in the direction whence came the sound of the water, evidently a stream. He was in hopes that on reaching the bank, and following along the water's edge, he might find the continuation of the road at some point where the stream was fordable. After making his way with much labour and loss of time through the labyrinthine tangle of the thicket, he arrived at the bottom of the cascade, just at the moment when Costal and Clara were about entering upon the ceremony of invoking the Siren.

Notwithstanding the desire which the dragoon captain had to escape as soon as possible from the dilemma into which chance had conducted him, the spectacle of this cascade—one of the most magnificent in America— drew from him a cry of wonder and admiration. For some minutes he stood regarding it with admiring eyes, inspired with those sublime feelings which such a grand sight is calculated to call forth.

At length other thoughts came before his mind; and he was about turning away to continue his explorations for a path, when an unexpected object presenting itself to his eyes, caused him to keep his place.

Chapter Eleven
A Ludicrous Spectacle

Amid the vapoury mist that soared above the foaming torrent, the tops of the two *ahuehuetes* could be seen only indistinctly, but the trunks and lower limbs were more palpably visible. On one of these, that projected obliquely over the water, the dragoon fancied he could perceive the figure of a man. On closer scrutiny he became certain it was the figure of a man, and the bronze-coloured skin told him the man was an Indian.

Looking further, he observed another apparition equally singular. Through the fork of the second *ahuehuete*, appeared a face with a complexion black as ebony. It could be no other than the face of a negro.

Here, then, were three distinct types of the human race met in this wild spot. Why he was himself there, Don Rafael knew well enough; but what had brought the Indian and negro into such a place, and at such an hour, was what was now puzzling him.

Without saying a word, he stood watching the movements of the two men, in hopes that the event would furnish him with an explanation. Soon the entire bodies of both negro and Indian appeared in sight, as the two men crawled outward on the overleaning limbs of the trees; but still more plainly, as, hanging by the branches, they let themselves down till their feet dipped in the foam; and swinging there, appeared to go through a series of the most grotesque contortions! The sight made the head of the officer to swim, as if suddenly struck with vertigo.

Thus engaged, neither of the two perceived Don Rafael, though he was standing upon a spot of open ground immediately below them.

For his life, the officer could not guess the nature of these singular proceedings. He concluded that some object—unseen to him—was engaging their attention; and he could not help fancying that it was some nymph of the waters, whom the negro appeared to be wooing, to judge by his impassioned gestures and animated physiognomy.

The large mouth of the darkey was open from ear to ear, displaying his double row of white teeth set in the most winning smile; while ever and anon he stretched his neck out over the water, as if the object of his regards was hid under the shining sheet of foam!

The Indian was acting in a similar fashion, but with a more serious expression of countenance, and greater dignity of manner.

The officer carefully scrutinised the whole surface of the cascade; but he could see nothing but the glistening sheen of the water, and the mass of white foam where it broke over the rock.

At that moment the Indian made a sign to the black to cease from his grimaces; and, letting go his hold with one hand, he swung his body wholly upon the other over the fearful abyss.

The recklessness of the action caused a renewed surprise to the spectator standing below, amounting almost to a feeling of awe. Before he had time to reflect upon it, a human voice reached his ears, rising high above the roaring of the torrent. It was the voice of the Indian, who, with outstretched arm, was chaunting a solemn invocation to the spirit of the waters. The words could not be distinguished, but Don Rafael saw, by the muscular play of the man's lips, that he was singing with all the strength of his lungs.

Curiosity might have prompted the dragoon captain to watch these strange proceedings to the end, but the desire of learning something about his route influenced him to act otherwise. He fancied that by waiting longer the opportunity might be lost. The two persons might disappear in a manner as mysterious as was their behaviour.

To attract their attention, therefore, he shouted, and at the top of his voice; but to no purpose. The deafening roar of the cataract hindered him from being heard; and partly, perhaps, the engrossing occupation in which the two men were engaged.

Failing to attract their notice, he resolved upon ascending the side of the ravine, and going round to the place where they were. For that purpose he retraced his steps through the thicket; and after a difficult climb he reached the top of the cliff, at the point where the *ahuehuetes* formed the arcade over the water. The two personages had disappeared!

Curious as to the object of their ludicrous proceedings, the dragoon climbed up one of the trees, and from a commanding point carefully scrutinised the water underneath. He there perceived nothing more than he had seen already—nothing to justify the strange conduct he had witnessed.

While in the tree, he looked down into the ravine below; first upon the frothing river, and then over the tops of the bushes that grew upon its bank. In an instant he perceived that some of these were in motion, as if some one was making way through the thicket which he had himself traversed.

Presently two men emerged from the cover, and stepped out upon the open bank, at the spot where but the moment before Don Rafael had stood. A glance satisfied him that they were the same he had seen upon the *ahuehuetes*—the negro and Indian.

The sun had already set, but there was still light enough, even in the bottom of the ravine, for Don Rafael to distinguish, not only the movements of the men, but the expression upon their features. Both wore a solemn cast, but those of the negro exhibited evidence of his being influenced by a secret fear.

Near the bank, and where the stream was shallow, a large round boulder of rock stood up out of the water. Towards this the two were directing their steps.

At a signal from the Indian, the negro collected a number of dry sticks; and having piled them upon the flat top of the rock, set them on fire.

In a short time the blaze shot up, and cast its red glare over the stream, tinging with purple flakes the foam of the cataract.

The negro, after kindling the fire, seated himself on the bank, and appeared to contemplate the blaze and its reflections with a feeling of awe. The Indian, on the other hand, threw off his hat, and untwined the plaits of his hair—black as the wing of the raven—whose age he expected to attain. Leaving the long tresses to fall wildly over his shoulders, he walked out into the water, and halted by the side of the rock. The dragoon now saw for the first time a huge sea-shell—a conch—in the hands of the Indian, which had hitherto hung by his side suspended in a string. Placing the conch to his month, he blew several loud, prolonged notes upon it, as if with the intention of arousing the spirit of the waters. Then suffering the shell to fall back upon its string, he commenced leaping around the rock in a sort of grotesque dance, splashing and plunging through the water until the spray rose up and wetted him over the crown of the head.

The whole spectacle was at once ludicrous and imposing. The stoical composure of the negro, who sat perfectly silent upon the bank watching with a solemn air the grotesque capers of his companion—the red light reflected upon the savage figures of the two men—reflected also upon the foaming cataract, which appeared to roll over the cliff like an avalanche of fire—all combined to form a scene in which the ludicrous and the sublime were singularly commingled.

Don Rafael might have desired to witness the *finale*; but time was pressing, and he had a strong motive urging him to proceed upon his journey.

"*Santos Dios!*" cried he, in an impatient tone, "I should like very well to wait and see what pagan divinity these droll savages are invoking; but it will not do to tarry longer here. I must onwards; and to find my way it will be necessary to interrupt their proceedings."

Saying this, the officer raised his voice and shouted "Hola!" with all the strength of his lungs.

The hail was not heeded: it was not heard.

"*Maldito!*" exclaimed he, "I must try some other means of drawing their attention."

A method at once suggested itself; and stooping, the officer took up a handful of small pebbles, and launched them down upon the two adorers of the demon.

So far as drawing their attention went, the means proved efficacious; for the instant that the pebbles fell upon the water, the Indian, with a stroke of his hand, swept the fire from the rock, and the ravine became instantaneously as dark as Erebus. The forms of the two water-worshippers disappeared in the gloom; and Don Rafael found himself alone in the presence of the foaming cataract.

Chapter Twelve
The Diadem

Chagrined at the result, the traveller had no course left but to return to the place where he had left his horse. He was now in a worse predicament than ever; since it had become dark, and it would be difficult not only to find a path, but to follow it when found. The moon, however, had already risen, or rather had been all the while above the horizon, but hidden by a thick band of cumulus clouds that hung over the west. As the clouds did not cover the whole canopy, and it was likely that the moon would soon be visible, the traveller saw that he had no other resource than to wait: in hopes that by her light he might extricate himself from the difficulty into which his mischances had guided him.

On arriving where he had left his horse, Don Rafael sat down upon a fallen tree; and, lighting a cigar, awaited the appearance of the moon. He knew he should not have long to wait, for the yellow sheen, which betokened the situation of the luminary of night, was at no great distance from the edge of the cloud.

He had not been seated more than a few seconds, when a singular sound fell upon his ear. It was not the rushing noise of the cascade—for to that he had been accustomed for some time—but a sound that resembled the scream of some wild animal, ending in a hoarse and fiercely intoned roaring. He had heard it once or twice before; and although he could tell that it was not the howl of the coyote, he knew not what sort of creature was causing it.

Despite his ignorance of the cause, there was something in the sound that denoted danger; and, instinctively influenced by this idea, the young officer rose from his seat upon the log; and, untying his horse, leaped into the saddle. It was not with the intention of moving away from the spot—for the moon was not visible as yet—but with the knowledge that on horseback he would be the better prepared for any event that might arise. Still further to provide against possible danger, he unbuckled the strap of his carbine, and tried whether the piece was primed and in order. Don Rafael, although young, had seen some military service on the northern frontier of Mexico—

where Indian warfare had taught him the wisdom of keeping habitually upon his guard.

Again he heard the wild lugubrious scream rising above the roar of the waters; and perceived that his horse, hearing it also, trembled between his thighs!

Coupling the sound with the strange spectacle to which he had just been a witness, the young officer could not help feeling a slight sensation of fear. He was a Creole, brought up consequently in the midst of ecclesiastical superstition, scarce less monstrous and absurd than that of pure paganism itself. He had heard in his youth how animals in presence of beings of the other world are seized with a shivering—such as that exhibited at the moment by his own horse—and he could almost fancy that the scene he had just witnessed was some evocation of the Prince of Darkness, to which the lugubrious sounds now reaching him were the response.

But Don Rafael was one of those bold spirits whom fear may visit but not subdue; and he remained immobile in his saddle, without showing any further symptoms of apprehension than by the twitching of his lips against his cigar, the light of which at intervals gleamed like a meteor through the darkness.

While thus patiently waiting the moonlight, the horseman fancied that he heard other sounds, and of a different import. Human voices they appeared to be; and it at once occurred to him, that it might be the two men whom he had disturbed and driven from their incantations. The voices were each moment more distinctly uttered; and it was evident that the speakers were approaching him. He perceived that it was probable they would come out somewhere near where he was stationed; and in order to have the advantage of a preliminary survey, in case they might turn out to be enemies, he drew his horse back under the darker shadow of the trees— placing himself in such a position that he commanded a view of the path.

The voices he heard were in reality those of the Indian and negro or Costal and Clara: for it need scarce be told that it was they who were the heroes of the mysterious spectacle of which Don Rafael had been the sole spectator.

The two worthies, on being interrupted in their pagan ceremony by the shower of pebbles, had given up the performance; and were now threading their way through the thicket to reach the road beyond it.

The Indian was venting his wrath against the unknown personage who had intruded upon their sacred devotions, and who had very probably hindered the Siren of the dishevelled hair from showing herself. The negro appeared to be equally indignant; but his anger was probably only pretended.

"Is it only at the first appearance of a new moon that the Siren shows herself?" inquired Clara, as if the opportunity for seeing her had escaped them.

"Of course," replied Costal, "only then; but if there is a profane person in the neighbourhood—and by profane I mean a *white*—the spirit will not appear."

"Perhaps she is afraid of the Inquisition?" naïvely suggested the negro.

"Bah! Clara, you're a ninny! Why the devil should you suppose that the powerful divinity of the waters has any fear of long-robed monks? It is they, more likely, who would have cause to tremble in her presence, and prostrate themselves before her."

"*Carrambo*! if she's afraid to show herself before one white man, more reason why she should fear a whole host of monks—who, it must be confessed, are ugly enough to frighten anything."

"May the devil drown the man who interrupted us!" cried Costal, rendered the more indignant by the justice of the negro's reasoning. "A few minutes more, and I am certain the Siren would have showed herself."

"Why did you extinguish the fire so soon? I think, friend Costal, you did wrong in that," remonstrated Clara.

"I did it to hide from the eyes of the profane white man the mystery about to be accomplished. Besides, I knew after what happened there was no chance of her appearing."

"So you really think it was some one who disturbed us?"

"I am sure of it."

"And is that how you account for the shower of stones?"

"Of course."

"By my faith, then," said the negro in a serious tone, "I differ with you in opinion about that."

"You do? And what is your opinion about it?" inquired Costal, stopping and turning his eyes upon his companion.

"I would stake my life upon it," replied the negro, still speaking seriously, "that while you were dancing around the rock, I saw the Siren."

"Saw the Siren?"

"Yes. Just where we had been—up by the *ahuehuetes*—I saw by the blaze of our fire a face, surrounded by a diadem of shining gold. What could that have been but the Siren?"

"You must have been mistaken, friend Clara."

"I was not mistaken. I saw what I tell you, and I shouldn't a bit wonder that what we took for pebbles were neither more nor less than a shower of *pepitas* (nuggets) of gold, which the spirit had thrown down to us."

"*Carajo!* why did you allow us to leave the place without telling me of this?"

"Because it has just occurred to me now that it was *pepitas*, and not pebbles; besides, our touchwood is all gone, and we could not have kindled another fire."

"We might have groped in the dark."

"Nonsense, friend Costal! How could we tell grains of gold from gravel or anything else in the midst of such darkness as there is down here. Besides, if I came away, it was only with the thought of returning again. We can come back in the morning at daybreak."

"Aha!" cried Costal, suddenly starting with an alarmed air, and striking his forehead with his hand. "We shan't return here to-morrow morning. *Carrai!* I had forgotten; we shall do well to get out of this ravine as quickly as possible."

"Why so?" hastily inquired the black, astounded beyond measure at the altered demeanour of his companion.

"*Carrai!* I had forgotten," said Costal, repeating his words. "To-night is new moon; and it is just at this season that the rivers rise, break over their banks, and inundate the whole country. Yes! the flood will come upon us like an avalanche, and almost without warning. Ha! I do believe that is the warning now! Do you not hear a distant hissing sound?" And as he said this the Indian bent his head and stood listening.

"The cascade, is it not?"

"No—it is very different—it is a distant sound, and I can distinguish it from the roar of the river. I am almost certain it is the inundation."

"Heaven have mercy upon us!" exclaimed the black. "What are we to do?"

"Oh! make your mind easy," rejoined Costal in a consolatory tone. "We are not in much danger. Once out of the ravine, we can climb a tree. If the flood should find us here, it would be all over with us."

"*Por Dios!* let us make haste then," said Clara, "and get out of this accursed place, fit only for demons and tigers!"

A few steps more brought the two adventurers out into the open ground; and close to the spot where the dragoon captain was sitting silently on his horse. The red coal glowing at the end of his cigar shone at intervals in the darkness, lighting up his face, and the gold band of lace that encircled his hat. Clara was the first to perceive this unexpected apparition.

"Look, Costal!" said he, hastily grasping his companion by the arm, and whispering in his ear; "look there! As I live, the diadem of the Siren!"

The Indian turned his eyes in the direction indicated, and there, sure enough, beheld something of a circular shape, shining in the glow of a reddish-coloured spot of fire.

He might have been as much puzzled to account for this strange appearance as was his companion; but at that moment the moon shot up from behind the bank of clouds that had hitherto hindered her from being seen, and the figures of both horse and rider were brought fully into the light.

Chapter Thirteen
Who goes there?

At a glance Costal saw what the strange object was—a broad band of gold lace encircling a *sombrero*, and placed, Mexican fashion, around the under edge of the brim. The cigar illuminating the lace had deceived the negro, guiding him to the idea of a diadem!

"*Carajo!*" muttered Costal between his teeth, "I told you so. Did I not say that some profane white had hindered the Siren from appearing?"

"You were right," replied Clara, ashamed at the mistake he had made, and from that time losing all belief in the *genius* of the cascade.

"An officer!" murmured Costal, recognising the military equipments of the dragoon, who, with a carbine in one hand, and his bridle in the other, sat smoking his cigar, as immoveable as a statue.

"Who goes there?" cried Costal, saluting him in a loud, bold voice.

"Say, rather, who stands there?" responded Don Rafael, with equal firmness, at the same moment that he recognised in the speaker the Indian whose incantation he had witnessed.

"Delighted to hear you speak at last, my fine fellows," continued the dragoon in his military off-hand way, at the same time causing his horse to step forward face to face with the adventurers.

"Perhaps we are not so much pleased to hear you," replied Costal roughly, as he spoke, shifting his gun from one shoulder to the other.

"Ah! I am sorry for that," rejoined the dragoon, smiling frankly through his thick moustache, "for I'm not inclined to solitary habits, and I'm tired of being here alone."

As Don Rafael said this, he placed his carbine back into its sling, and rebuckled the straps around it, as if it was no longer required. This he did notwithstanding the half-hostile attitude of the adventurers.

The act did not escape the quick perception of the Indian; and, along with the good-humour manifest in the stranger's speech, made an instantaneous impression upon him.

"Perhaps," added Don Rafael, plunging his hand into the pocket of his *jaqueta*, "you have no good feeling towards me for disturbing you in your proceedings, which I confess I did not understand. Neither did they concern me; but you will excuse a strayed traveller, who wished to inquire his way; and as I had no means of making myself heard to you, I was forced to adopt the method I did to draw your attention. I hope that on reflection you will do justice to my dexterity in taking care that none of the stones should hit you."

As he finished speaking the dragoon took a dollar from his purse, and offered it to the Indian.

"Thank you," said Costal, delicately refusing the piece, but which Clara, less scrupulous, transferred to his pocket. "Thank you, *cavallero*! May I ask where you are going?"

"To the hacienda Las Palmas."

"Las Palmas?"

"Yes—am I far from it?"

"Well," replied Costal, "that depends on the road you take."

"I wish to take the shortest. I am rather pressed for time."

"Well, then—the road which is the shortest is not that which you will find the most easy to follow. If you wish to go by the one on which there is the least danger of your getting astray, you will follow up the course of this river. But if you wish a shorter route—one which avoids the windings of the stream—you will go that way."

As Costal finished speaking, he pointed in a direction very different from that which he had indicated as the course of the river.

The Indian had no design of giving a false direction. Even had the little resentment, which he had conceived for the stranger, not entirely passed, he knew that he dared not mislead a traveller on the way to the hacienda, of which he was himself a servitor. But he no longer held any grudge against the young officer, and his directions were honestly meant.

While they were speaking, another of those terrible screams that had perplexed the traveller broke in upon the dialogue. It was the cry of the jaguar, and came from the direction in which lay the route indicated by Costal as the shortest.

"What on earth is that?" inquired the officer.

"Only a jaguar searching for prey," coolly responded Costal.

"Oh!" said the dragoon, "is that all? I was fancying it might be something more fearful."

"Your shortest route, then, lies that way," said Costal, resuming his directions, and pointing with his gun towards the spot where the howl of the tiger had been heard.

"Thank you!" said the horseman, gathering up his reins, and heading his horse to the path. "If that is the shortest, I shall take it."

"Stay!" said Costal, approaching a little nearer, and speaking with more cordiality than he had yet shown.

"*Oigate, señor cavallero*! A brave man like you does not need to be warned of every danger; but one ought to be informed of the dangers one must meet."

Don Rafael checked his horse.

"Speak, friend," said he; "I shall not listen to you ungratefully."

"To reach from here the hacienda of Las Palmas," continued Costal, "without going astray, or making détours, be careful always to keep the moon to your left, so that your shadow may be thrown on the right—a little slanting—just as you are at this moment. Moreover, when you have started, never draw bridle till you have reached the house of Don Mariano de Silva. If you meet a ditch, or brake, or ravine, cross them in a direct line, and don't attempt to go round them."

The Indian gave these directions in so grave a tone of voice, and with such solemnity of manner, that Don Rafael was struck with surprise.

"What frightful danger is it that threatens me?" he inquired at length.

"A danger," replied Costal, "compared with which that of all the tigers that ever howled over these plains is but child's play—the danger of the *inundation*! Perhaps before an hour has passed, it will come sweeping over these savannas like a foaming sea. The *arriero* and his mules, as well as the shepherd and his flocks, will be carried away by its flood, if they don't succeed in reaching the shelter of that very hacienda where you are going. Ay! the very tigers will not escape, with all their swiftness."

"I shall pay strict attention to the directions you have given me," said the officer—once more about to ride off—when just then he remembered his fellow-traveller whom he had left on the road.

In a few hurried words he made known to the Indian the situation of the young student of theology.

"Make your mind easy about him," replied the latter. "We shall bring him to the hacienda to-morrow, if we find him still alive. Think only of yourself, and those who might bewail your death. If you meet the jaguars don't trouble yourself about them. Should your horse refuse to pass them, speak to him. If the brutes come too near you, let them hear you as well. The human voice was given us to procure respect, which it will do from the most ferocious of animals. The whites don't know this—because fighting the tiger is not their trade, as it is that of the red man; and I can tell you an adventure of this kind that I once had with a jaguar—Bah; he's gone!"

The last exclamatory phrases were drawn from the speaker, on perceiving that the horseman, instead of staying to listen to his tale of adventure, had put spurs to his horse, and suddenly ridden away.

In another instant he was beyond earshot, galloping over the moonlit plain in the direction of the hacienda Las Palmas.

"Well!" cried Costal, as he stood gazing after him, "he's a frank brave fellow, and I should be very sorry if any mischance were to happen to him. I was not pleased about his interrupting us. It was a pity, to be sure; but after all, had I been in his place I should have done just as he did. Never mind," he added, after a pause, "all is not over—we shall find another opportunity."

"Hum!" said Clara, "I think the sooner we get out of the neighbourhood of these tigers the better for our skins. For my part, I've had enough adventure for one day."

"Bah! still frightened about the tigers! For shame, Clara! Look at this young man, who never saw a jaguar in his life; and heeds them no more than so many field mice. Come along!"

"What have we to do now?"

"The spirit of the waters," replied Costal, "does not show herself in the cascade alone. She appears also to those who invoke her with the conch, amidst the yellow waves of the inundation. To-morrow we may try again."

"What about the young fellow whom the officer has recommended to our care?"

"We shall go to look after him in the morning. Meanwhile, we must have some rest ourselves. Let us climb out of the ravine, and carry the canoe up to the summit of the *Cerro de la Mesa*. There we shall sleep tranquilly, without fear either of floods or jaguars."

"That's just the thing," said Clara, his black face brightening up at the prospect of a good night's rest. "To say the truth, friend Costal, I'm tired enough myself. Our gymnastics up yonder, on the *ahuehuetes*, have made every bone in my body as sore as a blister."

And as the two *confrères* ended their dialogue, they stepped briskly forward, and were soon at the top of the precipitous path that led up from the ravine.

Chapter Fourteen
Precious Moments

The Captain of the Queen's Dragoons continued his gallop towards the hacienda of Las Palmas.

For the first mile or two of his route, he passed over the broad plain that lay silent under the soft light of the moon. The frondage of the palms swayed gently under a sky sparkling with stars, and the penetrating odour of the guavas loaded the atmosphere with a delicious perfume. So tranquil was the scene, that Don Rafael began to think the Indian had been playing upon his credulity. Mechanically he relaxed his pace, and delivered himself up to one of those sweet reveries which the tropic night often awakens within the spirit of the traveller. At such an hour one experiences a degree of rapture in listening to the voices of earth and heaven, like a hymn which each alternately chants to the other.

All at once the traveller remembered what for the last two days of his journey had been perplexing him—the houses abandoned—the canoes suspended from the trees. Now, for the first time, did he comprehend the meaning of these circumstances, no longer strange. The canoes and *periaguas* had been thus placed as a last means of safety, for those who might be so unfortunate as to be overtaken by the inundation.

Suddenly rousing himself from his reverie, Don Rafael again spurred his horse into a gallop.

He had ridden scarce a mile further, when all at once the voices of the night became hushed. The cicadas in the trees, and the crickets under the grass, as if by mutual consent, discontinued their cheerful chirrup; and the breeze, hitherto soft and balmy, was succeeded by puffs of wind, exhaling a marshy odour, stifling as the breath of some noisome pestilence.

This ominous silence was not of long duration. Presently the traveller perceived a hoarse distant roaring, not unlike that of the cataract he had left behind him; but from a point diametrically opposite—in fact, from the direction towards which he was heading.

At first he fancied that in his momentary fit of abstraction he had taken a wrong direction, and might be returning upon the stream. But no: the moon was on his left; his shadow and that of his horse were projected to the opposite side. He must still be on the right road.

His heart began to bound more quickly within his breast. If the Indian had spoken the truth, a danger lay before him against which neither his carbine nor rapier—neither courage nor a strong arm—could avail him. His only hope rested in the speed and strength of his horse.

Fortunately, the long journey had not deprived the brave steed of all his vigour. With ears laid back, and muzzle stretched horizontally forward, he continued his rapid gallop; his spread nostrils inhaling the puffs of damp air which came like avant-couriers in advance of the troubled waters.

It was now a struggle between the horseman and the flood, as to which should first reach the hacienda of Las Palmas.

The officer slackened his bridle-rein. The tinkling rowels of his spurs resounded against the ribs of his horse. The trial of speed had commenced. The plain appeared to glide past him like the current of a river. The bushes and tall palms seemed flying backward.

The inundation was rolling from west to east. The horseman was hastening in the opposite direction. Both must soon come together; but at what place?

The distance between them was rapidly diminishing. The noise of the flood, at first low, like the muttering of distant thunder, was gradually growing louder. The palms still appeared to glide past like spectres, but as yet the belfry of the hacienda had not come in sight. Neither as yet was visible the threatening mass of the inundation.

At this perilous moment Don Rafael perceived that his horse was sensibly slackening his pace. The sides of the animal felt swollen, and heaved with a convulsive panting.

The air, so rapidly cut in his swift course, with difficulty entered his nostrils. A few seconds longer, and that in his lungs must give out.

The officer drew up for an instant. The breathing of his horse appeared obstructed, and the hoarse sound, caused by its inspiration, was a mournful accompaniment to the sough of the waters that were constantly advancing.

The traveller listened to these sounds with a sentiment of despair.

Just then he heard the clanging of a bell, as if hurriedly tolled. It was that of the hacienda, giving out its warning notes over the wide savanna.

A reflection crossed his mind. It had been partly suggested by the words of the Indian: "*Think only of those who may bewail your death.*" Was there in that hacienda, where he was hourly expected, one who would bewail it? Perhaps yes, and bitterly!

The thought would have urged him onward; but Don Rafael still remained halted. He saw that his horse required a moment of rest, in order to recover his wind, otherwise he could not have proceeded.

The dragoon had the presence of mind to perceive this imperious necessity; and, in spite of the danger that threatened he dismounted, loosened the girdle of his saddle, thus permitting the horse to breathe more freely.

Chapter Fifteen
A Friend in Need

He was counting with anxiety the minutes that passed, when at that moment there echoed upon his ear the hoof-strokes of another horse, going at full gallop.

It was a horseman following the same route, and running the same risk as himself. He was mounted upon a strong, swift animal, that appeared to pass over the ground like a bird upon the wing.

In an instant the horseman came up, and drawing vigorously on the bridle, halted alongside.

"What are you about?" cried the new-comer, speaking in hurried phrase. "Do you not hear the alarm-bell? Don't you know that the flood is coming down?"

"Yes; but my horse has given out. I am waiting till he recovers his wind."

The stranger cast a glance towards the bay-brown of Don Rafael, and then threw himself out of his saddle. "Take hold of this," he said, flinging his bridle to the officer. "Let me examine your horse."

Raising the saddle-flap, he placed his hand underneath, to feel the pulsations of the lungs.

"All right yet," he exclaimed, after a pause, apparently satisfied that the animal would recover.

Then stooping down, he took up a large stone, and began to rub it vigorously over the ribs and along the belly of the panting steed.

Don Rafael could not help gazing with curious interest on a man who, thus careless of his own life, was occupying himself so generously about the safety of another—that other, too, a perfect stranger!

The man was costumed as an *arriero* (muleteer). A species of tight-fitting blouse, of coarse greyish-coloured wool, striped black, covered the upper part of his body, over which, in front, hung a short leathern apron. Wide calzoneros of linen flapped about his legs. His feet were encased in buskins of brown goat-skin, while over his face fell the shadow of a broad-brimmed hat of coarse felt cloth.

He was a man of less than medium size; but with a sweet expression of features, from which his sunburnt complexion did not detract. Even at that terrible moment his countenance appeared calm and serene!

Don Rafael did not attempt to interrupt his proceedings, but stood regarding him with a feeling of deep gratitude.

For some moments the muleteer continued to use the stone. Then stopping the process, he placed his hand once more to feel the pulsation. This time he appeared less satisfied than before.

"He will founder," said he, "if something be not done to prevent it. He must have more breath through his nostrils. There is but one way to save him. Assist me to try it. We must haste, for the bell is tolling with double violence to give warning that the waters are near."

As he was speaking, he drew a cord from the pocket of his leathern apron; and, forming a running noose at one end of it, he drew it tightly around the muzzle of the horse, just above the nostrils.

"Now," said he, handing the cord to Don Rafael. "First cover the horse's eyes with your handkerchief; and then hold the cord with all your might."

While Don Rafael hastened to obey the directions, the muleteer took a knife from his belt, and with a quick cut divided the transparent partition between the nostrils of the animal. The blood gushed forth in copious jets; and the horse, notwithstanding the efforts of Don Rafael to hold him to the ground, reared up on his hind legs, and struck forward with his hoofs. A hollow gurgling noise came forth from his nostrils as the air rushed in through the opening that had been made.

"Now!" exclaimed the muleteer, "you need no longer fear for his wind. Your horse can run as far as his legs will carry him. You will be saved if you are to be saved."

"Your name," cried Don Rafael, stretching out his hand to the muleteer; "your name, that I may always keep it in remembrance."

"Valerio Trujano, a poor *arriero*; not very fortunate in his affairs, but who consoles himself with the belief that he has done his duty, and leaves the rest to God. Our lives are now in His hands. Let us pray that He may preserve them from the awful danger that is before us."

Repeating these words with an air of solemnity, the muleteer took off his hat, displaying to view a mass of black curling hair. Then kneeling upon the sand, he raised his eyes to heaven, and in a voice of prayer pronounced the words:—

"De profundis clamavi ad te, Domine! Domine, exaudi vocem meam!"

While the muleteer was engaged in his devotion, the dragoon tightened his girths for the last struggle; and both at the same time springing into their saddles, resumed the gallop that had been so unfortunately interrupted. The damp, chill wind which preceded the coming of the waters bore loudly to their ears the warning notes of the bell—mingled with the sinister sounds that betokened the approach of the inundation.

Chapter Sixteen
Las Palmas and its People

The southern portion of the state of Vera Cruz, bordering on Tehuantepec, exhibits a singular hydrographic system. A number of great rivers, as the *Rio Blanc*, the *Plaza Vicente*, the *Goazacoalcos*, and the *Papatoapan*, with many of smaller note, form a complete network over the country. Most of these rivers have their sources in the *Sierra Madre*, and traversing the plains of the *tierra calienté*, debouch into the Gulf of Mexico.

Every one has heard how profusely the rain falls in tropical countries during that period of the year known as the "rainy season." It is the American winter of these southern latitudes, commencing in the month of June, and ending in October. At this time the waters of the rivers above mentioned, augmented by torrents of rain falling daily, break over the boundaries of their channels, and, free as the wild horses upon their banks, rush impetuously over the surrounding plains.

Almost with the rapidity of a galloping steed, the yellow flood rolls onward, as if impelled by the breath of a demon, carrying terror and desolation in its track. Woe to the living thing unable to flee before its watery phalanx!

The inundations proceeding simultaneously from the different streams soon become joined to one another; and the waters, now spread over a vast tract of country, flow in a more tranquil current. Thus united together, they form an immense sea, covering the whole extent of the savannas; upon the tranquil surface of which may be seen the *débris* of their destructive violence, with the carcasses of all sorts of animals.

In the country thus inundated a singular spectacle may at this time be witnessed: villages completely surrounded by water, as if built upon islands; trees with their trunks submerged, their leafy tops alone visible; canoes and large *periaguas*, decked with flags and filled with people in their holiday suits, trying to outdo each other in speed or elegance of adornment; while groups of young girls, gaily dressed and crowned with flowers, may be seen seated in the boats, singing to the inspiriting accompaniment of the harp or mandolin.

The situation in which the hacienda of Las Palmas stood had been chosen with a view to provide against these annual floods. It was upon the north side of a plait apparently boundless towards the south, east, and west. The house stood upon an eminence of no great elevation—a sort of outlying spur of a higher ridge that backed it upon the north. It was isolated, however, and at some distance from the ridge, whose direction was eastward and westward. The hill upon which the hacienda stood was one of those singular eminences known in Spanish-America by the name of *mesa* (table). Its flat top formed an oblong parallelogram, at one end of which stood the dwelling-house, the other being occupied by the storehouses and stables. These were upon an extensive scale, all enclosed within a wall of strong mason-work. In the same enclosure were rows of chambers for the lodgment of the *peons, vaqueros*, and other retainers of the establishment.

The dwelling-house, standing upon the southern extremity of the *mesa*, fronted towards the great plain. In its centre a massive double door opened into the courtyard, or *patio*; and this entrance was reached by a broad causeway, sloping upward with a gentle declivity from the plain, and fenced along each edge by a parapet of strong mason-work. Thus situated, the hacienda of Las Palmas—so named from the numerous topes of palm-trees which mottled the plain in front—not only defied the flood, but might have served as a fortress of no despicable strength. The proprietor of this dwelling, as well as the extensive estate surrounding it, was Don Mariano de Silva.

The bell of the hacienda had tolled the evening *oration*, and the tinkling of the *angelus* was sounding the summons to prayer. At that moment might be witnessed an interesting spectacle upon the plain adjoining the dwelling of Don Mariano de Silva. The Indian labourers, who never work a moment beyond the prescribed time, at the first sound of the bell had all suddenly stopped as if struck by paralysis. The pickaxe raised aloft, the spade half buried in the earth, the goad lifted to prick forward the ox, fell simultaneously from their hands; while the oxen themselves, accustomed to imitate their drivers, came at once to a stand, leaving the plough in the half-finished furrow. The *vaqueros* galloped straight to their stables and unsaddled their horses; the peons came crowding in from the fields; and while the plain was thus deserted the corral and outhouses became crowded.

In the midst of this crowd women were seen hurrying to and fro, carrying hot plates of *comal, tortillas*, and *chile colorado*, destined for the evening repast.

The sun was yet shining brightly, and his last rays darted their golden light through the iron bars and green trelliswork of the windows of the hacienda. One, however, that looked eastward was sheltered from his beams; and a traveller coming in that direction might have observed that the lattice blind was raised up, and the rich amber-coloured curtains were visible behind it, although partially drawn. The window was at no great height from the ground, in fact on the ground-floor itself; but the house standing upon the pedestal of the *mesa* was elevated several feet above the level of the plain, and a horseman, however high his horse, could not have looked into the chamber thus situated.

There was no traveller, however, in sight; no one except some belated labourers, who, through the luminous haze of the setting sun, could be seen making their way towards the hacienda.

Any one who could have looked into this chamber would have there beheld a scene of more than ordinary interest. Though a mansion in the western world, the style and furnishing of the apartment exhibited a certain character of *orientalism*: for Mexico has long held traffic with the countries of the far East.

At that moment the chamber contained something of more interest than even its rich furniture. Three young girls graced it by their presence. Two of them were evidently sisters—judging by the air of familiarity that existed between them, rather than by any very marked personal resemblance. They were the daughters of Don Mariano, the proprietor of the mansion. The third was simply a servant—their waiting-maid.

Chapter Seventeen
A Creole Toilette

It is customary in Europe to accuse the Creole ladies of tropical America of the crime of indolence. This custom is common with those who talk of woman and her political rights, and who believe that woman was created to share man's labours instead of soothing them. He, however, who has looked upon these fair Creole women and observed their tranquil repose of spirit—perhaps a certain sensualism, which only adds to their beauty—he, I say, who has seen this, will be disposed to look with a more lenient eye upon their so-called indolence, and will scarce believe it a crime.

The two daughters of Don Mariano de Silva offered at this moment, though in degrees somewhat different, examples of this peculiar characteristic of their countrywomen. One of them, with her limbs crossed in the oriental fashion, was seated upon a Chinese mat. Her long black hair, that had been plaited in several tresses, and recently combed out, still preserved the wavy outlines of the plaits, as it fell profusely over her shoulders.

Perhaps there are no women in the world who take more pride in their hair than do the Creoles of Spanish-America. It is never desecrated by the touch of the scissors; and several hours of every day are bestowed upon the dressing of it. For all this, the young girl in question, as she sat with her head pensively inclined, seemed to give but little thought to those luxuriant tresses that, undulating over her white shoulders, lay in clusters upon the mat. She appeared rather to deliver them up mechanically to the hands of her attendant, who was occupied in arranging them.

The face encircled by these exuberant masses of glossy hair, possessed all the characteristics of the finest Creole beauty. Her features, at once proud and calm, denoted an ardent and enthusiastic spirit habitually hidden under an expression of indolent serenity. The elegance of the Spanish race was also manifest in her small white hands, and in those little feet possessed by Mexican and South American women of whatever class. Blue satin slippers covered those of the young girl, otherwise nude: for stockings are not a rigorous necessity of Creole costume.

The young lady thus described was Doña Gertrudis, the elder of the two daughters of Don Mariano.

The younger, Marianita, was scarce less beautiful, but her beauty was of a different style. Quick-witted, and prone to laughter, her sparkling glances formed a contrast to the calm yet brilliant gaze of her sister; while varying expressions passed as rapidly over her countenance as the fleeting shadows of an April sky. With Doña Gertrudis it was altogether different; she resembled the volcanoes of her country, with their perpetual fire hidden under a robe of snow.

Neither of the young girls had yet reached the age of womanhood. Gertrudis was only seventeen, while the other was a year and a half younger. Both, however, had acquired that full development of feminine beauty which a tropical climate often calls forth at a much earlier age.

While the hair of Gertrudis was being arranged by her waiting woman, Marianita was tying around her ankle the ribbons that were to confine the tiny slipper upon her pretty little foot.

The grand political events at this time occurring had disturbed the quietude of this family, as well as that of most others. There were some probabilities, too, of there being a difference of opinion among its members, for at the moment when our narrative commences, a marriage was on the *tapis* between a young Spaniard of the neighbourhood and Doña Marianita.

Previous to the Mexican revolution, the most ardent wish of a young Creole lady was to obtain for a husband some new arrival from the mother country—Spain. Gertrudis, nevertheless, had more than once declined this honour, which Marianita, as we have seen, had accepted. Why did the Doña Gertrudis form an exception to the general rule? The sequel will show.

We have presented these two young girls in the act of making their toilet; we may add, that these preparations were in view of the arrival of two gentlemen who were that evening expected. One was the young Spaniard, the betrothed lover of Marianita; the other Don Rafael Tres-Villas, Captain in the Queen's Dragoons. The former lived within less than two leagues of the hacienda Las Palmas, and might be expected at any moment—the other, having two hundred to travel, could scarce be looked for with equal punctuality; for although he had sent positive word that he would arrive on that evening, it was reasonable to suppose that upon such a long journey some incident might arise to derange his calculations. Was this uncertainty the reason why Gertrudis had scarce commenced making her toilet, while Marianita had finished hers? Was Don Rafael the only man in whose eyes Gertrudis cared to appear beautiful? We shall presently know.

One of the daily cares of a young Creole lady is to take down the abundant plaits of her hair, and combing out the separate tresses, leave them hanging over her shoulders, so that the air may circulate freely among them. As soon as the attendant of Gertrudis, charged with this duty in the present instance, had accomplished her task, she passed out of the chamber, and the two sisters were left alone.

There are certain subjects of conversation which young girls, of whatever country, love only to talk of between themselves, and in their own private apartment.

Scarce had the servant closed the door behind her, than Marianita — who had just finished placing some pomegranate flowers behind her tortoiseshell comb — glided eagerly towards the window. On reaching it she stood for some moments with her eyes bent inquiringly on the plain. Gertrudis had changed her oriental posture for a seat upon a leathern *fauteuil*. After casting back, by an indolent movement of her arms, the dark masses of her hair, she delivered herself up to a silent reverie.

"I have examined the plain with all my eyes," said Marianita after a while spent at the window; "it appears entirely deserted. I cannot see a human creature upon it, much less Don Fernando, or Don Rafael. Santissima! I fear I have had all this trouble for nothing; in half an hour it will be sunset."

"You need not be uneasy. Don Fernando will come," said Gertrudis, in a calm voice.

"Ah!" exclaimed Marianita, "one might tell by the tone in which you speak that you are not expecting your *novio* (betrothed), as I am. My very impatience makes me despair of seeing him. Ah! Gertrudis, you have never experienced the emotion of love."

"Were I in your place I should feel more chagrin than impatience."

"Chagrin, oh! no; if Don Fernando don't choose to come this evening, he will lose the pleasure of seeing me in this beautiful white dress which he admires so much, and with these purple pomegranates in my hair, which I put in just to please him. For my part I prefer the white blossoms of the orange; but they say that a woman when married must make some sacrifices, and I may as well accustom myself to them."

In saying these words the young girl snapped her fingers together till they cracked like castanets; while her countenance, instead of expressing any very painful emotion, exhibited an air of perfect contentment.

Gertrudis made no answer, except by a sigh, half-suppressed. She sat motionless, with the exception of her foot, which kept balancing upward and downward the little slipper of blue satin, while the fresh breeze of the evening blowing in from the window, caused a gentle tremulous movement among the tresses of her hair.

"It's very tiresome—this country life," continued Marianita; "it's true one can pass the day by combing out one's hair, and taking a siesta; but in the evening, to have nothing else to do but walk in the garden and listen to the sighing breeze, instead of singing and dancing in a *tertulia*! Oh, it is wearisome—very, very wearisome, I declare. We are here, like the captive princesses in an Eastern romance, which I commenced reading last year, but which I have not yet finished. Santa Virgen! I see a cloud of dust upon the horizon at last—a horseman! *Que clicha*! (what happiness!)"

"A horseman!—what is the colour of his steed?" inquired Gertrudis, suddenly aroused.

"Ha—ha! As I live his horse is a mule—what a pity it was not some knight-errant! but I have heard that these fine gentry no longer exist."

Gertrudis again sighed.

"Ah! I can distinguish him now," continued Marianita. "It is a priest who rides the mule. Well, a priest is better than nobody—especially if he can play as well on the mandolin as the last one that travelled this way, and stayed two days with us. He! He is coming on a gallop—that's not a bad sign. But no! he has a very grave, demure look. Ah! he sees me; he is waving a salute. Well, I must go down and kiss his hand, I suppose."

Saying these words, the young Creole—whose education taught her that it was her duty to kiss the hand of every priest who came to the hacienda—pursed up her pretty rose-coloured lips in a saucy mocking fashion.

"Come, Gertrudis!" continued she; "come along with me. He is just by the entrance gate!"

"Do you see no one upon the plain?" inquired Gertrudis, not appearing to trouble herself about the arrival of the priest. "No other horseman—Don Fernando, for instance?"

"Ah, yes!" answered Marianita, once more looking from the window. "Don Fernando transformed into a mule-driver, who is forcing his *recua* into a gallop, as if he wished the loaded animals to run a race with one another! Why, the muleteer is making for the hacienda, as well as the priest, and galloping like him, too! What on earth can be the matter with the people? One would think that they had taken leave of their senses!"

The clanging of bolts and creaking hinges announced the opening of the great gate; and this, followed by a confused clatter of hoof-strokes, told that the mule-driver with his train of animals was also about to receive the hospitality of the hacienda. This circumstance, contrary to all usage, somewhat surprised the young girls, who were wondering why the house was being thus turned into an hostelry. They were further surprised at hearing an unusual stir in the courtyard—the servants of the establishment talking in a clamorous medley of voices, and footsteps falling heavily on the pavements and stone stairs leading up to the *azotéa* of the building.

"Jesus!" exclaimed Marianita, making the sign of the cross; "is the hacienda going to be besieged, I wonder? Mercy on us! I hope the insurgent brigands may not be coming to attack us!"

"Shame, sister!" said Gertrudis, in a tone of calm reproach. "Why do you call them brigands?—these men who are fighting for their liberties, and who are led by venerable priests?"

"Why do I call them brigands?" brusquely responded Marianita. "Because they hate the Spaniards, whose pure blood runs in our veins; and because," continued she—the impetuous Creole blood mounting to her cheek—"because *I* love a Spaniard!"

"Ah!" replied Gertrudis, in the same reproachful tone; "you perhaps only fancy you love him? In my opinion, sister, true love presents certain symptoms which I don't perceive in you."

"And what matters if I do not love him, so long as he loves me? Am I not soon to belong to him? And why, then, should I think different to what he does? No, no!" added the young girl, with that air of passionate devotion which the women of her country and race lavish without limits on those whom they love.

At this moment, the sudden and unexpected strokes of the alarm-bell breaking upon their ears interrupted the dialogue between the two sisters, putting an end to a conversation which promised to engender ill-feeling between them—just as the same topic had already caused dissension in more than one family circle, breaking the nearest and dearest ties of friendship and kindred.

Chapter Eighteen
The Inundation

Just as Marianita was about to open the door and inquire the cause of the tumult, the *femme-de-chambre* rushed into the room; and, without waiting to be questioned, cried out—

"*Ave Maria, señoritas! the inundation is coming*! A vaquero has just galloped in to say that the waters are already within a league or two of the hacienda!"

"The inundation!" echoed both the sisters in a breath; Marianita repeating the sign of the cross, while Gertrudis bounded up from the *fauteuil*, and, gathering her long hair around her wrists, rushed towards the window.

"*Jesus! señorita*," cried the waiting-maid, addressing herself to Gertrudis, "one would think you were going to leap down to the plain, as if to save some one in danger."

"Don Rafael, God have pity on him!" exclaimed Gertrudis in a state of distraction.

"Don Fernando!" cried Marianita, shuddering as she spoke.

"The plain will soon be one great lake," continued the servant; "woe to them who may be caught upon it! But as for Don Fernando, you may make yourself easy, señorita. The vaquero who came in was sent by Don Fernando with a message to master, to say that he would be here in the morning in his boat."

After delivering this intelligence the attendant retired, leaving the young girls once more alone.

"In a boat!" exclaimed Marianita, as soon as the servant had gone out. "Oh, Gertrudis!" she continued, suddenly passing from sadness to a transport of joy, "won't that be delightful? We shall sail upon the water in our state barge crowned with flowers, and—"

As Marianita turned round, her transport of frivolous egotism was suddenly checked, as she saw her sister, with her long dark tresses hanging dishevelled around her, kneeling in front of an image of the Madonna. Giving way to a feeling of reproach, she also knelt down and mingled her prayers with those of Gertrudis, while the alarm-bell continued to peal forth to the four quarters of the compass its notes of solemn and lugubrious import.

"Oh, my poor Gertrudis!" said she, taking her sister's hand in her own, while her tears fell fast upon the glistening tresses; "pardon me if, in the fulness of my own joy, I did not perceive that your heart was breaking. Don Rafael—you love him then?"

"If he die I shall die too—that is all I know," murmured Gertrudis, with a choking sigh.

"Nay, do not fear, Gertrudis; God will protect him. He will send one of his messengers to save him," said the young girl, in the simplicity of her faith; and then returning, she mingled her prayers with those of her sister, now and then alternating them with words of consolation.

"Go to the window!" said Gertrudis, after some time had passed. "See if there is yet any one upon the plain. I cannot, for my eyes are filled with tears. I shall remain here."

And, saying these words, Gertrudis again knelt before the image of the Virgin.

Marianita instantly obeyed the request, and, gliding across the floor, took her stand by the open window. The golden haze that had hitherto hung over the plain was darkening into a purple violet colour, but no horseman appeared in the distance.

"The horse he will be riding," said Gertrudis, at the moment interrupting her devotions, "will be his bay-brown. He knows how much I admire that beautiful steed—his noble war-horse that carried him through all his campaigns against the Indians. I have often taken the flowers from my hair to place them upon the frontlet of the brave bay-brown. Oh! *Virgen Santissima*! O Jesus! sweet Lord! Don Rafael! my beautiful! my loved! who will bring you to me?" cried the young girl—her wild, passionate ejaculations mingling with the words of her prayer.

The plain was every moment becoming less visible to the eye, as the twilight deepened into the shadows of night, when all at once it was re-illuminated by the pale rays of the moon. Still no horseman could be seen either near or afar off—nothing but the tall, dark palm-trees that stood motionless in the midst of the silent savanna.

"He has been warned in time," suggested Marianita, in hopes of tranquillising her sister. "Most likely he will not have set out to-day."

"Oh, no—no!" cried Gertrudis, wringing her hands in anguish; "you are wrong. I know Don Rafael too well. I judge his heart by my own. I am sure he would try to be here this very evening. Another day would be too long for him. He would brave every danger, if only to see me a few hours sooner—I know he would. I know he will be coming at this moment!"

Just then a noise as of distant thunder was heard mingling with the metallic notes of the bell; and simultaneous with this ominous dialogue, between the hoarse muffled rumbling of the waters and the lugubrious clanging, a sheen of reddish light was seen to gleam suddenly over the moon-whitened plain, and, as it glared far into the distance, illuminating the dark forms of the palm-trees. It was proceeding from the beacon fires which Don Mariano had caused to be kindled both on the platform of the hacienda and on the higher ridge behind it—in hopes that their light might serve as a guide to those who might be still wandering upon the plain.

Both the eye and the ear were thus warned of the threatening danger; and, as the people moved around the blazing fires, their shadows, magnified to gigantic proportions, were projected far out upon the savanna.

The moments passed slowly, amidst fearful and ominous sounds. The muffled roar of the inundation was every instant heard more distinctly, as the exasperated flood came rolling onward. Already it resembled the noise of the loudest thunder, when the mass of dense waters was seen glistening under the light of the fires, only a few hundred paces distant from the western wall of the hacienda!

"Oh, sister!" cried Gertrudis, in a voice of despair, "look again! Is no one in sight? O mercy!"

Marianita still stood by the window, eagerly directing her glance over the plain, and endeavouring to penetrate the obscure gleam outside the circle lighted by the glare of the fires.

"No—no one," replied she; and then her tone suddenly changing into one of terror, she shrieked out—"O mercy! I see two horsemen—yes; they are horsemen. *Madre de Dios*! they are flying like the wind! Alas! alas! they will be too late!"

As she spoke, loud shouts were heard from above—from the *azotéa* of the house—to which Don Mariano and a crowd of servants had ascended. Other men, mounted on horseback, galloped along the terrace upon which the house stood, waving long lazoes around their heads, and ready to fling them out as soon as the two travellers should approach within reach. The men below were also uttering loud cries, unable to restrain their voices at the sight of the two horsemen thus desperately struggling to anticipate the approach of the mass of roaring waters. Already the flood was rushing forward upon the walls of the hacienda, approaching like waves of fire under the glare of the flaming beacons.

The sisters within the chamber heard the cries, without seeing those that gave utterance to them, or knowing aught of the movements that were being made for rescuing the two horsemen from their perilous position.

"Oh, Gertrudis!" cried Marianita, now leaning out from the window, and clinging convulsively to one of the iron bars, "come hither and see them! You can tell whether it be Don Rafael. I do not know him. If it be he, your voice might encourage him."

"I cannot—I cannot!" replied Gertrudis, in a voice quivering with emotion. "Oh, sister! I dare not look upon such a spectacle. 'Tis he—too well my heart tells me it is he—oh, I can only pray for him!"

"They are both mounted on dark-coloured horses. One of them is a little man. He is in the costume of an arriero. That cannot be Don Rafael!"

"The other? the other?" cried Gertrudis in a low but anxious tone.

"The other," answered Marianita, "is a head taller than the first. He sits his horse like a centaur. Now I can see his face distinctly. He has a fine noble countenance, with black moustaches. There is a band of gold lace on his hat. The danger does not appear to alarm him. Ah! he is a noble, handsome fellow."

"It is he!" cried Gertrudis, in a voice that could be heard high above the *mêlée* of sounds. "Yes—it is Don Rafael!" she repeated, springing to her feet, as if with the intention of beholding him once more before he should be engulfed in the flood of waters. "Where, sister? where?" she continued, gliding towards the window; but before she had made three steps across the chamber, her strength failed her, and she sank half-fainting upon the floor.

"Mercy!" exclaimed Marianita, half stupified with terror. "Oh! *Jesus Maria*! another bound of their horses, and they will be safe! *Valga me Dios*! too late—too late! there are the waters. Oh! their wild roar! hear how they beat against the walls. Mother of God! shield these brave men! They hold one another by the hand! They bury their spurs in their horses' flanks! They ride forward without fear! They advance upon the frothing flood, as if they were charging upon an enemy! Virgin of Paradise! one of them, the smaller, is actually chaunting a hymn!"

In effect, at that moment the voice of a man was heard above the rush of the water, crying out in measured accents—

"*In manus tuas, Domine! commendo animam meam!*"

"Merciful Father!" cried Marianita, "I see them no more, the waters are over them both!"

For a moment a death-like silence reigned in the apartment, broken only by the groaning of the waters, and the shouts of those clustering upon the *azotéa* without.

Gertrudis, prostrate amidst the tresses of her dishevelled hair, was no longer able to give utterance to a word even in prayer.

The voice of Marianita once more aroused her.

"Now I see them again," continued she, "but no, only one! There is only one of them in the saddle. It is the taller one—he with the moustache. The other is gone. No! I see him, but he is dismounted, and borne off upon the flood. There! the other has seized hold of him! he raises him up, and draws him across his horse. What a powerful arm the brave man must have—he lifts the other like a child! The horse too appears strong as his master. How gallantly he breasts the flood with both men upon his back! What a strange sound comes from his nostrils! Now they are heading for the walls. *Santissima Virgen*! will you allow this brave cavalier to perish? he who overcomes that which has rooted up the trees of the forest?"

"Oh!" cried Gertrudis, recovering her strength, and speaking in a burst of passionate pride; "it is Don Rafael, I am sure! No other could perform such a deed!"

Her heart suddenly sank again, as she observed that her sister once more spoke in a tone of anguish.

"Alas, alas!" cried Marianita, "an enormous tree is drifting towards them! Oh! it will strike the horse! they will be overwhelmed by it."

"Angel, whose name he bears!" shrieked Gertrudis, "angel, protect him! Virgin Mary, appease the rage of the waters, and shield him from destruction! Holy Virgin, save him, *and I vow to sacrifice my hair for his life!*"

This was the most precious offering the young Creole could think of making to the Virgin, and as if the vow had been accepted, the voice of Marianita was at that moment heard in a more cheerful tone.

"Blessed be God!" exclaimed she, "they will yet be saved! A dozen lazoes are around the tree. They have been thrown by people from the house. Good! the trunk no longer rolls onward. It is checked and held by the ropes. The brave horseman might easily mount upon it. But no! he will not abandon his noble horse, nor the man he is holding in his arms. See, he is riding around the tree, his brave steed plunging through the water with all his strength. Once more he is breasting the flood—on—on—ah! hear those shouts of triumph! He is up to the walls! he is saved!"

A loud triumphant cheer rising from below, and blending with a similar cry that pealed along the roof of the hacienda, confirmed the words of Marianita; and the two sisters rushing together became locked in a mutual embrace.

"Ah, Gertrudis!" said Marianita, after a moment, "you have vowed your hair to the Virgin? your beautiful hair, worth a kingdom!"

"Yes," responded Gertrudis, "and, were it worth a world, I should have given it all the same for the life of my noble Don Rafael. Ah! yes; and he shall cut it from my head with his own hands!"

Chapter Nineteen
The Last of the Zapoteques

At no great distance from the cascade already introduced to the reader, there rises a little hill, with a flat or table-shaped top, as if it had once been a cone, whose apex had been cut off by some freak of nature. As already observed, such eminences are not uncommon throughout the plains of America, where they are generally termed *mesas*, or *cerros de la mesa* (table hills). The archaeologists of the province, in speaking of the hill in question — which simply bore the name of *Cerro-de-la-mesa* — declared it to be an ancient shrine of the Zapoteques. Tradition says that a temple once stood upon it; but, if so, it must have been constructed of very perishable materials; since no ruin testifies to the truth of this tradition. Costal, however, believed it, for the *tigrero*, though apparently a Christianised Indian, was still a faithful believer in many of the pagan rites of his fathers; and, influenced by a superstitious feeling, he was in the habit of sleeping upon the summit of the *Cerro-de-la-mesa*, whenever the necessities of his calling compelled him to remain over night in that neighbourhood. A little hut which he had constructed out of bamboos, with the broad leaves of bananas thrown over it for thatch, served him sufficiently well for this occasional and temporary shelter.

Costal had told Clara no more than the truth. He was descended from the ancient Caciques of Tehuantepec; and, while wandering through the midst of the solitary savannas, the falling grandeur of his ancient race was often the subject of his thoughts. Perfectly indifferent to the political quarrels of the whites, he would have regarded the new insurrection of Hidalgo without the slightest interest or enthusiasm; but another motive had kindled within his breast the hope that in the end he might himself profit by the revolutionary movement, and that by the aid of the gold which he vainly dreamt of one day discovering, he might revive in his own person the title of Cacique, and the sovereignty which his ancestors had exercised. The pagan doctrines in which he had been brought up, the solitudes in which he dwelt while engaged in his calling of tiger-hunter, the contemplation of the boundless sea, whose depths he had often explored — for previous to his becoming a *tigrero* he had long practised the perilous profession of a pearl-diver—all these circumstances had contributed to give to his character a tone of singular exaltation which bordered upon frenzy.

Visionary dreamer though he was, he had acquired as much ascendancy over the negro Clara as ever Don Quixote had over his squire Sancho Panza. Nay more, for, unlike the *Manchego* gentleman, he might easily have persuaded his black associate that windmills were giants, since the latter had already taken a captain in the Queen's dragoons for the Siren with the dishevelled hair!

About an hour after this incident we find the two adventurers upon the summit of the *Cerro-de-la-mesa*. Thither they had just transported the canoe of Costal, which, being a light craft, they had carried up on their shoulders without much difficulty. They had placed it keel upwards close to the wall of the bamboo hovel.

"Ouf!" grunted the negro as he sat down upon it. "I think we have fairly earned a minute's rest. What's your opinion, Costal?"

"Didn't you travel through the province of Valladolid?" asked the Indian without replying to Clara's idle question.

"Of course I did," answered the black. "Valladolid, Acapulco, and several other of the south-western provinces. Ah, I know them well—from the smallest path to the most frequented of the great roads—every foot of them. How could I help knowing them? for, in my capacity of *mozo de mulas*, did I not travel them over and over again with my master, Don Vallerio Trujano, a worthy man, whose service I only quitted to turn proprietor in this province of Oajaca?"

Clara pronounced the word *proprietor* emphatically, and with an important air. His proprietorship consisted in being the owner of a small *jacal*, or bamboo hut, and the few feet of ground on which it was built—of which, however, he was only a renter under Don Mariano de Silva. To the haciendado he hired himself out a part of each year, during the gathering of the cochineal crop. The rest of his time he usually passed in a sort of idle independence.

"Why do you ask me these questions?" he added.

"I don't see," said Costal, speaking as much to himself as to his companion, "how we can enrol ourselves in the army of Hidalgo. As a descendant of the Caciques of Tehuantepec, I am not above hiring myself out as a tiger-hunter; but I can never consent to wear a soldier's uniform."

"And why not?" asked Clara. "For my part, I think it would be very fine to have a splendid green coat with red facings, and bright yellow trowsers, like one of these pretty parroquets. I think, however, we need not quarrel on that score. It's not likely that the Señor Hidalgo, though he is generalissimo of the American insurgent army, will have many uniforms to spare; and unless we enrol ourselves as officers, which is not likely, I fear—"

"Stay!" said Costal, interrupting him. "Why couldn't we act as guides and scouts, since you know the country so well? In that capacity we could go and come as we pleased, and would have every opportunity to search for the Siren with the dishevelled hair."

"But is the Siren to be seen everywhere?" naïvely inquired Clara.

"Certainly; she can appear at any place to her faithful worshippers, wherever there is a pool of water in which she can mirror herself, a stream or a cascade in which she may bathe herself, or in the great sea where she searches for pearls to adorn her hair."

"And did you never see her when you were yourself a pearl-fisher on the coast of the Gulf?"

"Certainly I have," replied Costal; "yes, more than once, too, I have seen her at night; and by moonlight I have heard her singing as she combed out her shining hair and twisted long strings of pearls about her neck, while *we* could not find a single one. Several times, too, I have invoked her without feeling the slightest sensation of fear, and intreated her to show me the rich pearl-banks. But it was all to no purpose: no matter how courageous one is, the Siren will not do anything unless there are two men present."

"What can be the reason of that?" inquired Clara. "Perhaps her husband is jealous, and don't allow her to talk to one man alone."

"The truth is, friend Clara," continued Costal, without congratulating the negro on the cleverness of his conjecture, "I have not much hopes of seeing her until after I am fifty years old. If I interpret correctly the traditions I have received from my fathers, neither Tlaloc nor Matlacuezc ever reveal their secrets to any man who is less than half a century old. Heaven has willed it that from the time of the conquest up to my day none of my ancestors has lived beyond his forty-ninth year. I have passed that age; and in me alone can be verified the tradition of my family, which has been passed down in regular succession from father to son. But there is only one day in which it may be done: the day of full moon after the summer solstice of the year, in which I am fifty. That is this very year."

"Ah, then," said the negro, "that will explain why all our efforts to invoke the Siren has proved fruitless. The time has not yet come."

"Just so," said Costal. "It will be some months yet before we can be certain of seeing her. But whatever happens we must start to-morrow for Valladolid. In the morning we can go to the hacienda in our canoe, and take leave of our master Don Mariano as two respectable servants ought to do."

"Agreed," said Clara; "but are we not forgetting an important matter?"

"What?"

"The student whom the officer left near the tamarind trees? Poor devil! he's in danger of being caught by the inundation!"

"I had not forgotten him," rejoined Costal. "We can go that way in the morning, and take him to the hacienda in the canoe along with us—that is, if we still find him alive. I hope he will have sense enough, before the flood reaches him, to climb into one of the trees."

As Costal said this, he rose from his seat, and glanced westward over the plain. Already the hoarse murmur of the inundation was making itself heard in the direction of the hacienda.

"Listen!" said he, "to the growling of the waters. *Carrambo!* Who knows if the officer himself has had time to escape? He would have done better had he passed the night with us here. He appeared so anxious about going on to the hacienda. Probably he has his own private reasons for that; besides, I never thought of asking him to stay with us."

"Well," said Clara, "we may congratulate ourselves upon being safe here; but I feel rather hungry just now; do you chance to have a bit of *tasajo* in any corner of your cabin? I could put up with that and a drink of water."

"I think I can manage to find a morsel or two," said Costal, going inside the hut, whither he was followed by the negro.

A fire of dried sticks soon crackled upon the hearth, among the embers of which, as soon as they had burnt to a certain degree of redness, Costal placed several pieces of jerked meat—which he had taken from a string suspended across the room. This species of viand requires but a slight process of cooking; and, as soon as it was deemed sufficiently done, the two adventurers entered upon their frugal repast, which a keen appetite rendered palatable, if not absolutely luxurious.

Supper over, they stretched themselves along the floor, and for a time lay listening to the hoarse mutterings of the flood that every moment grew louder and louder. To this, however, they paid but little attention, having full confidence in the security of their elevated position; and even the noise of the water as the great waves came dashing against the hill did not hinder Costal from falling into a profound slumber. The negro also fell asleep, but awoke from time to time—fancying that he heard the screams of the jaguars mingling with the confused surging of the waters! In truth it was no fancy. What the negro heard was in reality the voices of the savage creatures they had that evening encountered. On becoming aware of the approach of the inundation, all four of them had made for the *Cerro-de-la-mesa*; but perceiving that its summit was already occupied by the two men, they had halted by its base, and stood for some moments growling their chagrin. The near approach of the waters inspiring them with terror, started them off afresh; and bounding rapidly onward, they were soon far distant from the hill, fleeing at utmost speed from the danger of the inundation, well understood even by them.

Chapter Twenty
A Canopy of Jaguars

Considering the circumstances in which he has been left, it is time to return to the poor student of theology—Don Cornelio Lantejas. We left him sleeping in a hammock, between two great tamarind trees; and certainly it must have been his good star that had conducted him into that comfortable situation.

All at once he awoke with a start—his slumber having been interrupted by a chilly sensation that had suddenly crept upon him. On opening his eyes, he perceived that he was suspended over a vast sea that rolled its yellow waves beneath the hammock, and within six inches of his body! At this unexpected sight, a cry of terror escaped him, which was instantly responded to by a growling, sniffing noise, that appeared to proceed from the tops of the tamarinds over his head!

As yet he saw nothing there; but casting his eyes around, he perceived that the whole country was under water sweeping onward in a frothy, turbulent current!

A moment's reflection sufficed to explain to him this singular phenomenon. He now remembered having heard of the great annual inundation to which the plains of Oajaca are subject, and which occur almost at a fixed day and hour; and this also explained the circumstances which had been mystifying him—the abandoned dwellings, and the boats suspended from the trees. He had arrived in the midst of one of these great floods, which he might have shunned but for the slow and gentle gait at which his *cavallo de picador* had carried him along the route.

What was he to do? He scarce knew how to swim. But even had he been as accomplished in the art of natation as a pearl-diver himself, it would not have availed him in the midst of that immense sheet of water, on all sides apparently stretching to the limits of the horizon!

His situation, sufficiently unpleasant on account of the danger of the rising inundation, soon became absolutely frightful from another and a very different reason.

Some shining objects, which appeared to him among the leaves of the tamarinds, and that looked like burning coals, just then caught his glance; and a closer scrutiny convinced him that these could be no other than the eyes of some fierce animals that had taken refuge upon the trees—jaguars, no doubt: since he could think of no other creatures that could have climbed up the smooth trunks of the tamarinds!

His terror was now complete. Beneath rushed the surging waters. He knew not how soon they might mount higher and engulf him—for the flood might still be far from its maximum height! On the other hand, he dare not climb upwards. The fierce animals in the tree would be certain to dispute his ascent, even should they feel disposed to leave him unassailed where he was!

In this horrid state of uncertainty—dreading the double danger—he was compelled to pass the remainder of the night.

We need not detail the unpleasant reflections to which his situation gave rise: for a volume would scarce contain the thousand alternations from hope to fear that passed through his spirit before the light of the morning broke upon his longing eyes.

Though he had longed for morning to come, the daylight did not add much to the joyfulness of his situation. The animals, whose glancing orbs had kept him all night in a state of apprehension, were now plainly seen among the branches of the trees. They *were* jaguars—four of them—two large ones, and two others of smaller size, or *cachorras*. This was not all that Don Cornelio saw to alarm him. In addition to the fierce quadrupeds, the tops of the tamarinds were occupied by other living creatures of equally frightful aspect. These were reptiles: large serpents of hideous appearance twined spirally round the branches, with their heads projected outwards, and their forked tongues glistening beyond their teeth!

The terrified student cast an inquiring glance over the waters, to see if there was no means of escape from his perilous position. He saw only the bubbling surface, here and there mottled with huge uprooted trees, upon which appeared wolves and other wild animals half dead with affright. High overhead, eagles, vultures, and other birds of prey wheeled in circles through the air, uttering their piercing cries—fit accompaniment to this scene of desolation and death.

Don Cornelio again turned his eyes towards the fierce jaguars crouching among the branches of the trees. These brutes appeared to struggle against the ferocious instincts of their nature, which prompted them to seize hold of a prey almost within reach of their claws. Fear for their own lives alone prevented them from taking that of the student; and at intervals they closed their eyes, as if to escape the temptation caused by his presence!

At the same time the serpents, not far above his face, kept continually coiling their long viscous bodies round the branches, and rapidly uncoiling them again—equally uneasy at the presence of the man and the tigers.

Mechanically closing the folds of the hammock over him, and thus holding them with both hands, the student lay perfectly still. He feared either to speak or make a motion, lest his voice or movement might tempt either the reptiles or quadrupeds to make an attack upon him.

In this way more than an hour had passed, when over the surface of the waters, which now flowed in a more tranquil current, Don Cornelio fancied he heard a singular sound. It resembled the notes of a bugle, but at times the intonation was hoarser and more grave, not unlike a certain utterance of his two formidable neighbours, which from time to time the student heard swelling from the tops of the tamarinds.

It was neither more nor less than the conch of Costal; who, making his way towards the spot in his canoe, was employing the time to advantage in endeavouring to invoke the goddess of the waters.

Presently the student was able to make out in the distance the little canoe gliding over the water, with the two adventurers seated in the stem and stern. At intervals, the Indian, accustomed to this sort of navigation, was seen to drop his oars and hold the shell to his mouth. Lantejas then saw that it was from this instrument the sounds that had so puzzled him were proceeding.

Absorbed in their odd occupation, neither Costal nor Clara had as yet perceived the student of theology—hidden as he was by the thick network of the hammock, and almost afraid to make the slightest movement. Just then, however, a muffled voice, as of some one speaking from under a mask, reached their ears.

"Did you hear anything, Costal?" inquired the negro.

"Yes, I heard a sort of cry," replied Costal; "like enough it's the poor devil of a student who is calling us. *Carrambo*! where can he be? I see only a hammock hung between two trees. Eh! as I live, he is inside it. *Carrai!*"

As Costal finished speaking, a loud peal of laughter burst from his lips, which to him in the hammock appeared like heavenly music. It told him that the two men had discovered his situation; and the student at once fervently returned thanks to God for this interposition of His mercy.

Clara was sharing the mirth of the Indian, when music of a very different sort stifled the laugh upon his lips. It was the cry of the jaguars, that, suddenly excited by the voice of the student, had all four of them sent forth a simultaneous scream.

"*Carrambo!*" exclaimed Clara, with a fresh terror depicted upon his face; "the tigers again."

"Rather strange!" said the Indian. "Certainly their howls appeared to come from the same place as the voice of the man. Hola! Señor student," he continued, raising his voice, so as to be heard by him in the hammock, "are you making your siesta alone, or have you company under the shade of those tamarinds?"

Don Cornelio attempted to reply, but his speech was unintelligible both to the Indian and the negro. In fact, terror had so paralysed his tongue, as to render him incapable of pronouncing his words distinctly!

For a moment his arm was seen elevated above the folds of the hammock, as if to point out his terrible neighbours upon the tree. But the thick foliage still concealing the jaguars from the eye of Costal, rendered the gesture of the student as unintelligible as his cry.

"For the love of God, hold your oar!" cried Clara; "perhaps the tigers have taken refuge on the top of the tamarinds!"

"All the more reason why we should get up to them," replied the Indian. "Would you leave this young man to smother in his hammock till the waters had subsided?"

In saying this, Costal plied his oars more vigorously than ever; and, in spite of the remonstrances of his companion, headed the canoe in a direct line towards the hammock.

"If these be the same tigers we encountered yesterday," said Clara, in an anxious tone of voice, "and I am almost sure they are, by the mewing of their whelps, think for a moment, Costal, how desperately spiteful they will be against us."

"And do you think I am not equally spiteful against them?" replied Costal, urging his canoe onwards with more rapidity than ever.

A few strokes of the paddle brought the light craft within gunshot distance of the tamarinds; and now for the first time did Costal obtain a good view of the theological student couched within the hammock—where he appeared to be indolently reposing, like some Oriental satrap, under a daïs of tigers and serpents!

Chapter Twenty One
The Student Rescued

The odd spectacle once more overcame the gravity of the Indian; and, resting upon his oars, he delivered himself up to a renewed spell of laughter.

Through the network of the hammock the student could now note the movements of those who were coming to his rescue. He saw the Indian turn towards his companion, pointing at the same time to the singular tableau among the tops of the trees, which the negro appeared to contemplate with a countenance that betrayed an anxiety equal to his own.

Don Cornelio could not make out what there was to laugh at in a spectacle that for two mortal hours—ever since daybreak—had been causing him the extreme of fear; but, without saying a word, he waited for the explanation of this ill-timed hilarity.

"Let us get a little farther off!" stammered the negro; "we can deliberate better what we should do."

"What we should do!" cried Costal, now speaking seriously; "it needs no deliberation to tell that."

"Quite true," assented Clara, "it does not. Of course we should push off a little; and the sooner we do it the better."

"Bah!" exclaimed Costal, "that's not what I meant;" as he spoke coolly laying his paddle in the bottom of the canoe, and taking up his carbine.

"But what are you going to do?" anxiously asked Clara.

"*Por Dios*! to shoot one of the jaguars; what else? You shall see presently. Keep yourself quiet, Señor student," he continued, speaking to Don Cornelio, who still lay crouched up within the hammock, and who, from very fear, could neither speak nor move.

At this moment one of the jaguars uttered a growl that caused the blood to run cold through the veins of Clara. At the same time the fierce creature was seen tearing the bark from the tamarind with his curving claws; while, with mouth agape, and teeth set, as if in menace, he fixed his fiery eyes upon

Costal, who was nearest to him. His angry glance had no terrors for the *tigrero*, who, gazing firmly back upon the fierce brute, appeared to subdue him by some power of fascination.

Costal now raised the carbine to his shoulder, took deliberate aim, and fired. Almost simultaneously with the report, the huge animal came tumbling down from the tree, and fell with a dull, dead plash upon the water. It was the male.

"Quick, Clara!" cried the Indian. "A stroke of the paddle—quick, or we shall have the other upon us!"

And, as Costal spoke, he drew his long knife to be ready for defending himself.

Anxious as the negro was to get out of the way, and making all the haste in his power, his fears had so unnerved him that his efforts were in vain. The female jaguar, furious at the death of her mate, and anxious for the safety of her whelps, stayed only to utter one savage yell; and then, bounding downward from the branches, she launched herself upon the student. The hammock, however, oscillating violently to one side, caused her to let go her hold, and making a second spring, she dropped down into the canoe. The weight of her body, combined with the impetus which her anger had given to it, at once capsized the little craft; and Indian, negro, and jaguar went all together under water!

In a second's time all three reappeared on the surface—Clara half-frightened out of his senses, and striking out with all the energy of despair.

Fortunately for the negro, the old pearl-diver could swim like a shark; and, in the twinkling of an eye, the latter had darted betwixt him and the jaguar—his knife slung between his clenched teeth.

The two adversaries, now face to face, paused for an instant as if to measure the distance between them. Their eyes met—those of the tiger-hunter expressing coolness and resolution, while the orbs of the jaguar rolled furiously in their sockets.

All at once the hunter was seen to dive; and the jaguar, astonished at the sudden disappearance of her enemy, paused, and for a moment balanced herself in the water. Then turning round, she commenced swimming back towards the tree upon which she had left her young ones.

Before reaching it, however, she was seen to struggle, and sink partially below the surface—as if some whirlpool was sucking her underneath; then rising up again, she turned over on her back, and floated lifeless down the current. A long red gash appeared freshly opened in her belly; and the water around was fast becoming tinged with the crimson stream that gushed copiously from the wound.

The Indian, in turn, came to the surface; and, after casting a look around him, swam towards the canoe—which the current had already carried to some distance from the trees. Overtaking it, he once more turned the craft deck upwards; and, mounting aboard, paddled back towards the student.

Lantejas had not yet recovered from the surprise with which the encounter, as well as the audacious *sang-froid* exhibited by the *tigrero*, had inspired him, when the latter arrived underneath; and, with the same blade with which he had almost disembowelled the tiger, opened the bottom of the hammock by cutting it lengthwise. By this means he had resolved on delivering the student more easily than by endeavouring to get him out over the edge.

At that moment was heard the voice of Clara, still swimming about in the water.

"The skins of the jaguars!" cried he; "are you going to let them be lost? They are worth twenty dollars, Costal!"

"Well, if they are," replied the Indian, "swim after and secure them. I have no time to spare," added he, as he pulled Lantejas through the bottom of the hammock, and lowered him down into the canoe.

"*Dios me libre!*" responded Clara; "I shall do nothing of the kind. Who knows whether the life's quite out of them yet? They may go to the devil for me! Heigh! Costal! paddle this way, and take me in. I have no desire to go under those tamarinds—laced as they are by half a mile of rattlesnakes."

"Get in gently, then!" said Costal, directing the canoe towards the negro. "Gently, or you may capsize us a second time."

"Jesus God!" exclaimed Don Cornelio, who now for the first time had found the power of speech; "Jesus God!" he repeated, seeing himself, not without some apprehension, between two strange beings—the one red, the other black—both dripping with water, and their hair covered with the yellow scum of the waves!

"Eh! Señor student," rejoined Clara, in a good-humoured way, "is that all the thanks you give us for the service we have done you?"

"Pardon me, *gentlemen*," stammered out Don Cornelio; "I was dreadfully frightened. I have every reason to be thankful to you."

And, his confidence now restored, the student expressed, in fit terms, his warm gratitude; and finished his speech by congratulating the Indian on his escape from the dangers he had encountered.

"By my faith! it is true enough," rejoined Costal, "I have run some little danger. I was all over of a sweat; and this cursed water coming down from the mountains as cold as ice—*Carrambo!* I shouldn't wonder if I should get a bad cold from the ducking."

The student listened with astonishment to this unexpected declaration. The man whose fearful intrepidity he had just witnessed to be thinking only of the risk he ran of getting a cold!

"Who are you?" he mechanically inquired.

"I?" said Costal. "Well, I am an Indian, as you see—a Zapoteque— formerly the *tigrero* of Don Matias de la Zanca; at present in the service of Don Mariano de Silva—to-morrow, who knows?"

"Don Matias de la Zanca!" echoed the student, interrupting him; "why, that is my uncle!"

"Oh!" said Costal, "your uncle! Well, Señor student, if you wish to go to his house I am sorry I cannot take you there, since it lies up among the hills, and could not be reached in a canoe. But perhaps you have a horse?"

"I had one; but the flood has carried him off, I suppose. No matter. I have good reasons for not regretting his loss."

"Well," rejoined Costal, "your best way will be to go with us to the Hacienda las Palmas. There you will get a steed that will carry you to the house of your uncle. But first," added he, turning his eyes towards the tamarinds, "I must look after my carbine, which has been spilled out of the canoe. It's too good a gun to be thrown away; and I can say that it don't miss fire once in ten times. It should be yonder, where the brute capsized us; and with your permission, Señor student, I'll just go in search of it. Ho, Clara! paddle us back under the hammock!"

Clara obeyed, though evidently with some reluctance. The hissing of the serpents still sounded ominously in his ears.

On arriving near the spot where the canoe had turned over, Costal stood up in the bow; and then raising his hands, and joining them above his head, he plunged once more under the water.

For a long time the spectators saw nothing of him; but the bubbles here and there rising to the surface, showed where he was engaged in searching for his incomparable carbine.

At length his head appeared above water, then his whole body. He held the gun tightly grasped in one of his hands, and making a few strokes towards the canoe he once more climbed aboard.

The Tiger Hunter | 99

Costal now took hold of the paddle; and turning the head of the canoe in a westerly direction commenced making way across the turbid waters towards the Hacienda las Palmas.

Although the fury of the inundation had by this time partially subsided, still the flood ran onward with a swift current; and what with the danger from floating trees, and other objects that swelled the surface of the water, it was necessary to manage the canoe with caution. Thus retarded, it was near mid-day before the voyageurs arrived within sight of the hacienda. Along the way Don Cornelio had inquired from his new companions, what strange accident had conducted them to the spot where they had found him.

"Not an accident," said Costal; "but a horseman, who appeared to be in a terrible hurry himself, as *Por Dios*! he had need to be. He was on his way to the house of Don Mariano, for what purpose I can't say. It remains to be known, Señor student, whether he has been as fortunate as you, in escaping the flood. God grant that he has! for it would be a sad pity if such a brave young fellow was to die by drowning. Brave men are not so plentiful."

"Happy for them who are brave!" sighed Don Cornelio.

"Here is my friend, Clara," continued Costal, without noticing the rejoinder of the student, "who has no fear of man; and yet he is as much afraid of tigers as if he were a child. Well, I hope we shall find that the gallant young officer has escaped the danger, and is now safe within the walls of the hacienda."

At that moment the canoe passed round a tope of half-submerged palm-trees, and the hacienda itself appeared in sight, as if suddenly rising from the bosom of the waters. A cry of joy escaped from the lips of the student, who, half-famished with hunger, thought of the abundance that would be found behind those hospitable walls.

While gazing upon them a bell commenced to toll; and its tones fell upon his ears like the music of birds, for it appeared as if summoning the occupants of the hacienda to pass into the refectory. It was, however, the *angelus* of noon.

At the same instant two barges were seen parting from the causeway that led down in front, and heading towards the high ridge that ran behind the hacienda, at a little distance on the north. In the first of these boats appeared two rowers, with a person in a travelling costume of somewhat clerical cut, and a mule saddled and bridled. In the second were two gentlemen and the same number of ladies. The latter were young girls, both crowned with luxuriant chaplets of flowers, and each grasping an oar in her white delicate fingers, which she managed with skill and adroitness. They were the two daughters of Don Mariano de Silva. One of the gentlemen was Don Mariano himself, while the other was joyfully recognised by Costal as the brave officer who had asked him the way, and by the student as his *compagnon du voyage* of yesterday—Don Rafael Tres-Villas.

Shortly after, the two boats reached the foot of the Sierra; and the traveller with the mule disembarked. Mounting into his saddle, he saluted those who remained in the other boat; and then rode away, amidst the words oft repeated by Don Mariano and his daughters—

"*A dios! a dios! Señor Morelos! a dios!*"

The two barges now returned towards the hacienda, arriving there nearly at the same time as the canoe which carried the student of theology, the Indian, and the negro.

Don Cornelio had now a better opportunity of observing the rich freight carried in the larger of the two boats. The drapery of purple silk which covered the seats and fell over the sides of the barge, threw its brilliant reflections far out upon the water. In the midst of this brilliance appeared the young ladies, seated and bending languidly upon their oars. Now and then Marianita, in plunging her oar-blade into the water, caused the pomegranate flowers to rain down from her hair, as she shook them with bursts of laughter; while Gertrudis, looking from under the purple wreath, ever and anon cast stealthy glances at the cavalier who was seated by the side of her father.

"Señor Don Mariano!" said Costal, as the barge drew near, "here is a guest whom I have taken the liberty to bring to your hospitable mansion."

As the Indian delivered this speech he pointed to the student of theology still seated in the canoe.

"He is welcome!" rejoined Don Mariano; and then, inviting the stranger to disembark, all except Costal, Clara, and the servants, landed from the boats, and passed out of sight through the front gateway of the hacienda.

These taking the boats around the battlements of the building, entered the enclosure by a gate that opened towards the rear.

Chapter Twenty Two
Rafael and Gertrudis

As already stated, Don Luis Tres-Villas, the father of Don Rafael, was a Spaniard. He was one of those Spaniards, however, who from the first had comprehended the necessity of making liberal political concessions to the Creoles—such as those accorded to them by the enlightened Don José Iturrigaray. Even the interest of Spain herself demanded these reforms.

Don Luis, himself an officer in the vice-regal guard, had been one of the most devoted partisans of Iturrigaray; and when the latter was arrested by the more violent *Gachupinos* and sent prisoner to Spain, Tres-Villas saw that all ties of attachment between Spaniards and Creoles had been severed by the act; and that an open rupture was at hand. Unwilling to take part against the native people, Don Luis had thrown up his commission as captain in the vice-regal guards, left the capital, and retired to his estate of Del Valle.

This hacienda was situated on the other side of the ridge that bounded the plain of Las Palmas on the north, and about two leagues distant from the dwelling of Don Mariano de Silva. These two gentlemen had met in the metropolis; and the slight acquaintance there initiated had been strengthened during their residence in the country.

On receiving the news of Hidalgo's insurrection, Don Luis had sent an express messenger to his son Don Rafael, summoning him to the Hacienda del Valle. In obedience to the order of his father, the young captain of dragoons, having obtained leave of absence from his regiment, was on his way thither, when he overtook upon the road the student of theology. Nevertheless, Don Rafael had not deemed the order of his father so pressing as to hinder him from passing a day at the hacienda of Las Palmas, which lay directly in the route to that of Del Valle. This, therefore, he had determined upon doing.

A word about the antecedents, which led to this resolve on the part of the dragoon captain.

In the early part of the preceding year Don Mariano de Silva had passed three months in the Mexican metropolis. He had been accompanied by his daughter Gertrudis—Marianita remaining in Oajaca with a near relative of the family. In the *tertulias* of the gay capital the fair *Oajaqueña* had met the dashing captain of dragoons, and a romantic attachment had sprung up between them, mutual as sincere. To this there could be no objection by the parents on either side: since there was between the two lovers a complete conformity in age, social position, and fortune. In all likelihood the romance of courtship would soon have ended in the more prosaic reality of marriage; but just at that time the young officer was ordered upon some military service; and Don Mariano was also suddenly called away from the capital. The marriage ceremony, therefore, that might otherwise have been expected to take place, thus remained unconsummated.

It is true that up to this time Don Rafael had not formally declared his passion to the young Creole; but it is probable that she knew it without any verbal avowal; and still more that she fully reciprocated it. Neither had Don Mariano been spoken to upon the matter: the captain of dragoons not deeming it proper to confer with him till after he had obtained the consent of Gertrudis.

After the separation of the two lovers, by little and little Don Rafael began to doubt whether his passion had been really returned by the fair Oajaqueña. Time and absence, while they rendered more feeble the remembrance of those little incidents that had appeared favourable to him, increased in an inverse ratio the impression of the young Creole's charms — that in fancy now appeared to him only the more glowing and seductive. So much did this impression become augmented, that the young officer began to think he had been too presumptuous in aspiring to the possession of such incomparable loveliness.

His cruel doubts soon passed into a more cruel certainty; and he no longer believed that his love had been returned.

In this state of mind he endeavoured to drive the thoughts of Gertrudis out of his head: by saying to himself that he had never loved her! But this attempt at indifference only proved how strongly the sentiment influenced him; and the result was to force him into a melancholy, habitual and profound.

Such was the state of Don Rafael's mind when the soldier-priest, Hidalgo, pronounced the first *grito* of the Mexican revolution. Imbued with those liberal ideas which had been transmitted to him from his father—and even carrying them to a higher degree—knowing, moreover, the passionate ardour with which Don Mariano de Silva and his daughter looked forward to the emancipation of their country; and thus sure of the approbation of all for whom he had reverence or affection—Don Rafael determined to offer his sword to the cause of Independence. He hoped under the banners of the insurrection to get rid of the black chagrin that was devouring his spirit; or if not, he desired that in the first encounter between the royalist and insurgent troops, death might deliver him from an existence that was no longer tolerable.

At this crisis came the messenger from Del Valle. The message was simply a summons to his father's presence that he might learn from him some matters that were of too much importance either to be trusted to paper or the lips of a servant. The young officer easily conjectured the object for which he was summoned to Oajaca. Knowing his father's political leanings, he had no doubt that it was to counsel him, Don Rafael, to offer his sword to the cause of Mexican Independence.

The message, however significant and mysterious, partially restored the captain of dragoons to his senses. In the journey he was necessitated to make, he saw there might be an opportunity of sounding the heart of Gertrudis, and becoming acquainted with her feelings in regard to him. For this purpose he had determined upon frankly declaring his own. In fine, he had half resolved to renounce those chivalric sentiments, that had already hindered him from opening the affair to Don Mariano without the consent of Gertrudis. So profound had his passion become, that he would even have preferred owing to filial obedience the possession of her he so devotedly loved, than not to possess her at all.

Influenced by such ideas, no wonder that with feverish ardour he rushed over the hundred leagues that separated Mexico from Oajaca; and it was for this reason he was willing to risk the danger of perishing in the flood rather than not reach the Hacienda las Palmas, on the evening he had appointed to be there.

It may be mentioned that in sending back the messenger of his father, he had charged the man to call at the hacienda of Las Palmas and inform its proprietor of his—Don Rafael's—intention to demand there the hospitality of a night. Having calculated the exact time he might be occupied on his journey, he had named the day, almost the very hour, when he might be expected. Without knowing the importance which the young dragoon attached to this visit, Don Mariano was but too gratified to have an opportunity of showing politeness to the son of a gentleman who was at the same time his neighbour and friend.

With regard to the sentiments of Gertrudis, they are already known to the reader. What would not Don Rafael have given to have been equally well acquainted with them! Ah! could he have known the secret pleasure with which his arrival was expected—the ardent prayers, and that sacrificial vow registered in his favour, at the moment when he was struggling with danger—could he have known all this, it would have at once put an end to his melancholy!

At this time the insurrection was just beginning to make some stir at Oajaca. On throwing off the mask, Hidalgo had despatched secret agents to the different provinces of Mexico, in hopes that they might all join in the *grito* already pronounced by him in Valladolid. The emissaries sent to Oajaca were two men named Lopez and Armenta; but both, having fallen into the hands of the government authorities, were beheaded on the instant, and their heads, raised upon poles, were exposed upon the great road of San Luis del Rey, as a warning to other insurgents.

This rigorous measure had no effect in retarding the insurrection. Shortly after, a ranchero, named Antonio Valdez, raised the standard of independence, and, at the head of a small *guerilla* of country-people, commenced a war of retaliation. Many Spaniards fell into his hands; and their blood was spilled without mercy: for in this sanguinary manner did the Mexican revolution commence; and in such fashion was it continued.

Chapter Twenty Three
The Honest Muleteer

On the same day in which the student of theology arrived at the Hacienda las Palmas, and about four o'clock in the afternoon—just after the hour of dinner—the different members of the family, along with their guests, were assembled in one of the apartments of the mansion. It was the grand *sala* or reception room, opening by double glass doors upon a garden filled with flowering plants, and beautiful shade trees.

Two individuals, already known to the reader, were absent from this reunion. One was the student himself, who, notwithstanding that he was now in perfect security, had so delivered himself up to the remembrance of the dangers he had encountered while reclining under his terrible daïs of tigers and serpents, that he had been seized with a violent fever, and was now confined to his bed.

The other absentee was Marianita, who, on pretext of taking a look at the great ocean of waters—but in reality to ascertain whether the bark of Don Fernando was not yet in sight—had gone up to the *azotéa*.

Don Mariano, with that tranquillity of mind, which the possession of wealth usually produces—assuring the rich proprietor against the future— was seated in a large leathern *fauteuil*, smoking his cigar, and occasionally balancing himself on the hind legs of the chair.

Beside him stood a small table of ornamental wood, on which was placed a cup of Chinese porcelain containing coffee. It was of the kind known among Spanish-Americans as *café de siesta*; on the principle, no doubt, *lucus a non lucendo*: since it is usually so strong that a single cup of it is sufficient to rob one of the power of sleep for a period of at least twenty-four hours.

In the doorway opening into the garden stood Don Rafael, who appeared to be watching the evolutions of the parroquets, amidst the branches of the pomegranates, with all the interest of a naturalist.

Though his countenance was calm, his heart was trembling at the thought of the *entretien* he had proposed on bringing about.

Gertrudis, with head inclined, was seated near by, occupied with the embroidery of one of those scarfs of white cambric, which the Mexican gentlemen are accustomed to wear over their shoulders, after the fashion of the Arab burnouse, to protect them from the too fierce rays of the sun.

Despite the tranquil silence of the haciendado, at intervals a cloud might have been observed upon his brow; while the pale countenance of Don Rafael also exhibited a certain anxiety, belying the expression of indifference which he affected.

The spirit of Gertrudis in reality was not more calm. A secret voice whispered to her that Don Rafael was about to say something; and that same voice told her it was some sweet prelude of love. Nevertheless, despite the quick rush of her Creole blood, and the sudden quivering that rose from her heart to her cheeks, she succeeded in concealing her thoughts under that mask of womanly serenity which the eye of man is not sufficiently skilful to penetrate.

The only individual present whose countenance was in conformity with his thoughts, was the *arriero*—Don Valerio Trujano.

With hat in hand, and standing in front of the haciendado, he had come to say *adios*, and thank Don Mariano for the hospitality his house had afforded him.

To that easy gracefulness of manners common to all classes in Spanish-America, there was united in the person of the *arriero* a certain imposing severity of countenance, which, however, he could temper at will by the aid of a pair of eyes of mild and benevolent expression.

Notwithstanding that his social position was not equal to that of his host—for Mexico had not yet become republican—Valerio Trujano was not regarded as an ordinary guest either by Don Mariano or his daughters.

Independent of his reputation for honesty beyond suspicion—for profound piety as well—which he enjoyed throughout the whole country, he possessed other high qualities that had entitled him to universal esteem. The generosity and courage which he had exhibited on the preceding evening—when assisting a stranger at the risk of his own life—had only added to the great respect already entertained for him by the inmates of the Hacienda las Palmas.

Although the dragoon officer had in some measure requited the service, by afterwards snatching the *arriero* from the jaws of the devouring flood, he did not on that account feel a whit less grateful. Neither did Gertrudis, who with her thoughts of love had already mingled her prayers for him, who had a just title to be called the saviour of Don Rafael's life.

The man, Valerio Trujano, whose nature at a later period became immortalised by the siege of Huajapam, was at this time about forty years of age; but his fine delicate features, overshadowed by an abundance of glossy black hair, gave him the appearance of being much younger.

"Señor Don Mariano," said he, on coming into the presence of the haciendado, "I have come to bid *adios*, and thank you for your hospitality."

"What!" exclaimed Don Mariano, "surely you are not going to leave us so soon? No, no."

Gertrudis at the same time expressed her unwillingness that he should depart.

"I must leave you, Don Mariano," answered the *arriero*. "The man who has business to attend to is not always his own master. When his heart impels him to turn to the right, his affairs often carry him to the left. He who is *in debt*, is still less master of himself."

"You owe a sum of money, then?" said Don Rafael, interrogatively, at the same time advancing towards the *arriero* and offering him his hand. "Why could you not have told me of this? Whatever be the amount, I—"

"Ah! *cavallero*," interrupted Trujano, with a smile, "it is a bad plan to borrow from one for the purpose of paying another. I could not think of accepting a loan. It is not from pride, but a sense of duty that I decline your generous offer; and I hope you will not be offended. The sum I owe is not a very heavy one—a few hundred dollars. Since it has pleased God that my mules should find a shelter in the stables of Don Mariano, and thus escape the inundation, I can now take the road through the mountains to Oajaca, where the money I shall receive for my *recua* will, I hope, entirely clear me from debt."

"What!" cried Don Mariano, in a tone of surprise, "do you talk of selling your mules—the only means you have of gaining your livelihood?"

"Yes," modestly replied the muleteer, "I intend selling them. I do so in order that I may be able to go where my vocation calls me. I should have gone already; but being in debt up to this time, my life belonged to my creditors rather than to myself, and I had not the right to expose it to danger."

"To expose your life?" interrogated Gertrudis, with an accent that bespoke her interest in the brave man.

"Just so, Señorita," responded the *arriero*. "I have seen the heads of Lopez and Armenta exposed upon the high road of San Luis del Rey. Who knows but that my own may soon figure beside them? I speak openly," continued Trujano, looking round upon his audience, "and as if before God. I know that my host, no more than God himself, would betray a secret thus confided to him."

"Of course not," rejoined Don Mariano, with an air of hospitable simplicity such as characterised the earlier ages. "But here," he continued, "we are one and all of us devoted to the cause of our country's liberty; and we shall pray for those who aid her in obtaining it."

"We shall do more than that," said Tres-Villas in his turn; "we shall lend our help to her. It is the duty of every Mexican who can wield a sword and ride a horse."

"May all those who raise an arm in favour of Spain!" cried Gertrudis, her eyes flashing with patriotic enthusiasm, "may they be branded with infamy and disgrace! may they find neither a roof to shelter them, nor a woman to smile upon them! may the contempt of those they love be the reward of every traitor to his country!"

"If all our young girls were like you," said Trujano, looking gratefully towards Gertrudis, "our triumph would soon be attained. Where is the man who would not be proud to risk his life for one smile of your pretty lips, Señorita, or one look from your beautiful eyes?"

As the *arriero* said this, he glanced significantly towards the young officer. Gertrudis hung her head, happy at hearing this homage rendered to her beauty in presence of the man in whose eyes she alone cared to appear beautiful.

After a pause Trujano continued: "*Dios y Libertad*! (God and Liberty!) that is my motto. Had I been in a condition sooner to take up the cause of my country, I should have done so—if only to restrain the excesses that have already sullied it. No doubt you have heard of them, Señor Don Mariano?"

"I have," replied the haciendado; and the shadow that at that moment passed over his brow told that the news had troubled him.

"The blood of innocent Spaniards has been shed," continued the muleteer, "men who had no ill-will towards our cause; and, shame to say, the only one in this our province who now carries the banner of the insurrection is the worthless wretch, Antonio Valdez."

"Antonio Valdez!" cried Don Rafael, interrupting him. "Do you mean Valdez, a *vaquero* of Don Luis Tres-Villas—my father?" "The same," replied Don Mariano. "May it please God to make him remember that his master always treated him with kindness!"

The air of uneasiness with which Don Mariano pronounced these words did not escape Don Rafael.

"Do you think, then," said he, in a tone that testified his alarm, "do you think that my father, whose liberal opinions are known to every one, is in any danger from the insurgents?"

"No, I hope not," replied Don Mariano. "Señor Valerio," said Don Rafael, turning to interrogate the *arriero*; "do you know how many men this fellow, Antonio Valdez, may have under his command?"

"Fifty, I have heard; but I think it likely his band may have been greatly increased by accessions among the country-people—who have suffered even more than those of the town from the oppressions of the Spaniards."

"Señor Don Mariano," said the officer, in a voice trembling with emotion, "nothing less than news similar to what I have just now heard could have tempted me to abridge a sojourn under your roof, which I should have been only too happy to have prolonged; but when one's father is in danger—even to the risk of life—his son's place should be by his side. Is it not so, Doña Gertrudis?"

On hearing the first words of Don Rafael's speech, which announced the intention of a precipitate departure, a cry of anguish had almost escaped from the lips of the young girl. With the heroism of a woman's heart she had repressed it; and stood silent with her eyes fixed upon the floor.

"Yes, yes!" murmured she, replying to Don Rafael's question in a low but firm voice.

There was an interval of silence, during which a sort of sinister presentiment agitated the spirits of the four personages present. The homicidal breath of civil war was already commencing to make itself felt within the domestic circle.

Trujano was the first to recommence the conversation—his eyes gleaming as he spoke like one of the ancient prophets moved by Divine inspiration.

"This morning," said he, "an humble servant of the Most High, the obscure priest of a poor village, has left you to offer up his prayers for the insurgent cause. And now an instrument, not less humble, by the will of

God takes leave of you to offer it his arm, and if need be, his life. Pray for them! good and beautiful Madonna!" he continued, addressing himself to Gertrudis, and speaking with that religious and poetical fervour which was the leading trait in his character; "pray for them; and perhaps it will please the Almighty to show that from the very dust He can raise the power that may hurl the tyrant from his throne."

On saying these words, the *arriero* respectfully pressed the hands that were held out to him, and then walked out of the *sala*, followed by Don Mariano.

Chapter Twenty Four
The Lovers alone

It may be that the haciendado had reasons for thus leaving his daughter alone with Don Rafael, during the few short moments that should elapse previous to the departure of the young officer.

The voices of the muleteers, who were busily lading the *recua* of Don Valerio, scarce reached the ears of the lovers, who were now embarrassed by the profound silence that reigned in the *sala*. It was the first time they had found themselves alone, since the arrival of the officer at the hacienda.

The sun was gilding the tops of the pomegranate trees, where the parroquets were joyously performing their gymnastic exercises; and the breeze which caressed the plants in the garden, wafted into the saloon the perfumes of a thousand flowers. It was a solemn and decisive moment. Gertrudis, happy, yet trembling for the words of love she expected to hear, sat with her face partially concealed behind the folds of her silken *reboso*. In her fingers she still held the scarf she had been embroidering; but, seeing that this betrayed the trembling of her hand, she placed it on a table by her side, lest Don Rafael might observe the emotion of which he was the author. It was the last effort of virgin pride—its last attempt at resistance before avowing itself overcome.

"Gertrudis!" said Don Rafael, endeavouring to stifle the pulsations of his heart, "I have spoken to your father. I wish to consecrate these few moments—the last I may ever pass in your presence—to an explanation between us. I implore you, then, to speak, as I intend speaking myself, without reserve—without ambiguity."

"I promise you that, Don Rafael," responded Gertrudis; "but what mysterious secret have you been communicating to my father?" added she, in a tone of gentle raillery.

"I told him," replied the lover, "that I had come hither with my heart full of *you*; that my father's message summoning me to his presence had been received by me as a voice calling me to bliss: since it gave me this opportunity of once more being near you. I told him how I had hurried over the immense distance that separated us; and how, in order that I might see you an hour sooner, I had disregarded the howling of the jaguars, and the threatening voice of the inundation—"

Don Rafael became silent, perhaps from embarrassment, while Gertrudis still remained in a listening attitude. It was a melody to which she could have listened for ever!

"And when you told my father," said she, after a pause of silence, "that—that—you loved me—did he exhibit any astonishment at the unexpected revelation?"

"No, not any," replied the officer, himself a little surprised at the question thus put to him.

"That, then, must have been because I had already told him," said the young beauty, with a smile as sweet as her voice. "But my father—what answer did he give you?"

"'My dear Don Rafael,' said he to me, 'I would be most happy to see our families united. But this can only be with the consent of Gertrudis, and the free wish of her heart; and I have no reason to think that her heart is yours.' Those were the terrible words that proceeded from the lips of your father. Gertrudis, do your lips confirm them?"

The voice of Don Rafael quivered as he spoke; and this trembling of a strong man—who never trembled in the presence of danger—was so delicious to the heart of her who loved him, as to hinder her from hastening to make reply.

On hearing the answer which her father had given to Don Rafael, the carnation upon her lips became of a deeper hue. She was biting them to restrain a smile. Assuming an air of gravity, however, which had the effect of rendering her lover still more anxious, she at length made reply—

"Don Rafael!" said she, "you have appealed to my candour, and I shall speak frankly to you. But swear to me that you will not regard my sincerity as a crime."

"I swear it, Gertrudis! Speak without fear, though your words should crush a heart that is entirely your own."

"Only on one condition can I speak freely."

"Name it! it shall be observed."

"It is, that—while I am making my confession to you, you will keep your eyes fixed upon the tops of those pomegranate trees. Without doing that you might risk not hearing certain things—in short, an avowal—such as you might wish."

"I shall try to obey you," answered Don Rafael, turning his gaze towards the tops of the trees, as if about to study the domestic habits of the parroquets, that still continued their evolutions among the branches.

In a timid and trembling voice, Gertrudis commenced—

"One day," said she, "not very long ago—a young girl made a vow to the Virgin, to save the man she loved from fearful danger that threatened him. Don't you think, Don Rafael, that that man was dearly loved?"

"That depends upon the nature of the vow," replied the officer.

"You shall hear it. The young girl promised to the Virgin, that if her lover should escape from the danger, she would cause him to cut the hair— Oh! if you look at me I cannot go on—she would cause him to cut the hair from her head with his own hands—the long tresses which she herself highly valued, and which he had so passionately admired. In your opinion, was that man beloved?"

"Oh! who would not be proud to be so loved?" cried Don Rafael, casting a glance at his questioner that moved her to the depths of her soul.

"I have not yet finished," said she. "Turn your eyes upon the trees, or perhaps you may not hear the end of my tale, and that might vex you. When this young girl, who had not hesitated to sacrifice her hair—the object of her constant care—the long silken tresses that encircled her head like the diadem of a queen, and which, perhaps, were, in her lover's eyes, her greatest embellishment—when this poor girl will have cut—had cut them off, I should say—do you believe that her lover—you may look at me now, Don Rafael—I give you permission—do you believe that he would still love her as before?"

Don Rafael faced round suddenly at the question; not that he yet comprehended its import; but the tone of melancholy in which Gertrudis was speaking had profoundly moved him.

A tender tear—a tear of envy for the lot of this unknown, so passionately loved—glistened in his eye, as he made reply—

"Oh, Gertrudis!" said he, "no devotion could repay such a sacrifice as that; and the young girl you speak of, however beautiful she might be, could not be otherwise than an angel in the eyes of her lover."

Gertrudis pressed her hand over her heart, to stay the flood of joyful emotion that was rushing through it.

After a pause she continued, her voice quivering as she spoke—

"Once more, and for the last time, I desire you to raise your eyes towards heaven. We have reason to be thankful to it."

While Don Rafael obeyed the direction, Gertrudis permitted the *reboso* to fall from her shoulders; and with her fingers she removed the comb that imprisoned her shining hair, which, coiled up in two long plaited tresses, encircled her crown like a diadem. These she allowed to drop down at will, until they hung far below her waist. Then seizing in one hand the scissors she had just been using at her work, and with the other covering the crimson blush upon her cheek, she held forth the instrument, at the same time crying out—

"Now, Don Rafael! aid me in keeping my vow, by cutting for me the hair from my head."

"I?" exclaimed Don Rafael, in whose ear her voice had sounded like the voice of an angel. "I?" repeated he, astounded at the proposal. "Gertrudis! Gertrudis!"

"I have promised it to the Virgin for saving you last night. Now do you comprehend, Don Rafael—my dearly beloved Rafael?"

"Oh, Gertrudis!" cried the lover, in an ecstasy of joy, "you should have prepared me more gradually for so much happiness."

And kneeling in front of the young girl, he eagerly took hold of her hand, which no longer refused to let him touch it, but, on the contrary, was rather advanced to meet his lips.

"Is it my fault?" said Gertrudis, in a tone of sweet playfulness. "Is it my fault if men are slow at taking a hint? *Santissima!* for a full quarter of an hour, shameful as it may appear, have I been endeavouring to prepare you for what you call your happiness." Then suddenly laying aside her playful tone, she continued—"But now, my dear Rafael, I must remember my vow. I have made it, and you must assist me in its accomplishment."

"But why did you promise your hair?" inquired the lover, with a slight air of chagrin.

"Because I had nothing more valuable to offer in exchange for your life—mine perhaps as well. Oh! I am well repaid for the sacrifice by knowing that you love me. Come, Rafael! take the scissors."

"Oh! I could never manage with that weak instrument," said Don Rafael, speaking merely to gain time.

"Ah! are you going to complain of the trouble it will give you?" inquired Gertrudis, bending down towards her lover, who was still kneeling before her—"Come, my brave Rafael! Use these scissors. I command you."

Don Rafael took the shining instrument in his trembling hand, but still hesitated to use them—like the woodman, who, with his axe raised against some noble tree of the forest he has been ordered to cut down, hesitates before striking the first blow. Gertrudis would have smiled to encourage him, but at that moment, as she looked upon those gorgeous tresses, so long and carefully guarded, and which, if unfolded, would have covered her like a shawl, the poor young girl could not hinder a tear from escaping her.

"Stay, my Rafael—a moment yet," cried she, while the crimson blush mantled higher upon her cheeks. "I have long desired—dreamt of it as a supreme felicity—to entwine in these poor tresses the man whom I should one day love, and—and—"

Before she could finish speaking, Don Rafael had caught the perfumed tresses between his fingers, and rapturously kissing them, passed them around his neck.

"Now I am ready," continued she, raising the long plaits that encircled her lover's cheeks, and setting the captive free. "Go on, Rafael! I am ready."

"I should never have the courage to commit such a fearful act," cried the officer, flinging the scissors upon the floor, and crushing them under his heel.

"It must be done, Rafael; it must be done. God will punish me else. Perhaps He may punish me by taking away from me your love."

"Well, I shall do it," rejoined the reluctant lover, "but not yet awhile. On my return, Gertrudis. For my sake, leave it over till then."

The passionate appeal of Don Rafael at length obtained a respite, until the time fixed for his return; which was to be on the morrow—as soon as he should have assured himself of the safety of his father.

While their next meeting was being arranged between the two lovers, Gertrudis suddenly started up, like a young doe that springs from its perfumed lair at the first sound of the hunter's horn.

"Surely I heard a noise?" said she; "a strange noise. What could it mean?"

Don Rafael, whose senses had been entirely absorbed by his new-found happiness, sprang also to his feet, and stood listening.

They had scarce listened for a dozen seconds, when a well-known sound fell upon the ears of both—though well-known, a sound significant and ominous. It was the report of a gun, quickly followed by several others as if fired in fusillade.

At the same moment, Don Mariano and his daughter Marianita rushed into the room. They, too, had heard the reports, which were in the direction of the hills, and were proceeding to the rear of the hacienda to inquire the cause.

All remained listening and alarmed—Don Rafael, more than even the young girls: for too much happiness has the effect of weakening the heart. The most profound silence reigned throughout the building; for the firing, heard by the servants of the hacienda, had inspired one and all of them with the same mute alarm; just as pigeons asleep upon the tree aroused by the first scream of the kite, remain for some moments terrified and motionless in their places.

Chapter Twenty Five
A Mexican Major-Domo

Don Mariano, the dragoon officer, and the two sisters rushed up to the *azotéa*, the hearts of all filled with a dread presentiment.

From the roof, already crowded with servants, a view of the ridge could be obtained—its whole slope from top to bottom being visible at a single glance. A horrible spectacle came under the eyes of all at once.

At the upper end of the path which led towards the Hacienda del Valle, a horse and horseman were seen lying upon the road close to one another. Both appeared to be wounded—the man struggling to regain his feet—the horse making only the slightest motion, as if in the last moments of life.

"Haste!" cried Don Mariano to his domestics. "Haste! Procure a litter, and have the wounded horseman carried down here to the house."

"If my eyes don't deceive me," said the young officer, casting uneasy glances to the hill, "yonder unfortunate man is poor old Rodriguez, the oldest of my father's servants."

The head of the wounded horseman was in fact covered with grey hair, as could be seen from the *azotéa*.

"The name Antonio Valdez," continued Don Rafael, "now recalls to me some facts connected with that wretch. I remember something of a punishment inflicted upon him; and I have a dark presentiment— Oh, heavens! Señor Don Mariano, such happiness to be thus interrupted—"

And without finishing his speech, the young officer hastily pressed the hand of his host, and rushed for the postern that opened towards the hills.

In a few seconds after, he was seen climbing the ridge, followed by the domestics of Don Mariano, who carried a *litera*.

On reaching the wounded man, Don Rafael had no longer any doubts about his being old Rodriguez; though having seen the latter only in his childhood, he remembered little more than the name.

Rodriguez, enfeebled by the loss of blood, and by the efforts he had been making to get upon his feet, was fast losing consciousness.

"Hold!" said Don Rafael to the domestic. "It is useless placing him on the *litera*. He will not be able to endure the motion. His blood has nearly all run out by this terrible wound."

As the officer spoke he pointed to a large red spot upon the vest of the wounded man, beneath which the bloody orifice of a wound showed where the bullet had entered.

The dragoon captain had fairly won his spurs in the sanguinary wars of the Indian frontier. He had witnessed death in all its forms, and his experience had taught him to adopt the readiest means in such a crisis.

He first stopped the bleeding with his handkerchief, and then, taking the scarf of China crape from his waist, he bound it tightly over the wound. For all this he had but little hopes of the man's recovery. The bullet had entered between his shoulders, and passed clear through his body.

Don Rafael only anticipated that, the haemorrhage once stopped, the wounded man might return for a moment to consciousness, he was, no doubt, the bearer of some important message from his master, and it behoved Don Rafael to learn its purport.

Some time elapsed before the old servant opened his eyes; but one of Don Mariano's people at that moment came up, carrying a flask of *aguardiente*. A few drops were poured down his throat. Some of the liquid was sprinkled over his temples, and this had the effect of momentarily reviving him.

Opening his eyes, he beheld his young master bending over him. He had not seen Don Rafael since childhood, but he knew he was in the neighbourhood, and that the young officer must be he.

"It is I, Rodriguez," said Don Rafael, speaking close to his ear. "I—Rafael Tres-Villas. You have a message from my father? Why has he sent you?"

"Blessed be God that He has sent *you*," said the old man, speaking with difficulty. "Oh! Señor Don Rafael, I bring fearful news. The hacienda Del Valle—"

"Is burnt?"

The wounded man made a sign in the negative.

"Besieged, then?"

"Yes," replied Rodriguez in a feeble voice.

"And my father?" inquired the officer with a look of anguish.

"He lives. He sent me to you—to Don Mariano's—to ask assistance. I—pursued by the brigands—a bullet—here! Do not stay with me. Hasten to your father. If any misfortune happen—Antonio Valdez—Remember—

Antonio Valdez—miscreant—taking vengeance for—oh, young master! Don Rafael—pray for poor old Rodriguez—who nursed you when a child—pray—"

The sufferer could speak no more, even in whispers. His head fell back upon the turf. He was dead. When the litter was set down in the courtyard of Las Palmas it carried only a corpse! Don Rafael had turned back for his horse, and to bid a hasty adieu to the family of his host.

"If Costal were only here!" said Don Mariano. "Unfortunately the brave fellow is gone away. Only a few hours ago he came to take his leave of me, with another of my people—a negro whom I had no great fancy for. Both, I believe, are on their way to join the insurgent army in the capacity of scouts or guides. *Hola*!" continued the haciendado, shouting to one of the *peons*, "send hither the *mayor-domo*!"

This functionary soon made his appearance; not a house steward—as the name might seem to imply—in white cravat, stockings, and powdered wig; but, on the contrary, a strapping energetic fellow, dressed in full *ranchero* costume, with a pair of spurs upon his booted heels, whose enormous rowels caused him to walk almost upon his toes, and with long black hair hanging to his shoulders like the manes of the half-wild horses he was accustomed to ride. Such is the *mayor-domo* of a Mexican hacienda, whose duties, instead of confining him to the dwelling-house, consist in the general superintendence of the estate, often equal in extent to the half of a county. It is, therefore, necessary for him to be a man of the most active habits, a first-class rider, ever in the saddle, or ready to leap into it at a moment's notice. Such was the personage who presented himself in obedience to the summons of Don Mariano.

"Give orders," said the latter, addressing him, "to my two vaqueros, Arroyo and Bocardo, to saddle their horses and accompany Señor Don Rafael!"

"Neither Arroyo nor Bocardo can be found," replied the mayor-domo. "It is eight days since I have seen either of them."

"Give each of them four hours in the *xepo* (stocks), as soon as they return!"

"I doubt whether they will ever return, Señor Don Mariano."

"What! have they gone to join Valdez, think you?"

"Not exactly," replied the mayor-domo; "I have my suspicions that the brace of worthies have gone to get up a guerilla on their own account."

"Summon Sanchez, then!"

"Sanchez is laid up in bed, Señor Don Mariano. He has some bones broken by a wild horse—that he had mounted for the first time—having reared and fallen back upon him."

"So, Señor Don Rafael," said the haciendado with an air of vexation, "out of six servants which I counted yesterday I have not one to place at your service, except my mayor-domo here, for I cannot reckon upon those stupid Indian *peons*. The mayor-domo will attend you."

"No," rejoined Don Rafael; "it is not necessary. Let him remain here. I shall go alone to the assistance of my father, who, no doubt, will have plenty of people with him. It is more likely a leader that is wanted."

The mayor-domo, dismissed by this answer, hurried towards the stables, to see that Don Rafael's horse was made ready for the road.

Chapter Twenty Six
The Vow Performed

While these incidents were in course of occurrence, the two sisters had returned to their own chamber.

Alarmed by the coincidence, between the melancholy event that had just transpired and the procrastination of her vow, Gertrudis fancied she saw in it the finger of Providence; and, without further hesitation, she, with her own hands, completed the pious but painful sacrifice!

Shrouded under the folds of her *reboso*, her pale face appeared beneath a single band of hair that encircled her forehead—all that was left of that magnificent *chevelure*.

Marianita was in tears. It was she one would have thought that had suffered a misfortune; while Gertrudis, whose eyes shone with a sort of melancholy satisfaction for the act she had accomplished, appealed to be endeavouring to console her sister!

"Do not weep, my poor Marianita!" said she. "Perhaps, had it not been for my culpable weakness, in consenting to defer the fulfilment of my vow, this sad affair would not have arisen. Now I am more confident, that whatever danger he may run, God will restore Rafael safe to me. Go and tell him that I wait here to bid him *adios*. Bring him here, but stay with us yourself. Remember that, sister. Remain here along with us, for I cannot trust my strength. I might never allow him to leave me. Go, dearest, and return quickly!"

Marianita, covering her face with a kerchief, and endeavouring to dry her tears, hastened upon her errand.

Gertrudis, left alone, looked towards the two long plaits which she had placed beside her upon the table. The lips of Don Rafael had kissed them but the moment before; and, perhaps, influenced by this sweet souvenir, the young girl took them up and pressed them repeatedly to her own. Then laying them once more upon the table, she knelt down, to seek in prayer the strength of which she stood in need.

She was still upon her knees when Marianita, followed by Don Rafael, entered the chamber—that virgin sanctuary of the two sisters, where man, except their father, had never before penetrated.

A rapid glance told Don Rafael that the sacrifice had been accomplished. He was already too pale to change countenance.

Gertrudis rose and seated herself upon a *fauteuil*. Marianita also took a seat, but in a remote corner of the apartment. Don Rafael remained standing.

"Come here, Don Rafael!" said Gertrudis, "come near me. Kneel before me. No!—on one knee!—upon both only before God. So! Place your hands in mine! Look into my eyes."

Don Rafael obeyed these gentle injunctions without resistance or reluctance. What more could he wish, than thus to bend before her whom he loved? To press those white delicate fingers between his own strong hands? To drink from those swimming eyes as from the fountain of love? What more could man desire?

"Do you remember what you just now said to me, Don Rafael? '*Oh! Gertrudis, there is no love that could repay such a sacrifice! And however beautiful she might be, that young girl must appear in the eyes of her lover as beautiful as an angel!*' Are you still of the same opinion?" And with a sweet smile the questioner looked down in the face of her lover. "There, hush!" continued she, placing her little hand over his lips, "you need not make reply. Your eyes—you have beautiful eyes, my Rafael!—your eyes answer in the affirmative."

The simple and tender homage, thus rendered to the personal appearance of her lover, may appear a little *brave* in the opinion of those who pretend to love a man for the qualities of his mind and heart. I shall not discuss the point. I only design to draw a faithful picture, and exhibit in all its simple exaltation the love of a Creole maiden under the ardent sky of the tropics.

Reassured that she was still beautiful as ever in the eyes of her lover, the young girl proceeded—

"Do not tell me, Rafael, that you will ever love me more than you do now. It is sweet for me to know that you cannot love me more. Now!" she continued with faltering voice—"now we are about to part. I do not know—when one loves one always has fear. Take one of these tresses. I have been so happy while decking it with flowers for you. Take it! Keep it as a token—a souvenir. It will remind you, that you should never cease to love a poor girl, who knew of nothing more precious to offer to God in exchange for your life. The other I shall keep myself, as a talisman. Oh! it is a fearful thing I am now going to say to you. If one day you should cease to love me—if I should know this beyond all doubt—swear to me, Rafael, that, no matter in what place you may be—no matter at what hour it may reach you—when you receive this tress from me, that you will instantly come to see me. This silent messenger will say to you, *'The woman who sends you this token knows that you no longer love her; but, despite all, she cannot cease to love you, and she desires once more, only once more, to see you kneeling before her'* —as you are now, Don Rafael!"

"I swear it," cried the lover with emphasis. "I swear it; and though I were standing in front of my most mortal foe, with my sword raised to strike him, I should suspend the blow to obey that sacred message!"

"Your oath is registered in Heaven, Don Rafael," said Gertrudis. "But now the time presses. Accept from me this sun-scarf, which I have embroidered for you. Each thread of the embroidery will recall a thought, a prayer, or a sigh, of which you have been the object. Adieu, my beloved Rafael! You must go; your father may stand in need of your help. What is a mistress when compared with one's father?"

"It is time," said Don Rafael, suddenly awakening to a sense of his filial duty, "I shall be gone."

And yet he remained kneeling at the feet of Gertrudis, ever intending to go, and as often tarrying in his intent, adieu following adieu, like the eternal waves of the ocean!

"Say to him to go, Marianita," said Gertrudis with a sweet smile, "I have not the courage to tell him. One more kiss, Don Rafael, ere we part! let it be the pledge—"

The ardent pressure of her lover's lips interrupted her speech. One last fond embrace—a strange commingling of joy and sorrow—one wildly spoken "*Adios!*" and Don Rafael rushed from the apartment.

The clattering of hoofs, heard shortly after, told that he was galloping away from the hacienda.

Chapter Twenty Seven
Duty versus Love

The last beams of the sun were gilding the summit of the ridge that bounded the plain of Las Palmas, when Don Rafael Tres-Villas crossed it on his way to the hacienda Del Valle. To recover the time he had lost, he pressed his horse to his utmost speed, and descended the slope on the opposite side at a gallop. As the brave steed dashed onward, a hoarse snorting sound was heard to issue from his nostrils, caused by the singular operation which the *arriero* had performed upon him.

On reaching the level of the valley in which stood the hacienda Del Valle, the horseman drew bridle and listened, he was sufficiently near the house to have heard any unusual commotion that might be there going on. He fully expected to have distinguished the shouts of men engaged in fight, or the tumultuous murmur of a siege.

No sound, however, reached his ear—not a murmur. Silence ominous and profound reigned throughout the valley.

With clouded brow, and heart anxiously beating, the officer continued on his course. He had unbuckled his carbine from the saddle, and carried the piece in his hand ready for use.

The silence continued. Not a cry awoke the solitude—not the flash of a fusil lit up the darkness of the twilight. The sleep of death seemed to be upon everything.

As already stated, Don Rafael had not visited the hacienda of Del Valle since he left it when only a child: he therefore knew nothing of the way that led to it beyond the directions he had received from his late host.

He was beginning to think he had gone astray, when a long wide avenue opened before him. This was bordered on each side by a row of tall trees, of the species *taxodium disticha*—the cypress of America. He had been told of this avenue, and that at its extremity stood the hacienda he was in search of. The description was minute: he could not be mistaken.

Heading his steed into the avenue, he spurred forward beneath the sombre shadow of the trees. In a rapid gallop he traversed the level road, and had arrived nearly at its further extremity, when all at once the walls of the hacienda came in view directly in front of him—a dark mass of building, that filled up the whole space between the two rows of trees.

The main entrance in the centre appeared to be only half closed, one wing of the massive gate standing slightly ajar. But no one came forth to welcome him! Not a sound issued from the building. All was silent as the tomb!

Still pressing forward, he advanced towards the entrance—determined to ride in through the open gateway; but, just at that moment, his steed made a violent bound, and shied to one side.

In the obscurity of the twilight, or rather from the confusion of his senses, Don Rafael had not observed the object which had frightened his horse. It was a dead body lying upon the ground in front of the gateway. More horrible still, it was a body wanting the head!

At this frightful spectacle a cry broke from the lips of the officer—a cry of fearful import. Rage, despair, all the furious passions that may wring the heart of man, were expressed in that cry—to which echo was the only answer. He had arrived too late. All was over. The body was that of his father!

He needed not to alight and examine it, in order to be convinced of this terrible fact. On a level with his horse's head an object appeared hanging against one of the leaves of the great door. It was a head—the head that had belonged to the corpse. It was hanging from the latch, suspended by the hair.

Despite the repugnance of his horse to advance, Don Rafael drove the spur into his flank; and forced him forward until he was himself near enough to examine the fearful object. With flashing eyes and swelling veins, he gazed upon the gory face. The features were not so much disfigured, as to hinder him from identifying them. They were the features of his father!

The truth was clear. The Spaniard had been the victim of the insurgents, who had respected neither his liberal political sentiments, nor his inoffensive old age. The authors of the crime had even boasted of it. On the gate below were written two names, *Arroyo—Antonio Valdez*.

The officer read them aloud, but with a choking utterance.

For a moment his head fell pensively forward upon his breast. Then on a sudden he raised it again—as if in obedience to a secret resolve—saying as he did so, in a voice husky with emotion—

"Where shall I find the fiends? Where? No matter!—find them I shall. Night or day, no rest for me—no rest for them, till I have hung both their heads in the place of this one!"

"How now," he continued after a pause, "how can I combat in a cause like this? Can a son fight under the same flag with the assassins of his father? Never!"

"For Spain, then!" he cried out, after another short moment of silence. "For Spain shall my sword be drawn!" And raising his voice into a louder tone, he pronounced with furious emphasis—

"*Viva Espana! Mueran a los bandidos!*" (Spain for ever! Death to the brigands!)

Saying this, the dragoon dismounted from his horse, and knelt reverentially in front of that ghastly image.

"Head of my venerable and beloved father!" said he, "I swear by your grey hairs, crimsoned with your own blood, to use every effort in my power, by sword and by fire, to nip in the bud this accursed insurrection—one of whose first acts has been to rob you of your innocent life. May God give me strength to fulfil my vow!"

At that moment a voice from within seemed to whisper in his ear, repeating the words of his mistress:—

"*May all those who raise an arm in favour of Spain be branded with infamy and disgrace! May they find neither a roof to shelter them, nor a woman to smile upon them! May the contempt of those they love be the reward of every traitor to his country!*"

Almost the instant after, another voice replied—"*Do your duty, no matter what may be the result.*" In presence of the mutilated remains of his father, the son hearkened only to the latter.

The moon had been long up before Don Rafael finished the melancholy task of digging a grave. In this he respectfully placed the headless corpse, and laid the head beside it in its proper position. Then, drawing from his bosom the long plait of Gertrudis' hair, and taking from his shoulders the embroidered sun-scarf, with like respectful manner, he deposited these two love-tokens alongside the honoured remains of his father.

Convulsed with grief, he threw in the earth, burying in one grave the dearest *souvenirs* of his life.

It was not without difficulty that he could withdraw himself from a spot thus doubly consecrated by filial piety and love; and for a long while he stood sorrowing over the grave.

In fine, new thoughts coursing through his bosom aroused him to action; and, leaping into his saddle, he spurred his steed into a gallop, taking the road that conducted to the capital of Oajaca.

Chapter Twenty Eight
The Illustrious Morelos

Little more than twelve months after its first breaking out—that is, about the close of the year 1811—the Mexican revolution might have been compared to one of those great fires of the American prairies, whose destructive range has been checked by the hand of man. In vain the flames jet out on all sides, seeking fresh element. A wide space has been cleared around them. Soon the crackling of the large trees, and the hiss of the burning grass, cease to be heard; and the whole plain becomes enveloped under a cloud of smoke rising upward from the blackened ashes.

Such was the fate of the insurrection stirred up by the priest Hidalgo. From the little hamlet of Delores it had spread like fire over all the vice-kingdom of New Spain; but very soon the leaders were almost to a man made captives and shot—the venerable Hidalgo himself undergoing the same sad fate. A remnant of the insurgents, pressed on all sides by the royalist troops under General Calleja, had taken refuge in the little town of Zitacuaro, where they were commanded by the Mexican general, Don Ignacio Rayon. There they had established a *junta*, independent of the government; and continued to launch forth their proclamations, powerless as the glow of the prairie fire after its flames have been extinguished.

When such a fire, however, has been the work of men—when kindled by man's will and for man's purpose—and not the result of accident or spontaneity, then, indeed, the flames may be expected to burst forth anew at some other point of the prairie or the forest.

Just so was it with the Mexican revolution. Another champion of independence, of origin even more obscure than his predecessors—if that were possible—soon appeared upon the arena which they had quitted, and with an *éclat* likely to eclipse any of those who had preceded him.

This was the curate of Caracuaro, he whom historians designate as "*El insigne Morelos*" (the illustrious Morelos). The Mexican writers do not state in what year Morelos was born. Judging from the portraits I have seen of him, and comparing the different dates that have been assigned to his birth, he should have been about thirty-eight or forty years old, at the commencement of his career as a revolutionary leader. His native place was Talmejo, a small hamlet near the town of Apatzingam, in the state of Valladolid—now called *Morelia*, after the most illustrious of its sons. The only patrimony of the future heir of the Mexican independence was a small *recua* of pack-mules, left him by his father, who was a muleteer.

For a long time the son himself followed this humble and laborious calling; when, for some reason or other, the idea came into his head to enter holy orders. History does not say what was his motive for this resolution; but certain it is that Morelos proceeded to carry it out with that determined perseverance which was an essential trait in his character.

Having sold off his mules, be consecrated his whole time to acquire those branches of education, rigorously indispensable to the attainment of his purpose—that is to say, the study of Latin and theology. The college of Valladolid was the scene of his student life.

Having gone through the required course, orders were conferred upon him; but Valladolid offering to him no prospect of advancement, he retired to the little *pueblo* of Uruapam, where for a time he subsisted upon the scanty means supplied by giving lessons in Latin.

About this time the curacy of Caracuaro became vacant. Caracuaro is a village as unhealthy as poor, where no one could be supposed to reside from choice; and yet Morelos, lacking powerful friends, had great difficulty in getting appointed to the living.

In this miserable place had he resided in a state of obscure poverty, up to that hour, when, accidentally introduced to the reader, at the hacienda Las Palmas. Under the pretence of visiting the Bishop of Oajaca, but in reality for the purpose of fomenting the insurrection, Morelos had travelled through the province of that name; and at the time of his visit to Las Palmas, he was on his way to offer his services to Hidalgo, as chaplain of the insurgent army. The result of that application was, that instead of a chaplaincy to his army, Hidalgo bestowed upon the *cura* of Caracuaro, a commission to capture the fortified seaport of Acapulco. It was in reality rather as a jest, and to disembarrass himself of the importunities of Morelos, that Hidalgo bestowed this singular and important commission. How much Morelos merited the honour will appear in the sequel.

Chapter Twenty Nine
A Course of Study Interrupted

In the early part of January, 1812—about fifteen months after the scenes detailed as occurring near the hacienda Las Palmas—two men might have been seen face to face—one seated behind a rude deal table covered with charts and letters—the other standing in front, hat in hand.

This tableau was within a tent—the least ragged and largest, among a number of others that formed an encampment on the banks of the river Sabana, at a short distance from the port of Acapulco.

The person seated wore upon his head a checked cotton kerchief while his shoulders were covered with a *jaqueta* of white linen. It would have been difficult for any one not knowing him, to recognise in this plainly-dressed individual the commander-in-chief of the insurgent army encamped around, and still more difficult perhaps to have believed that he was the *ci-devant* "cura" of Caracuaro, Don José Maria Morelos y Pavon. And yet it was he.

Yes, the humble curate had raised the standard of independence in the southern provinces; had long been carrying it with success; and at this moment he was commander-in-chief of the insurgent forces besieging Acapulco—that very town he had been ironically empowered to take.

But notwithstanding the eccentric changes which civil war produces in the situations of men, the reader cannot be otherwise than greatly astonished when told, that the gentleman who stood in front of Morelos, encased in the somewhat elegant uniform of a lieutenant of cavalry, was the *ci-devant* student of theology—Don Cornelio Lantejas.

By what magical interference had the timid student of theology been transformed into an officer of dragoons—in the army of the insurgents, too, towards whose cause he had shown himself but indifferently affected?

To explain this unexpected metamorphosis, it will be necessary to enter into some details, continuing the history of the student from the time when we left him on a fevered couch in the hacienda of Las Palmas, till that hour when we find him in the marquee of the insurgent general.

It may be stated, in advance, however, that the extraordinary transformation which we have noticed, was entirely owing to a new act of parsimonious economy upon the part of Don Cornelio's father, conducting him into a series of perilous mishaps and desperate dangers, to which his adventure with the jaguars and rattlesnakes, while suspended between the two tamarinds, was nothing more, according to the simile of Sancho Panza, than *"tortus y pan pintado"* (couleur de rose). To proceed, then, with the promised details.

On recovering from his temporary illness, the student travelled on to the dwelling of his uncle. He had been mounted in a more becoming manner, on a fine young horse, which Don Mariano—who owned some thousands of the like—had presented to him.

Having sounded the dispositions of the uncle, according to instructions, he made all haste in returning to his father's house; which he reached in less than half the time he had employed upon his previous journey. Too soon, perhaps; for, had he been delayed, as before, two months upon the route, he might have escaped the series of frightful perils through which he was afterwards compelled to pass.

Before setting out on his mission to the bachelor uncle, he had finished his preliminary studies for the ecclesiastical calling; and it only remained for him to return to the college, and present his thesis before the faculty of examiners, to take out his orders. For this purpose it was necessary he should repair to Valladolid, where the university was. To make the journey, his father now provided him with an old she-mule of a most unamiable disposition, which he had obtained in exchange for the young horse—the gift of Don Mariano—with a goodly number of dollars in "boot."

Thus mounted, the student started on his new journey—carrying with him the paternal blessing, and a long chapter of instructions, as to how he should manage his mule, and keep himself clear of all meddling with insurrectionary matters.

After journeying for two days along the route to Valladolid, he had arrived within sight of the straggling huts that compose the little *pueblita* of Caracuaro, when three horsemen appeared upon the road in front, and riding towards him.

The student was at the moment occupied in passing through his mind the rudiments of his theological education—which he had gained from a crowd of books; and which, with some uneasiness, he found had been well nigh driven out of his head by his late adventures in the South.

Just at that moment, when he was paying not the slightest attention to his mule, the skittish animal, frightened by the approach of the horsemen, threw up her hind quarters, and pitched her rider upon the road. As the latter fell, his head came in contact with a large stone, and with such violence as to deprive him of consciousness.

On coming to his senses again, he found himself seated against the bank of the causeway, his head badly bruised, and above all without his mule. The animal, profiting by the opportunity when the three horsemen had alighted to look after her spilt rider, had headed about, and taken the back track at full gallop!

Of the three horsemen, one appeared to be the master, and the other two his attendants.

"My son!" said the first, addressing the student, "your situation, without being dangerous, is nevertheless sufficiently serious. You will stand in need of that which you cannot obtain in the poor village of Caracuaro, which is, moreover, nearly two leagues distant. The best thing you can do is to mount behind one of my attendants, and ride back with us to the hacienda of San Diego, which we shall reach in an hour. Your mule has taken that direction; and I shall have her caught for you by the *vaqueros* of the hacienda. You will need a day or two of repose, which you can there obtain. Afterwards you can resume your route. Where were you going?"

"To Valladolid," replied Lantejas. "I was on my way to the University, to enter into holy orders."

"Indeed! then we are of the same robe," rejoined the horseman with a smile. "I myself am the unworthy curate of Caracuaro—Don José Maria Morelos—a name, I presume, you have never heard before."

In truth the afterwards illustrious Morelos was at this time entirely unknown to fame, and of course Don Cornelio had never heard his name.

The student was no little astonished at the appearance of the man who had thus announced himself as the *cura* of Caracuaro. For one of the clerical calling his costume was altogether singular—to say nothing of its being rather shabby. A double-barrelled gun, with one barrel broken, hung from his saddle-bow, and an old rusty sabre in a common leathern scabbard dangled against his horse's side.

The two domestics were still more plainly attired; and each carried in his hand a huge brass blunderbuss!

"And you, Señor padre?" inquired the student in turn. "Where are you going, may I ask?"

"I? Well," replied the *cura*, smiling as he spoke, "just as I have told you—to the hacienda of San Diego. After that to Acapulco—to capture the town and citadel in obedience to an order I have received."

Such were at this time the equipment and warlike resources of the general, whose name afterwards obtained such heroic renown!

His response caused the candidate for holy orders to open his eyes to the widest. He fancied that in the confusion of his head he had not clearly comprehended the meaning of the *cura's* speech; and he preferred this fancy to the alternative of supposing that the worthy priest of Caracuaro was himself suffering from mental aberration.

"What! you an insurgent?" inquired Lantejas, not without some apprehension.

"Very true. I am, and have been for a long time."

As neither upon the head of the *cura*, nor yet of his two servants, there appeared those diabolical ornaments which had been promised them by the Lord Bishop of Oajaca, Don Cornelio began to think that perhaps all insurgents were not delivered over to the devil; and, as there was no alternative, he accepted the offer made to him, and mounted behind one of the attendants. He had made up his mind, however, not to accompany the curate of Caracuaro further than the hacienda of San Diego, and to make as short a stay as possible in such suspicious company. But he had scarcely completed this satisfactory arrangement with his conscience, when the burning rays of the sun shining down upon his head, caused a ferment in his brain of so strange a character—that not only did the idea of this insurrection, excited by priests, appear right and natural, but he commenced chanting at the top of his voice a sort of improvised war song, in which the King of Spain was mentioned in no very eulogistic terms!

From that time, till his arrival at the hacienda of San Diego, the student was altogether unconscious of what passed—and for several days after, during which he remained under the influence of a burning fever. He had only a vague remembrance of ugly dreams, in which he appeared constantly surrounded by armed men, and as if he was tossing about on a stormy sea!

At length his consciousness returned, and on looking around he was astonished to find himself in a small and poorly furnished chamber. He now remembered his tumble from the mule, and his encounter with the *cura* of Caracuaro. Finally, feeling himself strong enough to rise from his couch, he got up, and staggered towards the window—for the purpose of ascertaining the nature of a noisy tumult that was heard outside.

The courtyard under the window was filled with armed men—some afoot, others on horseback. Lances with gay pennons, sabres, guns, and other weapons were seen on all sides, glancing under the sunbeams. The horses were rearing and neighing—the men talking loudly—in short, the scene resembled the temporary halt of a *corps d'armée.*

His weakness soon compelled the invalid to return to his couch, where he lay awaiting impatiently—the more so that he was half-famished with hunger—the coming of some one who could give him an explanation of the strange circumstances by which he was surrounded.

Shortly after, a man entered the chamber, whom the student recognised as one of the attendants of the *cura* of Caracuaro. This man had come, on the part of his master, to inquire, the state of the invalid's health.

"Where am I, friend? tell me that," said Lantejas, after having answered the inquiries of the servant.

"At the hacienda of San Luis."

The student summoned all his recollections; but these only carried him as far as the hacienda of San Diego.

"You must be mistaken?" said he. "It is the hacienda of San Diego, is it not?"

"Oh, no," replied the domestic. "We left San Diego yesterday; we were no longer safe there. What folly of you, señor, to act as you did! No matter how good a patriot one may be, it's not necessary to proclaim it from the housetops."

"I do not comprehend you, my good friend," said Lantejas. "Perhaps it is the fever that is still troubling my head."

"What I have said is clear enough," rejoined the domestic. "We were obliged to quit San Diego, where the royalist troops would have arrested us—on account of the loud declaration of his political opinions made by a certain Don Cornelio Lantejas."

"Cornelio Lantejas!" cried the student, in a tone of anguish, "why that's myself!"

"*Por Dios*! I well know that. Your honour took good care everybody should know your name: since out of the window of the hacienda you shouted with all your voice—proclaiming my master Generalissimo of all the insurgent forces; and we had the greatest difficulty to hinder you from marching upon Madrid."

"Madrid—in Spain?"

"Bah! two hundred leagues of sea was nothing to you to traverse. '*It is I!*' you cried, '*I, Cornelio Lantejas, who take upon me to strike down the tyrant!*'

In fine, we were obliged to decamp, bringing you with us in a litter—for my master would not abandon so zealous a partisan, who had compromised himself, moreover, in the good cause. Well, we have arrived here at San Luis; where, thanks to a strong body of men who have joined us, you may have an opportunity of proclaiming your patriotism as loudly as you please. For yourself, it can do no further harm, since, no doubt, there is a price placed upon your head before this time."

The student listened with horror, and completely stupefied, to this account of his actions.

"And now, cavallero," continued the domestic, "my master, whom you were the first to proclaim Generalissimo, has not permitted you to go without your reward. He has appointed you an *alferez*, and named you to be his aide-de-camp. You will find your commission under the pillow."

Saying this, the servant left the room, leaving the unhappy *alferez* crushed beneath the weight of the astounding disclosures he had made to him.

Chapter Thirty
A Soldier against his Will

As soon as the man had gone out of the apartment the student looked under his pillow. Sure enough there lay a document, which proved upon examination to be an ensign's commission, granted to Don Cornelio Lantejas, and signed by the commander-in-chief of the insurgent army—Don José Maria Morelos y Pavon.

An overwhelming anguish seized the spirit of the student; and once more he sprang from his couch and rushed towards the window. This time it was with the design of disavowing all participation in the insurrection—like the early Christians, who in the midst of an idolatrous host of persecutors still continued to avow their faith in God.

But the evil genius of Don Cornelio was yet by his side; and, at the moment when he was about opening his lips to deny all complicity with the enemies of Spain, his senses again gave way; and, without knowing what came out of his mouth, he cried in a loud voice, "*Viva Mexico, muera el tyran!*" Then, overcome by the effort, he staggered back to his couch.

This time his syncope was of short duration. On recovering his senses, he perceived that his bed was surrounded by armed men; who, judging from their looks and speeches, were examining him with more than ordinary interest. Among others he recognised the voice of Morelos himself!

"How can one explain this sudden sympathy with our cause?" Morelos was inquiring. "It seems as if the young man was under the hallucination of his fever?"

"Something more than that, General," suggested an officer of the name of Valdovinos. "If the most ardent patriotism was not boiling at the bottom, the foam would not thus rise to the surface."

"No matter!" rejoined Morelos, "but I cannot think that my ascendancy—"

A new-comer interrupted the speech of the *cura* of Caracuaro, just as Lantejas had got his eyes fairly open. This was a man of robust and vigorous appearance, with a noble martial air, and a bold open countenance. His large beard, and hair slightly grizzled, betrayed his age to be somewhere near fifty.

"And why not, General?" said he, taking hold of the hand which Morelos stretched out to him. "Why should not this brave young man have submitted to your ascendancy at first sight, just as I have done? It is only this morning I have seen you for the first time, and yet you have no follower more devoted than myself. I shall answer for this young stranger. He is one of us, beyond doubt."

As the new-comer pronounced these words, he cast upon Lantejas a glance so winning and at the same time so severe, that it completely subjugated the spirit of the student with a sort of invincible charm, and hindered him from making any attempt to contradict the engagement which was thus made in his name. On the contrary, he rather confirmed it with an involuntary gesture, which he could not restrain himself from making.

The man who had thus intervened was he whom historians delight to call *the grand, the terrible, the invincible Hermenegildo Galeana*—the Murat of the Mexican revolution; he who afterwards, in more than a hundred actions, was seen to place his lance in rest, and dash into the thickest of the enemy's lines, like a god of battles, vociferating his favourite war-cry, *Aqui esta Galeana!* (Here comes Galeana!) A redoubtable enemy—a friend tender and devoted—such was Don Hermenegildo Galeana.

More fortunate than Murat, Galeana met his death on the battle-field, in the midst of hosts slain by his own hand. Still more fortunate than the French warrior, he died faithful to the principles as well as to the inn to whom he had consecrated his life.

"Well—however the thing may be," said Valdovinos, pursuing the subject of Don Cornelio's dubious patriotism, "I know this, that General Calleja has set a price upon this young man's head as well as on our own."

"Come, *Alferez* Don Cornelio!" added Galeana, "get ready to start in the morning; and show yourself worthy of the commission that has been bestowed upon you. You will soon find opportunity, I promise you."

At that moment the report of a cannon reverberated under the window, to the astonishment of Morelos himself: who had not yet been made aware that he had a piece of artillery under his orders.

"Señor General," said Galeana, explaining the presence of the gun, "that cannon is part of the patrimonial inheritance of our family. When a Galeana is born or one dies, it serves to signalise our joy or our sorrow. To-day we consecrate it to the service of the whole Mexican family. It is yours, as our swords and lives are yours."

As Galeana finished speaking, he advanced towards the window; and in that formidable voice which often struck terror into the hearts of the Spaniards, he cried out—"*Viva el General Morelos!*"

Responsive *vivas* rose up from the court below, mingled with the clanking of sabres, as they leaped forth from their scabbards, and the crashing jar of fusils dashed heavily against the pavement; while the horses, catching up the general enthusiasm, sent forth a loud, wild neighing.

In another instant the chamber was emptied of its guests. Morelos had gone down into the courtyard to press the hands of his new adherents, and the other officers had followed him.

Far from partaking of the universal warlike ardour, the student was suffering at the moment the most terrible anguish of heart. The thought of his theological studies being thus interrupted, in order that he might figure in the middle of an insurgent camp, was rendering him completely miserable; but still more the unpleasant information he had just received, that he had been declared a rebel, and that a price was set upon his head. All this, too, had been brought about by the shameful stinginess of his father, in providing him with that sorry mule—just as his former misfortunes had arisen, from his having no better horse than the old steed of the *picador*.

It is scarce necessary to say, that under these circumstances he passed a wretched night of it, and that his dreams were a continued series of horrid visions. He fancied himself engaged in numerous sanguinary battles: and that the insurgent army in which he was enrolled had suddenly changed into a legion of demons, with horns and hoofs!

On waking with the first dawn of day, his dreams, instead of being terminated, appeared to be continued. He heard a noisy tumult in the court below; and rising far above the general clamour could be distinguished a strange trumpet-like sound, now shrill, now hoarsely bellowing—as if the fiend himself was sounding the signal of "Boots and Saddles" to his infernal legions. Bathed in a cold sweat, he started up from his couch; and approaching the window, cast a glance into the courtyard. As before, he saw that it was crowded with armed men in every kind of equipment. The cannon was there, standing in the middle of the court. A negro was reloading it. It was not without surprise that Don Cornelio recognised in the negro the same man who, along with the tiger-hunter, had conducted him to the hacienda of Las Palmas.

Yes, the artillerist was no other than Clara; who was thus improvised as full commander of the solitary piece of cannon—the first which Morelos had at his disposal, and which, under the name of *El Nino*, became afterwards so celebrated in the history of the Mexican revolution. The student also saw the instrument that had been bellowing forth those infernal tones, which he had been fancying he had heard somewhere before. His fancy was not at fault, as he now ascertained—on seeing near the cannon a tall Indian, who was holding to his lips an immense sea-shell, from which proceeded the mysterious sounds. It was Costal and his conch, at that moment performing the *métier* of first bugler in the army of Morelos. Morelos himself, surrounded by a staff of officers, stood at one end of the spacious courtyard, in the act of distributing fusils to the newly enrolled troops.

Lantejas perceived the necessity of making ready for the departure which was evidently about to take place; and having dressed himself, he descended to the court and mingled among the other officers—beyond doubt the most lugubrious ensign in all the insurgent army.

The first person he encountered was the terrible Galeana; and he trembled lest the piercing glance of the warrior should detect under the lion's skin the heart of the hare.

Luckily for him, however, Galeana had at that moment something else to think of, than to scrutinise the thoughts of an obscure ensign; and all the rest were deceived by the martial air which he had done his best to assume.

Morelos, as stated, was at the moment making a distribution of fusils, a large quantity of which appeared by his side piled along the pavement of the courtyard.

It is necessary to explain how these arms had fallen so appropriately into the hands of the insurgent general—which they had done by a circumstance that might appear almost providential.

While retiring from the hacienda of San Luis, on account of the insane demonstrations of the student, and with the latter transported in a litter, Morelos encountered near San Diego the insurgent leader, Don Rafael Valdovinos. The latter, already at the head of a small *guerilla* was just on his way to join the *cura* of Caracuaro.

Having received information that the Spanish Government had forwarded a large number of fusils to the neighbouring village of Petitlan, for the purpose of equipping a corps of militia belonging to that place, the insurgent general thought that these guns might serve better in the hands of his own followers; and with the band of Valdovinos he made a rapid march upon Petitlan, and succeeded in capturing them.

The rumour of this dashing action had reached San Diego before Morelos himself; and, shortly after his arrival there, his troops were further strengthened by the followers of Galeana—who stood in need of this well-timed supply of weapons.

Almost on the instant that Lantejas presented himself in the courtyard, the cannon, El Nino, thundered forth another discharge. It was the signal of departure; and the little army, putting itself in motion, marched off from the hacienda of San Diego—the new *alferez* taking his place with the rest.

Morelos was shortly after joined by other partisans, till his troop had grown into a small army; and, after two months of long marches, and sharp skirmishes with the Spanish troops—out of which he always issued victorious—the insurgent general found himself in front of the town of Acapulco, on the Pacific Ocean. He was now besieging that place—which he had been ironically commanded to take—and with a fair prospect of obtaining its speedy surrender.

As for the student of theology, two months' campaigning had somewhat *soldierised* him. He had obtained a great reputation for courage; although his heart in moments of danger had often been upon the point of failing him.

On the first occasion that he was under fire, he was by the side of Don Hermenegildo Galeana, who had acquired a complete ascendancy over him, and whose terrible glances he more dreaded than even the presence of the enemy. Don Hermenegildo of course fought in the foremost rank; where, with his lance and long sabre, he was accustomed to open a wide circle around his horse, that no enemy dared to intrude upon, and which, for the sword of the trembling ensign, left absolutely nothing to do. Lantejas having learnt, in the first encounter, the advantage of this position, ever afterwards took care to keep well up with the redoubtable Don Hermenegildo.

There was another man, who, from habit, always fought alongside Galeana, and who scarce yielded to the latter either in courage or dexterity. This was Costal, the Zapoteque; and protected by these two, as by a pair of guardian angels, Lantejas scarce ran any danger in the hottest fight; while at the same time he was constantly gaining fresh laurels by keeping the position.

For all this, his glory sat upon him like a burden too heavy for his back, and one that he was not able to cast from his shoulders. To desert from the insurgent army was impossible: a price was set upon his head. Besides, Morelos had given to that corner of the Sabana river occupied by his camp the quaint title of *Paso de la eternidad* (the road to eternity)—to signify that, whoever should attempt either to abandon the entrenchments, or make an attack upon them, would be forced to embark upon that long journey.

Lantejas had already written to his father, informing him of all that had happened; how—thanks to the valuable roadster with which his parent had provided him—he was now sustaining his thesis with the sword; and that, instead of having only his hair shorn, he was more likely to lose his head.

To these letters—for there had been several written by him—he had at length received a response. This, after complimenting him upon the valorous deeds he had achieved—and which his worthy parent had hardly expected to hear of—ended by informing him that the latter had obtained from the Viceroy a promise of pardon for him, on the condition of his forsaking the insurgent cause, and throwing the weight of his sword into that of Spain.

This condition was hardly to the taste of Lantejas. In the ranks of the Spanish army he might seek in vain for two such protectors as he now had by his side. Moreover, were he to join the Spaniards, he might some day, as an enemy, be brought face to face with the formidable Galeana! The very thought of such a contingency was enough to make his hair stand on end!

It was some time before he could bring himself to any definite resolution as to what he should do. At length, however, he resolved upon a course of action. Instead of attempting to run away from the insurgent ranks, he determined to say nothing to the General about the contents of his father's letter, but to obtain from him, if possible, a short leave of absence: which it was his intention should be prolonged to an indefinite period.

It was for this purpose he had entered the General's tent, and was now standing, hat in hand, in front of the Commander-in-Chief of the besieging army.

Chapter Thirty One
Pepe Gago

Besides his military chapeau, the lieutenant of cavalry held in his hand a piece of folded paper; and although he had already stated his errand, his countenance exhibited considerable embarrassment.

"What, leave of absence?" said the General, smiling benignantly upon his aide-de-camp. "You, friend Lantejas—you think of quitting us? and at such a time, too, when all is going well!"

"It is necessity, General, that drives me to make the application. There are family affairs that require me at home, and—" Lantejas here paused, as if inwardly ashamed of the deceit he was practising. "Besides, General, to say the truth, this soldier's life is not suited to me, nor I to it. I was born to be a priest, and would greatly desire to complete my theological studies, and enter upon that career to which my inclinations lead me. Now that success has crowned your army, you will no longer require me?"

"*Vita Cristo*!" exclaimed Morelos, "not require you! Ah, friend Lantejas, you are too valiant a soldier of the Church militant to be spared so easily as that. Like that faithful adherent of some French king, whose name I do not now remember, you would be the very man to wish yourself hanged if Acapulco were taken without you. I must refuse your application, then, although I see it vexes you. I refuse it, because I am too well satisfied with your services to let you go. You were my first follower; and do you know what people say, that the three bravest men in our little army are Don Hermenegildo Galeana, Manuel Costal, and yourself? And what at this moment still more endears you to me is, that you propose leaving me just as fortune is showering her favours upon me; whereas, with most other friends, the reverse is usually what may be expected. I have just heard that the Captain Don Francisco Gonzales has been killed in the affair of Tonaltepec. You will replace him in the command of his company—Now? *Captain* Lantejas?"

The new captain bowed his thanks in silence, and was about to retire.

"Do not go yet!" commanded the General; "I have something more to say to you. You have, I believe, some relative or relatives living near

Tehuantepec. Well, I have a commission for some one to that part of the country, and I require a man of courage and prudence to execute it. I have thought of sending *you*, as soon as we have taken Acapulco—which I trust will be in a very short time."

Lantejas was about to open his mouth, and inquire the nature of this confidential mission, when he was interrupted by the entrance of two men into the tent. One of these was Costal the Indian; the other was a stranger both to Morelos and the captain. The latter was again about to retire, when Morelos signed him to stay.

"There's the General," said Costal, pointing out the commander-in-chief to the man who accompanied him, and who was in the costume of a Spanish officer.

The latter regarded for an instant, and not without surprise, the simply-clad individual whose name at that moment had become so widely renowned. Although evidently a person of imperturbable coolness, the stranger said nothing, leaving it to the General to open the conversation.

"Who are you, my friend, and what do you want?" inquired Morelos.

"To speak a word in confidence with you," replied the man. "This individual," continued he, pointing to Costal, "whom I encountered philosophising upon the sea-beach, has promised me that his word would enable me to obtain an interview with your Excellency, and safe conduct through your camp. On this promise I have followed him."

"Costal," said the General, "was my first bugler, and with his great conch sounded the signals to less than twenty horsemen, who at that time composed my whole army. I confirm the parole he has given you. Speak freely."

"With your Excellency's permission, then, my name is Pepe Gago. I am a Gallician, an officer of artillery, and command a battery in the castle of Acapulco—which your Excellency, if I am not mistaken, desires to capture."

"It is a pleasure which I intend affording myself one of these days."

"Perhaps your Excellency is confounding the castle with the town? The latter you can take whenever it pleases you."

"I know that."

"But you would not be able to hold it, so long as we are masters of the citadel."

"I know that also."

"Ah, then, your Excellency, we are likely to understand one another."

"It is just for that reason that I decline taking the town till I have first captured the castle."

"Now I think we are still nearer comprehending each other: since it is just that which you wish to have, that I come to offer you. I will not say to *sell*: for my price will be so moderate that it will deserve rather to be called a gift I am making you. *Apropos*, however, of the price—is your Excellency in funds?"

"Well, you have heard, no doubt, that I have just captured from the Spanish general, Paris, eleven hundred fusils, five pieces of cannon—to say nothing of the eight hundred prisoners we have made—and ten thousand dollars in specie. That is about ten times the price of a fortress, which in a short time I may have for nothing."

"Be not so sure of that, your Excellency. We have no scarcity of provisions. The Isle of Roqueta—"

"I shall capture that also."

"Serves us," continued the Spaniard, without noticing the interruption, "as a port of supply, by which the ships can always throw provisions into the castle. But not to dispute the point, am I to understand that your Excellency fixes the price at a thousand dollars? I agree to that sum. You say you have captured ten thousand. Unfortunately for me, I have the opportunity of selling the fortress only once."

"A thousand dollars down, do you mean?" inquired the General.

"Oh, no," replied the artilleryman; "what security would you have of my keeping my word? Five hundred, cash down, and the balance when the castle is delivered up to you."

"Agreed! And now, Señor Pepe Gago, what are your means for bringing about the surrender?"

"I shall have the command of the portcullis guard from two till five to-morrow morning. A lantern hung up on the bridge of Hornos to advise me of your approach—a password between us—and your presence. I presume your Excellency will not yield to any one the taking of the place?"

"I shall be there in person," replied Morelos. "With regard to the password, here it is."

The General handed to the Gallician a scrap of paper, on which he had written two words, which neither Costal nor Lantejas were near enough to read.

A somewhat prolonged conversation was now commenced between Morelos and Pepe Gago, but carried on in a tone so low that the others did not understand it import. At length the Spaniard was about to take his departure, when Costal, advancing towards him, laid his hand firmly on his shoulder.

"Listen to me, Pepe Gago!" said he to the Gallician in a serious voice. "It is I who am responsible for you here; but I swear by the bones of the Caciques of Tehuantepec—from whom I have the undoubted honour of being descended—if you play traitor in this affair, look out for Costal, the Zapoteque. Though you may dive like the sharks to the bottom of the ocean, or like the jaguars hide yourself in the thickest jungles of the forest, you shall not escape, any more than shark or jaguar, from my carbine or my knife. I have said it."

The Spaniard again repeated his declarations of good faith, and retired from the tent under the safe conduct of Costal.

"By-and-by," said the General to Lantejas when the others had gone, "I shall speak to you of the mission I intend sending you upon. Meanwhile, go and get some rest, as I shall want you at an early hour in the morning. At four o'clock I shall myself take a party of men up to the castle. As it is best that no one should know our intention, you and Costal must hang a lantern on the bridge of Hornos. That is to be the signal for our approach to the gate."

Saying this, the commander-in-chief dismissed his captain—who strode forth out of the marquee, with no very sanguine anticipations of obtaining a tranquil night's rest.

Chapter Thirty Two
The Secret Signal

The fortress castle of Acapulco stands at some little distance from the town, commanding the latter. It is built upon the summit of the cliffs that inclose the Acapulco Bay—against whose base the waves of the South Sea are continually breaking. On each side of the fortress a deep ravine or barranca pierces the precipice down to the depths of the ocean—so that the castle stands upon a sort of island promontory or *voladero*. The cliff upon the right flank of the castle is called the *Voladero de los Hornos*; and over the ravine between it and the citadel stretches a narrow bridge called *El Puento de los Hornos*.

Early in the following morning—while the insurgent camp was in some confusion consequent upon an unexpected order from the commander-in-chief; and while a strong detachment was getting under arms, not knowing where they were to be conducted—Captain Don Cornelio Lantejas and Costal the Indian were seen gliding silently along the sea-beach in the direction of the fortress.

The night was still dark—for it wanted yet two hours to sunrise—and both the town and castle were wrapped in the most profound slumber. The only sounds heard distinctly were the continuous murmuring of the waves as they broke along the beach.

The two men, after cautiously advancing towards the black cliff, on which stood the fortress, commenced climbing upward. It was not without much exertion, and danger too, that they at length succeeded in ascending to the bridge of Los Hornos.

The Indian now struck a light; and kindling a resin candle, which he carried inside his lantern, he hung the latter to a post that stood near the middle of the bridge, fixing it in such a manner that the light should shine in the direction of the fortress. It was the signal agreed upon by the Gallician; and as their part of the performance was now over, the two men sat down to await the attack which was soon to be made by the General in person.

The position which they occupied commanded an extensive view—taking in the town, the castle, and the ocean. Of the three, the last-mentioned alone gave out any sound; and Lantejas, after a time, ceased watching the two former, and involuntarily bent his regards upon the sea.

Costal was also turning his eyes upon the great deep, in which everything might also have appeared asleep, but that at intervals a narrow line of light might be seen gleaming along the black surface of the water.

"There's a storm in the air," muttered Costal to his companion in a solemn tone of voice. "See, how the sharks are shining in the roadway!"

As Costal spoke, half-a-dozen of these voracious creatures, in search of prey, were seen quartering the waters of the bay—crossing each other's course, and circling around, like fireflies over the surface of a savanna.

"What think you," continued the *ci-devant tigrero*, "would become of the man who should chance to fall overboard among those silent swimmers? Many a time, for all that, have I braved that same danger—in the days when I followed pearl-diving for my profession."

Don Cornelio made no reply, but the thought of being among the sharks at that moment sent a shivering through his frame.

"I was in no danger whatever," continued the Indian. "Neither the sharks nor the tigers—which I afterwards also hunted as a profession—could prevail against one destined to live as long as the ravens. Soon I shall be half-a-century old; and then *quien sabe*? At present, perhaps, no one here except myself could swim in the midst of those carnivorous creatures without the danger of certain death. *I* could do it without the slightest risk."

"Is that the secret of your courage, Costal—of which you give so many proofs?"

"Yes, and no," replied the Indian. "Danger attracts me, as your body would attract the sharks. It is an instinct which I follow—not a bravado. Another reason, perhaps, gives me courage. I seek to avenge in Spanish blood the assassination of my forefathers. What care I for the political emancipation of you Creoles? But it is not of this I wish to speak now. Look yonder! Do you see anything down there?"

A strange object just then came under the eyes of Lantejas, which caused him to make a movement of superstitious terror. Costal only smiled, while gazing calmly upon the object.

A dark human-like form, with a sort of tufted hair hanging loosely over its head, had emerged from the water, and was supporting itself by his two arms upon the beach—as if resting there like some bather fatigued with swimming.

"What is it?" inquired Lantejas in a troubled tone—the more so that a plaintive whine seemed to proceed from this singular object, which, with somewhat of the form of a woman, had nothing human in its voice.

"A *manatee*," responded Costal; "an amphibious creature we call *pesca-mujer*—that is, half-fish, half-woman. Dare you stand face to face with a creature still more human-like in form—ah! more perfect than any human creature?"

"What do you mean?" inquired Lantejas.

"Señor Captain Don Cornelio," continued the Indian, "you who are so brave in the face of the enemy—"

"Hum!" interrupted Lantejas with an embarrassed air, "the bravest has his moments of weakness, do you see?"

An avowal of his want of courage—though on certain occasions the ex-student of theology was not lacking this quality—was upon the tongue of Lantejas, when Costal interrupted him with a rejoinder—

"Yes, yes. You are like Clara—although a little braver than he, since he has not had such an opportunity to cultivate an acquaintance with the tigers, as you. Well, then, if you were to see down on the beach yonder, in place of the manatee, a beautiful creature rise up out of the deep—a beautiful woman with dishevelled locks—her long hair dripping and shining with the water, and she singing as she rose to the surface; and were you to know that this woman, although visible to your eyes, was only a spirit, only of air—what would you do?"

"A very simple thing," answered the ex-student, "I should feel terribly afraid."

"Ah! then I have nothing more to say to you," replied the Indian, with an air of disappointment. "For a certain object I had in view, I was in search of a comrade, one with more courage than Clara. I must content myself with the negro. I expected that you—never mind—we need not talk any more about the matter."

The Indian did not add a single word; and the officer, whose fears were excited by the half-confidences of his companion, was silent also. Both awaiting to hear the sounds of the attack upon the castle, continued to gaze upon the vast mysterious ocean, in which the luminous tracks of the sharks and the dark body of the manatee alone animated its profound solitude.

They were thus seated in silence, with their eyes wandering over the dark blue surface of the water, when all at once the manatee was heard to plunge under the waves, uttering a melancholy cry as it went down. Just then the loud booming of a cannon drowned the voice of the amphibious creature.

"The castle is taken!" cried Lantejas.

"No," replied Costal, "on the contrary, Pepe Gago has betrayed us. I fear our General has been tricked."

Several discharges of cannon followed on the instant, confirming Costal's surmise; and the two men, hastening to leave their dangerous post by the bridge of Hornos, retreated towards a narrow defile called the *Ojo de Agua*. There they saw the Mexican detachment scattered, and in full retreat towards their encampment. A man standing in the middle of the path was trying to intercept their flight.

"Cowards!" cried he, "will you pass over the body of your general?"

Many halted, and, returning, made an attack upon the works of the citadel. But it was to no purpose: the gate was too well defended; and a discharge of grape had the effect not only of terrifying the assailants, but also killed several of their number.

Morelos now saw that he had been betrayed, and caused the retreat to be sounded. It was the first check he had experienced during a victorious career of months.

The day had not yet dawned, when two men were seen advancing from the direction of the insurgent camp toward the bridge of Los Hornos. One of these men was Costal, but this time he was accompanied by Clara the negro. The resin candle still burned within the lantern, but giving out a more feeble light, as the first streaks of day began to succeed to the darkness of night.

"You see that lantern, Clara?" said Costal, pointing out the glimmering light to his companion. "You know what it was hung there for: since I have just told you. But you haven't yet heard the vow I have taken against the traitor who has so played with us. I shall tell you now."

And Costal proceeded to disclose to his old camarado the oath he had registered against Pepe Gago.

"Devil take me!" said Clara in reply, "if I can see how you will ever be able to fulfil your vow."

"No more do I," rejoined Costal, "but as I have promised Pepe Gago that he should not forget the lantern on the bridge of Los Hornos, and as I am determined he shall have a sight of it now and then, to keep his memory awake, I don't see why I should leave it here to be picked off by the first comer. At all events, it is no longer needed as a signal."

Saying this, the Indian took down the lantern from the post, and blew out the light.

"Here, Clara," he continued, "help me to make a hole. I intend hiding it—so that I can get it again, whenever I may want it."

The two men kneeling down, and using the blades of their knives, soon carved out a hollow place, in which Costal deposited the lamp still containing the resin candle.

"Now, friend Clara," said the Indian, as soon as they had covered it in, "sit down here, and let us try if we can't think of some way to capture this castle, as well as the *picaro* who is within it."

"Willingly, I will," answered the black; and seating themselves side by side, the two associates commenced with all due gravity their important deliberation.

Chapter Thirty Three
The Isle of Roqueta

While thus on the summit of the *Voladero de los Hornos* the Indian Costal and the negro Clara were debating between themselves how the castle might be captured—the same subject was being discussed by two persons of more importance in the tent of the insurgent general. These were Morelos himself, and Don Hermenegildo Galeana—now usually styled the "Marshal," to distinguish him from another Galeana, his own nephew, who was also an officer in the insurgent army.

The countenance of Morelos had not yet cast off the shadow caused by the failure of their assault upon the castle; and his garments were still soiled with dust, which, under the agitation of violent passions, he disdained to wipe off.

The brow of the Marshal was also clouded; but that was rather by reflecting the unpleasant thoughts that were troubling the spirit of his well-beloved General: for no care of his own ever darkened the countenance of the warlike Galeana.

A chart of the bay and roadstead of Acapulco lay upon the table before them, illuminated by two candles, whose light was every moment becoming paler, as the day began to break into the tent.

They had been for some time engaged in discussing the important matter in question. The Marshal had been endeavouring to press upon the General the necessity of at least capturing the town: since the troops were not only badly provided with tents and other equipage, but were in such a position among the burning sands, that it was difficult to transport provisions to the camp. Moreover, the situation on the river's bank was exceedingly unhealthy; and fever was daily thinning the ranks, and prostrating some of their best soldiers. The Marshal urged, that, once inside the town, they would at least be better lodged, while many other evils might be avoided. The town could not hold out against a determined assault. It might be, carried by a *coup de main*.

"I know all that, my dear Marshal," said Morelos, in reply to the arguments of Galeana; "we can easily take the town, but the castle will still hold out, provisioned as it can always be through this unfortunate isle of Roqueta, with which the garrison is able to keep up a constant communication."

The isle in question lay in the roadway of Acapulco, two short leagues from the town. There was a small fort upon it, with a Spanish garrison; and at the anchorage connected with this fort the Spanish ships, occasionally arriving with supplies for the fortress, could discharge their cargoes, to be afterwards transported to the castle in boats.

"Let us first capture Roqueta, then?" suggested Galeana.

"I fear the enterprise would be too perilous," replied Morelos; "we have scarce boats enough to carry sixty men—besides, the isle is two leagues out to sea; and just at this season storms may be looked for every hour—to say nothing of a mere handful of men landing to attack a strong garrison behind their entrenchments."

"We can take them by surprise," continued the intrepid *Mariscal*. "Leave it to me, General; I care not for the danger. In the glory of your name I shall undertake to capture La Roqueta."

"A perilous enterprise!" repeated Morelos, half in soliloquy. "Yes, friend Galeana," continued he, once more addressing himself to his Marshal, "although you have taught me to believe in the success of any enterprise you may undertake, this is really of such a nature as to require serious consideration."

"Never fear for the result, Señor General! I promise to capture the isle on one condition."

"What is it?"

"That as soon as you see my signal, announcing that I have mastered the garrison of Roqueta, you will take the town of Acapulco. Your Excellency will agree to that?"

Morelos remained for a moment thoughtful, and apparently reluctant to permit so perilous an attempt.

Just at that moment a rocket was seen ascending into the air, and tracing its curving course against the still sombre background of the sky. It had evidently been projected from the fort of Roqueta, which in daylight would have been visible from the camp of the insurgents. Morelos and his Marshal, through the open entrance of the marquee, saw the rocket and conjectured it to be some signal for the garrison on the isle to the besieged within the fortress. Almost on the instant, this conjecture was confirmed by another rocket seen rising from the citadel upon the summit of the cliffs, and in turn tracing its blue line across the heavens. It was evidently the answer.

For some minutes the General and Galeana remained within the marquee, endeavouring to conjecture the object of these fiery telegraphs. They had not succeeded in arriving at any satisfactory conclusion, when the General's aide-de-camp, Captain Lantejas, entered the tent. His errand was to announce to the Commander-in-chief that Costal, the scout, had just arrived in the encampment as the bearer of some important intelligence.

"Will your Excellency permit him to come in?" requested the Marshal. "This Indian has always some good idea in his head."

Morelos signified assent, and the next moment the Indian entered the tent.

"Señor General!" said he, after having received permission to speak, "I have just been up to the cliff of Los Hornos, and through the grey dawn I have seen a schooner at anchor by the isle of Roqueta. She must have arrived during the night: since she was not there yesterday."

"Well, what of it, friend Costal?"

"Why, General, I was just thinking how easy it would be for a party of us, after it gets dark, to slip up alongside, and take possession of her. Once masters of that schooner—"

"We could intercept all the supplies destined for the castle," impetuously interrupted Galeana; "and then we shall reduce it by famine. Señor General, it is God who speaks by the mouth of this Indian. Your Excellency will no longer refuse the permission which I have asked?"

It is true, the danger apprehended was not diminished by the presence of the schooner; but, overcome by the earnest appeals of the Marshal, and the prospect of the important results which would certainly arise from the possession of the vessel, Morelos at length consented to the attempt being made.

"If I know how to read the clouds," said Costal, whose counsel on this point was now requested, "I should say, from the way in which the sun is now rising, we shall have a dark calm day and night—at least, until the hour of midnight—"

"After midnight?" demanded the Marshal.

"A tempest and a howling sea," replied Costal. "But before that time the schooner and the isle of Roqueta may be ours."

"*Shall* be ours!" cried Galeana, with enthusiasm.

In fine, and before the council broke up, the enterprise was planned. The expedition was to be commanded by the Marshal, accompanied by his nephew, the younger Galeana, while Lantejas was to be the captain of a canoe, with Costal under his orders.

"The brave Don Cornelio would never forgive us," said Galeana, "if we were to perform this exploit without him."

The Captain smiled as he endeavoured to assume a warlike expression of countenance. He thought to himself, however, how much more to his taste it would be to have been deprived of the privilege accorded to him. But according to the habit he had got into, and in conformity with the energetic Spanish refrain: *Sacar de tripas corazon* (Keep a stout heart against every fortune), he pretended to be delighted with the honour that was yielded to him.

The prognostic of Costal about the weather appeared likely to be realised. During the whole day, while they were making preparations for their night expedition, the sky remained shadowed with sombre clouds; and, as evening arrived, the sun went down in the midst of a thick cumulus of vapour.

Chapter Thirty Four
An Enterprise by Night

As soon as darkness had fairly descended over the deep, the men took their places in the boats.

The flotilla was comprised of three barges or whale-boats, and a small canoe—in which altogether not more than fifty men could be embarked; but as it was at this period the sole fleet possessed by the insurgents, they were forced to make the best of it.

With oars carefully muffled, they rowed out from the beach; and, thanks to the darkness of the night, they succeeded in passing the castle without causing any alarm.

They were soon out of sight of the shore; and after rowing a mile or so further, the dark *silhouette* of the cliffs ceased to be visible through the obscurity.

The canoe commanded by Captain Lantejas carried, besides himself, Costal and two rowers. As it was the lightest vessel in the flotilla, it was directed to keep the lead, as a sort of *avant-courier*, to announce whatever might be seen ahead.

Costal sat in the stern guiding the craft; and while engaged in this duty, he could not resist the temptation of pointing out to his captain what the latter had already tremblingly observed:—three or four great sharks keeping company with the canoe.

"Look at them!" said the Indian; "one might almost imagine that the instinct of these fierce sea-wolves told them—"

"What?" inquired Lantejas, with an anxious air.

"Why, that this vessel we are in is not sea-worthy. She is as rotten and ricketty as an old tub; and very little—Bah! I only wish that my friend Pepe Gago was one of those fellows in the water, and I had nothing more to do than leap in and poniard him in presence of the others!"

"What! are you thinking still of that fellow?"

"More than ever!" replied Costal, grinding his teeth; "and I shall never leave the army of Morelos—even when my time of service is out—so long as there's a hope of capturing the castle of Acapulco, and getting my hands on the miserable traitor."

Lantejas was paying only slight attention to what the Indian said. The doubt which the latter had expressed about the sea-worthiness of the canoe, was at that moment occupying his thoughts more than Costal's project of vengeance; and he was desirous that they should reach the island as soon as possible. Even an engagement with a human enemy—so long as it should take place on *terra firma*—would be less perilous than a struggle in the water with those terrible monsters—the sharks.

"The canoe goes very slowly!" remarked he to Costal mere than once.

"Señor Don Cornelio!" exclaimed the Indian with a smile, "you are always in a hurry to get into the fight; but we are now approaching the isle; and, with your permission, I think we would do well to obtain leave from the admiral (by his title Costal designated Don Hermenegildo) to go a little more in advance, and reconnoitre the way for the others. The canoe can approach near the schooner without much risk of being seen; whereas those great whale-boats would just now stand a pretty fair chance of being discovered. That's my advice—do you agree to it, Captain?"

"Willingly," replied Lantejas, scarce knowing between the two dangers which might be the greatest.

At a command from Costal the two rowers now rested upon their oars; and, shortly after, one of the barges arrived alongside. It was that which carried the admiral.

"What is it?" inquired the latter, seeing that the canoe had stopped for him. "Have you discovered anything?"

Don Cornelio communicated to him the proposition of Costal. The idea appeared good to the Marshal; and, in accordance with it, the three barges were ordered to lie to, while the lighter craft glided on in advance.

In a short time the isle appeared in sight—a dark spot upon the bosom of the water, like some vast sea-bird that had settled down upon the waves, to rest a moment before resuming its flight.

Presently, as they drew nearer, the dark mass appeared to grow larger, but still lay buried in sombre silence, with no light nor any visible object distinguishable through the gloom.

Still drawing nearer, they at length perceived, rising over the tops of the trees that thickly covered the island, the tall tapering masts and cross-yards of a ship. It was the schooner they were in search of.

Continuing their course, in a few moments they were able to make out her hull against the white background of the beach, and then the two cabin windows in her stern. Through these, lights were shining, that in two broad bands were flung far over the surface of the water. In the darkness, the vessel might have been likened to some gigantic whale that had risen a moment, and was bending its huge eyes to reconnoitre the surface of the sea.

"We must change our course," muttered Costal. "If the canoe gets under that light, some sentry on the quarterdeck may see us. We must make a détour, and approach from the other side."

In saying this the Indian shifted the rudder, and turned the head of the craft into a new direction, while the rowers still continued to ply their muffled oars.

The sharks turned at the same time, and kept on after the canoe, as could be told by the luminous traces left by their viscous bodies in passing through the water.

Beyond, the surface was sparkling with phosphoric points, as if the sky, now covered with a uniform drapery of dark clouds, had dropped its starry mantle upon the sea.

At intervals there came a slight puff of wind, and the water curling under it glanced more luminously; while an occasional flash of lightning announced that the clouds above were charged with electricity.

In all these signs Costal recognised the precursors of a storm.

The canoe had now passed far out of sight of the barges, and was circling around, to get upon the other side of the schooner—still followed by five of the shining monsters of the deep.

Both Costal and the Captain believed themselves too far distant from the schooner to be seen by any one aboard when all at once a brilliant light enveloped the Spanish vessel, revealing her whole outlines from stem to stern. Those in the canoe had just time to perceive that it was the blaze of a cannon, when the report followed, and the hissing of a ball was heard. Almost on the instant the little craft received a terrible shock; and, in the midst of a cloud of spray thrown around it, the two rowers were seen tumbling over the side and sinking below the surface of the water. Two of the sharks disappeared at the same moment!

Costal, seated in the stern, at once perceived that the canoe no longer obeyed the rudder; and Lantejas, who was more amidships, saw to his horror that the vessel was sinking at the forward part, where she had been struck by the ball.

"*Por los infiernos!* an unlucky shot!" cried Costal.

"What will be the result?" anxiously demanded Lantejas.

"Why, a very simple thing: the bullet has crushed in the bow of the craft, and she will go down head foremost, I suppose."

"*Por Dios!* we are lost then!" cried Don Cornelio in a voice of terror.

"Not so sure of that yet," calmly returned Costal, at the same time rising and stepping forward in the canoe. "Keep your place!" whispered he to Lantejas, "and don't lose sight of me."

Notwithstanding the assuring air with which the Indian spoke, the third rower, under the excitement of a terrible alarm, at this moment rushed up and caught him around the knees—as if clinging to him for help.

"Ho!" cried Costal, endeavouring to disengage himself, "hands off there, friend! Off, I say—here it is every one for himself!" And as he said this he pushed the man backward.

The latter, staggering partly under the impulsion he had received, and partly under the influence of his fright, tumbled back into the water. At the same instant a third shark disappeared from the side of the canoe, while a cry of despair appeared to rise up from the bottom of the sea!

"It was his own fault," said the impassable Zapoteque, "his example should be a warning to others!"

At this frightful innuendo the ex-student of theology, more dead than alive, commenced invoking God and the saints with a fervour such as he had never felt in all his life.

"*Carrambo!* Captain," cried the imperturbable pagan, "put more confidence in your own courage than your saints. Can you swim?"

"Only a few strokes," feebly replied Lantejas.

"Good! that will be enough. There is only one way to hinder the canoe from going head downwards. Look out, then, and keep close by my side!"

Saying this, Costal waited until the canoe rose upon the top of a wave; and then, throwing all his strength into the effort, he kicked the craft, overturning it keel upwards.

Both men were for the moment under water; and Lantejas, on coming to the surface, felt himself violently grasped by the garments. He fancied it was one of the sharks that had seized hold of him; but the voice of Costal close to his ear once more reassured him.

"Do not fear: I am with you," said the Indian, dragging him through the water towards the capsized canoe, which was now floating wrong side up.

The efforts of the Indian, joined to those which Lantejas mechanically made for himself, enabled the latter to get astride the keel of the canoe; where Costal, after swimming a few strokes through the water, mounted also.

"Another minute," said the Indian, "and the old tub would have gone to the bottom. Now she may keep afloat till the whale-boats get up—that is, if the storm don't come down before then."

Lantejas cast a despairing glance towards the distant ocean, which, lashed by the wind, had already commenced under its mantle of foam. The sight drew from him a fresh invocation to the saints, with an improvised but earnest prayer for his own safety.

"*Carrambo!*" cried the pagan Costal, "keep a firm seat, and don't trust too much to your gods. If you let yourself be washed off, you'll find they won't do much for you. Stay! you've nothing to hold on by! let me make a catch for you."

Saying this, Costal bent towards his companion; and with the blade of his knife commenced opening a hole in the keel of the canoe. In the worm-eaten wood this might be easily effected; and, working with all the *sang-froid* of a wood-carver, in a few seconds Costal succeeded in making an aperture large enough to admit the hand. Through this Lantejas thrust his fingers; and, clutching firmly underneath, was now in a condition to maintain his seat against the waves that were threatening every moment to roll over the spot.

Costal, having thus secured his companion, and provided for his own safety in a similar fashion, now commenced peering through the darkness in hopes of seeing the barges.

In this he was disappointed. Though the lightning now flashed at shorter intervals, its gleams revealed only the dark and scowling water, the isle sleeping in sullen gloom, and farther off the frowning mass of the fortress-crowned cliff.

Notwithstanding that the castaways now shouted at the highest pitch of their voices, there was no response from the whale-boats. Their cries pealed along the seething surface of the waters, and died without even an echo.

Chapter Thirty Five
Fearful Fellow-Swimmers

The shipwrecked sailor, floating upon his frail raft, or some spar of his shattered vessel, could not be more at the mercy of wave and wind, than were the two men astride of the capsized canoe. Their situation was indeed desperate. The stroke of a strong sea would be sufficient to swamp their frail embarkation; and, should the tempest continue to increase in fury, then destruction appeared inevitable.

Despite the imminent danger, Lantejas still indulged a hope that the intrepidity of the Zapoteque might rescue him from the present danger, as it had from many others. Sustained by this vague belief, he kept his eyes fixed upon the countenance of Costal, while endeavouring to read in its expression the condition of the Indian's spirit.

Up to that time the imperturbable coolness exhibited by the *ex-tigrero* had favoured the hopes of his companion. As the time passed, however, and nothing was seen of the whale-boats, even the features of Costal began to wear an expression of anxiety. There is a difference, however, between anxiety and despair. The spirit of the Indian had only succumbed to the former of these two phases.

"Well, Costal, what think you?" demanded Lantejas, with a view of breaking the silence, which appeared to him of ill omen.

"*Por Dios!*" replied the Indian, "I'm astonished that the barges have not moved up on hearing that shot. It's not like the Marshal to hang back so. He don't often need two such signals to advance—"

A blast of wind sweeping past at the moment hindered Lantejas from hearing the last words of his companion's speech. He saw, however, that the latter had relapsed into his ominous silence, and that the cloud of inquietude was growing darker over his countenance. It was almost an expression of fear that now betrayed itself upon the bronzed visage of the Indian.

The Captain well knew that the least display of such a sentiment on the part of Costal, was evidence that the danger was extreme. Not that he needed any farther proof of this, than what he saw around him; but, so long as the Zapoteque showed no signs of fear, he had entertained a hope that the latter might still find some resource for their safety.

He almost believed himself saved, when the voice of the Indian once more fell upon his ear, in a tone that seemed to betray an indifference to their present situation.

"Well, Señor Don Cornelio," said Costal, "what would you give now to be lying in a hammock, with a canopy of jaguars and rattlesnakes over you? Eh?"

Costal smiled as he recalled the scene of the inundation. His gaiety was a good sign. Almost immediately after, however, he muttered to himself, in a tone of inquietude—

"Can it be possible that the barges have gone back?"

In situations of a frightful kind the smallest suspicion soon assumes the form of a reality; and the Captain did not doubt but that the barges had returned to the shore. Not that there was the slightest reason for this belief. On the contrary, it was more natural to suppose that they were still in the place where they had been left—awaiting the return of the canoe, and the news it might bring them. This was all the more likely: since they in the barges could not fail to have heard the shot from the schooner, and would be awaiting an explanation of it.

The probability of all this—especially of the boats being still in the same place—did not fail to strike Costal, who for some seconds appeared to be reflecting profoundly.

Meanwhile the waves had increased, and had all the appearance of soon becoming much larger. Already the frail embarkation was tossed about like an egg-shell.

"Listen to me, Señor Don Cornelio Lantejas!" said Costal.

"Ah!" woefully murmured the Captain, on hearing his patronymic pronounced; for ever since his proscription as Cornelio Lantejas, he had held his own name in horror. Never did it sound to him with a more lugubrious accent than now.

"Listen!" said Costal, repeating himself with emphasis; "I know you are a man for whom death has no terrors. Well, then! I think it would not be right of me to conceal from you—a fact—"

"What fact?"

"That if we stay here one hour longer, we must both go to the bottom. The waves are constantly growing bigger, as you see—"

"And what can we do?" demanded Lantejas, in a despairing tone.

"One of two things," replied Costal. "The barges are either waiting for us where we left them, or they are directing their course towards the isle. It is absurd to suppose they have returned to the town. When one receives an order from a great general to attack any particular point, one does not return without making an attempt. The boats, therefore, must still be where we parted from them."

"Well, what would you do?"

"Why, since it is easy for me to swim to them—"

"Swim to them!"

"Certainly. Why not?"

"What! through the midst of those monsters who have just devoured our comrades under our very eyes?"

A flash of lightning at that instant lit up the countenance of Costal, which exhibited an expression of profound disdain.

"Have I not just told you," said he, "that I am perhaps the only man who could pass among these sharks without the least danger? I have done it a hundred times out of mere bravado. To-night I shall do it to save our lives."

The thought of being left alone caused the Captain a fresh alarm. He hesitated a moment before making a reply. Costal, taking his silence for consent, cried out—

"As soon as I have reached one of the barges I shall cause a rocket to be sent up as a signal that I am aboard. Then you may expect us to come this way; and you must shout at the top of your voice, in order that we may find you."

Don Cornelio had not time to make answer. On finishing his speech the *ci-devant* pearl-diver plunged head foremost into the water.

The Captain could trace a luminous line as he swam for some seconds under the surface; and could also see that the fierce denizens of the deep— as if they recognised in him a superior power—had suddenly glided out of his way!

Don Cornelio saw the intrepid swimmer rise to the surface, at some distance off, and then lost sight of him altogether behind the curling crests of the waves. He fancied, however, he could hear some indistinct words of encouragement borne back by the wind. After that, the only sounds that reached his ear were the hoarse moanings of the surf, and the ominous plashing of the waves against the quivering timbers of his canoe.

Chapter Thirty Six
Unpleasant Swimming Companions

A shark may be driven off for a time by the efforts of a human enemy, but his natural voracity will soon impel him to return to the attack. When the Indian therefore rose to the surface of the water—remembering his old practice as a pearl-diver—he cast around him a glance of caution. Having shouted back to his companion in misfortune some words which the latter had indistinctly heard, he placed his knife between his teeth, and swam straight onward.

It was not fear that caused him to take this precaution. It was merely an act of habitual prudence.

As he struck out from the canoe, he perceived that two monsters of the deep, far more formidable than those of the forest, were proceeding in the same direction as himself. One was about twenty feet from him on the right; the other appeared at an equal distance on his left; and both were evidently *attending* upon him!

Unpleasant as two such companions might be deemed, the swimmer at first paid but slight attention to their movements. His mind was pre-occupied with a variety of other thoughts—especially with the doubt as to whether he might be able to find the barges. On the wide surface of the sea, and in the midst of the profound darkness, it would be but too easy to pass without perceiving them, and very difficult indeed to find them. This apprehension, combined with those fearless habits in the water, which he had contracted while following the life of a pearl-diver—and furthermore his belief in a positive fatalism—all united in rendering the Zapoteque indifferent to the presence of his two terrible attendants.

Only at intervals, and then rather from prudence than fear, he turned his head to the right or left, and glanced in the direction of his *compagnons du voyage*. He could not help perceiving moreover that at each instant the sharks were drawing nearer to him!

By a vigorous stroke on the water he now raised his body high over the surface; and, there balancing for a moment, glanced forward. It was an eager glance; for he was looking for that object on the finding of which his life must depend. He saw only the line of the horizon of dull sombre hue—no object visible upon it, except here and there the white crests of the waves.

A sudden glance to the right, and another to the left, showed him the two fearful creatures, now nearer than ever. Neither was more than ten feet from his body!

Still the swimmer was not dismayed by their presence. Far more was he daunted by the immense solitude of the watery surface that surrounded him.

However bold a man may be, there are moments when danger must necessarily cause him fear. Costal was in a position sufficiently perilous to have unnerved most men. Swimming in the midst of a rising sea—beyond sight of land, or any other object—escorted by two voracious sharks—with a dark sky overhead, and no precise knowledge of the direction in which he was going—no wonder he began to feel something more than inquietude.

However strong may be a swimmer, he cannot fail after long keeping up such vigorous action as it requires, to become fatigued, and worn out: the more so when, like Costal, he carries a knife between his teeth—thus impeding his free respiration. But the ex-pearl-diver did not think of parting with the weapon—his only resource, in case of being attacked by the sharks—and still keeping his lips closed upon it, he swam on.

After a time, he felt his heart beating violently against his ribs. He attributed this circumstance less to fear than to the efforts he was making; and, taking the knife from his mouth, he carried it in one of his hands.

The pulsations of his heart were not the less rapid: for it may be acknowledged, without much shame to him, that Costal now really felt fear. Moreover, swimming with one hand closed, it was necessary for him to strike more rapidly with the other.

The precaution of holding his knife ready in hand, was not likely to prove an idle one. The two sharks appeared gradually converging upon the line which the swimmer must take, if he continued to swim directly onward.

On observing this convergence of his silent and persevering pursuers, Costal suddenly obliqued to the right. The sharks imitated his movement on the instant, and swam on each side of him as before!

For a few minutes—long and fearful minutes—he was forced to keep on in this new direction. He began to fancy he was swimming out of the way he should have taken; and was about to turn once more to the left, when an object came before his eyes that prompted him to utter an ejaculation of joy.

In spite of himself, he had been guided into the right direction, by the very enemies from whom he was endeavouring to escape; and it was the sight of the barges that had drawn from him the joyful exclamation.

The moment after, he uttered a louder cry, hailing the boats.

He had the satisfaction of hearing a response; but as no one saw him through the darkness, it was necessary for him to continue swimming onwards.

By this time the two sharks had closed on each side, and were gliding along so near, that only a narrow way was open between them. Costal felt that he had not sufficient strength to make a détour; and the only course left him, was to swim straight for the nearest boat. He kept on therefore, his heart beating against his ribs, and with his knife firmly held in his grasp—ready to bury the weapon in the throat of the first that should assail him. With the last efforts of his strength he lunged out right and left, by voice and gesture endeavouring to frighten off the two monsters that flanked him; and he proceeded onward in this way like some doomed ship, struggling between black masses of rocky breakers.

By good fortune his efforts proved successful. The hideous creatures, glaring upon him with glassy eyeballs, were nevertheless frightened by his menacing gestures, and for the moment diverged a little out of his way.

Costal took advantage of this precious moment; and, swimming rapidly forward, succeeded in clutching the side of one of the barges.

A dozen friendly arms instantly drew him aboard; but as his comrades bent over him upon the deck, they perceived that he was unconscious. The effort had been too much for his strength. He had sunk into a syncope.

The presence of Costal in such sad plight sufficiently revealed the fate of the canoe and its occupants. Words could not have made the history of their misfortune more clear.

"It is no use remaining longer here," said the soldier-admiral. "The canoe must have gone to the bottom. Now, my braves! we shall pull straight for the isle."

Then raising his sombrero in a reverential manner, he added—

"Let us pray for the souls of our unfortunate comrades—above all, for Captain Lantejas. We have lost in him a most valiant officer."

And after this laconic oration over Don Cornelio, the barges were once more set in motion, and rowed directly towards the isle of Roqueta.

Meanwhile the unhappy Lantejas sat upon the keel of the broken canoe, contemplating with horrible anxiety the waves of the ocean constantly surging around him, and gradually growing fiercer and higher. Now they appeared as dark as Erebus; anon like ridges of liquid fire, as the lightning flashed athwart the sky, furrowing the black clouds over his head.

He listened attentively. He heard the wind whistling against the waves, and lashing them into fury—as a horseman rouses his steed with whip and spur; he heard the groaning of the surge, like an untamed horse rebelling against his rider.

Fortunately for him, it was yet but the prologue of the storm to which he was listening; and he was still able to maintain his seat upon the frail embarkation.

At short intervals he shouted with all his might, but the wind hurled back his cries, mingled with the spray that was dashed in his face.

No succour appeared within sight or hearing. Costal had no doubt been either drowned or devoured; and the unhappy officer had arrived at the full conviction, that such was to be his own fate; when, all of a sudden, some object came under his eyes that caused him to quiver with joy. Under the glare of the lightning, the barges were visible mounted on the crest of a huge dark wave!

Only a momentary glance did he obtain of them; for, after the flash had passed, the boats were again shrouded in the obscurity of the night.

Do Cornelio raised a loud cry, and listened for the response. No voice reached him. His own was drowned; midst the roaring of the waters, and could not have been heard by the people on board the boats.

He shouted repeatedly, but with the like result—no response.

Once more was he plunged into the deepest anxiety—approaching almost to despair—when on the next flashing of lightning he once more beheld the barges at a little distance from him, but in a direction altogether opposite! They had passed him in the darkness, and were now rowing away!

This was his reflection, though it was an erroneous one. The boats were still in the same direction as at first, but now appeared in the opposite quarter. This deception arose from Don Cornelio himself having turned round on the broken canoe, which kept constantly spinning about upon the waves.

At this moment a rocket shooting up into the dark sky inspired the castaway with fresh hope; and he once more raised his voice, and shouted with all the concentrated power of throat and lungs. After delivering the cry, he remained in breathless expectation, equally concentrating all his strength in the act of listening.

This time a responsive cry came back—a sound all the more joyful to his ears from his recognising it as the voice of Costal.

Don Cornelio now repeated his cries, thick and fast after each other, until his throat and jaws almost refused to give out the slightest sound. Nevertheless he kept on shouting, until one of the barges, bounding over the waves, forged close up to the side of the canoe. Then he felt himself seized by strong arms—they were those of Costal and Galeana—and the moment after he was lifted into the boot, where, like the ex-pearl-diver, but from a very different cause, he fell fainting upon the deck.

It was fortunate for Don Cornelio that Costal had remained only a short time under the influence of his syncope. Recovering from it, the Indian had, in a few words, revealed the situation of the canoe. The signal agreed upon was at once made; and led, as described, to the rescue of his companion from his perilous position.

Chapter Thirty Seven
A Deed à la Cortez

Notwithstanding the alarm given by the schooner, the barges of Galeana found no difficulty in effecting a landing upon the isle—but on the opposite side to that where the war vessel lay. The stormy night favoured the attempt; the garrison of La Roqueta not dreaming that on such a night any attack would be made upon the fort.

Lantejas still remained unconscious; and, when at last he came to his senses, he found himself on land, the branches of tall trees extending over him, through which the wind was whistling with all the fury of a tempest. The rustling of the leaves was the sweetest melody he had ever heard: since it told him he was once more on *terra firma*—though at the same time the thunder rolling around appeared to shake the foundations of the isle.

On awakening to consciousness, he looked around him. He saw men reclining, or sitting in groups—most of them with arms in their hands. He recognised them as the people of the expedition.

Costal, asleep, was lying upon the ground close at hand.

"Where are we, Costal?" inquired Lantejas, after rousing the Indian from his slumber.

"Where? *Por Dios*! where should we be, but on the isle of Roqueta?"

"But how did we get ashore?"

"Easily enough, Señor Capitan. We had no opposition to contend against. Not one of the Spanish garrison suspects our presence here; for who would think of sixty men venturing to sea on such a night as this? We shall take the enemy completely by surprise."

"And what hinders the Marshal from attacking them now?"

"We have not yet found them. We neither know where the fort is, nor where we are ourselves. Don't you see that the night is as dark as the inside of a cannon, and one can't make out his finger before him? They're safe enough while this storm lasts; and, by good luck, so are we."

It was in truth to the storm that the Mexicans owed their present security. Few in numbers, and ignorant of the locality in which they had landed, an attack by the troops of the garrison might have proved fatal to them. Thanks to the tempestuous character of the night, they had not only found an opportunity of debarking on the isle, but time to mature their plans for assaulting the fort.

It was now about four in the morning, and the wind, still blowing with all its fury, was causing the large waves to roll up against the beach, threatening to break the cables by which the barges were moored to the shore. Don Cornelio cast glances of fear upon that mighty ocean that, but a few hours before, had come so near engulfing him within its dark depths.

While he sat with his face turned seaward, his eye fell upon the figure of a man who was passing from the spot where the groups were scattered downward to the beach. This man having approached the place where the barges were moored, for some moments appeared to be occupied with them, as if looking to their security. This was Don Cornelio's first impression on seeing the figure bending over the cables; but the moment after, the blade of a knife glancing in the man's fingers, was revealed by a flash of lightning; and this gave a sudden turn to the captain's thoughts.

"What is he about to do?" inquired he of Costal, at the same time pointing out the individual so mysteriously occupied about the barges.

"*Carrambo!* he is cutting the cables!" cried the Indian, springing to his feet, and rushing towards the boats, followed by Don Cornelio.

On drawing nearer the beach, both recognised, under the pale reflection of the foaming waves, the Marshal himself—Don Hermenegildo Galeana!

"Ah! Captain Lantejas, it is you!" cried the Marshal as they approached. "Good. I want you to lend me a hand here in cutting these hawsers: they are hard as iron chains."

"Cut the hawsers!" echoed the astonished captain. "And what, General, if we are compelled to retreat before a superior force?"

"That's just what I wish to provide against," replied Don Hermenegildo, laughing. "Some people fight but poorly when they know they may run away; and I wish our people to fight well."

Don Cornelio saw it was no use to attempt remonstrance with the chivalric Galeana, and both he and Costal went to work to assist the Marshal in his daring design.

"All right, comrades!" cried Don Hermenegildo, as soon as the three hawsers were parted; "it only remains for us to get the signal rockets out of the boats, and then let them go to sea of themselves."

So saying, the energetic leader stepped aboard one of the barges, seized hold of the rocket case, and, assisted by Costal and Don Cornelio, carried it on shore. Then, giving each of the boats a shove from the beach, the Marshal had the satisfaction—not shared by the Captain, however—of seeing all three of them the next moment carried far away from the shore, and still tossing seaward on the crests of the foaming waves! Retreat was no longer possible. The people of the expedition must either conquer or succumb.

"Now, Captain Lantejas," said the Marshal, addressing Don Cornelio, "you had better go and get some sleep. You have need of rest, after what you have passed through. I shall cause you to be awakened in good time. Meanwhile Costal will make a reconnaissance, to discover, if possible, the whereabouts of our enemy. By daybreak both the fort and schooner must be ours."

With this finish to the conversation, Don Hermenegildo folded his cloak around him and walked away. Costal and the captain returned to the temporary encampment among the trees. There the Indian, without communicating his thoughts to his companion, silently divested himself of the little remnant of clothing that remained to him, and glided off among the bushes—like a jaguar advancing through the underwood to surprise the gaunt alligator on the bank of some solitary lagoon.

Chapter Thirty Eight
The Capture of La Roqueta

It was in vain that Don Cornelio attempted to sleep. Although more than a year of campaigning and the experience of many sanguinary engagements had inured him to danger, there was something in the peril to which he was now exposed that was altogether novel and unpleasant.

Their leader had provided against retreat, and to conquer or die had become a positive obligation of the expeditionary force. This was sufficient to keep the involuntary soldier awake for the remainder of the night.

He passed the time in reflecting upon the singular *contretemps* that had so interfered with his plans of life, and changed, as it were, his very destiny. He could now only entertain but one hope and wish, and that was that the fortress of Acapulco should be taken as soon as possible: since upon that event being completed, Morelos had promised to grant him leave of absence from the army.

In about an hour afterwards, Costal returned from his scout, and reported to him the result of his explorations, which he had already detailed to the Marshal.

According to the information collected by the Indian, the Spanish garrison consisted of about two hundred men; who were entrenched in a small earthwork on the southern side of the isle, and not more than cannon-shot distance from the Mexican encampment. Two field pieces, set in battery, defended the work; and the schooner, whose unlucky shot had swamped the canoe, lay at a cable's length from the land, in a little bay that ran up to the fort.

The Mexican leader now knew the position of his enemy, their numbers, and means of defence; and, as soon as the dawn began to appear, he summoned his little band, and formed them into rank. At the same time he caused the signal rockets to be carried to an eminence that was near their encampment.

"Now, *muchachos*!" said he, addressing his soldiers in an undertone, "whatever point we attack, may be considered as taken. We are about to assault the enemy. We may therefore at once announce to our general-in-chief, without fear of disappointment, that the isle and fortress of La Roqueta are in our hands. I have promised it."

And without awaiting a reply from any one, the Marshal took the cigar from his lips, and held the burning end of it to the fuse of one of the rockets.

The piece of hemp became kindled at the touch, and the moment after the rocket rose hissing into the air, and described a circle of vivid red against the grey background of the sky. A second rocket was sent up, which traced an ellipse of white light; and then a third, whose reflection was a brilliant green.

"Red, white, and green!" cried Galeana, "our national colour. It is the signal I agreed upon with our General, to announce to him the capture of the isle. Our comrades in the Mexican camp have by this time seen the signal. They believe we have triumphed, and we must not deceive them. Forward to victory!"

On issuing the command, Galeana bounded lightly forward and placed himself at the head of his men; and the whole troop, guided by Costal, advanced at a rapid pace towards the enemy.

As they approached the fort, cries of distress were heard in that direction, which at first filled the assailants with surprise. The cause, however, was soon apparent. The cries came not from the fort, but from the schooner, which was now seen through an opening between the trees struggling against the storm, and fast drifting among breakers! A row of jagged rocks stretched along to leeward; and from driving upon these rocks, the sailors aboard of her were vainly endeavouring to restrain the ill-fated vessel.

The latter, during the violence of the wind, had dragged her anchors, and was now fast hastening to destruction.

"*Jesus Maria*!" exclaimed Galeana at the sight. "Comrades, what a pity! She will undoubtedly be lost, and I had counted upon this magnificent bounty. *Carrambo*! we shall get nothing but a wreck."

The dangerous situation of the schooner was of course known in the fort, where it had already created considerable confusion. This was now changed into consternation by the approach of the insurgents; and the wild war-cry of Galeana, as he sprang forward to the walls, echoed by his followers, and accompanied as it was by loud peals of thunder, produced something like a panic among the ranks of the Spanish garrison. So sudden was the attack, and so completely unexpected, that it could scarcely fail of success; and indeed, after a short hand-to-hand combat, one portion of the garrison fled, while the other surrendered without conditions to the triumphant Galeana.

Scarcely had the last shot been fired, and the fort delivered up to the victors, when the schooner, striking violently upon a sharp reef, leant over to one side, and, like a steed gored by the horns of the bull, the sides of the vessel were opened, and she began to sink among the foaming waves. The victors on shore thought no more of enemies, but now bent all their energies towards saving the unfortunate mariners, whose lives were thus placed in peril. By means of lazoes flung from the beach, most of the latter were rescued from the death that threatened them.

The sun soon after cast his yellow beams over the agitated bosom of the ocean, but his rising had no effect in calming the tempest. The storm continued to rage as furiously as ever.

Just as the last of the shipwrecked sailors had been got safely on shore, a flag running up to the signal-staff of the fort announced that a new sail was seen in the offing. In a few minutes after a vessel was perceived in the roadstead of the bay, struggling against the storm, and endeavouring to stand outward to sea.

This intention the adverse winds seemed trying to prevent; and driven by these out of her course, the strange ship passed so near the isle of Roqueta that those in the fort could see the people on board, and even distinguish the uniforms and faces of the officers upon the quarterdeck. It was evident that the vessel thus coasting past Acapulco was a man-of-war; and the uniforms of the officers aboard of her could plainly be distinguished as that of the Spanish navy. One was dressed somewhat differently from the rest. His costume was military, not naval. It was that of an officer of dragoons. Costal, Clara, and Captain Lantejas were standing on the parapet of the fort, observing the manoeuvres of the strange ship, when the keen eyes of the Indian became fixed on this officer.

He was a man in the full vigour of youth and strength—as was testified by his erect and graceful figure, and by the rich masses of dark hair that clustered under his laced cap; but an air of profound melancholy seemed resting upon his features, and it was evident that some secret care was occupying his thoughts far more than the storm or its dangers!

"Do you recognise the officer, yonder?" inquired Costal pointing him out to Clara and Don Cornelio.

"No," replied Lantejas, "I don't remember ever having seen him before."

"He is the same," rejoined Costal, "whom we three formerly knew as a captain of the Queen's dragoons—Don Rafael Tres-Villas. He is now *Colonel* Tres-Villas."

"*Por Dios!*" interposed a soldier who was standing near, and who had come from the state of Oajaca. "Colonel Tres-Villas! That is he who nailed the head of Antonio Valdez to the gate of his hacienda!"

"The same," assented Costal.

"*Carrambo!*" cried another soldier, "that is the officer who, after capturing the town of Aguas Calientes, caused the hair to be cropped from the heads of three hundred women who were his prisoners!"

"It is said that he had his reasons for doing so," muttered Costal, in reply.

"Whether or no," said the soldier, "if he comes this way, he'll get punished for it."

Just as the soldier spoke, the ship became enveloped in a mass of fog— at that moment spreading over the water—and was lost to the view of the people on the isle. When she became visible again, it was seen that she was standing out to sea. By a favourable turn which the wind had taken, she was enabled to gain the offing, and was soon receding from view upon the distant horizon.

Costal was correct in his identification. The officer thus accidentally seen, and who was a passenger on board the man-of-war, was indeed Don Rafael Tres-Villas, who from one of the northern ports was now on his return to Oajaca, bearing with him to the shores of Tehuantepec a profound and incurable melancholy.

The capture of the isle of La Roqueta was an important step towards the taking of Acapulco. The town itself had fallen into the hands of the insurgents, almost at the same instant; for Morelos, according to agreement, on perceiving the signals of Hermenegildo, had directed his attack upon the town, and so brusquely that the place was carried by a *coup de main*.

The possession of La Roqueta enabled the insurgent general to intercept the supplies of the citadel garrison; and shortly after the fortress itself was compelled to surrender.

This conquest, with which the humble *cura* had been derisively entrusted, rendered him master of the whole southern part of Mexico—from the shores of the Pacific Ocean, almost to the gates of the capital of New Spain. Twenty-two battles had he gained from that day, when, accompanied by his two domestics, he rode forth from the village of Caracuaro to raise in Oajaca the banner of the insurrection. To that province, after the taking of Acapulco, it was necessary for him to proceed with his victorious army — in order to assist the insurgents then besieged in the town of Huajapam. Thither, but some days preceding him, shall we conduct the reader, in order that we may once more return to the hero of our predilection.

Chapter Thirty Nine
The Plain of Huajapam

It was a morning of June, just before the commencement of the rainy season—at that period of the day and year when the tropic sun of Southern Mexico is least endurable. His fervid rays, striking perpendicularly downward, had heated like smouldering ashes the dusty plain of Huajapam, which lay like a vast amphitheatre surrounded by hills—so distant that their blue outlines were almost confounded with the azure sky above them. On this plain was presented a tableau of sadness and desolation, such as the destructive genius of man often composes with demoniac skill.

On one side, as far as the eye could reach, horsemen could be seen hurrying about the plain in the midst of pillaged houses—some of which had been given to the flames. Under the hoofs of these horses, as they dashed recklessly to and fro, were crushed rich treasures that had been sacked from the deserted dwellings, and now lay scattered upon the ground, tempting only the hand of the thievish camp-follower. The soil, defiled in every way, presented only a scanty growth of bruised herbage, upon which the horseman disdained to pasture his steed.

Here and there groups of black vultures told where some dead body of horse or rider had been abandoned to their voracity; while the *coyotes* trotted in troops far out from the mountain ridge, going to or returning from their hideous repast.

Looking over the plain in another direction, the standard of Spain could be seen floating over the tents of the royalist camp, whose night-fires still sent up their lines of bluish smoke; while from the same quarter could be heard the neighing of horses, the rolling of drums, and the startling calls of the cavalry bugles.

Farther off in the same direction—above the low, flat-shaped *azotéas* of a village—could be seen the domes and belfries of several churches, all breached with bombs or riddled with round shot. This village lay at the distance of a few hundred yards from the lines of the royalist camp, and was evidently besieged by the latter. Rude earthworks could be perceived extending between the scattered suburbs, upon which a few pieces of cannon were mounted, and pointing towards the entrenchments of the Spanish encampment. Between the hostile lines the plain was unoccupied, save by the dead bodies of men and horses that lay unburied on the dusty surface of the soil.

The village in question—or town it might rather be called—was the famous Huajapam, that now for more than three months had been defended by a body of three hundred insurgents against a royalist force of five times their number! The heroic leader of this gallant resistance was Colonel Don Valerio Trujano.

At mention of this name the reader will call to mind the noble muleteer Trujano, whose firm voice he has heard intoning the *De profundis* and *In manus* while struggling against the inundation. Beyond a doubt his religious zeal had inspired the besieged of Huajapam: for, every now and then, from out the sad and desolate town may be heard the voices of his men, chanting in chorus some sacred song or prayer to the God of battles!

In that moment when the priests of Huajapam have left the altar to take part in the defence of their town, there will be observed, neither in their acts nor words, aught to recall their former profession. At such a time Don Valerio Trujano may be said to reproduce one of those ascetic heroes of the old religious wars—great repeaters of *paternosters*, whose blows always fell without mercy, and who marched into battle reciting quotations from Scripture. Perhaps he might be more happily likened to one of the old Templars, careless of personal renown, kneeling to pray in front of the foe, and charging upon the Saracen to the accompaniment of that famous psalm, "Quare fremuerunt gentes?"

Such was the appearance which the plain of Huajapam presented on the morning in question: houses smoking and in ruins—dead bodies scattered over the ground—vultures wheeling above—the royalist banner face to face with the banner of the insurrection.

We shall first enter the camp of the besiegers, where the Brigadier Bonavia, governor of Oajaca, held command—assisted by the Spanish generals, Caldelas and Regules.

At an early hour of the morning two dragoons, who had been scouring the distant plain, were seen returning to the lines of the encampment, conducting with them a third horseman, evidently a stranger to the camp. This was on the side, opposite to that on which lay the town of Huajapam. The horseman, guided by these dragoons, was costumed as a vaquero— that is, he wore a jacket and wide calzoneros of brick-coloured deerskin, with a huge sombrero of black glaze on his head, and a speckled blanket folded over the croup of his saddle. He had already reported himself to the dragoons as the bearer of a message to the colonel—Don Rafael Tres-Villas. Furthermore, in addition to the horse on which he rode, he was leading another—a noble steed of a bay-brown colour.

This animal, startled at the sight and smell of the dead bodies among which they were passing, gave out from time to time a snorting of a peculiar character, which had drawn the attention of the dragoons.

These, after conducting the vaquero through a portion of the camp, halted in front of one of the largest tents. There a groom was saddling another steed, in strength and beauty but little inferior to that led by the vaquero. It was the war-horse of Colonel Tres-Villas, of whom the groom in question was the *assistente*.

"What is your name, *amigo*?" demanded the latter, addressing himself to the vaquero.

"Julian," replied the stranger. "I am one of the servitors of the hacienda Del Valle. Colonel Tres-Villas is its proprietor, and I have a message for him of great importance."

"Very well," responded the other, "I shall tell the Colonel you are here."

So saying, the *assistente* entered the tent.

On that day the besieging army was about to make the fifteenth attack upon the town, defended by Colonel Trujano, and Don Rafael was dressing himself in full uniform to assist at the council of war, called together to deliberate on the plan of assault.

At the word "messenger" pronounced by his military servant, a slight trembling was seen to agitate the frame of Colonel Tres-Villas, while his countenance became suddenly overspread with pallor.

"Very well," stammered he, after a moment's hesitation, and in a voice that betrayed emotion. "I know the messenger; you may leave him free; I shall answer for him. Presently let him come him in."

The *assistente* stepped out of the tent and delivered this response of the Colonel. The dragoons rode off, leaving the vaquero free to communicate to his master the message of which he was the bearer.

It is here necessary for us to detail some portion of the history of Don Rafael, from the time when he took his departure at full gallop from the hacienda Del Valle, up to that hour when we again encounter him in the royalist camp before Huajapam.

When the first shock of grief, caused by the murder of his father—when that terrible struggle betwixt love and duty, had passed, and his spirit become a little calmer—the only line of conduct that appeared possible for him, was to repair at once to Oajaca; and, having found its governor, Don Bernardino Bonavia, obtain from him a detachment of troops, with which he might return and punish the insurgent assassins.

Unfortunately for Don Rafael, notwithstanding the distinguished reception accorded to him by the governor, the latter could not place at his disposal a single soldier. The province was already in such a state of fermentation, that all the men under his command were required to keep in check the revolt that threatened to break out in the provincial capital itself. Don Rafael therefore could not prevail upon the governor to enfeeble the garrison of Oajaca, by detaching any portion of it on so distant a service as an expedition to the hacienda Del Valle.

While negotiating, however, word reached him of a royalist corps that was being raised at no great distance from Oajaca, by a Spanish officer, Don Juan Antonio Caldelas. Don Rafael, urged on by a thirst for vengeance, hastened to join the band of Caldelas, who on his part at once agreed to place his handful of men at the disposal of the dragoon captain for the pursuit of Valdez. Of course Caldelas had himself no personal animosity against the insurgent leader; but believing that the destruction of his band would crush the insurrection in the province, he was the more ready to co-operate with Don Rafael.

Both together marched against Valdez, and encountered him and his followers at the *cerro* of Chacahua, where the ex-vaquero had entrenched himself. An action was fought, which resulted in Valdez being driven from his entrenchments, but without Don Rafael being able to possess himself of his person, a thing he desired even more than a victory over his band.

A fortnight was spent in vain searches, and still the guerilla chief continued to escape the vengeance of his unrelenting pursuer. At the end of that period, however, the insurgents were once more tempted to try a battle with the followers of Don Rafael and Caldelas. It proved a sanguinary action, in which the royalists were victorious. The scattered followers of Valdez, when reunited at the rendezvous agreed upon in the event of their being defeated, perceived that their leader was missing from among them.

Alive they never saw him again. His dead body was found some distance from the field of battle, and around it the traces of a struggle which had ended in his death. The body was headless, but the head was afterwards discovered, nailed to the gate of the hacienda Del Valle, with the features so disfigured that his most devoted adherents would not have recognised them but for an inscription underneath. It was the name of the insurgent, with that of the man who had beheaded him, Don Rafael Tres-Villas.

Valdez had fled from the field after the defeat of his followers. Before proceeding far, he heard behind him the hoarse snorting of a steed. It was the bay-brown of Don Rafael.

In a few bounds the insurgent was overtaken. A short struggle took place between the two horsemen; but the ex-vaquero, notwithstanding his equestrian skill, was seized in the powerful grasp of the dragoon officer, lifted clear out of his saddle, and dashed with violence to the earth. Before he could recover himself, the lasso of Don Rafael—equally skilled in the use of this singular weapon—was coiled around him; and his body, after being dragged for some distance at the tail of the officer's horse, lay lifeless and mutilated along the ground. Such was the end of Antonio Valdez.

Chapter Forty
Fatal Misunderstandings

The death of this first victim, offered to the manes of his murdered father, had to some extent the effect of appeasing the vengeful passion of Don Rafael. At all events his spirit became calmer; and other sentiments long slumbering at the bottom of his heart began to usurp their sway. He perceived the necessity of justifying his conduct—which he knew must appear inexplicable—to the inhabitants of the hacienda Las Palmas. Had he done so at that moment all would have been well; but unfortunately a certain spirit of pride interfered to hinder him. A son who had punished the murderer of his father, ought he to excuse himself for what he felt to be a holy duty? Moreover, could he expect pardon for becoming the enemy of a cause he could no longer call his own?

This haughty silence on the part of Don Rafael could not do otherwise than complete the ruin of his hopes, and render still more impassable the gulf that had been so suddenly and unexpectedly opened up between his love and his duty.

The news of Valdez' death—brought to the hacienda of Las Palmas by a passing messenger—together with the tenour of the inscription that revealed the author of it, had fallen like a bomb-shell into the family circle of Don Mariano de Silva. Unfortunately the same messenger had failed to report the assassination of Don Luis Tres-Villas—for the simple reason that he had not heard of it. His hosts, therefore, remained ignorant of the cause of this terrible reprisal.

From that moment, therefore, the family of Las Palmas could not do otherwise than regard the dragoon captain as a traitor, who, under the pretence of the purest patriotism, had concealed the most ardent sympathies for the oppressors of his country. Nevertheless the love of Gertrudis essayed that justification, which the pride of Don Rafael had restrained him from making.

"O my father!" exclaimed she, overwhelmed with grief, "do not judge him too hastily. It is impossible he can be a traitor to his country's cause. One day—I am sure of it—one day, he will send a message to explain what has occurred."

"And when he does explain," responded Don Mariano, with bitterness, "will he be less a traitor to his country? No—we need not hope. He will not even attempt to justify his unworthy conduct."

In fine, the message came not; and Gertrudis was compelled to devour her grief in silence.

Nevertheless the audacious defiance to the insurrection implied in the act of Don Rafael, and the inscription that announced it, had something in it of a chivalric character, which was not displeasing to the spirit of Gertrudis. It did not fail to plead the cause of the absent lover; and at one time her affection was even reconquered—that is, when it came to be known that the head of the insurgent chief had replaced that of Don Rafael's father, and that it was blood that had been paid for blood.

If in that crisis the captain had presented himself, Don Mariano, it is true, might not have consented to his daughter forming an alliance with a renegade to the Mexican cause. The profound patriotism of the haciendado might have revolted at such a connection; but an explanation, frank and sincere, would have expelled from the thoughts both of himself and his daughter all idea of treason or disloyalty on the part of Don Rafael. The latter, ignorant of the fact that the news of his father's death had not reached Las Palmas—until a period posterior to the report of that of Valdez—very naturally neglected the favourable moment for an *éclaircissement*.

How many irreparable misfortunes spring from that same cause—misunderstanding!

The two captains, Caldelas and Tres-Villas, soon transformed the hacienda of Del Valle into a species of fortress, which some species of cannon, received from the governor of the province, enabled them to do. In strength the place might defy any attack which the insurgent bands of the neighbourhood could direct against it.

During the constant excursions which he made against the other two assassins of his father, Arroyo and Bocardo, Don Rafael left the charge of their citadel to the Captain Caldelas.

Listening only to the whisperings of his heart, he had finished by making a compromise between his love and his pride. Repelling the idea of communicating by a messenger, he had at one time resolved to present himself in person at the hacienda of Las Palmas; but, carried forward by the ardour of his vengeance, he dreaded that an interview with Gertrudis might have the effect of weakening his resolution; and for this reason he deferred seeking the interview, until he should complete the accomplishment of that rash vow made over the grave of his murdered parent.

Notwithstanding the almost superhuman efforts which he daily made in the pursuit of the insurgents, the result was not such as to appease his spirit of vengeance. Man by man did he accomplish the destruction of their band; but both the leaders still contrived to escape. In fine, after more than two months had passed since the death of Valdez, the rumour became spread throughout the neighbourhood that Arroyo and Bocardo had quitted the province of Oajaca, and gone northward with the remnant of their guerilla to offer their services to General Hidalgo.

On receiving this news Don Rafael, who had been absent on a protracted scout, returned to the hacienda Del Valle. During his absence, an order had arrived from the general-in-chief of the vice-regal army, commanding him to return to duty with his regiment—the Queen's dragoons.

Before obeying this order, however, he resolved on devoting one day to the affairs of his heart; and, permitting his love to conquer his pride, he determined on presenting himself at the hacienda of Las Palmas.

Alas! it might now be too late. A justification in the eyes of Don Mariano would now be more difficult than it might have been two months before. During that time appearances had been converted into realities, suspicions into certainties, and Don Rafael was for him no longer aught but a common renegade. Certain words which he was in the habit of repeating to his daughter, told too plainly his opinion of the dragoon captain; and these words rang in the ears of Gertrudis as a sad presentiment which she almost believed already accomplished.

"Do not weep for the defection of Don Rafael," said the haciendado, endeavouring to dry his daughter's tears. "He will be false to his mistress, as he has been to his country."

What appeared a strange circumstance in the eyes of the father—these words only caused Gertrudis to weep the more abundantly and bitterly!

Nevertheless, such had been the former friendship of Don Mariano for the young officer—such the tender passion kindled in the heart of Gertrudis—that it is possible, had Don Rafael even then presented himself before them—his countenance open and beaming with the manly pride of accomplished duty—the frankness of his bearing, and the loyalty of his speech, might have still dissipated the clouds that hung over the heads of all.

Unfortunately destiny had decided otherwise. It was not decreed by fate that at that hour Don Rafael should enter, as a friend, the hospitable gates of the hacienda Las Palmas.

Chapter Forty One
A Rude Reception

Don Rafael had now become known throughout all Oajaca as one of the most energetic foes of the insurrection. Among the country-people, therefore—the majority of whom were of Creole blood, and of course revolutionary in principle—he need not expect to meet many friends. Every man whom he might encounter was pretty certain of being his enemy. For this reason, although it was only a league from the hacienda Del Valle to that of Las Palmas, he deemed it prudent to take half-a-dozen of his troopers along with him—a wise precaution, as the event proved.

After crossing the chain of hills that separated the two estates, the dragoon captain and his escort rode direct for the postern of the hacienda Las Palmas, that opened to the rear of the building. This, for some reason, had been recently walled up; and it became necessary for them to go round to the main entrance in front. Scarce, however, had the horse of Don Rafael doubled the angle of the wall, when he and his little band were suddenly confronted by a score of horsemen of ruffianly aspect, who opposed the passage, the leader of them vociferating loudly:—

"Muera al traidor—mueran *los coyotes*!" (Death to the traitor!—death to the jackals!)

At the same instant one of the assailants, charging recklessly forward, brought his horse into collision with that of Don Rafael, and with such a violent shock that the steed of the dragoon officer was thrown to the ground.

In this crisis the agility of Don Rafael, along with his herculean strength, enabled him to save himself. Instantly disengaging his limbs from the body of his horse, he sprang upon that of one of his escort who had just fallen from his saddle, thrust through by one of the insurgents; and after a short struggle, in which several of the assailants succumbed, Don Rafael, with his five remaining followers, was enabled to retreat back to the ridge, where their enemies had not the courage to follow them.

One of his men killed—with the loss of his favourite bay-brown—such was the result of Don Rafael's attempt to justify his conduct after two months of silence! No wonder that with bitter emotions he retraced his steps to the hacienda Del Valle.

His heart was wrung with grief and disappointment. This hacienda of Las Palmas, where two months before he had been the honoured guest, now sheltered the enemies that were thirsting for his blood.

These, after their unsuccessful attempt to possess themselves of the person of Don Rafael, hastened back towards the entrance of the building.

"You stupid sot!" exclaimed one of them, speaking in angry tones, and addressing a companion by his side; "why did you not allow him to get into the hacienda? Once inside, we should have had him at our mercy, and then— *Carajo!*"

The speaker, a man of ferocious and brutal aspect, here made a gesture of fearful meaning, as an appropriate finish to his speech.

"Don Mariano would not have permitted it," rejoined the other, by way of excusing himself for having been the cause of the dragoon officer's escape. "Once under his roof, he would never have consented to our molesting him."

"Bah!" exclaimed the first speaker. "It's past the time when we require to ask Don Mariano's permission. We are no longer his servants. The time is come when the servants shall be the masters, and the masters the servants, *Carajo!* What care I for the emancipation of the country? What I care for is blood and plunder."

The fierce joy that blazed in the eyes of the speaker as he pronounced the last words, told too plainly that these were his veritable sentiments.

The second of the two brigands who, though smaller in size and of a more astute expression of countenance, was equally characterised by an aspect of brutal ferocity—for a moment appeared to quail before the indignation of his companion.

"*Carajo!*" continued the first, "we have got to shift our quarters. If that furious captain finds out that *we* are here, he will set fire to the four corners of the hacienda, and roast us alive in it. Fool that I was to listen to you!"

"Who could have foreseen that he would get off so?" said the lesser man, still endeavouring to excuse himself.

"You, *Carrai!*" thundered the bandit; and overcome by rage and chagrin at the escape of his mortal enemy, he drew his poignard, and struck a left-handed blow at the bosom of his associate. The latter severely wounded, uttering a cry of pain, fell heavily from his horse.

Without staying to see whether or not he had killed his comrade, the guerillero dashed through the gate of the hacienda; and, dismounting in the courtyard, ran, carbine in hand, up the stone stairway that led to the *azotéa*.

Meanwhile Don Rafael and his five horsemen were ascending the hill that sloped up from the rear of the building.

"*Santos Dios*! it is very strange!" remarked one of the troopers to a companion. "It's the general belief that Arroyo and Bocardo have quitted the province, but if I'm not mistaken—"

"It was they, to a certainty," interrupted the second trooper. "I know them well, only I didn't wish to tell our captain. He is so furious against these two fellows, that if he had only known it was they who attacked us, we should not have had much chance of being permitted to retreat as we have done."

The man had scarce finished speaking when the report of a carbine, fired from the roof of the hacienda, reverberated along the ridge, and the trooper fell mortally wounded from his saddle.

A bitter smile curled upon the lips of Don Rafael, and a sharp pang shot through his heart, as he compared the adieu he was now receiving from the inhabitants of the hacienda, with that which had accompanied his departure but two months before.

The fatal bullet had struck that very trooper who had judged it prudent to conceal from his officer the names of his assailants.

"'Tis Arroyo who has fired the shot!" involuntarily exclaimed the other, who also believed that he had recognised the insurgent.

"Arroyo!" exclaimed the captain, in a tone of angry surprise; "Arroyo within that hacienda, and you have not told me!" added he, in a furious voice, while his moustachios appeared to crisp with rage.

The trooper was for the moment in great danger of almost as rude treatment as Arroyo had just given his associate. Don Rafael restrained himself, however; and, without waiting to reflect on consequences, he ordered one of his followers—the best mounted of them—to proceed at once to the hacienda Del Valle, and bring fifty men well armed, with a piece of cannon by which the gate of Las Palmas might be broken open.

The messenger departed at a gallop, while Don Rafael and his three remaining troopers, screening themselves behind the crest of the ridge, sat in their saddles silently awaiting his return.

It was long before Don Rafael's blood began to cool; and in proportion as it did so, he experienced a degree of sorrow for the act of hostility he was about to undertake against the father of Gertrudis.

A violent contest commenced within his breast, between two opposing sentiments of nearly equal strength. Whether he persisted in his resolution, or retreated from it, both courses seemed equally criminal. The voice of duty, and that of passion, spoke equally loud. To which should he listen?

The struggle, long and violent, between these antagonistic sentiments, had not yet terminated, when the detachment arrived upon the ground. This decided him. It was too late to retire from his first determination. On towards the hacienda! Don Rafael drew his sword, and, placing himself at the head of his troop, rode down the hill. The bugle sounding the "advance," warned the inhabitants of the hacienda that a detachment of cavalry was crossing the ridge.

A few minutes after, the squadron halted before the great gate, at a little distance from the walls. A horseman advanced in front of the line, and once more having sounded the bugle, in the name of Don Rafael Tres-Villas, Captain of the Royalist army, summoned Don Mariano de Silva to deliver up, dead or alive, the insurgents, Arroyo and Bocardo.

The demand having been made, Don Rafael, with pale face, and heart audibly beating, sat motionless in his saddle to await the response.

Silence—profound silence alone made reply to the summons of the horseman and the sound of his trumpet.

Chapter Forty Two
Bearding a Brigand

In addition to the consequences that would arise from his resolve—already foreseen by Don Rafael Tres-Villas—there was one other of which he could not have had any foresight.

A glance into the interior of the hacienda will proclaim this consequence.

Within that chamber, already known to the reader, were Don Mariano de Silva, with his two daughters; and their situation was enough to justify the silence which succeeded to the summons of the dragoon. Inside the closed door, and by the side of the two young girls, stood Arroyo and Bocardo. Poignard in hand, the brigands were tracing out to Don Mariano the line of conduct he should pursue.

"Listen to me, Don Mariano de Silva," said the former, with an air of brutal mockery that was habitual to him, "I rather think you are too loyal a gentleman to dishonour the laws of hospitality by delivering up your guests."

"It is true," replied the haciendado, "you may rest assured—"

"I know it," continued Arroyo, interrupting him; "you would not betray us of your own accord. But this demon of a dragoon captain will break open the gate, and take us in spite of your intreaties. Now, listen! and hear what I wish you to do."

"Can you suggest any means of preventing him from acting thus?"

"Nothing more simple, good Señor de Silva. This *coyote* of the devil is your personal friend. If in the quality of your serving-man—that is, in times past—I chanced to apprehend a little of what was going on, you cannot blame me. If I am not mistaken, the dragoon captain has a little weakness for the pretty Doña Gertrudis. For that reason he will pay some regard to the danger that now hangs over the young lady's head."

"Danger! I do not comprehend you."

"You will, presently. You may say to the captain outside there, that if he persists in breaking open your gates, he may capture *us* alive. That he may do, beyond doubt; but as to yourself, and your two daughters, he will find nothing more of you than your dead bodies. You understand me now?"

Arroyo need not have been so explicit. Half the speech would have been enough to explain his fearful meaning. The air of ferocity that characterised his features was sufficiently indicative of his thoughts.

The daughters of Don Mariano, terrified at his looks, flung themselves simultaneously into the arms of their father.

At that moment the notes of the bugle resounded through the building; and the voice of the dragoon was heard for the second time pronouncing his summons.

The haciendado, troubled about the fate of his children—thus completely in the power of his unfaithful vaqueros, whose companions crowded the corridor—permitted the second summons to pass without response.

"*Mil Devionios!*" cried the bandit, "why do you hesitate? Come! show yourself at the window, and make known to this furious captain what I have told you. *Carrai*! if you do not—"

The bugle sounding for the third summons drowned the remainder of the brigand's speech. As soon as the trumpet notes had ceased to echo from the walls, a voice was heard from without, the tones of which produced within the heart of Gertrudis at the same moment both fear and joy.

It was the voice of Rafael.

Quickly following it were heard the cries of the troopers as they called aloud—

"Death to the enemies of Spain!"

"One moment!" shouted Don Mariano, presenting himself at the window, where he could command a view of the plain below; "I have two words to say to your captain: where is he?"

"Here!" responded Don Rafael, riding a pace or two in front.

"Ah! pardon," said the haciendado, with a bitter smile; "I have hitherto known Captain Tres-Villas only as a friend. I could not recognise him in the man who threatens with ruin the house where he has been a guest."

At this imprudent speech—whose irony Don Mariano had not been able to conceal—the face of the Captain, hitherto deadly pale, became red.

"And I," he replied, "can only recognise in you the promoter of an impious insurrection, which I have striven to crush, and the master of a mansion of which brigands are the guests. You have understood my summons? They must be delivered up."

"In any case," rejoined the haciendado, "I should not have betrayed those I had promised to protect. As it is, however, I am not left to my own choice in this matter; and I am charged to say to you, on the part of those whom you pursue, that they will poignard my two daughters and myself before suffering themselves to fall into your hands. Our lives depend on them, Captain Tres-Villas. It is for you to say, whether you still persist in your demand, that they be delivered up to you."

The irony had completely disappeared from the speech and countenance of the haciendado, and his last words were pronounced with a sad but firm dignity, that went to the heart of Don Rafael.

A cloud came over it at the thought of Gertrudis falling under the daggers of the guerilleros, whom he knew to be capable of executing their threat; and it was almost with a feeling of relief that he perceived this means of escaping from a duty, whose fulfilment he had hitherto regarded as imperious.

"Well, then," said he, after a short silence, and in a tone that bespoke the abandonment of his resolution, "say to the brigand, who is called Arroyo, that he has nothing to fear, if he will only show himself. I pledge my solemn word to this. I do not mean to grant him pardon—only that reprieve which humanity claims for him."

"Oh! I don't require your solemn word," cried the bandit, impudently presenting himself by the side of Don Mariano. "Inside here I have two hostages, that will answer for my life better than your word. You wish me to show myself. What want you with me, Señor Captain?"

With the veins of his forehead swollen almost to bursting, his lip quivering with rage, and his eyes on fire, Don Rafael looked upon the assassin of his father—the man whom he had so long vainly pursued—the brigand, in fine, whom he could seize in a moment, and yet was compelled to let escape. No wonder that it cost him an effort to subdue the impetuous passions that were struggling in his breast.

Involuntarily his hand closed upon the reins of his bridle, and his spurs pressed against the flanks of his horse, till the animal, tormented by the touch, reared upwards, and bounded forward almost to the walls of the hacienda.

One might have fancied that his rider intended to clear the obstacle that separated him from his cowardly enemy—who, on his part, could not restrain himself from making a gesture of affright.

"That which I wish of the brigand Arroyo," at length responded the Captain, "is to fix his features in my memory, so that I may know them again, when I pursue him, to drag his living body after the heels of my horse."

"If it is to promise me only such favours that you have called me out—" said the bandit, making a motion to re-enter the chamber.

"Stay—hear me!" cried Don Rafael, interrupting him with a gesture; "your life is safe. I have said it. Humanity has compelled me to spare you."

"*Carrambo*! I am grateful, Captain; I know the act is to your taste."

"Gratitude from you would be an insult; but if in the red ditch-water that runs through your heart there be a spark of courage, mount your horse, choose what arms you please, and come forth. I defy you to single combat!"

Don Rafael in pronouncing this challenge rose erect in his stirrups. His countenance, noble and defiant, presented a strange contrast to the aspect of vulgar ferocity that characterised the features of the man thus addressed. The insult was point blank, and would have aroused the veriest poltroon; but Arroyo possessed only the courage of the vulture.

"Indeed?" responded he, sneeringly. "Bah! do you suppose me such a fool as to go down there? fifty to one!"

"I pledge my honour, as a gentleman," continued the captain, "as an officer, in the presence of his soldiers; as a Christian, in the presence of his God—that whatever may be the issue of the combat—that is, if I succumb—no harm shall happen to you."

For a moment the bandit appeared to hesitate. One might have fancied that he was calculating the chances of an encounter. But the address and valour of the dragoon captain were known to him by too many proofs, to allow him to reckon many chances in his favour. He dared not risk the combat.

"I refuse," he said, at length.

"Mount your horse. I shall abandon mine, and fight you on foot."

"*Demonio*! I refuse, I tell you."

"Enough. I might have known it. One word more then, I shall still agree to your life being spared. I solemnly promise it, if you will allow the inmates of this hacienda to leave the place, and put themselves under the safeguard of a loyal enemy."

"I refuse again," said the bandit, with a demoniac sneer.

"Away, poltroon! you are less than man; and, by the God of vengeance, when this hand clutches you, you shall not die as a man, but as a mad dog."

After delivering this terrible adieu, the captain put spurs to his horse, turning his back upon the bandit with a gesture of the most profound contempt.

The bugle sounded the "forward;" and the detachment, wheeling around the wall of the hacienda, once more took the road that led over the ridge.

Among other bitter reflections, with which this interview had furnished Don Rafael, not the least painful was his apprehension for the safety of Gertrudis. No wonder he should have fears; considering the character of the ruffians in whose power he was compelled to leave her.

The apprehensions of Don Rafael were only realised in part.

Two days afterwards he received information from one of his scouts—sent to Las Palmas for the purpose—that Arroyo and Bocardo had quitted the neighbourhood—this time in reality—and that Don Mariano and his daughters had suffered no further injury from them, beyond the pillage of their hacienda. This the robbers had stripped of every valuable that it was convenient for them to carry away.

Chapter Forty Three
Roncador Restored

Captain Tres-Villas, now compelled to obey the order he had received from the commander-in-chief, proceeded to rejoin his regiment. Caldelas, at the same period, promoted to the rank of commandant, was summoned away from Del Valle; and the garrison of the hacienda which still remained fell under the command of Lieutenant Veraegui, a Catalan.

During the events which followed, Don Rafael saw a great deal of active service. He bore a conspicuous part in the battle of Calderon, where the Royalist general, Calleja, with only six thousand soldiers, routed the undisciplined army of Hidalgo, numbering nearly an hundred thousand men!

After being carried by the chances of the campaign into almost every province of the vice-royalty, Don Rafael was at length ordered back to Oajaca, to assist in the siege of Huajapam. It was while on his passage to this latter province from the fort of San Blas, that he appeared for a moment off the isle of Roqueta.

At the siege of Huajapam, his old comrade Caldelas re-appears as a general; while Don Rafael himself, less fortunate, has not risen above the rank of a colonel.

Such, briefly, is the history of the dragoon captain up to the time when the vaquero, Julian, arrived in the camp at Huajapam.

The announcement of this messenger caused within the bosom of Don Rafael an emotion sudden and vivid. Absence, remarks a moralist, which soon dissipates a slight affection, has the very opposite effect upon a profound passion. It only inflames it the more—just as the wind extinguishes the flame of a candle, while it augments the blaze of a conflagration. Absence had produced upon Don Rafael an effect of the latter kind. He lived in the hope that Gertrudis might some day send him a message of pardon and love. No wonder, then, that he was moved by the arrival of a messenger from that part of the country.

"Well, Julian," said he, in a tone of assumed carelessness, "you have news for me—what is it, my lad? I hope the insurgents have not captured our fortress?"

"Oh no, master," replied Julian; "the soldiers at the hacienda only complain of having nothing to do. A little scouting through the country— where they might have the chance of sacking a rich hacienda—would be more to their taste and fancy. As to that, the news which I bring to your Honour will probably procure them this opportunity."

"You bring news of our enemy, I presume?"

The tone of disappointment in which the interrogatory was put, was sufficiently marked to strike even the ear of Julian.

"Yes, Captain," replied he, "but I have other messages; and, to begin with that which is least important, I fancy it will be agreeable to your honour to know that I have brought along with me your favourite, Roncador."

"Roncador?"

"Yes; the brave bay-brown you lost in your affair at Las Palmas. He has been recovered for you, and taken care of. Ah! he has been marvellously cared for, I can assure your Honour. He was sent back to the hacienda."

"Who sent him?" hastily inquired Don Rafael.

"Why, who could it be, your Honour, but Don Mariano de Silva. One of his people brought the horse to Del Valle three days ago—saying that he supposed the owner of such a fine animal would be pleased to have him again. As the saddle and bridle had been lost, a new saddle and bridle were sent along with him. Ah! splendid they are—the bridle, with a pretty bunch of red ribbons on the frontlet!"

"Where are these ribbons?" hastily asked Don Rafael, carried away by the thought that a sight of them might enable him to divine whether the hand of Gertrudis had attached them to the frontlet.

"One of our people—Felipe el Galan—took them to make a cockade with."

"Felipe is a silly fellow, whom, one of these days, I shall punish for his indiscretion."

"I told him so, your Honour; but he would take them. I should add, your Honour, that the servant of Don Mariano also brought a letter for you."

"Ah! why did you not tell me so at first?"

"I began at the beginning, your Honour," replied the phlegmatic Julian. "Here is the letter."

The messenger drew from the pocket of his *jaqueta* a small packet done up in a leaf of maize, inside which he had prudently concealed the letter. Unfolding the leaf, he handed the note to Don Rafael, whose hand visibly trembled on taking it.

In vain did he attempt to dissemble his emotion under the studied air of coolness with which he received the letter, which he permitted to remain unopened.

This letter, thought he, should be from Gertrudis; and he dwelt on the voluptuous pleasure he was about to enjoy while reading it alone.

"Well, Julian," said he, after a pause, "anything else have you to tell me of?"

"Yes, your Honour; the most important of all. Arroyo, Bocardo, and their bandits have returned to the neighbourhood; and Lieutenant Veraegui has charged me to say to you—"

"Arroyo! Bocardo!" interrupted Don Rafael, all at once re-awaking from his sweet dreams to thoughts of vengeance. "Tell Lieutenant Veraegui to give double rations to his horses, and get them ready for a campaign. Say that in two or three days I shall be with him, and we shall enter upon it. The last assault upon Huajapam is to be made this very day, and the place must either fall, or we raise the siege. I shall then obtain leave from the Commander-in-chief, and by the Virgin! I shall capture these two ruffians, or set the whole province on fire. *Vaya, Julian!*"

Julian was about to depart, when Don Rafael's eye, once more alighting upon the little billet which promised to yield him a moment of sweet happiness, called the messenger back to him.

"Stay a moment!" said he, looking around for his purse, "you have been the bearer of good news, Julian. Here!"

And, as he said this, he placed in the hands of the messenger an *onza* of gold.

Julian accepted the douceur with eagerness—not without profound astonishment at being so generously recompensed for reporting the re-appearance of Arroyo and his band! Nevertheless, his satisfaction at the perquisite far exceeded his surprise.

As soon as he had gone out of the tent, Don Rafael took the letter from the table—where he had for the moment deposited it—and held it for some seconds in his hand without daring to open it. His heart rose and fell in violent pulsations, for he had no doubt that the letter was from Gertrudis, and it was the first souvenir he had received from her for nearly two years—since he had embraced the Royalist cause.

In fine, he opened the note. Although written in a feminine hand, it was more like that of Marianita than Gertrudis, and contained only the following words:—

> "The inmates of Las Palmas are not forgetful that they have received a kindness from Don Rafael Tres-Villas under very critical circumstances; and they believe that the Colonel Tres-Villas might be gratified at having restored to him the noble steed which the Captain Tres-Villas had such reason to esteem."

"A kindness!" exclaimed Don Rafael, with bitter emphasis, "what ingratitude! A service rendered by the betrayal of an oath sworn over the head of my murdered father! They call it a kindness—an act of simple politeness, forsooth! Oh! I must endeavour to think no more of those who have forgotten me."

And with a bitter sigh the Colonel strode forth from his tent, and proceeded towards the marquee of the Commander-in-chief—where the council of war was at that moment assembling.

Notwithstanding his chagrin, however, Don Rafael did not tear up the letter that had caused such disappointment, nor yet did he fling it away. Perhaps it had been touched by the hand of Gertrudis; and, with this thought passing through his mind, he placed the billet in a little pocket in his uniform, which chanced to be on the left side, just over his heart.

While passing towards head-quarters, another reflection crossed his mind, that exerted a consolatory influence upon his spirits. Gertrudis knew how much he prized the noble bay-brown—so often caressed by her hand. Was it for that reason the horse had been sent back to him? Was it she who had attached the rosette of ribbons to the bridle, to recall the flowers of the grenadine which in happier times she had placed upon his frontlet?

It was sweet happiness to believe it was she.

Chapter Forty Four
The Council of War

The Commander-in-chief Bonavia, the generals of brigade—Caldelas and Regules—were seated around a table covered with a green cloth, when Don Rafael entered the marquee. The council had not yet commenced.

"Ah! Colonel," cried Bonavia, addressing Don Rafael, as he entered, "I understand you have received a message from Del Valle. Is it of a private nature, or one that may assist the Royalist cause?"

"The lieutenant who commands the garrison of Del Valle informs me that those two guerilleros, whom both sides now regard as outlaws— Arroyo and Bocardo, I mean—have returned to Oajaca with their band. I have the honour to solicit from your Excellency that, after this place is taken, you will grant me permission to go in pursuit of these brigands, and hunt them as wild beasts."

"You shall have leave to do so, Colonel. I know no one better qualified to perform such a duty."

"I can promise your Excellency that no one will set about it with more zeal, nor follow it up with more perseverance."

The war council was then inaugurated without further delay.

Without reporting all that passed at Huajapam, we shall give a few details that may render more clear the relative situation of the besieged and the besiegers at this memorable blockade of Huajapam.

"Gentlemen," began Bonavia, addressing himself to his assembled officers, "it is now one hundred and fourteen days since we opened siege upon this paltry town. Without counting skirmishes, we have made fourteen regular attacks upon it; and yet we are at this hour no nearer capturing it than we were on the first day!"

"Less nearer, I should say," interposed Regules, when the Commander-in-chief had ceased speaking. "The confidence of the besieged has grown stronger by the success of their obstinate resistance. When we first invested the place, they possessed not a single cannon. Now they have three pieces, which this Colonel Trujano has caused to be cast out of the bells of the churches."

"That is as much as to say that General Regules is of opinion we should raise the siege?"

This speech was delivered by Caldelas in a tone of irony, which plainly expressed that a certain animosity existed between these two generals. Such was in reality the fact—a feeling of rivalry having long estranged them from each other. Caldelas was an energetic officer, brave, and of undoubted loyalty; while Regules, on the other hand, was noted for unnecessary severity, while his courage was more than questionable.

"It is just that question I have summoned you to discuss," said Bonavia, without giving Regules time to reply to the taunt of his rival, "whether we are to raise the siege or continue it. It is for Colonel Tres-Villas, who is the youngest of you, and of lowest grade, to give his advice first. Pronounce, Colonel!"

"When fifteen hundred men besiege a place like Huajapam, defended by only three hundred, they should either take it, or to the last man die upon its ramparts. To do otherwise, would be to compromise not only their own honour but the cause which they serve. That is the opinion I have the honour of submitting to your Excellency."

"And you, General Caldelas, what is your advice?"

"I agree with the Colonel. To raise the siege would be a pernicious example for the Royalist troops, and a deplorable encouragement to the insurrection. What would the brave Commander-in-chief of our army— Don Felix Calleja—say to our raising the siege? During a hundred days he besieged Cuautla Amilpas, defended by a general far more skilful than Trujano—Morelos himself—and yet on the hundredth day he was master of the town."

"Morelos evacuated the place," interposed Regules.

"What matter if he did? By so doing, he acknowledged himself defeated; and the Spanish flag had the honours of a successful siege."

It was now the turn of Regules to give his opinion.

He reviewed at full length the delays and difficulties they had experienced; the fruitless assaults and sanguinary skirmishes they had made. He argued that it was impolitic to stand upon an empty point of honour consuming the lives and courage of one thousand soldiers in front of a paltry village, while Morelos was at that moment marching on the capital of Oajaca.

"And when I say a *thousand* soldiers," continued he, "I do not speak without reason. The Colonel, in speaking of fifteen hundred, must have counted our dead along with the living. Up to the present time, in all other parts of the vice-kingdom, our troops have only encountered enemies, inspired by what they please to designate 'love of their country;' while here, in our front, we have a host of religious fanatics, whom this droll muleteer, Trujano, has imbued with his own spirit, and it must be confessed, with his courage as well. It is not three hundred enemies against whom we are contending, but a thousand fanatics who fight under the influence of despair, and die with a song upon their lips. While we are here wasting time in useless attempts, the insurrection is spreading in other parts of the province, where we might be profitably employed in crushing it. My advice, then, is to raise a siege that has been disastrous in every point of view."

"The besieged no doubt recall the exploits of Yanguitlan," ironically remarked Caldelas. "That is why they defend themselves so well."

At this allusion to Yanguitlan, which will be understood in the sequel, Regules bit his lips with suppressed chagrin, at the same time darting a look of concentrated hatred upon his rival.

To the view of the case presented by Regules, the General-in-chief was disposed to give in his adhesion. Less accessible to mere punctilios of honour than his younger officers, he saw in the advice of the brigadier reasons that were not wanting in a certain solidity. Without, however, availing himself of the full authority of his rank, he proposed an intermediate course. It was, that on the morrow, they should try one last and powerful attack; and if that should prove a failure then they might raise the siege.

While Bonavia was still speaking a singular noise reached the tent, as if coming from the besieged town. It appeared as a chorus of many voices intoning some solemn chaunt. This was followed by the clangour of horns and trumpets, and the explosion of fireworks—as if let off upon the occasion of a jubilee.

"These rejoicings," remarked Regules, "are an ill omen for us. It is not to-morrow that the siege should be raised, but this very day."

"That is to say," rejoined Caldelas, "that we should take to flight before an exhibition of fireworks!"

"Or, like the walls of Jericho, fall down at the sound of trumpets!" added the Colonel.

"Well," said Regules, "perhaps before long you may learn to your cost that I have been right."

In spite of his opinion, however, a last assault was determined upon, to take place on the following morning; and after the plans were discussed and arranged, Bonavia dissolved the council; and the officers proceeded to their respective tents.

Don Rafael hastened towards his: he was anxious to be alone. He desired to indulge in reflection—to ponder upon the meaning of the message he had received—and above all to caress the sweet ray of hope which had lately entered his heart, so long desolate and sad.

He did not even deign to lend an ear to the tumultuous rejoicings that came swelling from the beleaguered town; although the whole Royalist camp was at that moment occupied with these demonstrations, the soldiers deeming them, as Regules had pronounced, sounds of sinister import.

Chapter Forty Five
Valerio Trujano

In Colonel Valerio Trujano the reader will recognise the ex-muleteer, who, it will be remembered, declined exposing his life to the chances of war before paying his debts. Though in full command at Huajapam, he was simply a leader of guerilleros—nothing more; and in these partisan chieftains the country at the time abounded. The renown, however, which Trujano had gained within the narrow sphere of his exploits, had already rendered him a subject of constant inquietude to the government of Oajaca; and to crush this formidable enemy had been the object of the march upon Huajapam, where Trujano chanced to be at the time. The Royalist officers believed that a favourable opportunity had offered, in the absence of two of Trujano's ablest supporters—Miguel and Nicolas Bravo—both of whom had been summoned by Morelos to assist at the siege of Cuautla.

Such was the importance attached to the defeat of the religious insurgent, that the government employed against him nearly every soldier in the province—concentrating its whole force upon Huajapam.

The little town was at the time entirely without fortifications of any kind, and on all sides open to an enemy. All the more does the remarkable defence made by Trujano deserve to be immortalised. Fortunately for him the place was well supplied with provisions.

For all this, resistance against such a superior force would have been impossible, according to the ordinary rules of war; and it was not by these that Trujano succeeded in making it.

His first act was to store all the provisions in a common magazine; and these were served out every morning in rations to each soldier and each head of a family among the citizens. He also established a code of discipline, almost monastic in its severity; which discipline, from the first hour of the siege, in the midst of its most sanguinary episodes, during the long period of nearly four months, he managed to maintain without the slightest infraction. The energy of his character, combined with the prudence of his dispositions, obtained for him an irresistible ascendency over both soldiers and citizens.

The time was distributed for various purposes in the same manner as in a convent; and the most part of it that was not taken up by military duties, was spent in prayers and other devotional exercises. Orations and vespers were performed in public—every one, both soldiers and citizens, taking part; and in this remote village, cut off from all communication with the world, amidst a population little used to the pleasures of life, hourly prayers were offered up with that fervour with which the mariner implores the protection of God against the fury of the storm.

It must be acknowledged that these dispositions were somewhat droll and eccentric. They were prudent, however; since the followers of the insurgent chieftain, thus continually kept in occupation, had no time to become discouraged. If provisions were becoming scarce, they knew nothing about it. No curious gossips were permitted to explore the magazines, and report upon their emptiness. No indiscreet tongue was allowed to talk of approaching starvation. This arrangement could only lead to one of two issues: either the besiegers must destroy the last man in Huajapam, or themselves abandon the siege.

During more than a hundred days, as already stated, this strange condition of things existed in the town; and in all that time only one attempt had been made from without to relieve the place. This was by the insurgent leaders, Colonel Sanchez and the priest Tapia. The attempt had proved a failure; but even that did not shake the constancy of Trujano and his followers. The discouragement was altogether on the side of the Royalists.

Among the besieged perfect confidence was placed in their leader—a truly extraordinary man—one in whom were united the most brilliant qualities, and even those of a kind that are rarely found existing together.

Never did he permit the ardour of his courage to interfere with the prudence of his plans; and never did he advance them too hastily to maturity. Brave almost to rashness, he nevertheless calculated minutely the chances of a combat before commencing it. His frank open countenance had something so winning in it, that all freely yielded up their secret thoughts to him, while no one could penetrate his.

His gentleness towards his soldiers, tempered with a due measure of justice, had the effect of gaining their obedience by love rather than fear. An indefinable charm, in short, emanated from his person, which excluded all idea of disobedience to his will.

It may here be observed that at this period of the Mexican Revolution (1812), the Spaniards were in possession of all the resources of administration—the posts, and express couriers, with the principal highways of the country. The insurrectionary forces were in scattered and isolated bodies, either besieged in towns or pursued among the *sierras*. Bearing these facts in mind, it will not be wondered at, that although, while Trujano was besieged in Huajapam, and Morelos was in Cuautla, at the distance of only two or three days' journey, the Mexican general was entirely ignorant of the situation of the ex-muleteer! Even a month after Morelos had evacuated Cuautla, and retired upon Isucar, the position of his compatriot still remained unreported to him. Fortunately Trujano had learnt the whereabouts of the general, and had despatched a messenger to him demanding assistance.

Enclosed as Huajapam was by the enemy—who guarded every approach with the strictest vigilance—it seemed impossible that any messenger could make his way through their lines. Several days had passed since the man—an Indian—had gone out of the town; but whether he had succeeded in safely reaching Morelos' camp, or whether he might be able to return with the answer, were questions of prime importance to the plans of Trujano.

On that same day in which the council of war was held in the Spanish camp, Trujano had ordered a mass to be performed—specially devoted to prayer for the return of his messenger. It was in the evening, the hour succeeding twilight, that this mass was held; and all the population of the town, including the soldiers, was assembled in the public piazza, which was illuminated by torches of *ocote*, although the moon was shining brilliantly above. A church, whose dome was shattered with bombs, and rows of houses in ruins, surrounded the square. The temple in which the offering was made was the Piazza itself, and the roof was the starry canopy of the sky. There, under the red glare of the torches, might be seen the assembled people of Huajapam; the priests who assisted at the ceremony in their robes, covering a military garb underneath; the women, children, and aged, grouped around the walls of the houses; the soldiers, in ragged uniforms, with guns in hand; and the wounded seated upon doorsteps with bloody bandages—having dragged themselves thither to take part in the sacred ceremonial.

Profound silence reigned throughout the Piazza.

On the appearance of a man who advanced into the centre of the square, his countenance calm, and his eye beaming with religious enthusiasm, every head was uncovered, or bent in obeisance. This man was Trujano.

Stopping in the midst of the multitude, he made sign that he was about to address them. The silence, if possible, became more profound.

"Children!" he commenced in a sonorous voice, "the Scripture saith, 'except the Lord keep the city, the watchman waketh but in vain.' Let us pray, then, to the God of battles to watch with us!"

All bent down at the summons, the speaker kneeling in their midst.

"This evening," said he, "we celebrate mass for a special purpose. Let us pray for our messenger; let us pray to God to protect him on his journey, and grant him a safe return. Let us sing praises to that God, who has hitherto preserved from evil the children who have trusted in Him!"

The speaker then intoned the verse of the well-known psalm—

"His truth shall be thy shield and buckler. Thou shalt not be afraid of the terror by night, nor for the arrow that flieth by day; nor for the pestilence that walketh in darkness; nor for the destruction that wasteth at noon day."

After each verse of the psalm, the people repeated—

"Lord have compassion upon us! Lord have mercy upon us!"

The devout Colonel, as if he expected that God would show him some signal mark of his favour, in more emphatic tone chanted the verse—

"I will deliver him because he hath known My name; I will protect him because he hath loved Me."

And as if in reality the Divine interpretation had been granted, the messenger at that moment appeared entering the Piazza!

The man had seen Morelos, and brought back the glad news that the insurgent general would instantly place his army *en route* for the relief of Huajapam.

Trujano, raising his eyes to heaven, cried out—

"Bless the Lord! oh, bless the Lord, all ye who are His servants!"

He then proceeded to distribute the supper rations—giving them out with his own hands—after which the torches were extinguished, and the besieged betook themselves to sleep, trusting in Him who never slumbers, and whose protection was to them as a shield and buckler.

Chapter Forty Six
A Walking Corpse

While the mass was being performed in the Piazza, the Spanish sentries, who guarded the trenches outside, could distinctly hear the voices of those who took part in it; and could even distinguish the words of the sacred song, which alone broke the silence of the night.

The sentinel whose post was nearest to the entrenchments of the town, had for his companions a number of dead bodies of the enemy, who had fallen during a sortie of the insurgents, and whose corpses their comrades had no opportunity of interring. These, as already mentioned, were all more or less mutilated by their cruel foes, who oft-times revenged themselves on the dead for defeats they had suffered from the living.

The sentry in question walked to and fro upon his prescribed rounds, alternately turning face and back upon the mangled corpses. On each occasion, as he faced round half mechanically he counted them, by way of killing the time, at the same time preserving between them and himself a respectable distance.

After a short while spent in this melancholy pastime, the sounds accompanying the ceremony of the mass attracted his attention; and, as a change, he commenced endeavouring to make out the words that were being spoken or chaunted.

A distant voice exclaimed—

"A thousand shall fall at thy side, and ten thousand at thy right-hand; but it shall not come nigh thee."

"What the devil can it mean?" soliloquised the soldier. "Latin it must be! Some prayer for these dead rebels, I suppose!"

While thus alluding to the corpses that lay near, he once more glanced towards them. All at once it appeared to him that their number had increased!

"I must have made a mistake," muttered he to himself; "I surely counted only nine of them a moment ago; and yet now there was surely ten—one, two, three—yes, ten!"

He again lent his ears to listen to the chaunting of the psalm —

"Thou shalt tread upon the lion and the adder; the young lion and the dragon shalt thou trample under foot."

"Ah!" exclaimed the sentry, "they are talking of dragoons — the Queen's dragoons, I suppose?"

On making this remark, he paused suddenly in his steps. He had been timing his paces with that regular tread habitual to sentries, and in such a fashion as to maintain the same distance between himself and the corpses — which he had no inclination to approach. This time, on turning his face, it appeared to him that he had got much nearer to one of them; and at the next turn nearer still! This induced him to count the steps he was taking; and though on each round he made exactly the same number, he could not resist the conviction that he was constantly approximating to the corpse. Either he must be mistaken, or the dead body must have moved from its place! The latter was, of course, the more probable supposition; but, to assure himself, he approached the corpse to examine it. The dead man was lying upon his side; and a blotch of crimson colour conspicuous behind his cheek, marked the place where his ear had been cropped off.

A brief examination satisfied the sentry that the man was dead. It followed, therefore, that he himself must have been labouring under an illusion as to the distance. He almost gave way to an impulse to thrust his bayonet through the corpse; but a dead body, seen under the shadows of night, inspires a certain air of imposing solemnity, which repels profanation; and this, acting upon the spirit of the sentinel, hindered him from yielding to the temptation.

"If it were possible for dead men to get upon their legs and walk, I should say these fellows could do so. I am almost sure I counted only nine at first. Now there are ten; and devil take me if that fellow, whom I have examined, does not look as if he wished to have a chat with me, for the fun of the thing. *Carrambo*! the voices of those rebels in the town are not very gay at the best; but for all that they are pleasanter to bear than the silence of these companions here. There goes the sing-song again!"

The chaunt continued —

"Lift your hands through the night, and bless the Lord. His truth shall be thy shield and buckler. Thou shalt not be afraid of the terror by night!"

Although to the ears of the sentry the chaunting of the besieged was merry as a drinking song compared with the melancholy silence of the dead bodies, yet the time seemed long enough to him; and every now and then he looked towards the camp, in hopes of hearing some sound that would indicate the approach of the relief guard.

None was heard; and he continued to walk his round, as before measuring the ground with exact steps.

The dead body which was nearest appeared to remain in the same place; and the mind of the soldier was becoming gradually tranquillised, when all at once, on turning sharply round, he perceived that this corpse was no longer where he had last seen it. At the same instant his eye caught the shadow of an upright figure gliding rapidly off, in the direction of the town!

Terror at the unexpected resurrection hindered him for a while from making any movement; and when this had passed, and he was able to reflect more calmly, he comprehended all. He had simply been duped by an Indian ruse; which explained the mysterious addition to the number of the corpses, and the lessened distance between himself and that which had been lying nearest.

It was now too late to arrest the progress of the Indian by firing after him; and, as the giving an alarm would only be to disclose his own negligence, the sentry prudently maintained silence, and permitted the man to continue his course.

To account for the absence of ears, which had led the soldier to mistake the Indian for a corpse, it is necessary to mention an episode of the insurrectionary war, which had happened some weeks before. The scene of the episode was the village of Yanguitlan, where the cruel Spanish general, Regules, having captured a number of Indian insurgents, had caused the ears of a score of them to be cropped off, so close to their heads, that many of them died of the haemorrhage which followed. The others succeeded in making their way to Huajapam; and the Indian, who had so cleverly duped the Spanish sentry—and who was no other than the messenger whose return was at that moment being prayed for within the town—was one of the survivors of the horrible outrage.

It was to this affair that Caldelas had derisively alluded during the sitting of the war council.

"*Mil Rayos!*" hissed out the sentry, in a frenzy of rage and chagrin; "*Demonios!* there may be more of these fellows alive! I shall take care that no other gets to his feet, and runs off like the one who has so cleverly tricked me. Now, then!"

Saying these words the sentry turned his fusil in his hands; and, rushing towards the corpses, did not leave off thrusting till he had passed his bayonet two or three times through each of them.

Not one of the bodies showed the slightest signs of life; and the only sounds that troubled the tranquillity of the scene, were the angry breathings of the soldier, as he performed his ghastly work, and the chaunting of the besieged that still swelled in melancholy intonation upon the night air.

"Chaunt away, you cowardly devils," cried the terrified soldier; "chaunt away! You have reason, if it were only to mock me for keeping such careful guard over you. *Chingarito!*"

And the Spaniard, as he uttered this emphatic shibboleth, gnashed his teeth with vexation.

Shortly after, the voices within the Piazza became hushed. As we have stated, the messenger had arrived, and delivered his welcome tidings to the insurgent leader.

Chapter Forty Seven
A Decoy Sentry

On the same evening while the besieged were celebrating mass in the Piazza of Huajapam, other scenes were occurring not many leagues distant. Behind the chain of hills which bounded the plain of Huajapam, and in the rear of the Royalist encampment, a third army had suddenly made its appearance—though still invisible to the Spanish sentries. Morelos, true to his promise, with a thousand soldiers under his command, was hastening forward to the relief of Trujano. These were all the regular troops at his disposal; as he had been compelled to leave a strong garrison in the town of Chilapa, which he had also recently taken from the Royalists.

Besides his regulars, however, he was accompanied by a large force of Indians, armed with bows and slings.

At a short distance behind the General-in-chief, the Marshal Galeana and Captain Don Cornelio Lantejas were riding side by side.

Notwithstanding the distinguished position which he held in the insurgent army, the ci-devant student of theology seemed ill at ease. Some secret grief was troubling his spirit.

"The General is quite right in refusing you leave of absence," said Galeana. "A brave and experienced officer like you cannot be well spared; and your persistence in asking for leave has greatly offended him, I can assure you. As for that, my dear Lantejas, leave it to me. I am much mistaken if I don't soon find you an opportunity of achieving some bold deed, which will be certain to reinstate you in the General's favour. You will only have to slay three or four Spanish soldiers, or a Royalist officer of high rank, and that will set you all straight with Morelos."

"I should prefer slaying the officer, I think," answered Lantejas, scarce knowing what to say in reply.

To him, who had hitherto been only a hero by simple accident, the idea of premeditating any act that would distinguish him, only brought a fresh shadow upon the horizon of his future; and he would gladly have resigned the honours he had already gained for leave to escape being the candidate for new ones.

As soon as Morelos' army had halted for the night, the General and Galeana commenced deliberating on some plan by which they might give the enemy a decisive blow. The strategy which appeared most to recommend itself was to get the Royalist army between two fires; that is, while the troops of Morelos himself assaulted the Spanish camp in the rear, those of Trujano should make a sortie from the town, and attack the enemy on his front.

To the carrying out of this design the chief obstacle that presented itself was the difficulty of communicating with the besieged. The messenger of Trujano had left the camp of Morelos before the idea of such an attack had been conceived. Was there any one in the insurgent army who could pass the Royalist lines, and carry a message into the town? That became the question, which, as it so happened, Don Cornelio Lantejas was able to answer in the affirmative.

The Captain was in command of the Indians, one of whom had informed him that he knew a secret way by which the town could be entered. The patriotic Indian at the same time declared his willingness to carry a message to Colonel Trujano.

On communicating this information to the General, Lantejas had no thought of the honourable commission it would be the means of obtaining for himself. Perhaps, had he suspected what was in store for him, he would have withheld it. He did not do so, however; and, on disclosing the fact to Morelos, the General at once ordered him to accompany the Indian, taking along with him some half-dozen of his trustiest men.

An honour thus offered by the Commander-in-chief of an army cannot, without difficulty, be declined; and Don Cornelio was constrained to accept it.

Choosing for his companions Costal and Clara, with some half-dozen others, and, preceded by the Indian guide, he set forth towards the town.

After two hours spent in climbing the hills, they came within sight of the bivouac fires of the Spanish camp—towards which they proceeded without making stop, until they had arrived near the line of pickets. Here the guide halted the party, concealing them behind a ruined wall.

From this point a road, deeply sunk below the surface of the plain, ran past the place where one of the Spanish pickets held post. It was the same post where, but a short while before, the earless Indian had succeeded in deceiving the sentry. The one now on post was not the same. The guard had been meanwhile relieved and another sentry had taken the place; who, by the uneasy glances which, from time to time, he kept casting around him, was evidently under the belief that his position was a dangerous one.

Many causes combined to render the new sentinel sufficiently uncomfortable. The night was disagreeably cold; the companionship of the corpses, whose mutilated state presented death before his eyes in its most hideous aspect; their odour horribly infecting the air;—all these causes, coming together, could not fail to inspire the soldier with a secret fear.

To chase away his unpleasant reflections—as well as to keep his blood warm against the chill breeze—he walked to and fro in double quick time. The only moments when he remained motionless were at those intervals when it was necessary for him to pause and call out the usual phrase: "*Alerta, centinela!*"

"I am sorry for the poor devil!" said Costal, "we must send him to keep guard in the next world."

The wall behind which they had halted, although tumbled down and in ruins, still rose sufficiently high to screen the party from the eyes of the sentinel. Moreover, between the latter and the ruin, the ground was thickly studded with aloe plants and bushes of wild wormwood.

"Let us first get rid of the sentry," said Costal; "that accomplished, scatter yourselves among the bushes, and leave the rest to me."

On giving this counsel, the Zapoteque borrowed a sling from one of the Indians, in which he placed a stone carefully chosen. Then ordering two others to make ready their bows, he continued, addressing himself to Don Cornelio—

"You, Señor Captain, can give the signal. Take two stones—strike them together so that the fellow may hear you—strike them twice. And you," continued he, turning to the bowmen, "on hearing the second stroke, take good aim, and let fly your arrows."

Costal stood holding the sling in readiness. It was one of those rare occasions when the bow and the sling serve better than any kind of firearm.

Lantejas brought the two stones into collision with a loud crack.

The sentry heard the concussion, suddenly halted in his steps, brought his piece to the "ready," and stood listening.

The Captain gave the second signal. The stone and arrows hissed simultaneously through the air; and, struck by all three, the soldier fell dead without even uttering a cry.

"Go! scatter yourselves among the bushes," cried Costal, hurriedly; "the rest I can manage better without you."

Don Cornelio and the Indians, in obedience to Costal's injunction, glided from behind the wall, and crept forward among the aloes.

As they were advancing, directly in front of them, there arose the cry, "*Alerta, centinela!*" It came from the place where the sentry had just fallen; and Don Cornelio, on looking in that direction, perceived, to his horror and surprise, that the man was once more upon his feet, and walking his rounds as if nothing had happened!

Lantejas turned to demand an explanation from Costal, but the latter was nowhere to be seen. The Captain then faced towards the other Indians; but these, instead of concealing themselves any longer behind the bushes, had risen erect, and were running past the sentinel, who seemed to take no notice of them!

A ray of light broke upon the mind of the innocent Lantejas.

"*Santissima!*" cried he, "the sentinel—it must be Costal himself!"

And so it was. The living had replaced the dead; and so aptly did Costal imitate the voice and movements of the soldier who had fallen, that the other sentries along the line had not the slightest suspicion of the change that had taken place.

On comprehending the situation of affairs, Don Cornelio sprang to his feet; and, passing the decoy sentinel, ran on at full speed towards the walls of the town—where his Indians had already preceded him.

Seeing his captain clear through the lines, Costal flung away the shako and musket of the soldier, and hastened after.

Soon overtaking Don Cornelio, he cried out, "Quicker, run quicker, Señor Captain! The others will give the alarm as soon as they have missed their comrade!"

As he spoke, he caught Don Cornelio by the wrist, and dragged him along at such a rate that the Captain was scarce able to keep upon his feet.

In a few seconds they reached the line of the Mexican sentries, who, already warned of their approach by the Indians, permitted them to enter the town without opposition. On entering the Piazza they encountered Trujano himself; who, with his sword girded on, was making a round of the village before retiring to rest.

While Don Cornelio was delivering to him the message of Morelos, the Colonel directed scrutinising glances both upon the Captain and his Indian companion. He had some vague recollection of having once before seen the two men, but he could not remember where. At the moment that Don Cornelio finished speaking, his recollection had become more clear upon the point, "Ah!" exclaimed he, "I was thinking where I had met you. Are you not the young student who had such confidence in the mandate of the

Bishop of Oajaca, and who, at the hacienda of Las Palmas, denounced the insurrection as a deadly crime?"

"The same," answered Lantejas, with a sigh.

"And you," continued Trujano, addressing himself to Costal, "are you not the tiger-hunter of Don Mariano de Silva?"

"The descendant of the caciques of Tehuantepec," answered Costal proudly.

"God is great, and his ways are inscrutable," rejoined the ex-muleteer, with the inspired air of a prophet of Judah.

After having more substantially repeated his message, Don Cornelio was conducted by the Colonel to his quarters, and shown the apartment in which he was to sleep.

It only remained for him to seek the few hours' rest that would intervene before daybreak—the hour fixed for the decisive battle which was to take place. Wrapped in his cloak, he flung himself upon the wooden bench that served for a bed—vowing to himself as he fell asleep to attempt no heroic deeds on the following day, beyond those which were rigorously necessary for the defence of his own person.

Chapter Forty Eight
The Morn of the Battle

Not until several hours after the arrival of Don Cornelio did the insurgent Colonel warn his troops of the coming event. Then they were instructed to be ready at the first dawn of day, for a sortie against the Royalist camp—which at the same instant of time was to be attacked by Morelos on the opposite side.

While the shadows of night were still hanging above the beleaguered town, a singular noise was heard proceeding from the Piazza. It resembled the creaking of a watchman's rattle, or rather half-a-dozen of these instruments that had been sprung together. Such in reality it was: for since the church bells had been converted into cannon, the rattles of the *serenos* had been substituted as a means by which to summon the inhabitants to prayers!

According to the monastic regulation, which Trujano had imposed upon the besieged, they were each day called together to *oration*. On this morning, however, their reunion was earlier than usual: since it had for its object not only the ordinary prayers, but preparation for the combat that was to decide the issue of a long and irksome siege.

At the same hour the Royalist camp was aroused by the beating of drums and bugles sounding the *reveille*; while behind the chain of hills that bounded the plain Morelos was silently setting his army in motion.

In a few minutes the Piazza of Huajapam was filled with citizens and soldiers, all armed for the fight. They stood in silent groups, awaiting the prayer that would endue them with the necessary energy and enthusiasm. The horsemen were dismounted—each man standing by the head of his horse, and in the order in which they were accustomed to range themselves.

Trujano appeared in his turn, his countenance solemn, yet smiling, with confidence in his heart as upon his lips. He was armed, according to his custom, with a long two-edged sword, which he had oft-times wielded with terrible effect. By his side marched Captain Lantejas, who for the time being was acting as an aide-de-camp. Behind them came a soldier, holding in hand two horses fully equipped for the field. One of these was the war-horse of Trujano himself; the other was intended for the aide-de-camp. Over the withers of the animal destined for the ex-student of theology rose a long lance, strapped to the stirrup and the pummel of the saddle.

Don Cornelio would have had a difficulty in declaring why he had armed himself in this fashion. In reality, the lance was not a weapon of his own choosing, since he had never had any practice in the handling of one; but the horse had been brought to him thus equipped, and he passively accepted the lance, for the same reason that he was allowing himself to be led into the fight:—because he could not help it.

The matin prayers were not extended to any great length of time. The dawn was already commencing to show itself in the east; and it would not be a great while before the sun would cast his golden bearing over the plains of Huajapam.

The religious insurgent was deeply versed in Scripture. Many portions of the Bible were so familiar to him, that he could correctly repeat them without referring to the sacred book. In a voice, every tone of which was heard to the most distant corner of the Piazza, he repeated the following verses—the meaning of which was rendered more solemn by the circumstances under which they were recited:—

"The people who walk in darkness have seen a great light. The dawn is come to those who dwell in the region of the shadow of death."

"Lord, thou hast blessed thy land; thou hast delivered Jacob from captivity. Glory to the most high."

A thousand voices repeated "Glory to the most high!"

By little and little the eastern horizon exhibited a brighter dawn; and the clouds that floated over the heads of those people so piously bent, becoming tinged with purple, announced the rising of the sun.

It will be remembered that, at the council of war, the Spanish general had decided not to make his attack till after the hour of noon. No preparations, therefore, had as yet been made in the Royalist camp.

As Bonavia was still ignorant both of the proximity of Morelos and Trujano's intention to make a sortie, the double attack was likely to fall upon the Spanish camp with the suddenness of a thunderbolt.

The Spanish army was divided into three brigades, that might almost be said to occupy three separate encampments. The first, commanded by Regules, held position nearest to the walls of the town. The second, under the immediate orders of Bonavia himself, occupied the centre; while the third, in command of Caldelas, formed the rearguard.

According to this disposition, Trujano, in sallying from the town, would come immediately into collision with the brigade of Regules; while Morelos, approaching from the mountains, would direct his attack against that of Caldelas. In this case, Bonavia, from the centre, could march to the assistance of whichever of his two brigadiers should stand most in need of it.

The Colonel Tres-Villas was second in command in the brigade of Caldelas, and his tent was of course in the rear.

During the night he had slept but little.

Sometimes during a storm the thick mantle of clouds which covers the sky breaks suddenly apart, disclosing an almost imperceptible portion of the azure canopy. Only for a moment the blue spot is visible, after which the dull vapoury mass closes over it, and again hides it from view.

Such was the ray of hope that had lately shone into the heart of Don Rafael. His habitual melancholy had assumed the ascendant, and the cloud had returned.

The man who passionately loves, and he who scarce loves at all, are equally unable to tell when their love is reciprocated. His violent passion blinds the judgment of the one; while indifference renders the other inattentive. Neither is capable of perceiving the tokens of love which he may have inspired, and which pass unnoticed before his eyes.

In the former situation was Don Rafael. Despite the proofs which Gertrudis had given him, his thought was, *not that he was no longer loved, but that he had never been loved at all*! He, who had almost sacrificed his love to his pride, could not perceive that the pride of a woman may also have its days of revolt against her heart. Hence arose the profound discouragement which had taken possession of him, and extinguished the ray of hope that had gleamed for a moment in his breast.

Wearied with tossing upon a sleepless couch, he rose at the first call of the *reveille* bugle; and ordering his horse to be saddled, he rode forth from the camp, in hopes that a ride would afford some distraction to his thoughts.

The aspect of the desolated fields—from which every vestige of a crop had disappeared—reminded him of his own ruined hopes: like the bud of a flower plucked from its stem, before it had time to blossom.

Occupied with such reflections, he had ridden nearly a league beyond the lines of the camp, without taking note of the distance. In the midst of the deep silence which reigned around him, he all at once heard a noise—at first low, but gradually becoming louder. This instantly roused him from his reverie—causing him to draw bridle and listen.

During the different campaigns he had made, Don Rafael had learnt to distinguish all the sounds which indicate the march of a *corps d'armée*. The cadenced hoof-stroke, the distant rumbling of gun-carriages and *caissons*, the neighing of horses, and the clanking of steel sabres were all familiar to his ear—and proclaimed to him the movement of troops, as plainly as if they were passing before his eyes.

He had no doubt that what he now heard was the approach of a body of the insurgents, advancing to the relief of the town. The alarm given by the sentinels upon the preceding night—the death of one of the number—the vivas and other strange exclamations of the besieged, within the town—left him no room to question the correctness of his conjecture.

Sure of the fact—and not wishing to lose a moment by listening longer—he wheeled around; and, putting spurs to his horse, galloped back to the camp where, on his arrival, he at once gave the alarm.

Chapter Forty Nine
Between Two Fires

After the first moment of confusion had passed, the Royalists commenced preparing to receive the attack, with that coolness which springs from practised discipline. In a short while every one was at his post.

The sun was just appearing above the horizon, disclosing to each army the view of its antagonist. The advanced sentinels along the lines had already retired from their posts, and were hurrying towards the camp. In the town could be heard the voices of the besieged, in solemn chorus chaunting the psalm *"Venite exultemus Domine,"* while shouts of *"Viva Morelos!"* came from the opposite direction, and loud above all could be heard the noted war-cry of the marshal, *"Aqui esta Galeana!"*

Almost at the same instant a double fusillade opened its formidable dialogue from the two separate wings of the Spanish army. Trujano and Morelos replied to it; one attacking in front, and the other upon the rear. The hour of retaliation had come: the besiegers were now besieged in their turn.

Meanwhile Morelos, having given orders to Galeana to direct the movement, had posted himself upon a little hill; where, telescope in hand, he stood watching the progress of the action.

After having coolly arranged his plan of attack, Trujano impetuously launched himself upon the camp of Regules, at the same instant that Galeana was advancing upon that of Caldelas.

On both sides the firing was of short duration. Neither the Marshal nor Trujano were the men to remain long at a distance from their enemy; and both, charging impetuously forward, brought their men hand to hand with the Royalists.

Although inferior in numbers to their enemies, the *guerilleros* of Trujano made such a desperate attack upon the soldiers of Regules, that the latter, unable to sustain the shock, were thrown for a moment into confusion. Their general, however, succeeded in rallying them; and Trujano, with his handful of men, was held for a time in check.

Meanwhile, Bonavia and Caldelas, having united their forces, were using all their efforts to resist the desperate charges made by Galeana; who, notwithstanding the impetuosity of his attack, found himself unable to break through their line and form a junction with Trujano.

There are men in whose company it is impossible not to feel brave—or at least have the appearance of it—especially when fighting by their side. Trujano was one of this character. His ardent valour was contagious; and alongside of him, Lantejas had no difficulty in sustaining his reputation for courage.

Nevertheless, the battle seemed to the Captain to be hanging a long time undecided; and he was growing fearfully troubled that the day would go against them, when Trujano, wiping the perspiration from his forehead, cried out to him—

"Captain Lantejas! I fear we shall never be able to break their line with such a handful of men. Put spurs to your horse, and gallop round till you find General Morelos. Ask him to reinforce me with two or three battalions. Say that I have great need of them, and that the success of the day depends upon it. Ride quickly; and I shall endeavour to sustain the attack till your return. *Vaya! Capitan!*"

The aide-de-camp, on receiving the order, went off at a gallop, lance in hand.

At the same instant an officer rode forth from the camp of Regules, on a similar mission to the Commander-in-chief of the Spanish army. The latter, however, succeeded in executing his commission more promptly than Don Cornelio; and Bonavia hastened, notwithstanding the protest of Caldelas, to send to Regules the reinforcement he had demanded.

"That man will be our ruin," said Caldelas to Tres-Villas, as the battalions were drawn from his brigade.

Don Rafael, mounted upon his favourite steed, El Roncador, was at this time making every effort to reach the Marshal, whose defiant war-cry, so often pealing in their ears, was beginning to create terror among the ranks of the Royalists.

"*Mil demonios!*" exclaimed Caldelas, "if Regules prove the cause of our defeat, I shall blow out his brains, and afterwards my own!"

As the brigadier pronounced this threat, his soldiers, pressed by a violent movement in front, commenced to give ground; and that which he had foreseen was likely to be realised. His brigade, weakened by the battalions sent as a reinforcement to Regules, was unable to withstand the desperate charges of Galeana; and, in a minute or two after, his troops broke line, fell back, and then scattered in full retreat.

Blinded by rage, Caldelas turned his horse, leaving to Don Rafael the duty of collecting the dispersed soldiers, and, furiously plying the spur, he galloped off towards the ground where Regules was still contesting the issue with Trujano.

Meanwhile Don Cornelio was going at full speed on his message to Morelos. He was not proceeding in a very direct line, however. Not desiring to get again embroiled in the battle, he had resolved on making a wide circuit round a vast field of maize, that extended along the edge of the plain, and slightly elevated above it. Every now and then he endeavoured to discover whether he was opposite the position held by Morelos; but in this he was unsuccessful; for the blades of the maize plants rising above his head hindered him from having a view over the plain. He at length reached a crossroad; and, deeming that he had ridden far enough to put him beyond the ground occupied by the Royalist forces, he turned his horse along the road, still going at a gallop.

The combatants were hidden from his view by a thicket of low bushes that skirted the side of the road. This, however, at length terminated abruptly; and Don Cornelio, riding into the open ground, all at once found himself in the presence of a large body of Spanish soldiers, who appeared in front of him forming a semicircle of swords, bayonets, and lances.

Terrified at the excess of his involuntary boldness, he turned his horse upon the instant, and plunged back into the crossroad; but he had scarce made three lengths of his horse in the back direction, when he saw riding towards him a Spanish officer, who, pistol in hand, and with a countenance red with rage, was uttering the most emphatic threats and protestations. In another instant they must meet face to face.

The advancing horseman had his eyes fixed upon the field of battle; and, although he did not appear to be aware of the approach of Don Cornelio, the latter had no other belief than that he himself was the object of the blasphemous menaces. If the Spaniard was not expressly searching after him to kill him, why should he thus cut off his retreat by the crossroad — the only direction that offered him a chance of escape?

Believing that the horseman was advancing to assail him, and suddenly nerved by despair, the Captain, on his side, charged forward; and delivering a vigorous thrust with the lance, he pierced his unsuspecting antagonist through the body, striking him lifeless out of his saddle!

A cry of grief reached the ears of the ex-student, coming from another part of the field; but not staying to see who had uttered it, he again spurred his steed along the crossroad — determined this time to make a détour sufficiently wide before heading towards the position of Morelos.

He had not gone far, however, when he heard a loud voice hailing him from behind; while the hoarse snorting of a horse was mingled with the cries—a snorting that resembled the roaring of a jaguar, and for that reason awakened within him the most terrible souvenirs.

"It is surely the horse of the Apocalypse?" muttered the ex-student of theology, while using every effort to maintain the distance that lay between himself and this mysterious pursuer.

In order to gallop more freely, he had flung away the lance, and was now plying the spurs with all the energy of a racing jockey; but still the singular snorting appeared to grow louder, and the pursuer was evidently gaining upon him.

To say the least, the situation of Captain Lantejas was becoming critical—to judge by the fierce zeal exhibited by his pursuer. Perhaps in all his life the ex-student had never been in a position of greater peril than at that moment.

Just as he was about reaching the crossing of the roads, he heard close behind him the breathing of the man who was in pursuit of him; and, glancing over his shoulder, he saw the head of the animal he had termed the horse of the Apocalypse—almost on a level with the croup of his saddle.

In another moment, a vigorous hand seized him by the collar, that lifting him out of his stirrups, dragged him backward, till he felt that he was lying across the pummel of his adversary's saddle.

Don Cornelio now saw a poignard raised to strike, which flashed before his sight like the sword of an archangel. He closed his eyes, believing his last hour had come; when all at once the arm fell, and a voice cried out—

"*Toma!* Why it is Don Cornelio Lantejas!"

The ex-student reopened his eyes; and, looking up, recognised the young officer in whose company he had journeyed, on his way to San Salvador, whom he had afterwards met at the hacienda Las Palmas.

Chapter Fifty
A Splendid Stroke

Surrounded by his staff, Morelos still continued to watch the progress of events. From the commanding position which he held, almost every incident of the battle could be observed. Even those occurring at the most distant point of the field were observable through the medium of the telescope. Among other objects that had attracted his notice was a horseman going at full gallop along the crossroad, which led from the field of maize to the Royalist encampment.

"Ha!" exclaimed he to an officer of his staff; "if I'm not mistaken, it is our Captain Lantejas who is galloping down yonder. Where can he be going? No doubt he is about to strike one of those improvised, decisive blows in which he excels—as when at Cuautla, he dashed his horse full tilt against the gigantic Spanish cuirassier, and received the sabre stroke that might else have fallen upon my own skull. Fortunately his sword turned in the hand of the Spaniard, and Don Cornelio was struck by the flat side of the blade, which only knocked him out of his saddle, without doing him any great injury."

"Señor General," remarked the officer, with some show of hesitation; "there are evil-disposed persons, who pretend to say that—that—"

"What do they pretend to say?" demanded Morelos.

"Why, that on the occasion of which your Excellency speaks, the horse of Señor Lantejas was running away with him."

"An odious calumny!" pronounced Morelos, in a severe tone. "Envy is always the proof of merit."

At this moment, Don Cornelio disappeared from off the crossroad; and Morelos now saw coming in the same direction a Spanish officer also going at a gallop.

"*Santissima!*" cried Morelos, recognising the latter through his glass. "As I live, it is the brave Caldelas, who also appears to have been seized with vertigo! What can all this galloping mean?"

It was in reality Caldelas, who, pistol in hand, was searching for Regules, to accomplish the threat he had made.

Just then Don Cornelio again appeared in the crossroad; but this time going in the opposite direction, as if charging forward to meet Caldelas.

"See!" cried Morelos to his staff. "Look yonder—an encounter between Caldelas and the Captain! Ha! what was I saying to you? *Viva Dios!*—did you ever see such a beautiful *coup de lance*? He has struck down the most formidable of our enemies. Huzza! Victory is ours! The Spaniards are scattering! They yield the ground, and all because their bravest leader has been slain. Now, sir!" continued the General, turning to the officer who had doubted the courage of Don Cornelio; "will that silence the detractors of Señor Lantejas? To whom, if not to him, are we indebted for this splendid victory? Presently you will see him ride with his accustomed modesty, to say that he has simply done his duty. Otherwise, should he present himself to be complimented, he shall find his mistake: I must reprimand him for being too rash."

"Happy is he whom your Excellency is pleased to reprimand in such fashion," said the officer, withdrawing to one side.

"Let us onward!" exclaimed Morelos. "The action is over—the siege is raised, and our enemies are in full retreat. To Yanguitlan, and then—to take up our winter-quarters in the capital of Oajaca!"

On pronouncing these word, Morelos remounted his horse and rode off, followed by his officers.

We return to Colonel Tres-Villas and the ex-student of theology.

Notwithstanding the violent wrath of Don Rafael against the man who had killed his brave comrade, Caldelas, there was something so ludicrously comic in the countenance of the ex-student—so much innocent simplicity in its expression—that the resentment of Don Rafael vanished upon the instant. Then, quick as a flash of lightning, came over him the remembrance of that day—at the same time terrible and delightful—when parting from the student of theology, he had hurried forward to see Gertrudis, and receive from her the avowal of her love—alas! too soon forgotten!

These souvenirs—but more especially that recalling the daughter of Don Mariano—formed the aegis of the ex-student. A bitter smile curled upon the lip of Don Rafael, as he looked upon the pale and feeble youth within his grasp. "If such a man," thought he, "has been able to give his death-blow to the valiant Caldelas—whose very glance he could scarce have borne—it must be that the hours of the vice-royalty are numbered."

"You may thank your stars," he continued, addressing himself to Lantejas, "for having fallen into the hands of one, who is hindered by old memories from revenging upon you the death of the valiant Caldelas, the bravest of the Spanish chiefs."

"Ah! is the brave Caldelas dead?" inquired Don Cornelio, scarce sensible of what he was saying. "Is it possible? But it must be so, if you say it. In any case, I pardon him, and you too."

"Very gracious of you," rejoined Don Rafael, with a sarcastic smile.

"More than you think," replied the ex-student, a little restored to his senses at finding his exploit was to be forgiven. "You have no idea of the terrible fright that he and you caused me just now. But, Señor Don Rafael—with your permission—I am in a *very* uncomfortable position for conversing—"

"Perhaps you will pardon me again for setting you safe and sound upon your feet?" said Don Rafael, permitting the captain to slide gently to the ground. "Adieu, then, Captain!" continued he, about to ride away. "I leave you, regretting that I have not time to inquire how it is that the peace-loving student, so terribly frightened at the mandate of the Bishop of Oajaca against the insurrection has become transformed into an officer of the insurgent army?"

"And I," replied Lantejas, "I should like to know how it is that a captain in the Queen's Dragoons, who did not appear to view that same mandate with a favourable eye, is to-day one of the bitterest adversaries of the insurrection? If it pleases you, Señor Don Rafael, to sit down here beside me, and let us discourse a bit—like the old Paladins, who often interrupted their deadliest combats for such a purpose—it would be much more agreeable to me than returning to the battle-field."

A sombre shadow passed over the countenance of Don Rafael at the allusion made to the change of his opinions. Both officers presented a striking example of how little man can do to direct his own destiny, and how much he is the sport of circumstances. Both were, in fact, serving the cause opposed to that of their heart's choice.

Just then a series of loud huzzas and *vivas* of triumph came from both sides of the battle-field; but it was impossible for either of them to tell upon which side the victory had declared itself.

"Ah! Señor Don Rafael," cried the ex-student, "if our side has succumbed, then I am your prisoner."

"And if you are victorious, I am *not* yours," responded the Colonel, casting towards Lantejas a glance of contempt that he could not conceal—while at the same time he gathered up the reins of his bridle.

As he did so, at both extremities of the road appeared a number of mounted men, whose half-military equipments proclaimed them to be insurgents. One was heard to call out—

"Señor Colonel! Yonder he is—Don Cornelio still living and well!"

It was Costal who spoke.

In another moment both the Captain and Don Rafael were surrounded by the horsemen.

Chapter Fifty One
A Generous Enemy

The situation of Don Rafael had now become as critical as was that of Lantejas but the moment before. His pistols had been discharged; his sabre, broken in the battle, he had flung from him; and the only arm of which he could now avail himself was the dagger so near being sheathed in the heart of Don Cornelio.

During the Mexican revolutionary war but few prisoners were taken by the Royalists; and the cruelties exercised upon those that were, naturally led to retaliation. On both sides it was a war of extermination. The lives of captives were rarely spared, even after they had voluntarily surrendered.

Don Rafael, therefore, had made up his mind to sell his life as dearly as he could, rather than fall into the hands of his enemies, when one of them, an officer, addressing Lantejas, called out, in a voice which the latter recognised —

"Ah! Captain Lantejas! haste and come this way. The General wishes to thank you for the victory which you have given us."

Don Rafael also recognised the officer, who was advancing at a gallop; and brave though Tres-Villas was, it was not without satisfaction that the enemy he saw coming towards him was Colonel Trujano, the ex-muleteer.

Trujano, on his side, at the same instant recognised the royalist officer.

Don Rafael, too proud to appeal to old friendships for protection — even to one whose life he had saved, in return for a similar service — put spurs to his horse, and galloped towards Trujano. With such impetuosity did he ride, that in another instant the two horses would have come into collision, had not the bridle of Don Rafael's been grasped by a hand — the hand of Lantejas! The Captain, at the risk of being crushed under the hoofs of both horses — moved by the generosity which Don Rafael had so lately bestowed upon him — rushed between the two horsemen as a mediator.

"Colonel Trujano!" cried he, "I do not know what you mean in saying that the General is indebted to me for a victory; but, if I have done anything that deserves a recompense, I do not wish any other than the life and liberty of Don Rafael Tres-Villas."

"I ask favours from no one," interrupted Don Rafael, with a haughty glance towards Trujano.

"You will grant me one—that of giving me your hand," said the ex-muleteer, at the same time cordially holding out his own.

"Never to a conqueror!" exclaimed Don Rafael, though evidently affected, in spite of himself, by the action and speech of his generous enemy.

"Here there is neither conqueror nor conquered," rejoined Trujano, with that winning smile that gained all hearts. "There is a man, however, who always remembers a service done to him."

"And another who never forgets one," repeated Don Rafael, with warmth, at the same time grasping the hand that was still held towards him.

Then the two horsemen drew their horses nearer, and exchanged the most cordial greetings.

Trujano profited by this occasion to whisper in the ear of his enemy, and with a delicacy which still further moved Don Rafael, whose pride he had treated with such condescension—

"Go—you are free. Only promise not to cut the hair off the heads of any more poor women; although it is said there was one whose heart trembled with pride that the conqueror of Aguas Calientes should send her such a terrible souvenir. Go!" added he, withdrawing his hand from the convulsive grasp of Don Rafael, "deliver yourself up a prisoner at the hacienda Las Palmas, where the road is open for you, believe me."

Then, as if he had too long occupied himself with the trivial affairs of the world, the countenance of Trujano resumed its expression of ascetic gravity, and when the eye of Don Rafael was interrogating it, in hopes of reading there the true signification of the last words, the insurgent chieftain called out—

"Let Don Rafael Tres-Villas pass free! Let every one forget what has occurred."

Saying this, he formally saluted the Royalist colonel with his sword, who could only return the salute with a glance of the most profound gratitude.

Don Rafael pressed the hand of the Captain; and bowing coldly to the other insurgents, rode out from their midst. Then, urging his horse into a gallop, he followed the road that led outward from the plain of Huajapam.

On finding himself alone, he reduced the speed of his horse to a walk, and became absorbed in a reverie of reflection. The last words of Trujano—what could they mean? *"The road is open for you, believe me."* Was it an assurance that he should be welcomed at the hacienda of Las Palmas? Should he proceed thither, as the insurgent colonel had counselled him? or should he go direct to Del Valle, to make arrangements for his last campaign against the brigand Arroyo?

Once more had commenced the struggle between love and duty.

Don Rafael would not have hesitated long as to the course he should pursue, had some good genius only made known to him a certain fact—that at that same hour an accident was occurring at the hacienda Del Valle, of a nature to reconcile the two conflicting sentiments that had warped the thread of his destiny.

A messenger from Don Mariano—the same who had brought back Roncador to Del Valle—had on that very day again presented himself at the hacienda. This time his errand was one of a purely personal nature—to Don Rafael Tres-Villas himself.

"Where are you from?" demanded Veraegui of the messenger, in his usual blunt Catalonian fashion.

"Oajaca!"

"Who has sent you?"

"Don Mariano de Silva."

"What do you want with the Colonel?"

"I can only declare my errand to the Colonel himself."

"Then you will have to go to Huajapam first—that is, unless you prefer to wait till he arrives here. We expect him in three or four days."

"I prefer going to Huajapam," rejoined the man "my errand is of such a nature that it will not bear delay."

This messenger was on his way to Huajapam, and not more than thirty leagues from the town, at the moment when Don Rafael was leaving it to proceed in the opposite direction.

Meanwhile Trujano, returning to the field of battle covered with the bodies of his dead and wounded enemies, caused all his soldiers to kneel, and publicly render thanks to God for having delivered them from their long and painful siege. Morelos at the same moment ordered his troops to prostrate themselves in prayer; and then a psalm was sung by all in chorus, to consecrate the important victory they had gained.

Don Rafael was still not so distant from the field but that he could hear the swelling of many voices in the pious chaunt. The sounds fell with melancholy effect upon his ears, until the tears began to chase themselves over his cheeks.

In reviewing the circumstances which had influenced him to change his line of conduct in regard to this revolution, he reflected that had he given way to more generous instincts, and not allowed himself to be forced astray by the desire of fulfilling a rash vow, his voice would at that moment have been mingling with theirs—one of the loudest in giving thanks for the success of a cause of which he was now the irreconcilable enemy!

With an effort he repulsed these reflections, and sternly resolved upon going to the hacienda Del Valle, to re-steel his heart over the tomb of his father.

A perilous journey it would be for him. The whole province—the capital and one or two other places excepted—was now in the hands of the insurgents; and a royalist officer could not travel the roads without great risk of falling into their hands.

"God protects him who does his duty," muttered Don Rafael, as he again turned his horse to the roads, spurring him into a gallop, in order that the sound of his hoofs might drown that pious song, which, by stirring up sad souvenirs, was fast weakening his resolution.

In another hour he had crossed the Sierra which bounded the plain of Huajapam, and was following the road which led southward to the hacienda Del Valle.

Chapter Fifty Two
Rude Guests

Let us now recount the events which took place at the hacienda Las Palmas from the day on which Captain Tres-Villas was compelled to leave Don Mariano and his two daughters at the mercy of the ferocious robbers Arroyo and Bocardo.

The two guerilleros had sought refuge there, with the remnant of their band—most of which had been already destroyed by Tres-Villas and Caldelas. From the moment of first entering his house, they had insisted upon a footing of perfect equality between themselves and their old master. Even Gertrudis and Marianita were not exempted from this compulsory social levelling. The brigands ate at the same table with Don Mariano and his daughters—were waited upon by the servants of the hacienda—and slept in the very best beds the house afforded.

All the while Bocardo was observed to cast covetous glances on the silver plate—which, as is customary in the houses of Mexican *ricos*, was massive and abundant.

In Don Mariano's presence he was in the habit of frequently making allusion to the richness of the Royalists; and behind his back he had several times endeavoured to persuade Arroyo that one who was the proprietor of such wealth, as was enjoyed by the haciendado, could not be otherwise than an enemy to the insurgent cause, and, at the bottom of his heart, a friend to the oppressors of the country.

"Look at us, poor insurgents!" he would say, "often reduced—especially when absent from this hospitable mansion—to use our fingers for forks, and our *tortillas* for spoons!"

And the wind-up of his argument always was, that they "ought to treat as a Royalist a master who dined every day upon silver plates—that Don Mariano should be reduced to the same condition as other patriotic insurgents, and use his fingers for forks, while his plates should be converted into piastres."

Up to a certain period Arroyo rejected these proposals of his comrade. Not that he had any more respect for the property of Don Mariano than his associate had; but rather that he was not yet sufficiently hardened to reckless outrage, as to perpetrate such an audacious robbery on one who was publicly known to be a friend to the insurgent cause. We say, up to a certain time Arroyo preserved these egotistical scruples; but that time terminated on the day and hour when, in the presence of his old master, and the whole household of Las Palmas, he was forced to endure the terrible insults inflicted upon him by the dragoon captain. From that moment he transferred a portion of his vengeful hatred for Don Rafael to the haciendado and his daughters; and it is possible that on his leaving Las Palmas the night after—which the dangerous proximity of Del Valle influenced him to do— he would have left bloody traces behind him, but for the interference of his associate Bocardo.

The latter, in his turn, had counselled moderation. More covetous of gold, and less thirsty of blood than Arroyo, the astute brigand had represented, that "there could be no great blame attached to them for using the silver of Don Mariano to serve the good cause of the insurrection; that the more needy of the insurgents might justly demand aid from their richer brethren, but not their lives or their blood."

Arroyo no longer combated the proposals of his *confrère*. To him they now appeared moderate; and the result was, that the two *forbans* collected all of Don Mariano's silver they could lay their hands upon, with such other valuables as were portable—and, having made a distribution among their followers, decamped that night from Las Palmas, taking good care in their *Haegira* to give the hacienda of Del Valle a wide berth.

With regard to Don Mariano and his daughters, they were only too happy that nothing worse than robbery had been attempted by the brigands. They had dreaded outrage as well as spoliation; and they were rejoiced at being left with their lives and honour uninjured.

Made aware, by this episode, of the danger of living any longer in a house isolated as Las Palmas—which might be at the mercy any moment of either royalists or insurgents—Don Mariano bethought him of retiring to Oajaca. He would be safer there—even though the town was thoroughly devoted to the cause of the king; for, as yet, his political opinions had not been declared sufficiently to compromise him. For some days, however, circumstances of one kind or another arose to hinder him from putting this project into execution.

The hacienda of San Carlos, inhabited by the man who was about to become his son-in-law—Don Fernando de Lacarra—was only a few leagues distant from that of Las Palmas; and Marianita did not like the idea of leaving the neighbourhood. Without stating the true one, she urged a thousand objections to this departure. Gertrudis was also against it. The souvenirs which Las Palmas called up were at once sweet and sad; and the influence which sorrow has over love is well-known—especially within the heart of woman.

In the hacienda Las Palmas sad memories were not wanting to Gertrudis. How often, at sunset, did she sit in the window of her chamber, with her eyes bent in dreamy melancholy over the distant plain—deserted as on that evening when Don Rafael hastened to arrive, risking life that he might see her but an hour sooner!

When Don Rafael, in the first burst of his grief and vengeance, indulged in that wild pleasure which is often felt in breaking the heart of another, while one's own is equally crushed—when he galloped off along the road to Oajaca, after burying the *gage d'amour* in the tomb of his father—thus renouncing his love without telling of it—then, and for some time after, the young girl waited only with vivid impatience. The pique she had at first felt was soon effaced by anxiety for his safety; but this at length gave place to agony more painful than that of suspense—the agony of suspicion.

We have already related, by what insensible and gradual transitions the family of Don Mariano de Silva had become confirmed in the belief, that Don Rafael had proved traitor to his mistress as to his country.

Nevertheless, at that moment when he presented himself, to demand the surrendering of the brigands, the sound of his voice falling upon the ears of Gertrudis had come very near vanquishing her wounded pride. That manly voice—whether when exchanging a few words with her father, or hurling defiance at the ferocious Arroyo—had caused her heart to tremble in every fibre. She required at that moment to summon up all the resentment of love disdained, as well as all the natural modesty of woman, to hinder her from showing herself to Don Rafael, and crying out—

"Oh, Rafael! I can more easily bear the dagger of Arroyo, than your desertion of me!"

"Alas! what have you done, *mio padre*?" cried she, addressing herself to her father, as soon as Don Rafael had gone; "you have wounded his pride by your irritating words, at the very moment when, out of regard for us, he has renounced the vengeance which he had sworn on the grave of his father! It may be that the words of oblivion and reconciliation were upon his lips; and you have hindered him from speaking them now and for ever. Ah! *mio padre*! you have ruined the last hope of your poor child!"

The haciendado could make no reply to speeches that caused his own heart to bleed. He deeply regretted the allusions he had made, towards an enemy to whose generosity he was now indebted for the lives both of himself and children.

Chapter Fifty Three
Love's Malady

After the departure of the bandits, a mournful tranquillity reigned in the hacienda of Las Palmas. Gertrudis, asking herself at every moment of the day whether Don Rafael really no longer loved her, could only answer with certainty that she loved him, and should do so for ever.

One afternoon—it was the third after Arroyo had gone—she sat looking over the plain as the sun was sinking slowly to the horizon. It was just such an evening as that on which she had awaited the arrival of Don Rafael. Now, however, the floods had retired, and the landscape had assumed a more verdant and joyous aspect.

All at once, half-a-dozen horsemen appeared before her eyes, as if just coming from the hills in the rear of the hacienda. The Spanish pennants floating from their lances proclaimed them to be Royalist dragoons. One rode a little in advance of the rest, evidently their leader. Several other horsemen appeared, following them: until a large troop was seen defiling across the plain.

Gertrudis heeded not those in rank. Her eyes were solely occupied by the one who rode in front. He was too distant to be recognised by the sight, but her heart told her who it was.

"I, too," murmured she to herself, "I have been rash in my words—in pronouncing an anathema against those sons of our country who should betray its cause. What matters it to the woman who loves, what flag her beloved may fight under? His cause should be hers. Why did I not do as my sister? Ah! why, indeed? Marianita is now happy, while I—" A sigh choked her utterance, and with tears falling from her eyes she continued silently to gaze after the horsemen, until their retreating forms melted away into the golden haze of the sunset.

Not even once had their leader turned his face towards the hacienda, and yet it was Don Rafael!

It was in reality the dragoon captain, going off in obedience to the order he had received; and who, to conceal from his soldiers the anguish of his spirit, had thus ridden past the hacienda without turning his head to look back.

From this time it should have mattered little to Gertrudis where she might reside. For her, Las Palmas had now only sad memories; but even these seemed to attach her to the place; and she could not help thinking, that her departure from Las Palmas would break the last link that bound her to him she so devotedly loved.

When Don Rafael no longer breathed the same air with her, she found a melancholy pleasure in taking care of his beautiful steed—the bay-brown Roncador—that, having galloped off after the encounter with the men of Arroyo, had been recaught by Don Mariano's vaqueros, and brought back to the hacienda.

Shortly after the marriage of Marianita with Don Fernando de Lacarra was celebrated. This union had been arranged, long previous to the breaking out of the insurrection, and found no opposition on the part of Don Mariano. Don Fernando was a Spaniard, it is true; but he had already obtained the consent of the haciendado. Even under the changed circumstances in which the revolution had placed the country, it would not have been refused. Like many other Spaniards at this time, Don Fernando had chosen for his country, that which held the object of his affections; and his sympathies had become enlisted in favour of the land of his adoption.

A few days after his marriage, he bore his young bride home with him to the hacienda of San Carlos. His mansion was situated not far from the hacienda of Del Valle, lying, as the latter did, on the banks of the river Ostuta which separated the two estates, and not far from the lake of the same name.

Most of the people on the estate of Don Fernando—less given to insurrectionary views than those of Las Palmas—had remained faithful to its owner. On this account, it appeared to offer a more secure abode during the troublous times of the insurrection; and Don Fernando wished to give an asylum to his father-in-law and his family. Don Mariano, however, had declined the offer, in hopes that amidst the stirring life and society of a large town he might find distraction for the melancholy of Gertrudis. He preferred, therefore, retiring to Oajaca, and a few days after his daughter's marriage had set out. Gertrudis refused to use the *litera* that had been prepared for her on the journey. She preferred riding the beautiful bay-brown, that had so often carried Don Rafael; and the fiery Roncador, as if conscious that he was object most dear to his master, suffered himself to be guided with as much docility by the fair frail hand of Gertrudis, as if his rein had been held in the vigorous grasp of Don Rafael himself.

Contrary to Don Mariano's expectation, the sojourn in Oajaca proved ineffectual in removing the melancholy under which his daughter suffered. Insensible to all the attractions offered by the best society of the place, the time hung heavily upon Gertrudis. One moment of happiness she enjoyed: and that was when public rumour announced that Colonel Tres-Villas, after capturing the town of Aguas Calientes, had caused the hair to be shorn from the heads of three hundred women!

As Trujano had already hinted—having heard it from Marianita, at the house of whose husband he had spent several days—this news had for a moment filled the heart of the young Creole with happiness and pride. Amidst the general surprise at this act of singular severity, she alone knew why it had been accomplished. Don Rafael did not wish that she should be the only woman who, by this insurrection, should lament the loss of her hair. Gertrudis, nevertheless, did not fail to reproach herself, for indulging in this moment of selfish happiness.

"*Pobres mujeres!*" (poor women!) exclaimed she, as she drew her fingers through the ebony locks that already replaced the long luxuriant tresses she had sacrificed. "*Pobres mujeres!* They have not had, as I, the good fortune to make the sacrifice for the life of those they loved."

After this occurrence, months passed, without her receiving any news of Don Rafael; and her cheek, gradually growing paler, with the blue circles darkening around her eyes, bore witness to the mental torment she was enduring.

For the long period of two years this agony continued—the young girl in vain endeavouring to stifle the passion that was devouring her life. Both spirit and body, enfeebled by solitude, by silence, and the sedentary character of the life she now led, had not the strength to continue the struggle much longer.

Don Rafael had the advantage in this respect. He carried his grief from one end of the kingdom to the other; and the constant change of scene, along with the distraction caused by the excitement of battles, were to him a species of relief.

Such advantages were wanting to Gertrudis. Happily, however, God has granted to woman, in a large degree, the virtue of resignation—often her sole defence against sorrow.

Gertrudis made no complaint, but suffered in silence—concealing, as well as she could, the dark chagrin that was consuming her. In long sleepless nights, when resignation appeared as if it would soon succumb, a feeble ray of hope would sometimes break upon her spirit, and for the moment restore its equanimity.

It was then she thought of her first resource—that which she intended to make use of when her power of resistance should be gone—that supreme resource that still existed in the tress of hair she had so carefully cherished and preserved.

The sending back to Don Rafael his horse had already cost her a pang. It had been a step on her part towards compromising the strife between her love and pride. Still more painful would it be to resort to that last measure, and avail herself of the permission, alas! so prophetically asked for.

Chapter Fifty Four
Topographical Details

In proportion as the insurrection spread through the province of Oajaca did the Royalists increase their watchfulness in the capital; and Don Mariano, having become suspected of a leaning towards the insurgent cause, was ordered to leave the place.

Before taking his departure, he had despatched a messenger—the same already made mention of—to the hacienda Del Valle. Upon what errand? We shall know presently.

On the same day that the messenger had presented himself to the Catalan lieutenant, and almost at the same hour, Don Rafael Tres-Villas was galloping as a fugitive through the plain of Huajapam. On that morning, also, Don Mariano de Silva took his departure from Oajaca, *en route* for the hacienda San Carlos. The haciendado was accompanied by his daughter Gertrudis, borne in a litter, and attended by a number of mounted domestics. The pale cheeks of the young girl, contrasted with the purplish circles around her eyes, proclaimed the mental agony she had endured.

Finally, on that same day, only at a later hour, another important personage of our history—the Captain Don Cornelio Lantejas—rode out from the camp of Morelos—evidently bent upon a journey, as was testified by the travelling costume that had replaced his military uniform. He was accompanied by two men, easily recognised as the scouts Costal and Clara.

Don Cornelio had been ordered by the insurgent general on a mission, confidential as it was dangerous.

The summer solstice was close at hand; and the black and the Indian—the latter having now accomplished his half century of years—were discussing between themselves the best plan for raising the Siren of the dishevelled hair from the waters of the mysterious lake, Ostuta, on whose banks they expected to encamp, before Don Cornelio had finally accomplished his mission.

Although this mission was of a secret and confidential character, it will be no betrayal of confidence on our part to state at once what it was.

The taking of the capital of Oajaca would not only render Morelos master of the whole province, but of all the southern part of New Spain—from the Atlantic to the Pacific Ocean. The insurgent general was, therefore, anxious to complete this magnificent conquest before the closing of that year's campaign.

Nevertheless, in the prospect of attacking a town so populous and well garrisoned as Oajaca, he deemed it prudent to gain some information as to its actual resources; and it was chiefly upon this errand he had despatched his aide-de-camp Lantejas.

The mission of the Captain had another object, of secondary importance, which, however, was the first to be accomplished. To the honour of the cause which Morelos upheld, it was of urgent necessity to put an end to the depredations of the two notorious guerilleros, Arroyo and Bocardo; whose deeds of cruel atrocity were rapidly producing the effect of rendering the insurrection as odious to its partisans as to its enemies. The force which these two leaders had under their command was as little known as the whereabouts in which they might be found; but their bloody deeds had rendered them as much dreaded as if a numerous army had been under their orders. The rapidity of their movements gave them the opportunity of multiplying, to an indefinite extent, their acts of ferocity, though at the same time a pursuer in search of them might easily have found them by the ensanguined track which marked their passage.

Arroyo, ever ready to imbrue his hands in blood—no matter whose—seemed to find a savage pleasure in destroying life; and one of his favourite habits was to be himself the executioner of his victims. He was endowed with some brute courage, a quality altogether wanting to his associate, Antonio Bocardo; for the latter was both cowardly and cruel, though in general more inclined to robbery than murder.

Morelos had been apprised of the outrages committed by these two bandits; and a message to them was one of the commissions with which Captain Lantejas had been charged. The message was in the form of a simple threat—it was to say to them, on the part of the insurgent general, that, unless they discontinued those outrages which had so long dishonoured the insurgent cause, they should both be drawn and quartered.

From the reputation which these two brigands had acquired, of being little mindful of military authority—as well as on account of the rigid guard which the Spaniards had established in Oajaca—it will be seen that we have spoken only the simple truth in saying that the mission of Captain Lantejas was anything but a safe one. With melancholy mien, therefore, he traversed the road leading from Huajapam to the Ostuta river—upon the banks of which it was reported that Arroyo and his band were at that time encamped.

Before proceeding farther, it will be necessary to give, at a bird's-eye view—if we may use the expression—the topography of the country lying in the triangle between Huajapam, Oajaca, and the Lake Ostuta: for this is now to become the arena of the future events of our narrative.

Regarding Huajapam and the town of Oajaca as on the same line, we find a road running from each—the two gradually converging until they meet. The point of union is upon the banks of the Ostuta river, not far from the lake, and where a ford crosses the stream. Before arriving at this ford, the hacienda Del Valle lies to one side of the Oajaca road, while about an hour's journey after crossing the river the domain of San Carlos is reached. These two estates—each embracing an immense tract of territory—would be contiguous to each other, but for the river which flows between and separates them.

Arroyo, having returned to the neighbourhood, with the number of his followers augmented by recent successes, as well as by the more favourable prospects of the insurrection, had sworn not to leave a stone of the hacienda Del Valle standing in its place; and to accomplish this vow was the object of his presence on the banks of the Ostuta.

His band, divided into two encampments, held both sides of the river, just by the crossing. Thus disposed, he could direct himself at will either against San Carlos or Del Valle.

It was not only possible, but probable, that the messenger of Don Mariano de Silva, going from Del Valle to Huajapam, would meet Don Rafael coming in the opposite direction, and about half way; since, as already stated, both had set out about the same time. It was also likely enough that Don Mariano and his daughter, *en route* for San Carlos, would encounter Captain Lantejas, travelling from Huajapam somewhere not far from the crossing of the Ostuta. The time at which both had started on their respective journeys would favour this probability. Finally, Don Rafael, making for the hacienda Del Valle, unless some accident should detain him, might meet all those personages almost at the same instant of time.

The principal characters of our history would thus be once more united on the banks of the Ostuta.

Chapter Fifty Five
Sunrise in the Tropics

On the fourth day after the siege of Huajapam, let the reader fancy himself transported to the banks of the Ostuta, where he will behold one of the most magnificent natural landscapes of American scenery.

The sun has not yet risen, and the *mäipouri* (tapir), before seeking his forest lair, plunges once more under the shadowy waves of the river. The Mexican roebuck, more timid than the tapir, trembling at the slightest sound among the leaves, watches while drinking for the first signs of daybreak—its signal to conceal itself in the thickets of sassafras and tall ferns. The solitary heron, standing statue-like upon its long legs, and the red flamingoes ranged in silent ranks, await, on the contrary, the coming of the dawn to commence their matutinal fishery.

There is a profound silence over all, save those vague sounds heard at this hour even in the most solitary places—where the different guests of the forest, according to their nature, are either awaking to begin their day, or retiring to their haunts for rest and concealment.

Although the darkness of night has disappeared, the eye cannot yet make out, amidst the whitish vapour that overhangs the stream, with what species of vegetation its banks are adorned. The crowns of palm-trees rising high above the other foliage—like noble knights of the olden time above the mêlée of common warriors—can alone be distinguished. To a superficial observer, the banks of the Ostuta might appear as much of a solitude as in those days before the children of Europe had set foot upon American soil; but the eye of one scrutinising the scene more narrowly would discover this deserted appearance to be altogether a deception.

Along the right bank of the river—near its main crossing—might be distinguished a number of scattered fires, scintillating through the nocturnal vapour, like stars in a cloud-covered sky.

On the left bank also, and opposite the first, others appear, irregularly gleaming along the edge of the river. Both lines of fires betoken an encampment—the same, though separated into two divisions by the stream.

At a considerable distance from the crossing, and contiguous to the road leading from Huajapam to the hacienda Del Valle, in the midst of a little glade, might be seen a group of eight horsemen, at the moment apparently engaged in some consultation among themselves. Still nearer to the river, and at the distance of some three or four hundred yards from this group, two pedestrian travellers appeared, cautiously advancing along the road, where it wound through an extensive wood of guiacum and cedrela trees.

Finally, between the eight horsemen and the two foot travellers, and at about mid-distance from each party, a single individual might have been seen, who could not be called either horseman or pedestrian, and who could neither be said to be occupied in any way. In fact, this personage was fast asleep, though in a most singular situation and attitude: that is to say, fast bound with a scarf of scarlet silk between the two main branches of a tree, and at a height of over ten feet from the ground.

The thick foliage so completely concealed him, however, that an Indian spy might have passed under the tree without suspecting his presence.

The individual who occupied this aerial couch was no other than Colonel Don Rafael Tres-Villas.

There are occasions when extreme bodily fatigue has the effect of causing apprehension in the spirit; and Don Rafael had found himself in one of these occasions.

Wearied, after three days' journey under a hot sun, and having had no sleep on the night before setting out, in spite of the uncomfortable position in which he had placed himself, Don Rafael was enjoying that deep repose which is often granted to the tired soldier, even on the eve of a sanguinary battle.

Leaving him, therefore, to indulge in his lofty siesta, and passing to some distance from the spot, and along the road leading to Oajaca, we shall encounter another group, differing from any yet mentioned. At a short distance from the river Ostuta, and near the lake of this name, a little before daybreak, might be seen a small party of travellers, about to resume their journey interrupted for the night. From the haste exhibited in making preparations for departure from their bivouac, it would appear as if they were in dread of some danger. Two of them were busy in extinguishing the remains of a fire, lest its light might still betray them; two others saddled the horses; while a fifth, who stood by the half-opened curtains of a *litera*, appeared to be reassuring a young lady who was inside.

It is scarce necessary to say that the travellers in question were Don Mariano de Silva, his daughter, and their domestics.

In the midst of the solitudes of transatlantic scenery, there are two solemn hours out of the twenty-four, in which all created nature seems more especially to rejoice—the hours of sunrise and sunset.

The eternal horologe is about to sound the first. A fresh breeze arising, gently stirs the leaves of the trees, and, playing over the surface of the water, dispels the nocturnal vapours. The eastern sky is becoming tinged with bright yellow streaks, mixed with the purple of the aurora, which proclaims the approach of the rising sun. His coming is saluted by the voices of myriads of bright birds that flutter among the trees of the forest.

The jackal flying to his den, utters his parting growl, and the funereal voices of the night-birds are heard for the last time. The mäipouri and roebuck have already disappeared within the thickets, where they have chosen their respective dens.

Finally, the clouds redden like the wings of the flamingoes, as the sun, shooting upward, gleams with golden brilliance upon the fronds of the palms, and discloses in all their splendid variety the trees of the American forest.

The tall ebony trees, with their bunches of golden flowers, the guiacums and perfumed liquidambars—like pyramids of solid vegetation—the mahogany and cedrela trees, and the princely palms towering over gigantic tree-ferns, and fanciful festoons of parasitical climbers, that form a flowery cortège around their stems.

In the midst of the almost impenetrable labyrinths formed by these various kinds of trees, glades may here and there be encountered, and paths leading from one to another, trodden only by wild animals, or savage bulls, the descendants of those introduced by the great Cortez into the province of Oajaca. These, maddened by thirst, may be seen pressing through the thick undergrowth towards the river, or standing, half immersed, with their black muzzles buried under water. Here and there pieces of the flowery turf, detached by their hooves, float down the stream, while birds alighting upon these miniature islets, joyfully flap their wings, as if celebrating a triumphal procession upon the water.

Such, in all its primitive splendour, was the aspect of the Ostuta on the morning in question, at that solemnal hour, when the sun proclaimed his presence upon the eastern horizon.

Chapter Fifty Six
The Bandit Camp

The bivouac fires appearing by the ford of the Ostuta were those of Arroyo and his guerilla.

At sunrise, this temporary encampment of the guerilleros presented a scene sufficiently animated and picturesque. A hundred men might be seen occupying themselves in grooming their horses. This they did in the most primitive fashion, some rubbing them down with bunches of dry grass, others with the first stone that offered, while still others, mounted on the bare backs of the animals, were swimming them through the stream, in order to wash and refresh them. On the bank the saddles were placed in a sort of irregular alignment, in the midst of bales of goods laid open, and of which only the coverings remained upon the ground, to tell of plunder taken from some unfortunate *arriero*.

On the right bank of the river—that side on which lay the hacienda San Carlos—was the principal encampment. There stood a large, rudely-shaped tent, constructed out of the covers of the despoiled packages—pieces of coarse hempen canvas and sack cloth, woven from the fibres of the maguey.

Two guerilleros, armed from head to foot, with carbines, swords, pistols, and knives, mounted guard on each side of it, pacing to and fro, but at such a distance from the tent that neither could hear what might be said within.

This rude marquee was the head-quarters of the two leaders, Arroyo and Bocardo, both of whom were at that moment inside. They were seated upon the skulls of bullocks, which served them for chairs, each smoking a cigarette rolled in the husk of Indian corn. From the attitude presented by Arroyo—his eyes bent upon the ground, which was cut up by the long heavy rowels of his spurs, it was evident that his astute associate was employing arguments to influence him to some deed of crime.

"Most certainly," said the latter, with an air of drollery, "I am disposed to do justice to the good qualities of the Señora Arroyo; they are truly admirable. When a man is wounded, she volunteers to sprinkle red pepper over his wounds. Nothing can be more touching than the way she intercedes for the prisoners we condemn to death—that is, that they may be put to death as slowly as may be—I mean as gently as possible."

"Ah, that is not selfishness on her part," interrupted the husband. "She does so to please me rather than herself—poor thing."

"True, she is greatly devoted to you—a worthy woman, indeed! Still, camarado," continued Bocardo with a hesitation that told he had finished speaking the praises of Madame Arroyo; "you will acknowledge she is neither young nor very pretty."

"Well—say she is old and ugly," answered Arroyo, "she suits my purpose for all that."

"That's strange enough."

"It's less strange than you think for. I have my reasons. She shares with me the execration of the public; and if I were a widower—"

"You would have to bear it all on your own shoulders. Bah! they are broad enough for that!"

"True," replied Arroyo, flattered at the compliment, "but you, *amigo*, have also a share of that load. It isn't often that the name of Arroyo is cursed, without that of Bocardo being mixed up in the malediction."

"Ah, there are too many lying tongues in this world!"

"Besides," continued the brigand, returning to the subject of Madame Arroyo, "I have another good reason for wishing that no harm should come to my wife. She is in possession of a scapulary, blessed by the Pope of Rome; which has the wonderful power of causing the husband of whatever woman may carry it to die at the same time that his wife does."

"Oh!" rejoined Bocardo in a tone of repudiation, "I did not mean that you should kill the Señora Arroyo—nothing of the kind. My idea is that she should be sent to a convent of penitents, where she might occupy her time in praying for the salvation of her soul, as well as that of her husband. Then replace her by a pretty young damsel, with eyes and hair as black as night, lips as red as the flowers of the grenadine, and skin as white as the *floripondio*. Now you can tell what for the last half-hour I have been killing myself to make you comprehend."

"And do you know of such a pretty young damsel?" inquired Arroyo after an interval of silence, which proved that the arguments of his associate were not lost upon him.

"Of course I do, and so do you as well—one that you could lay your hands on at any moment."

"Where?"

"Where? At the hacienda of San Carlos. Where else should she be?"

"You mean the Doña Marianita de Silva?"

"Precisely so."

"*Mil demonios, camarado*! Do you intend us to save every hacienda in the country? Of course it is for the sake of pillaging the house, that you wish me to possess myself of its mistress?"

"The owner of San Carlos is a Spaniard," rejoined Bocardo, without making any direct reply to the insinuation of his associate. "It would surely be no great crime to take either the wife or property of a *Gachupino*."

"Hold, *amigo*! that Gachupino is as great a friend to the insurgent cause as you or I. He has furnished us with provisions, and—"

"True; but he does it out of pure fear. How can you suppose that any one is a true insurgent, who has chests filled with bags of dollars, drawers crammed with silver plate, and besides," added Bocardo to conceal his true designs, "such a pretty young wife by his side. Bah! we were fools that we did not also take Don Mariano's two daughters from him, at the same time that we disembarrassed him of his plate. We should have been better off now, and I too should have possessed a beautiful creature, whereas I am still a solitary bachelor. But it's my luck, camarado, always to sacrifice my own interests to yours!"

"Look here, Bocardo!" said the brigand leader after a moment of pensive silence, in which he appeared to reflect upon the proposals of his astute associate, "we shall get ourselves into trouble, if we carry on in this fashion. It may end in our being hunted down like a pair of wild beasts."

"We have a hundred and fifty devoted followers," simply replied the other, "every one of them brave and true as his dagger."

"Well!" said Arroyo, still speaking in a reflective tone, "I do not say, but—I shall think it over."

The eyes of Bocardo flashed with a fierce joy as he perceived the undecided bearing of his associate. Well knew he that, before the end of that day, he should be able to obtain Arroyo's full consent and co-operation in the dark and terrible deed he had designed to accomplish.

Chapter Fifty Seven
A Real Virago

The two brigands remained for some time without saying a word, both reflecting on the scheme of murder and pillage which they now premeditated. At this moment the tent flap was raised, and a figure appeared in the entrance. It was a woman of masculine mien—a true virago—robust and hale; but whose countenance betrayed the ravage of evil passions rather than time. Her coarse hair clubbed around her head, and held in its place by a large tortoiseshell comb with gold pendants, showed no sign of advanced age. It was black as ebony. Around her neck were hung numerous chains of gold and glass beads, to which were attached a number of crosses, scapularies, and other golden ornaments; but in spite of this gaudy adorning her countenance was hideous to behold, and did not belie the portrait of Arroyo's wife which had been sketched by Bocardo, for it was she. As she presented herself at the opening of the tent, rage was depicted in her countenance, exhibiting itself in the swollen veins of her neck and forehead, and in the rolling of her bloodshot eyes.

"A shame on you!" cried she, casting on Bocardo, whom she both hated and despised, the angry look she feared to give her husband, "a shame on you, that after the oath you have taken, there should still remain a stone of this nest of vipers, or a man to defend it!"

"Well—what now?" demanded Arroyo, in an ill-humoured tone. "What nest of vipers are you speaking of?"

"The hacienda Del Valle—what other should it be? There our men—the greater number of them at least—have been besieging it for three days without any result. No, not without result, for I've just this moment learnt that three of our people have been killed in a sortie, and that this accursed Catalan, who commands the place, has nailed their heads over the door of the hacienda!"

"Who has told you this?" quickly demanded Arroyo.

"Gaspacho. He is outside awaiting your orders. He has been sent to ask for a reinforcement."

"By all the devils!" cried Arroyo in a rage. "Woman! who has given you the privilege of interrogating the couriers that are sent me?"

As he put this interrogatory the brigand sprang to his feet; and, seizing the bullock's skull upon which he had been seated, made a motion as if he would crush with it that of his amazonian partner. Perhaps, influenced by the late councils of Bocardo, he would have decided on bearing the public execration upon his own shoulders, had it not been for that scapulary blessed by the Pope, and whose fatal influence he at the moment remembered.

Bocardo paid no attention to the threatening demonstration of his associate, but sat phlegmatically silent.

"*Maria Santissima*!" exclaimed the virago, as she retreated before the angry menace of her husband. "Will you not protect me, Señor Bocardo?"

"Hum!" replied the latter, without moving from his seat, "you know the proverb, worthy Señora? Between the tree and the bark—you understand? These little domestic broils—"

"Must not occur any more," interposed Arroyo, quieting down; "and now, Señora," continued he, addressing himself to his helpmate, "before receiving Gaspacho, I have a commission for you to execute."

"What may that be?" brusquely demanded the woman, elevating her tone in proportion as that of her husband became lowered.

"It is a magnificent scheme conceived by me," interrupted Bocardo.

"Ah!" exclaimed the virago, "if you had only as much courage as intelligence, Señor Bocardo!"

"Bah! Arroyo has courage enough for both of us."

"That," said Arroyo, suddenly turning his anger upon his associate, who had not the advantage of possessing a charmed scapulary, "that is as much as to say that you have the intelligence for both of us?"

"God forbid I should either say or think so," rejoined Bocardo in an humble tone; "you are as intelligent as you are brave, Señor Arroyo."

"Wife!" continued Arroyo, without appearing to listen to the fulsome flattery of his associate, "go and interrogate once more the prisoner we have taken. Find out if possible what errand he was on—"

"The bird still sings the same tune," responded the woman; "he repeats that he is in the service of Don Mariano de Silva; and that he is the bearer of a message to that mad Colonel, as you call him, Don Rafael Tres-Villas."

At this hated name the shade deepened upon the brow of the bandit.

"Have you found out what this message is?" he inquired.

"The fellow insists upon it that it is of no importance. What do you suppose I found in his pockets, when we were searching him?"

"A vial of poison, perhaps?"

"No; but something equally droll. A packet carefully put up, enclosing a small cambric handkerchief, sweetly scented with perfume, and inside this a tress of hair—a woman's hair, long and beautiful, by my faith!"

"Indeed!" exclaimed Bocardo, in a significant tone; "and what have you done with it, Madame Arroyo?"

"What should I have done with it?" said the virago, with a disdainful toss of her head—"what but fling it back in the face of the messenger—the worthless thing. No doubt it is a love-token sent to this colonel of the devil."

"The messenger took it back then?"

"Ah, indeed—with as much eagerness as if it had been a chain of gold."

"So much the better," said Bocardo, with a significant gesture. "I have an idea," he continued, "if I am not mistaken—a superb idea! With this messenger and this love-token, we can give the Colonel Tres-Villas a rendezvous, where, instead of meeting his sweetheart, he may tumble into the middle of a score of our fellows, who may take him alive without the slightest difficulty. The thing's as good as done. Only put me in communication with this messenger, and I'll answer for the rest. What say you, Arroyo? What shall we do with the Colonel Tres-Villas?"

"Burn him over a slow fire—roast him alive!" responded the guerillero, with an expression of ferocious joy.

"But your wife will intercede for him?" ironically added Bocardo.

"*Carrambo*! Yes!" exclaimed the hag, "to burn him over the slow fire, and roast him alive—that I shall."

And with a hideous laugh she walked out of the tent to give place to Gaspacho, who the next moment entered.

The courier thus named had all the appearance of an original character. He was tall and thin as the blade of a rapier, with a cynical expression of countenance, and long snaky tresses of hair hanging down over his shoulders, like thongs of smoked leather.

"Speak!" commanded Arroyo, as he entered. "Thou bearer of evil tidings, what have you to tell us now?"

"Perhaps, Señor Captain," responded the brigand, who, notwithstanding his habitual air of importance, was evidently cowed by the scowl of his superior, "perhaps I have some good news as well?"

"First, then, deliver your bad ones!"

"Well, then, Señor Captain, there are not enough of us to take this hacienda by assault. The den of coyotes has proved stronger than we expected; and I am sent to ask for a reinforcement of men."

"Who has sent you?—Lieutenant Lantejas?"

"Lieutenant Lantejas will never send another message. This morning his head was nailed over the gate of the hacienda along with that of Sergeant Yañez."

"Tripes of the fiend!" exclaimed the guerilla leader, "Yañez, too!"

"Their heads are not the only ones, Captain. Besides them are those of Salinas and Tuerto, to say nothing of Matavidas, Sacamedios, and Piojento, who were taken prisoners and hung alive by the feet from the parapet of the building. We had to fire at them and kill them with our carbines, in order to put an end to their sufferings."

"They deserved it—a fig for their lives! Why did they allow themselves to be taken alive?"

"That's just what I told them," said Gaspacho, with an air of assent. "I warned them that your honour would be very angry about it. But they did not mind what I said for all that."

"So then there are now only forty-four of you laying siege to the accursed place?"

"Your pardon, Captain. I did not yet mention four others who have been hung up by the necks. Upon these we were not obliged to spend our powder—as they were dead enough already."

"*Carajo!*" vociferated the brigand with a furious accent. "Ten of my men gone already! *Demonios*! Am I to lose this band like the other? Go on! You have given me enough of ill news. Let me hear some of what you call good ones!"

"Yesterday evening a horseman approached the hacienda riding towards it, as if he had nothing to do but present himself at the gate and be admitted. Before getting near, however, he was seen by two of our videttes, who at once charged upon him. After a fight, in which the horseman made a fierce resistance, he managed to escape."

"*Carajo!*—the stupids!"

"Don't be angry with the poor fellows, Señor Captain. I assure you they did not let him go without a struggle, which ended in one of them getting his shoulder fractured by a pistol-shot, and the other having his horse fall under him. Pressed by the latter, the Royalist horseman turned upon him, and rushing against his horse, brought the animal to the ground. Then grasping the vidette by the collar, he lifted him clean out of his stirrups, and dashed him to the earth, as one would do a cocoa-nut to break its shell. It was full two hours before the poor fellow came to his senses."

"I know only one man strong enough to accomplish that feat," said Bocardo, turning pale—"the damned Colonel Tres-Villas. It was just in that way that he killed Antonio Valdez."

"It was Colonel Tres-Villas," added Gaspacho. "Pepe Lobos is sure of it. He heard the snorting of that strange horse—the same he rode upon the day he came to Las Palmas. Besides, Pepe recognised his figure, and the sound of his voice—notwithstanding that it was in the night. Ten of our men have gone in pursuit of him, and by this he ought to be taken."

"Holy Virgin!" exclaimed the guerillero chief, turning his eyes towards heaven, "I promise you a wax candle as big as a palm tree, if this man falls into our hands!"

"As big as a palm tree!" exclaimed Bocardo in astonishment.—"Camarado, do you mean it?"

"Hush!" said the other in a low voice. "Hold your tongue, Bocardo; it's only to humbug the Virgin!"

"Well," replied Bocardo, "whether they capture him or not, it don't much matter. We shall take him all the same. If I understand his history, and the meaning of the message which this coyote has for him, he can be lured by it to the farthest corner of the earth."

At this moment the wife of Arroyo re-entered the tent, her face exhibiting a still stronger expression of fury than before.

"The cage is empty!" cried she, "the bird has flown, and along with it the guardian left to watch it—the worthless Juan de Zapote!"

"Blood and fire!" vociferated Arroyo, "quick, pursue them! Hola!" continued he, raising the flap of his tent, "twenty men to horse! Scour the woods and the river banks. Bring back the two fugitives bound hand and foot. Above all, bring them back *alive!*"

The order created a brisk movement throughout the camp, where each seemed to compete with his fellow as to who should be the first to enter on the pursuit.

"*Jesus Santo!*" muttered Bocardo to himself, "if this Colonel should escape, and also the messenger, adieu to all my fine combinations! Well!" he continued, after the wife of Arroyo had gone out of the tent to hasten the departure of the pursuers. "Well, Señor Arroyo! if he should get away from us it will be a great pity sure enough. Still we shall find consolation at the hacienda San Carlos."

"True," replied the other, "and I have need of some distraction just now. This evening I mean to amuse myself. To-morrow we shall storm the fortress of Del Valle with all our force; and may the devil scorch me, if I leave one stone of it standing upon another!"

"Yes; to-morrow let us set seriously about it," said Bocardo, gleefully rubbing his hands together. "But see!" he continued, glancing out of the tent, "our fellows are ready to start. If you take my advice, instead of twenty men, you'll send only ten. That will be quite sufficient to capture those two droll devils who have escaped from us. After you have sent the reinforcement to Del Valle we'll have no great number of men to remain at head-quarters here."

The guerillero chief yielded to the counsel of his associate; and choosing from the horsemen that were ready ten of the best mounted, he directed them to enter upon the pursuit. The others were at the same time ordered to proceed to the hacienda Del Valle to reinforce the party already besieging the place.

Chapter Fifty Eight
An Unexpected Reception

From that portion of Gaspacho's report which related to Don Rafael Tres-Villas, the reader will easily guess the purpose of the eight horsemen assembled in the glade of the forest of Ostuta: they were no other than the soldiers who from the besieging party had gone in pursuit of the Royalist Colonel. It will be remembered, however, that ten was the number mentioned by Gaspacho, while only eight now composed the group that occupied the clearing.

We shall presently learn how their number became thus reduced: but first let us recount the adventures of Don Rafael himself—from the time of his quitting the camp of Huajapam, to the moment when we find him asleep upon his arboreal couch.

As soon as the song of triumph raised by the soldiers of Trujano had ceased to echo in his ears, Don Rafael proceeded to reflect upon his own situation. He perceived at once that, in order to traverse with safety some thirty leagues of a country almost entirely in the hands of the insurgents, certain precautions would be absolutely necessary. His gold-laced uniform, his helmet, all his equipments, in short, would betray him to an insurgent enemy. Moreover he was badly armed—having broken his sword in the conflict; and for such a perilous journey it was necessary to be provided with better weapons than a dagger and pistols.

He knew it was impossible to return to his marquee to re-equip himself. The camp was already filled with the insurgent soldiers, and no doubt his tent had been pillaged long before that time.

After a moment's reflection it occurred to him that on the field of battle—that part of it most distant from Huajapam, where Callejas had sustained the first shock of Morelos' army—he might find the necessary articles he desired; and turning a little out of his course, he directed himself thither.

His judgment proved correct. A two-edged sword soon rewarded his search; and he was able to exchange for his dragoon helmet the felt hat of an insurgent soldier, with a brass front-plate, bearing in ill-formed letters the inscription, *Independencia o' muerte*!

Scornfully tearing off the tablet and trampling it under his feet, Don Rafael placed the felt hat upon his head, and continued his explorations. Shortly after he exchanged the *jaqueta* of an insurgent soldier for his cavalry uniform; and then looking to the state of his pistols, and seeing that his cartridge-box was well garnished he put spurs to Roncador and rode briskly away from the ground.

It is not necessary to detail the many precautions which he adopted from hour to hour to keep out of the hands of the insurgents, who were on all sides scouring the country through which he had to pass. Suffice it to say that for the most part he journeyed only by night. Even travelling thus, he was not always safe; and more than once he found occasion to employ all the courage and presence of mind with which Nature had endowed him.

On the evening of the third day, just at the hour of twilight, he arrived in the neighbourhood of his own hacienda. He was expecting soon to be in security within its walls, when the two videttes already mentioned perceived and rushed forward to capture him. This behaviour was in conformity with the orders of Arroyo, who had commanded that every one seen near the hacienda should be made prisoner and brought into his presence.

Don Rafael was at first uncertain as to the enemy with which he had to deal; but he was not the man to submit tamely to conduct so brusque and uncourteous as was that of the videttes. His resistance ended in putting both of them *hors de combat*; but the circumstances of the encounter, for certain reasons, had been somewhat misrepresented by Gaspacho.

It is true that one of the two soldiers had his shoulder fractured by a shot; but the bullet had also passed so near his heart, that the man was dead in an hour after. As to the other, it was true that the Colonel dashed him to the ground as described; but, before doing so, he had taken the precaution to plunge his dagger into the breast of this second adversary.

Although he had left both deprived of the power to give the alarm, unfortunately the report of his pistol had betrayed his presence to the guerilleros. In a few moments half a score of them were riding in pursuit; for, by the orders of their chief, one half their horses were kept saddled and bridled both day and night.

After disembarrassing himself of his two adversaries, the Colonel had hesitated a moment, as to whether he should return on his path or continue on to the hacienda. It was during this interval of hesitation that the pursuing horsemen drew near, and that one of them (Pepe Lobos by name) caught sight of and recognised him, while the snorting of Roncador as he galloped off confirmed the guerillero in his belief.

It is likely enough that the extreme hatred which Arroyo bore for the Colonel was at this crisis the means of saving his life. The guerilleros, knowing the desire of their chief that Tres-Villas should be captured alive, reflected upon the rich recompense they might expect if they should so take him. Otherwise the volley of carbine shots, which they would have delivered on the instant, might have terminated the existence of their dreaded foe.

On seeing the horsemen, Don Rafael suddenly wheeled round and galloped back as he had come. His hope lay in being able to distance his pursuers, and afterwards find a temporary refuge in the thick forest he had just been traversing, and through which ran the road to Huajapam. With this purpose in view, he returned along the route at full gallop.

When he deemed himself at a sufficient distance in advance of his pursuers, he wheeled suddenly from the road and headed his steed into the thick underwood, through which he spurred onward, until his passage was fairly barred up by an impenetrable network of vines and bushes. Here he halted; and, dismounting, led his horse to a tree. He then commenced groping about, to find some spot where he might in safety obtain a few hours of repose, after the fatigues he had encountered during the day.

A few paces further on he perceived a cedrela tree of gigantic dimensions, and so thickly loaded with leaves that it seemed to promise a secure hiding-place among its branches. Still apprehensive that his pursuers might discover his track, Don Rafael resolved to climb the cedrela, whose dark foliage would screen him from the sharpest eyes. On approaching the tree, he perceived by the vast circumference of its trunk that he could not climb up by embracing it. Neither could he reach to even the lowest of its limbs. A means, however, presented itself of getting over the difficulty.

An enormous lliana, stretching from among the top branches, reached the ground in a diagonal direction; and up this Don Rafael was enabled to make his ascent.

Placing his body between two large boughs, he disposed himself, as best he could, to pass the remainder of the night, leaving it for the day to bring him to some further determination.

He commenced reflecting upon the pursuit. He was in hopes that his pursuers, having lost his track, might separate into small parties of two or three, in order the more thoroughly to scour the woods. In this case, he might be able to defeat the whole party, taking them in detail, and favoured by his own superior courage and strength, in which he felt the most perfect confidence.

The night had already advanced, and the moon from the high vault of the starry heavens poured down her floods of light over the spray of the forest. A few feeble raylets, penetrating through the thick masses of foliage, reached the retreat where Don Rafael had hidden himself.

He remained for some moments listening attentively. He could hear nothing—at least no sound that betokened the presence of human beings. The breeze sighing among the leaves, the distant howl of the coyote, the sweet note of the mimic night-thrush, or perchance the rustling caused by the iguana as it scampered over the dead leaves, were the only sounds that broke the stillness of the night.

The fresh balmy air that he was breathing, the shadow of night that enwrapped him, the imposing tranquillity that reigned around, all conspired to beget the desire for repose. He felt his eyelids gradually grow heavier and heavier; and after a while an invincible torpor seized upon his whole frame.

Without being in any great degree uneasy about his situation, Don Rafael nevertheless felt the necessity of keeping awake as long as he might be able. With this intent he struggled for a time against sleep, but in vain. Seeing that it was about to overpower him, he unwound the sash from his waist, and with this attached himself firmly between the branches. Having thus provided against the danger of a fall, he surrendered himself the moment after to a profound and silent slumber.

Chapter Fifty Nine
A Careless Search

Most of the guerilleros of the band of Arroyo were country-people—rancheros, vaqueros, and the like. Many of them, from their habits of life, were skilled in following the tracks of animals. It was not likely, therefore, they should fail to discover the place where the Colonel had turned off from the road; and in reality they perceived it, and there came to a halt. The uncertain light of the moon, however, hindered them from following his tracks through the underwood; and, unable to guess the direction he had taken, they remained for some minutes deliberating on what was best to be done.

To go forward in a body would be to diminish the chances of finding his traces—more especially if they proceeded on horseback. It was resolved, therefore, that all should dismount; and, separating into twos, thus scour the thicket in front. Afterwards, if unsuccessful in their search, they were to reunite in the glade where they had picketed their horses.

This resolution was carried out; and in pairs the guerilleros scattered off into the wood.

Although adopting all necessary measures of prudence, on account of the terrible name of him they were in search of, at first the pursuers conscientiously performed their work. By little and little, however, their ardour became abated; and then a very similar idea presented itself to the minds of all of them at the same time. They remembered how easily the Colonel had overcome his two adversaries, the videttes; and it now occurred to them that *they* had acted very rashly in thus weakening their strength by division.

As it would never do to return at once to the appointed rendezvous, each couple perceived the necessity of allowing some time to elapse before going back, for the sake of saving appearances. They continued their search, therefore; but rather by way of passing the time than with any ardour in the accomplishment of their original design.

"*Carrambo!* what a lovely moon!" remarked Pepe Lobos to his partner in the search; "it gives me an idea—"

"That the Colonel may see us before we discover him?" interrupted his companion.

"Bah! nothing of the kind," rejoined Pepe; "that devil of a royalist is not to be found. What I was thinking of is, that, since it is almost as clear as daylight, there's a good opportunity for your showing me that which you have so long promised."

"What is it, camarado?"

"The trick of cards by which one may always win an *albur* at monte."

"Of course I cannot show you without having the cards."

"But I have them, hombre—a brand-new pack too."

"Ah! it is easier to do that trick with an old pack," replied Pepe's comrade with a knowing shrug of the shoulders. "However, since I have promised you, and, as you justly remark, there is no chance of finding this royalist colonel, I agree to your request."

The two insurgents seated themselves on the turf—in a spot where the moon fell with a clear light—and Pepe Lobos, having drawn a pack of cards from his pocket, the lesson commenced. Between the ardour of the master and the docility of the pupil, the lesson was prolonged to such a time, that the Colonel, asleep between his two branches, could have dreamt all the dreams that might present themselves to his imagination before either of these worthies was likely to awaken him.

Not far distant two others of the searchers put in practice, as regards Don Rafael, a very similar courtesy.

"So, Suarez," said the first of these two to the other, "five hundred dollars, isn't it, that the Captain promises the man who may take this royalist colonel alive?"

"Yes," replied Suarez, "five hundred dollars, and a good round sum it is. But should one get an arm shot off, or a leg disabled, in capturing the *demonio*, will the Captain allow anything extra for that, do you think?"

"Ah! I can't say. I should fancy so."

"Well, then, hear me, friend Suarez. I have no doubt it will be a good thing; and for you who are married and have a family to support, this five hundred dollars would be a windfall. I am single, and don't require it. I am therefore willing to surrender my chance to you, and you can look for the Colonel by yourself."

Saying this, the soldier stretched himself along the grass, and disposed himself for a sleep.

"For the last two nights," continued he, "I haven't had a wink, and I can't keep my eyes open any longer. When you have captured the Colonel, come back and rouse me; but, whether you take him or no, mind you, good Suarez, come this way and wake me before daylight—else I may sleep too long."

"Coward!" exclaimed Suarez, "I shall keep on without you, and get the reward for myself."

The answer to these remarks was a loud snore, for Suarez' comrade had fallen asleep on the instant.

Of the ten enemies of Don Rafael three had thus withdrawn themselves from the pursuit.

Two others, at no great distance off, held the following conversation.

"*Santissima*!" exclaimed one, looking up to the sky. "Did you ever see a moon so ridiculously clear? This Royalist Colonel, if hidden about here, cannot fail to see us."

"That would be unfortunate," rejoined the second. "If he should see us, he would be certain to make off."

"Ah! hum!" muttered the first speaker, "I'm not so sure about that: he's not one of the kind that cares about making off. Have you heard how he lifted Panchito Jolas out of his stirrups?"

"Yes; I have myself had some falls from a horse, but when I think of poor Jolas it makes my blood run cold. *Ave Maria*! did you not hear something?"

The two searchers stopped in their tracks, and stood listening: with far more fear in their hearts than could be in that of him for whom they were searching.

It was only a false alarm; but it had the effect of causing them to betray to one another the dread with which the fame of the Colonel had inspired them. The mask thus removed, mutual confidence became established between the two; and both were equally agreed upon the prudence of at once returning to the appointed rendezvous.

The other four pursuers continued to advance; but with such easy nonchalance that in two or three hours afterwards eight of the ten had returned to the glade, all equally unsuccessful in their search.

As to the two who were still missing the reason for their absence was simple enough. As soon as Suarez had parted from his somnolent companion, the thought occurred to him that since the latter, only a single man, was so careful of his life, he, being married, and with a family, had still greater reason for being careful of his. Having given his companion a proof of his courage, which had cost him nothing, he resolved to imitate the latter in another respect. After going a hundred paces farther, he also stretched himself along the grass, and entered into the land of dreams— perhaps dreaming of his wife; and how upon his bed of moss he was enjoying the good fortune of escaping from her ill temper. Before falling asleep he had promised himself to awake at an early hour, and after rousing his companion to abuse him for his cowardice.

Unfortunately for Suarez, he reckoned without his host, when supposing he could awake himself; and both he and his partner slept, until long after the other eight had reassembled at the rendezvous, and commenced deliberating upon a more earnest prosecution of the search.

The moon had already gone down, and the day was beginning to dawn. The grey light falling upon the group of insurgent horsemen—dressed in their half-military, half-peasant costumes, soiled and tattered by long campaigning—presented a tableau of the most picturesque character.

Around the glade, their horses, tied to the trees, were endeavouring to satisfy their hunger by gnawing at the leaves and twigs. Even this miserable pasture was scarce attainable, on account of the bits which the animals still had in their mouths, and which were heard constantly clanking between their teeth. The eight insurgents had seated themselves in the centre of the glade; and with their carbines resting across their knees, and their daggers sticking in their boot tops, were listening to the discourse of Pepe Lobos.

"Suarez and Pacheco will never return," continued Pepe, in answer to the conjectures of his comrades. "It is as good as certain that this Colonel of Beelzebub has settled the affair with both—just as he did with poor Panchito Jolas; and since we have searched all night without finding any trace—"

"We explored our route with the greatest care!" interrupted one of the beaters who had exhibited the greatest dread of encountering the Colonel.

"We have done the same," added Pepe Lobos. "Ask my partner there. Although his trace has escaped our observation, it is evident the Royalist is somewhere in this wood—else what has become of Suarez and Pacheco? Yes, he is in it yet, be assured; and my advice is that we go back to the place where he left the main road, and follow the track of his horse from there. That will be the more likely plan to bring us to the place where he is at this minute."

The other seven gave in their consent to this plan, and it was resolved that it should be carried into execution.

"As for the reward of five hundred dollars," continued Pepe Lobos, "that's all very well. But I say vengeance before everything; and we will do better to kill this fierce devil at once. A fig for the bounty, say I!"

"Perhaps the Captain will pay one half, if we bring him in dead?" suggested one of the insurgents.

"When we have ascertained exactly where he is hid," continued Pepe, without heeding the suggestion, "we can then separate into two parties of four each. One can approach from one side, and the other party in the opposite direction. We shall thus have him between us; and let whoever sets eye on him fire at him as at a mad dog. That is the only way to make sure; besides, if he should be only wounded and we can carry him to camp with a little life in him, we shall still be entitled to the reward."

The counsel of Pepe Lobos met with a universal approbation; and it was finally resolved that as soon as day had fairly broken, they should all return to the main road and recommence the search.

Just as the sun commenced gilding the lofty summits of the palm-trees, the eight guerilleros scattered themselves along the road to examine the hoof tracks, and if possible discover the point at which Don Rafael had turned off into the woods. This was by no means so easily accomplished: for the ground was now trodden by their own horses in such a fashion that it seemed impossible to distinguish which of the trails was that of the Royalist dragoon. A native of Europe would have examined them in vain; but to a vaquero of Mexico, a gaucho of Chili, or in fact a native peasant of any part of Spanish-America, it was simply a work of time and patience. In fact, scarce ten minutes had passed, before Pepe Lobos called to his comrades to announce that he had discovered the track they were in search of.

Besides the hoof-prints of a horse, a twig broken from the branch of a tree, and some fresh leaves of sassafras laurel lying upon the ground, showed clearly the place where Don Rafael had passed through the underwood.

After following his trail for some paces, all believed that the fugitive could not be far distant from the spot. The two parties were then formed: one to advance directly on the trail, the other to make a circuit and enter the thicket from the opposite direction.

While the latter was executing the movement agreed upon, the four men who composed it came suddenly upon the horsemen whom Arroyo had sent in pursuit of Juan de Zapote and the fugitive messenger. By their known watchword the two parties of insurgents recognised each other; and, after joining their forces, they agreed to separate again into three bodies, and thus advance towards the spot where it was conjectured Don Rafael might be hidden. Four parties were now closing in upon a common centre; and just in that centre stood the great cedrela in which Don Rafael had ensconced himself.

As all four were acting under a common understanding that the Royalist Colonel was to be shot down upon sight, it will be perceived that the position of Don Rafael was now one of imminent danger. The very least misfortune that seemed to menace him would be to have the opportunity to die sword in hand—fighting to the death: for this would be far preferable to falling into the hands of his pitiless foeman, the brigand Arroyo. With the Royalist Colonel it was in reality a moment of extreme peril.

Chapter Sixty
El Zapote and Gaspar

Just about the moment when Pepe Lobos and his comrades had made their dispositions for advancing into the thicket, Don Rafael awoke from his prolonged slumber. On first opening his eyes, the glare of the sunlight so dazzled them, that he inquired of himself where he was. Presently, however, objects appeared more distinctly; and he became aware of the extraordinary situation in which he had placed himself.

He had scarce time for a single reflection, when his attention was drawn to a rustling among the leaves at a short distance off; and, looking diagonally downward, he perceived two men on foot advancing towards the cedrela.

On first awaking, he had felt such an extreme lassitude throughout all his limbs, that he could scarce believe himself to have slept as long as he had done. The height of the sun, however, proclaimed that he had slumbered for many hours.

Notwithstanding the strong desire he had to descend from his uncomfortable couch, at the sight of the two men he prudently deferred his intention. He took the precaution, however, to untie the sash that bound him to the branches—doing this as gently as possible—while he kept his eyes fixed upon the new-comers, who, to say the least, presented a suspicious appearance.

The costume of both was odd enough, and altogether unsuited for traversing such a thorny jungle as that through which they were passing. It consisted merely of a shirt and cotton drawers—while each of them carried in hand a large parcel. Although the night had been dry throughout, the garments of both pedestrians appeared saturated with water!

Without the slightest suspicion that Don Rafael was in the tree, or that any other human being was near, the two men were nevertheless moving with cautious steps. Now they looked to the right, and then to the left, with quick earnest glances—as if they were either searching for something, or in dread that an enemy might be concealed in the bushes.

"These droll fellows," said the Colonel to himself, "are either searching for some one, or fear that some one is searching for them—which of the two?"

He watched them, listening attentively.

The same reason which had induced Don Rafael to select this part of the wood as a hiding-place—that is the impenetrability of the thicket that surrounded it—seemed to have influenced in like manner the two thinly-clad pedestrians.

"We had better stop here," said one to the other, as both came to a halt, "at least until we can put on our clothes again."

"Agreed," was the response; "but we must make our stay as short as possible: we should by this time have been far along the road to Huajapam."

Each at the same moment untied the parcel which he carried, and which consisted of his upper garments that had been kept dry. Then stripping off their wet shirts and drawers, they commenced dressing themselves in their proper habiliments.

"So, amigo!" said the first speaker, pointing to a small packet which the other had been carrying, "that, you tell me, is worth its weight in gold?"

"Yes; and you shall soon find that you have nothing to regret in helping me to escape, and sharing with me the douceur we shall receive on presenting it. If we are only lucky enough to get away from this neighbourhood—I have no doubt they will pursue us."

"We may be certain of that, *compadre*; but don't be uneasy about their finding us. If we should fall into the hands of any of those who are besieging Del Valle, trust me for getting clear of them. As they are my comrades, and don't know yet that I have run away, I shall be able to mislead them. I can tell them, that I have been sent along with you, to receive the ransom of one of our prisoners."

"What if they should carry us back to Arroyo's camp?"

"Why, in that case we shall both be hanged. What matters it, a little sooner or later—it is the common lot?" philosophically added Juan el Zapote—for it was he, in company with the messenger whom he had aided in making his escape. "Never mind, *compadrito*," he continued in a more cheering tone, "I shall do my best to get *you* clear of the scrape anyhow."

"*Santa Virgen!*" mentally ejaculated the Colonel. "This droll fellow, who thinks it is the lot of all men to be hanged sooner or later, appears to be so sure of the fact, that it would not expose him to much more risk to conduct me also to a safer harbour."

And in making this reflection, Don Rafael caught hold of the llianas by which he had climbed up; and at the risk of leaving some of his garments behind him, sprang out from between the branches, and dropped down between the two pedestrians with a suddenness that stupefied them.

The man who was to pay so dear for the precious packet sent him by Gertrudis, was now face to face with the messenger who bore it; and yet neither of them knew the other!

"Hush!" said the Colonel, taking the initiative, "you have nothing to fear. I promise you my protection; but first lay down your arms!"

Zapote had drawn his long dagger, and stood ready to use it against the first enemy who came near, with that indifference peculiar to one who believed in the rope or garotte as the necessary termination of his life. But Don Rafael had at the same instant caught hold of his arm, which he held with a grasp, that proved he could also become as terrible an antagonist as he might be a powerful protector.

"Who are you?" simultaneously inquired the two fugitives.

"Ah! it might be indiscreet in me to tell you that," replied Don Rafael. "I am a young man who has just sprung down from the tree above you, as you may see by my hat still sticking up there among the branches."

Without letting go his hold of Zapote the Colonel raised himself on his toes; and, stretching his arm upwards, proceeded to disengage the insurgent's hat from among the branches.

"So, amigos!" continued he as soon as he had recovered his hat. "You are fleeing from the guerilleros of Arroyo? Well—so am I: that is enough for you to know at present. You are two and I only one; but let me plainly tell you, that if you do not make common cause with me, I shall be under the necessity of killing you both. Now you may choose—Yes or no!"

"*Carrambo!*" exclaimed Zapote, not ill pleased with the frank, off-hand manner of the stranger, "what a capital trader you would make with your roundabout way of coming to terms! Well, cavallero! what can we do for you?"

"Pass me off with these fellows of Arroyo: as you are intending to do your comrade here. Say that I am charged with the ransom of a prisoner at the hacienda Del Valle, and thus obtain for me permission to pass the lines. If you do this, I promise you a recompense. And since you are both about to share the bounty of some one between you—"

"Only a little commission," interrupted Zapote; "and if you knew what it is—"

"Oh, I have no intention of claiming my third in the reward. I don't care to know what it is."

"But you shall know, for all that," replied Zapote, apparently carried away by an irresistible desire of giving his confidence. "Among friends—for we are so at present—there should be no concealment."

"Well, then, what is it?" inquired the Colonel.

"It is the will of a rich uncle in favour of a nephew who believed himself disinherited, and to whom we are now taking it. You may fancy whether we have just grounds for expecting a good perquisite."

"Are you sure that the will is not a false one?" inquired the Colonel, not without suspicions as to the veracity of Zapote.

"Neither of us knows how to read," replied the ex-guerillero, with an air of affected innocence.

"But take my word for it, cavallero," he hastily added, "we had better get out of this place as quickly as we can. We have already lost too much time."

"But my horse," objected the Colonel, "what's to be done with him?"

"Oh, you have a horse? Well, then, the best way is to leave him behind: he will only embarrass you."

"He would certainly do so," interrupted the messenger, "if he was like a horse I once knew. Ah, that was a devil of an animal! If you had only heard—"

The man was alluding to a horse he had once seen in the stables of his master, Don Mariano de Silva, and which was no other than Roncador himself. He was about to recount the peculiarities of this famous steed— which would no doubt have led to a recognition between himself and Don Rafael—when his speech was interrupted by voices heard in different directions, as if men were approaching the spot from different sides.

Both Don Rafael and the messenger interrogated with anxious regard the countenance of Zapote.

"*Carrambo!*" exclaimed the latter, "it may be more serious than I thought."

The voices had now broken forth into shouts and cries—as if uttered by men engaged in a chase; and the sounds expressed a sort of vengeful resolve—on the part of those who uttered them—not to show mercy or give quarter.

El Zapote looked for some moments with fixed gaze upon the royalist fugitive, who with the felt hat of an insurgent, the jacket of an infantry soldier, and the pantaloons of a dragoon officer, presented a somewhat motley appearance.

"You are a man who has just dropped down from a tree," said he. "I will not deny that fact; but if you are the only one about here, I should say there is a royalist in this wood, that these fellows are about to hunt to death."

"On my side I shall be frank with you," answered Don Rafael. "You have guessed rightly: I am in the King's cause."

"These shouts," continued Zapote, "the meaning of which I understand full well, denote that there is a royalist hidden in these woods, who is to be taken dead or alive. Have the men who are pursuing you ever seen you?"

"I killed two of their number yesterday evening. There were others who, no doubt, saw me."

"Then there is no hope of my being able to pass you off as an ordinary prisoner, like my companion here, who is neither royalist nor insurgent."

"It is very doubtful, to say the least," remarked Don Rafael, in a desponding tone.

"Altogether impossible; but I can promise you one thing, however: that we shall not betray you, should we fall in with these pursuers. Moreover, I shall endeavour to throw them off your scent: for I am beginning to tire of this brigand life of theirs. On one condition, how ever."

"Name it!" said the Colonel.

"That you will permit us to part company with you. I can do nothing to save you—you know it—while you may only ruin us, without any profit to yourself. On the other hand your fate has become in a manner linked with ours; and to abandon you in the midst of danger would be a baseness for which I could never pardon myself."

There was in the words of Zapote an accent of loyalty, which moved the Colonel to admiration, in spite of himself.

"Have no care for me," resolutely rejoined Don Rafael. "Go which way you please without me; and I hope," he added with a smile, "that you will reach that nephew you speak of, and safely deliver to him his uncle's will!"

"After all, *amigo*," he continued in a more serious tone, "I have but little reason to care for life more than yourself. A little sooner or a little later, what matters it? Only," added he, smiling, "I should not exactly fancy to be hanged."

"Thanks for your permission that we should part from you," said Zapote; "but, Señor Cavallero, a word before you go. If you take my advice, you will climb back into that tree where no one will suspect your presence."

"No," interrupted Don Rafael. "Up there I should be as a jaguar pursued by hounds—without the power to defend myself; and I am like the Indians, I wish, on entering the other world, to send as many enemies before me as possible."

"Well, then, do better still—make towards the river; keep due south from this place; and, on reaching the banks of the Ostuta, you will see a vast thicket of bamboos—in which my comrade and myself have just found a refuge, and where we might have remained safe from enemies till the day of judgment, had we not to go forward upon our errand. If you can only succeed in reaching the bamboos, you are saved."

Saying this El Zapote, followed by his companion, turned his face northward, and striking off into the thicket but were soon lost to Don Rafael's sight.

Chapter Sixty One
The Fugitives in Danger

El Zapote and his confrère, the messenger, after making a wide détour through the forest, came out on the Huajapam road. Their intention was to journey on to Huajapam—where they supposed the royalist army still held the place in siege, and where they expected to find Colonel Tres-Villas, to whom the messenger had been sent. Little did either the ex-guerillero or his companion suspect that it was the colonel himself from whom they had just parted.

"By my faith!" remarked the messenger, as they journeyed along, "it's a pity now that we did not ask that gentleman his name. It is likely enough that he is some grand officer belonging to the royalist army."

"Bah!" replied Zapote. "What good would it be to us to know his name? He's a lost man, I fear. It matters little, therefore, what name he carries."

"*Quien sabe?*" doubtingly rejoined the messenger.

"I am more vexed," continued Zapote, "that we were not able to do anything for him. It can't be helped, however; and just now, let me tell you, my brave Gaspar, that we have got to look out for ourselves. We are yet far from being out of danger."

The two men pursued their route, gliding silently and cautiously under the shadow of the underwood.

Scarce ten minutes had elapsed when they again heard the voices of those who were beating the wood in search of the hiding-place of Don Rafael. Both stepped behind a screen of bushes and listened. In the midst of a profound silence, they heard the crackling of branches; and the moment after a man appeared at a short distance from where they stood. He was advancing with stealthy step, carbine in hand, and almost at the same instant two others made their appearance, coming up behind him, and moving forward with like caution.

All three were stealthily gliding from tree to tree—making a temporary rampart of the trunks, as they reconnoitred the ground before them.

One of these men was recognised by Zapote as an old comrade.

"Eh, Perico!" cried he, speaking loud enough to be heard by the men.

"Hola! Who calls me?" responded Periço.

"I—Juan el Zapote."

"Zapote! how is it that you are here? Where did you come from?"

"From the camp," replied Zapote, with wondrous impudence. "Our Captain has sent—"

"Oh! the Captain knows, then, that we are in pursuit of a royalist who has taken shelter in the *chapparal*? We have had a time of it after him, and he's not found yet. We have scoured the thicket all the night in search of his hiding-place; and, out of ten of us who came after him, eight only remain. Two, Suarez and Pacheco, he has killed somewhere; but if I may judge by the signal cries to which we have responded, there should be at least twenty of our comrades at present looking after him."

At this moment another man joined company with the three already on the ground. Fortunately for Juan el Zapote and the messenger, these four were precisely the same whom Pepe Lobos had ordered to go round by the Huajapam road, and as they had not yet been in communication with the party from the camp, they were ignorant of the fact that their old comrade, Zapote, was himself being pursued as a deserter. "Well," continued Zapote, "as I was saying, our Captain has sent me on an errand with my companion, Gaspar, here; and we are in the greatest haste."

"What errand?" demanded Perico.

"*Carrambo*! A secret mission; one that I daren't disclose to you. *Adios, amigo*! I am in a terrible hurry."

"Before you go," cried one of the men, "tell us if you saw anybody?"

"Saw anybody? Who? The royalist you are in search of?"

"Yes; the mad Colonel."

"No; I met no mad colonel," said Zapote, turning away.

"Eh! *hombre*?" exclaimed Perico, with a significant glance; "make it appear you are ignorant that it is the Colonel Tres-Villas we are pursuing? You know that well enough. You wish to capture him alone, and get the five hundred dollars to yourself?"

"Colonel Tres-Villas?" cried Zapote and the messenger in the same breath.

"Five hundred dollars reward!" exclaimed Zapote the instant after, raising his hand to his head, as if about to pluck out a fistful of his hair.

"Certainly, that same; a grand gentleman, with black moustachios, a felt hat of the same colour, a soldier's infantry jacket, and gold-laced cavalry pantaloons."

"And he has killed two of our people?"

"Four. Since Suarez and Pacheco have not returned, we may also reckon them as dead men."

Zapote no longer doubted that the man from whom they had just parted was he to whom they were bearing the message of Gertrudis de Silva, in other words, the Colonel Tres-Villas. He exchanged a significant glance with the messenger.

For a moment the new resolution of honesty made by the ex-bandit wavered upon its foundation, still but weakly laid; but the mute appealing glance of Gaspar, and the remembrance of the promise of fidelity he had just made, conquered the instinct of cupidity that had momentarily been aroused within him.

"Well—we have neither met nor seen any one," he remarked drily; "but we are losing our time. *Adios!*"

"*Vete con Dios!*" (God be with you), responded Perico.

Zapote and Gaspar, saluting the others, walked away—going at a moderate pace so long as they were in sight of the insurgents; but as soon as they were behind the bushes advancing with all the speed in their power.

Their object now was to put themselves as distant as possible from the danger; since their projected journey to Huajapam was no more to be thought of. When they had got to such a distance as not any longer to fear pursuit, Zapote flung himself down upon the grass with an air of profound disappointment.

"What are we to do now?" inquired Gaspar, in a lugubrious tone.

Zapote, overcome by his emotions, made no reply. About a minute after, however, he sprang suddenly to his feet, as if some interesting idea had occurred to him.

"A grand idea!" he exclaimed, "a superb idea!"

"Ah! What is it?"

"Listen, *camarado!* I am known to those who are laying siege to the hacienda Del Valle: you are known to those who defend it. Well, we shall thus be able to get in. Once inside, you can pass me off for one of the servants of your master, Don Mariano de Silva."

"That might be possible, my dear Zapote," naïvely answered Gaspar, "if it were not for your devil of a physiognomy."

"Never mind that. I shall alter it to suit the occasion. You shall see. All I ask is, that if I extricate the Colonel from his present dilemma, I am to have a reward of a thousand dollars. I risk my life for it; and the sum would be only a fair one. I shall take fifty men, and deliver him from danger. As to your message, he will pay for that separately, and you may have all the bounty to yourself."

"It would be a great stroke of business, if we could so manage it," assented Gaspar.

"You see, after all," philosophically remarked the ex-bandit, "that honesty is the best policy."

"But suppose the Colonel should be taken prisoner, or killed?" suggested Gaspar.

"We must take the chance of that. If he be, we shall endeavour to capture Arroyo. In either case, I ought to have a reward; and, cost what it will, I mean to try for one."

"It is possible," again suggested Gaspar, "the Colonel may be able to reach the bamboo brake on the river bank. If so, we might still be in time to save him."

"In less than two hours we can get back here with the men to rescue him. They can easily make a sortie from Del Valle, now that nearly all the others are scouring the forest. Quick, then, let us make for the hacienda."

Excited by the hope of being able to accomplish their design, the two adventurers started off, gliding through the thicket as rapidly as they could make their way in the direction of the hacienda Del Valle.

Chapter Sixty Two
Escaping the Toils

Left to himself, Don Rafael calmly considered the circumstances that surrounded him. He could not help feeling a conviction that his chances of escape were of the most doubtful kind; and that, unless some unforeseen accident should favour him, he had but a very poor prospect of being able to extricate himself from the danger that threatened. Such an accident he had no reason to expect.

The sun was now high in the heavens, and his bright beams penetrating through the foliage, illuminated even the darkest labyrinths of the forest. It would be eight or nine hours before he would set again; for it was near the summer solstice, when the days of the year are longest. Don Rafael now regretted having slept so long. Had he awoke before sunrise, there might still have been time to have secured his retreat. He further regretted not having declared his name and rank to the two men who had just parted from him. It was possible that, by the offer of a large recompense, he might have induced them to attempt making an entrance into the hacienda Del Valle, and warning Lieutenant Veraegui of his perilous situation.

He was far from suspecting at that moment, that a providential chance was about doing for him the very thing which his reflection had now too late suggested he should have done before.

Notwithstanding the danger in which he was placed, Don Rafael, who had not eaten for many long hours, began to feel hungered. This, however, gave him but little concern; since in the tropical forests of Mexico, the anona, the corosollo, the aguacate, and other fruit-bearing trees, yield spontaneously their delicious produce, sufficient for the sustenance of human life.

These reflections once made, Don Rafael was not the man to waste time in vain regrets. He resolved to act at once.

He hesitated only an instant, to reflect upon what he should do with his horse. At first he thought of abandoning him; but then it occurred to him, that while passing along his tortuous track through the chapparal, the animal might prove useful. He might serve as a sort of moveable rampart, behind which he could shelter himself from the bullets of the carbines, that might be fired by his assailants. Moreover, should he succeed in getting clear of the thicket, by flinging himself in the saddle he would still have a chance of escape, through the superior swiftness of Roncador. For this reason he decided upon going in search of the horse.

The thicket in which he had hidden him was at no great distance from the cedrela; and finding his own traces, Don Rafael returned on them with stealthy tread. The silence that reigned throughout the forest was for the moment profound; and he knew that the slightest sound, even the snapping of a stick, might betray his presence to some lurking foe.

He had advanced only a few paces, when a vague clamour of voices reached his ear. He listened for some seconds; but as the voices did not appear to come any nearer, he again moved forward.

At length he succeeded in reaching the thicket, where Roncador had been left. The poor animal, though devoured by thirst—and suffering from hunger as well—had made no effort to free himself from his fastenings. He was still standing by the tree, to which Don Rafael had attached him. At the approach of his master he uttered a joyous neigh.

Notwithstanding the fear which Don Rafael had that the noise might be heard by his pursuers, he could not help feeling a joyful emotion at being thus saluted by his old companion in many a scene of peril; and, while caressing the horse, he felt a certain remorse at the *rôle* he had just designed him to play. It was, however, one of those crises, when the instinct of self-preservation is at variance with the desire of the heart.

Leading his steed by the bridle, Don Rafael advanced as rapidly as was possible through the labyrinth of bushes and climbing plants that thickly covered the ground. The sun occasionally coming in view, enabled him to guide his course towards the south—the direction which Zapote had counselled him to take.

The advice given by the latter seemed to Don Rafael worth following. If he could only pass through the line of those seeking for him, and reach the cane-brake on the Ostuta, he might there conceal himself until after sunset. By night he might again attempt to enter the hacienda, and with a better chance of success; since he was now aware of its being surrounded by the insurgent guerilleros.

In order to give him more freedom in his movements, he cast away his sword-belt and scabbard; and with the bare blade in one hand, and his bridle-rein in the other, he continued to advance as silently as possible. He had determined to make use of his pistols—only as a last resource.

It was not long, however, before he was forced out of his direct course—not by the thickness of the jungle, but on hearing in front of him the voices of several men. These calling to one another, appeared to be directing a movement among themselves, as if advancing towards him in an extended deployment.

Singly, each of those who were approaching would have caused Don Rafael no more uneasiness than does the solitary hunter the lion who reluctantly retreats before him; but it was evident from the number of voices that a large party of men were in the wood; and should they all fall upon him simultaneously, there would be no alternative but to succumb. He therefore renounced the desperate idea that for a moment had occurred to him: of rushing upon the nearest, and putting an end to him without noise.

He perceived, at the same time, that, in the midst of the dense chapparal where he then was, a resolute man would have a decided advantage over enemies who were so scattered, and who were constantly warning him of their whereabouts as they advanced; while he, keeping silence, left them ignorant of his own.

The men were evidently getting nearer, and Don Rafael heard their voices with anxiety. He listened also to hear if any others replied to them in the opposite direction; since in that case he would be in danger of being surrounded. He knew not the number of his enemies; but he could tell by the sounds that their cordon had not yet been completely drawn around him, and there might still be a chance of escaping from it.

While thus listening, with all the eagerness of a man whose life was depending on the acuteness of his hearing, a noise reached him, which he knew was not made by a human being. It was the distant and sonorous tapping of a woodpecker upon the trunk of a dead tree—a sound often heard in the depths of an American forest. The sound fell upon his ear like the voice of a friend. It seemed to say that, in the direction whence it proceeded, no human creature would be found to trouble the solitude of the forest.

The hint was sufficient for one skilled in wood-lore, as Don Rafael was. Without a moment's hesitation, he faced in the direction of the sound, and commenced advancing towards it—guided by the measured strokes given by the beak of the bird.

He was still at some distance from the dead-wood, where the woodpecker was employed seeking its food, when the bird, perceiving him, flew off amidst the trees.

Don Rafael now halted, and once more bent his ear to listen. To his joy he perceived that the voices of the searchers had receded to a distance. This proved that he had passed out of their way; and, if they should not find reason to return on their tracks, his chances of escape were becoming more favourable.

To make more sure of not being followed, he adopted a ruse, which he had learnt during his Indian campaigns. Taking up two dry sticks of guiacuni wood, he struck one against the other, thus producing a sound that resembled the tapping of the woodpecker's beak; and, after repeating this for a number of times, he returned by a détour to the same direction from which he had been forced on hearing the voices.

After a half-hour's advance through the thicket, he halted to refresh himself by eating some fruits of the pawpaw that grew by the path. Their juicy pulp served for a moment to satisfy the craving of both appetites — relieving at the same time both hunger and thirst.

Mid-day had already passed, and the sun was beginning to fling his rays obliquely through the branches, when Don Rafael resumed his route; and shortly after, through the last straggling trees of the forest, he perceived the crystal current of the Ostuta running its tranquil course between banks thickly covered with tall bamboos.

The breeze blowing freely over the water stirred the long lance-like leaves of the gigantic canes; among whose moveable stems the caimans had sought protection from the hot sun, and were awaiting the freshness of the night to return to the channel of the river. Here, too, like them, was Don Rafael to find an asylum that would shelter him till sunset.

He was not long in choosing a place of concealment. The selvage of the forest through which he had come, extended to within a few paces of the bamboo brake; and, crossing the intervening space as rapidly as possible, the fugitive plunged in among the canes.

Once hidden by the gigantic reeds, he felt more secure; and had now an opportunity to reconnoitre to some extent a portion of the surrounding neighbourhood. From certain large rocks, which he saw lying in the mid-channel of the stream, he recognised the place, and knew that he was not far distant from the ford of the Ostuta — where, two years before, the pursuit of Arroyo and his brigands had more than once conducted him. He saw, moreover, on the opposite side of the stream, the rude tent of the guerillero chief, and the horsemen of his band galloping up and down the bank. The sight aroused all his fiery passions, and he could not restrain himself from raising his clenched hand, and stretching his arm in menace across the water.

All at once he heard shouts behind him, and the trampling of horses. These sounds were caused by the party sent in pursuit of him by Arroyo, and who were now returning to the camp. It need not be said that they had been unsuccessful, as they brought back with them, instead of the Colonel and the two runaways, only Suarez and Pacheco, still alive and well, but terribly frightened.

For better security, Don Rafael advanced still further among the bamboos, carefully parting them with his hands as he moved forward; and the horsemen, though they rode past along the bank, only a short distance from where he was concealed, had not the slightest suspicion their enemy was so near. The most sharp-sighted eye could not have discovered his place of concealment.

Still continuing to listen, he heard the plashing of the horses as they forded the crossing; and a few minutes after a profound silence reigned over the scene.

Chapter Sixty Three
An Unwilling Ambassador

On the afternoon of that same day—a little after the time when Don Rafael buried himself among the bamboos—the ex-student of theology, accompanied by Costal and Clara, was riding along the Huajapam road, at no great distance from the ford of the Ostuta. When near to this famous crossing, the three halted; and while their horses were picking up a little grass, Costal kept on a little further afoot—for the purpose of reconnoitring the ground upon the banks of the river.

Meanwhile Clara busied himself in roasting, over a fire he had kindled, some green ears of maize corn, which, with a few pieces of dried beef (*cecina*), were to constitute the dinner of the party. Clara had taken the materials from his *alforjas*.

After an interval of silence, the Captain commenced a conversation with the object of making to the negro a communication evidently deemed by him of some importance.

"Listen to me, Clara!" said he; "we are entrusted with a commission which I need not tell you will require us to act with the greatest circumspection. I need not tell you that our carrying to this Captain Arroyo the threats of the General is a sufficiently dangerous errand. No more need I assure you that to enter the town of Oajaca is of a similar character. There the Royalists think no more of the head of an insurgent, than you of one of those ears of corn that you are roasting in the fire. What I wish of you, then, is—that you will drop the bad habit you have of calling me by the name of Lantejas; which, up to the present time, has brought me nothing but ill fortune. It was under that name I was proscribed; and I beg of you, therefore, that, for the future, both you and Costal will know me only by the name of *Don Lucas Alacuesta*. This last is the name of my mother's family, and it will serve my purpose as well as any other."

"Enough said, Captain," rejoined the negro; "I shall not forget to obey your orders—even though I should have the axe of the executioner raised over my neck."

"I am satisfied you will not. Meanwhile, until Costal returns, you may serve me with some of those morsels you are roasting, which seem to be done enough. I am dying of hunger."

"And I too," added the negro, casting a greedy glance towards the *cecina*.

Clara spread out before the Captain his saddle-cloth to serve as a napkin; and, taking some pieces of the broiled meat from the coals, placed them upon it. To this he added two or three of the roasted ears. Then, seating himself close to the fire, he drew from the ashes the remaining portions of meat, and commenced eating with an earnestness that was likely to prove fatal to Costal's share in the banquet.

"Ho!" cried the Captain, "if you continue on in that fashion, your comrade Costal will be likely to go without his dinner."

"Costal will not eat before to-morrow," replied the negro in a grave tone.

"That I can easily believe," assented Don Cornelio. "There will be nothing left for him to eat, I fancy."

"You misunderstand me, Señor Captain. To-day is the third after midsummer, and to-night the moon will be at the full. That is why Costal will not eat, in order that by fasting he may prepare himself to hold communion with his gods."

"You fool! Do you believe in the wretched fables of the pagan Costal?"

"I have reason to believe them," gravely replied the negro. "The God of the Christians dwells in the sky; those of Costal inhabit the Lake of Ostuta, Tlaloc, the god of the mountains, lives on the summit of Monopostiac; and Matlacuezc his wife, the goddess of the water, bathes herself in the waters of the lake that surround the enchanted mountain. The third night after the summer solstice—at the full of the moon—is the time when they show themselves to the descendants of the caciques of Tehuantepec—to such as have passed their fiftieth year—and Costal intends to invoke them this very night."

As Don Cornelio was about endeavouring to bring the negro to a more rational religious belief, Costal strode silently up.

"Well," said the Captain, "is our information correct? Have you learnt whether Arroyo is really encamped on the banks of the Ostuta?"

"Quite true," answered the Indian, "a *peon* of my acquaintance, whom I chanced to meet, has told me that Arroyo and Bocardo are by the ford, where they intercept the passage of all who come this way. It is close by, so that this evening you can deliver your message. After that is done, I would ask leave of absence for Clara and myself for the night. We wish to spend it on the shore of the Sacred Lake."

"Hum!" muttered Don Cornelio, without noticing the request. "So near!" continued he, speaking to himself, and abruptly ceasing to eat. "What else did your *peon* acquaintance make known about Arroyo and Bocardo?"

"Only that they are more thirsty than ever—the one for blood, the other for plunder."

Costal imparted this information in a tone but little calculated to inspire the Captain with a relish for his mission.

He endeavoured to conceal his uneasiness, however; and, raising his voice to a tone of assumed boldness, he inquired:—

"It is to the ford of the Ostuta, then, we are to go?"

"Yes, Señor Captain, whenever it pleases your honour to move forward."

"We have plenty of time," replied Don Cornelio, evidently reluctant to make any further advance. "I wish to take a few hours of rest before going thither. And your old master, Don Mariano de Silva—did you hear anything of him?"

"Yes. He has long ago left the hacienda Las Palmas, and is living in Oajaca. As to that of Del Valle, it is still occupied by the Royalist garrison."

"So then we have enemies on all sides of us?" rejoined the Captain.

"Arroyo and Bocardo," said Costal, "should scarcely be enemies to an officer bearing despatches from the General Morelos. As for Clara and myself, we are that sort whom these bandits never frighten."

"I agree with you there," rejoined the Captain, "certainly I do— meanwhile—nevertheless—I should prefer—ah! who is that horseman who is galloping in this direction, carbine in hand?"

"If one may judge the master by the servant, and if this fellow chances to have a master, that master ought to be one of the greatest rogues on earth."

As Costal was delivering this figurative speech, he stretched forth his hand and seized hold of his own old and trusty piece.

The horseman in question was no other than Gaspacho—the courier who had brought to Arroyo the evil news from the hacienda Del Valle.

He rode forward as one rides in a conquered country; and without making any obeisance addressed himself to the Captain—who, from being a white, appeared to him the most considerable of the three strangers.

"Tell me, friend—" said he.

"Friend!" cried Costal, interrupting him, and evidently ill pleased with his looks, "a captain in the army of General Morelos is no friend to such as you."

"What does this brute of an Indian say?" demanded Gaspacho, regarding Costal with an air of contempt.

The eyes of Costal fairly blazed with rage; and his movements promised for Gaspacho a terrible chastisement, when Don Cornelio interposed to prevent it. "What is your wish?" asked he of the follower of Arroyo.

"To know if you have seen anything of that rascal, Juan de Zapote, and his worthy companion, Gaspar?"

"We have seen neither Zapote nor Gaspar."

"If they're not found, then, my friend Perico—who met and permitted them to pass him—is likely to spend a most uncomfortable quarter of an hour—when he appears in the presence of our Captain Arroyo."

"Ah! you are in Arroyo's service then?"

"I have the honour."

"Perhaps you can tell me where I shall be most likely to find him?"

"*Quien sabe*? By the ford of the Ostuta you may find him—if he's not gone elsewhere—to the hacienda of San Carlos, for example."

"This hacienda does not belong to the royalists then?" inquired the Captain.

"Perhaps I may be mistaken," ironically answered Gaspacho. "In any case, if you wish to see the Captain—which rather astonishes me— you will have to cross the ford all the same; and there you may hear of his whereabouts. My faith! that is a splendid cloak you have got on your shoulders. It appears a mile too big for you; and looks as if it would just fit a man of my dimensions."

On saying these words, the bandit put spurs to his horse and galloped off—leaving Don Cornelio with an unpleasant impression upon his mind, caused by his ambiguous speeches and the admiration the stranger had expressed for his cloak.

"I fear we have fallen among wicked people here," said he, addressing himself to Costal. "You see how little this ragged fellow makes of an officer of Morelos; and doubtless his master will make still less. Well—we must be prudent, and wait until night before we attempt to go forward among them."

"Prudence is not always a bad substitute for courage," remarked Costal, with a shrug. "We shall do as you desire, Señor Captain; and I shall be careful we do not fall either into the hands of the loyalists, or those of the followers of Arroyo, before arriving in the presence of that gentleman himself. Otherwise, I might lose the one peculiar day of my life, that I have so long looked forward to. Trust to me. I think you can say that I never let you remain long in a dangerous situation?"

"You are my providence," cried the Captain, with friendly warmth. "It is true; and it will always give me pleasure to acknowledge it."

"No, no," interrupted Costal, "what I may have done for you is not worth talking about. Meanwhile, we will act wisely to take a wink of sleep— Clara and myself more especially: since, during all this night, we shan't have another opportunity to close our eyes."

"You are right—I perfectly agree with you. Let us all have some sleep then."

As the sun was still hot, Clara and Costal stretched themselves under the shadow of a spreading tree, and both, with that indifference to danger to which a life of adventures had habituated them, were soon buried in profound slumber; during which the negro was constantly endeavouring, in dreams, to capture the Siren with dishevelled hair, and force her to reveal to him some rich *placer* of gold.

As for Don Cornelio, he lay for a long time awake: anxious and apprehensive about the result of his approaching interview with the guerilla chief. At length, imitating the example of his two *compagnons de voyage*, he also fell asleep.

Chapter Sixty Four
The Talisman Transmitted

It was only after a long and desperate effort to subdue the passion with which Don Rafael Tres-Villas had inspired her, that Gertrudis de Silva resolved upon making use of the talisman she had so carefully preserved—that message, which Don Rafael had sworn to obey without a moment's hesitation—even though it should reach him on the instant when his hand was raised to strike down his most mortal enemy.

When the young girl at length reluctantly yielded to the determination of once more seeing Don Rafael, her first emotion was one of profound pleasure. She could not convince herself of the fact, that her former lover could now be indifferent, or that from his mouth she should hear the avowal that he no longer loved her. She believed that the message would convey to him a happiness similar to that she herself felt in sending it; and it was for this reason, and also the better to secure his fidelity and zeal, that she had led the messenger to expect a magnificent reward, on the accomplishment of his errand. Under the critical circumstances in which the messenger found himself, after setting out from Oajaca, it was well that such a golden lure glistened before his mental vision—else the precious talisman might have stood less chance of arriving at its destination.

On the departure of the messenger, Gertrudis felt as if inspired with new life; but this joyful state was but of short duration. Doubt soon took the place of certainty. Between herself and her lover more than one misunderstanding had arisen, all the result of imperious circumstances. She was no longer loved—this was her reflection. The distant proof she had for a while believed in—the affair of Aguas Calientes—was perhaps only a wild freak on the part of the Colonel; and if he no longer loved her, it was because he loved another.

Moreover, her messenger would have to traverse a country disturbed by civil war, and there was every chance of his failing to accomplish his mission. This doubt also added to the torture she was undergoing.

Overcome by such sad thoughts, and at times devoured by black and bitter jealousy, her heart was lacerated to the extreme of endurance. Her cheek had paled to the hue of the lily; while the purple circle round her eyes told of the mental agony the young Creole was enduring.

In this condition was she when Don Mariano set out on the journey from Oajaca—only three days after the departure of the messenger Gaspar.

The fond father beheld with apprehension the extreme melancholy that had taken possession of his daughter; and, convinced of the inutility of the efforts he had already made to cure her of her passion for Don Rafael—by representing the latter as unworthy of her—he had altogether changed his tactics in that regard. He now endeavoured to extenuate the faults of the Colonel; and, in the place of an accuser, became his benevolent champion.

"The nobility and frankness of his character," Don Mariano would say, "is enough to set aside all suspicion of his perfidy. His silence may be explained by the events through which he has been involuntarily borne, and by the political relationships that surround him."

Gertrudis smiled sadly at the words of her father, but her heart was not the less torn with grief.

In this unpleasant state of mind they passed three days, while journeying from Oajaca to the borders of the lake Ostuta. On the route they had met with no particular adventures nor encountered any obstacle; though from rumours that reached them from time to time—of the sanguinary deeds perpetrated by the ferocious Arroyo—they could not help experiencing a certain amount of apprehension.

It was on the third evening of the journey that they reached the Ostuta river and had halted upon its banks at the spot already described. During the night Don Mariano, rendered uneasy by hearing certain confused noises in the adjoining forest, had despatched one of the trustiest of his servants in the direction of the crossing, with directions to reconnoitre the place.

Two hours afterwards the domestic returned, with the report, that, near the ford he had seen numerous fires blazing along the bank of the river and on both sides of the ford. These could be no other than the fires of Arroyo's camp: since they had heard several times along their route, that the brigand was encamped at the crossing of the Ostuta.

The servant added, that in returning from his reconnaissance he was under the belief that some one had followed him, as dogging his steps through the forest. It was for this reason that Don Mariano had caused the fires of his bivouac to be extinguished, and had so suddenly taken his departure from the place.

By going some distance down the river, and making the circuit of the lake into which it flowed, the servant of Don Mariano believed he could find a crossing, by which they might reach the hacienda of San Carlos on a different road. Although this détour would make their journey nearly one day longer, it would still be preferable to falling into the company of Arroyo and his brigands.

Among all the places in America, sacred to the worship of the native races, perhaps none enjoys a greater celebrity than the lake of Ostuta, and the mountain which rises up out of the bosom of its waters.

The mountain is called Monopostiac, or the *Cerro encantado* (enchanted hill). It has long been the locale of Indian tradition; and the singularly lugubrious aspect of the lake and its surrounding scenery would seem to justify the legendary stories of which it has been made the scene. It was to the borders of this lake, that the necessity of seeking his own and his daughter's safety, was now conducting Don Mariano de Silva.

The journey proved long and arduous. The feebleness of Gertrudis would not permit her to travel fast, even in her easy *litera*; and the bad state of the roads, which would scarce admit the passage of the mules, contributed to retard their advance.

It was near midnight before they came within sight of the lake,—its sombre waters suddenly appearing through an opening in the trees. At the point where they approached, it was bordered by a thick forest, whose dark shadowy foliage promised them an impenetrable asylum where they might pass the night safe from discovery or pursuit.

In this forest Don Mariano resolved to make halt, and wait until the light of day might enable him to discover the crossing, by which, as his servant had assured him, they might reach the by-road leading to the hacienda of San Carlos.

Chapter Sixty Five
Lantejas Beheaded

The short interval of bluish light between daybreak and sunrise in the tropics was nearly over, when Captain Lantejas and his two trusty followers climbed into their saddles to proceed towards the ford of the Ostuta. A difficulty yet lay in the way of their reaching it: since before gaining the river it would be necessary for them to pass within sight of the hacienda Del Valle, and they might be seen, as they supposed, by the sentinels of the royalist garrison. As yet the three travellers were ignorant that the place was blockaded by the guerilla of Arroyo.

"If we were to pass it by night," said Costal, "it would look more suspicious. Better to go in full daylight. Clara can ride ahead of us. If any one stops him, he can ask permission for a merchant and his servants who are travelling southward. If, on the other hand, he sees no one, he may ride on; and we can follow him without further ceremony."

The advice was to the liking of the Captain; and they accordingly commenced advancing along the road that would conduct them past the hacienda.

In about a quarter of an hour they arrived in front of it, near the end of the long avenue already mentioned. Costal and Don Cornelio halted at some distance behind while Clara rode forward; and, to make sure that no one was there, even entered the avenue itself.

Not a human being could be seen. The place appeared deserted—all was silent as upon that night when Don Rafael rode up to the house to find only desolation and death.

Still further to guard against surprise, Clara rode on up the avenue; but he had scarce gone a hundred paces from the main road when a soldier appeared behind the parapet of the hacienda, evidently watching his approach.

The black seeing that he was discovered kept on straight for the building.

The distance hindered Don Cornelio and Costal from distinguishing the words that passed between Clara and the sentry; but they could see that the latter was pointing out something to the black which was to them invisible. Whatever the object was, it appeared to excite the risible faculties of the negro: for, distant as he was, they could distinctly hear him laughing.

Meanwhile the sentinel disappeared, and as Clara continued to indulge in his hilarity, it was evident he had obtained the permission asked for. At all events, Don Cornelio and Costal regarded his behaviour as a good omen.

Nevertheless he seemed to hesitate about returning to the road; and instead of doing so, the moment after, he made signs to Don Cornelio and Costal to advance up the avenue.

Both instantly obeyed the invitation; and when they had arrived near the walls, Clara, still shaking his sides with laughter, pointed out to them the object which had given origin to his mirth.

On beholding it, Don Cornelio believed that his eyes were deceiving him. In truth the spectacle, to which he was thus introduced, had very little in it to justify the merriment of the black. In place of the heads of wolves and other noxious animals, which may often be seen nailed up against the walls of country houses, here there were three human heads! They were not yet desiccated, but appeared as if freshly cut off from the bodies to which they belonged.

"Wretched man!" cried Don Cornelio, addressing himself to Clara, "what is there in such a sight to excite your gaiety?"

"*Carrambo!*" exclaimed the negro, answering to the reproach by a fresh burst of laughter,—then, in a whisper, he continued, pointing to one of the heads—

"Señor Captain, don't you see? One of the heads is yours!"

"Mine?" muttered the ex-student, suddenly turning pale, though, as he felt his head still upon his shoulders, he believed that the negro was only mocking him.

"So the sentry has just told me," affirmed Clara, "but, Señor Captain, you who know how to read may satisfy yourself."

As the negro spoke he pointed to an inscription, that appeared over one of the heads. Don Cornelio, despite the gloomy shadow which the tall cypresses cast over the wall, was able to read the inscription: "*Esta es la cabeza del insurgente Lantejas.*" (This is the head of the insurgent Lantejas.)

It was in reality the head of an insurgent of the same name as Don Cornelio himself—one of Arroyo's followers, who, as already known, by the report of Gaspacho, had been captured during a sortie of the besieged.

Don Cornelio turned his eyes away from the hideous spectacle presented by the head of his namesake; and anathematising once more the unfortunate name which he had inherited from his father, made all haste to ride off from the spot.

In proportion as the distance between him and the hacienda increased, his terror became diminished, and at length ended in a melancholy smile at the odd coincidence of the encounter with his beheaded homonyme.

But the profound silence that surrounded him as he journeyed along, and the knowledge that in a few minutes he would find himself face to face with the redoubtable guerillero, once more imbued the mind of the Captain with the darkest presentiments.

Without permitting his companions to suspect the sentiments that were troubling him, he would willingly have proposed deferring for another day his interview with the bandit chief. Both Costal and Clara, however, as they rode along by his side, presented an appearance of such stoical indifference to danger, that he felt ashamed of showing himself less brave than they; and, thus restrained, he continued to travel on in silence.

Shortly after, they came in sight of the river, and at the same time could command a view of the banks on both side of the ford. Don Cornelio became reassured at the sight. Neither horse, horseman, nor tent, was to be seen. Noisy and bustling as the place had been in the morning, it was now in the evening completely silent and deserted. Not a trace remained of the encampment of Arroyo—save the smouldering bivouac fires, and the débris of various articles that lay scattered over the ground.

"If I know," said Costal to the Captain, "how to pick the truth from the lies which that scurvy fellow has told us—he who took such a marvellous fancy to your cloak—I should say we are on the road that will guide us to the man you are in search of. He is at this moment, I venture to say, at the hacienda San Carlos—notwithstanding that the droll humbug appeared to make such a mystery of his whereabouts."

"But suppose the hacienda San Carlos to be occupied by a Spanish garrison?" suggested the Captain.

"Let us first cross the river," said Costal, "you can remain upon the other side with Clara, while I go forward and make a reconnaissance."

This proposition was agreed to by Don Cornelio; and the three travellers having forded the stream, Costal prepared to separate from them.

"Be cautious, good Costal," said Lantejas, "there is danger on every side of us."

"For me and Clara," remarked the Indian, with an ironical smile; "one who has already lost his head should have nothing more to fear, Señor Captain!"

Saying this, Costal went off at a trot, leaving the Captain and Clara on the bank of the river.

The Indian had scarce passed out of sight, when a plunging in the water announced that horses were crossing the ford. Looking around, Don Cornelio beheld two horsemen riding out on the bank where he and Clara had halted. One of them carried behind him a pair of canvas alforjas, which appeared to have some large roundish objects inside. Merely exchanging a brief salute, the horsemen were passing on; when the Captain, in hopes of obtaining some information from them, inquired if the hacienda of San Carlos was far distant.

"No," replied one, "only about a quarter of a league."

"Are we likely to be well received there?" further asked Don Cornelio.

"Ah!" replied the second horseman, "that depends—"

The muttered voice, and the distance which he had already gained, hindered Don Cornelio from perceiving the tone of irony in which he spoke; but almost at the same instant the speaker elevated his voice to a high pitch, though only the last words were heard with distinctness.

These were, "*Mejico e independencia.*"

The phrase was well-known to Don Cornelio.

"What word came before it?" inquired he of his companion; "*viva*, was it not?"

"No, it was *muera*," replied the negro.

"You are mistaken, I think, Clara."

"No, I repeat it,—it was *muera*!"

Not having inquired from the horsemen whether San Carlos was in the power of the royalists or insurgents, Don Cornelio remained as undecided upon that point as ever.

A considerable time passed, and still Costal did not return.

"Suppose I gallop forward a bit," suggested Clara, "and see whether I can meet him?"

The Captain having become uneasy about the prolonged absence of Costal, assented to this proposition; but at the same time directed the black to return in a quarter of an hour, if Costal did not make his appearance within that time.

Chapter Sixty Six
Don Cornelio a Captive

Almost as soon as Clara had ridden out of sight, Don Cornelio began to count the minutes. The quarter of an hour appeared a whole one; and, when it had passed, with no signs of either returning, he became more than uneasy—he felt alarm.

In order to create some distraction for his thoughts, he rode gently forward—on the same path by which his two companions had gone. Not meeting either, he kept on for another quarter of an hour. Becoming still more alarmed, he was about to make a halt, when he saw lights that seemed to go and come along the summits of the trees that appeared at some distance before him. These lights had flashed into view at a turn of the road.

On looking more attentively, he perceived that the ground sloped up from the place which he occupied; and he was now enabled to distinguish the outlines of a vast building, the windows of which were so brilliantly illuminated from the inside, that one might have fancied the house to be on fire. Outside, upon the *azótea*, blazing torches appeared to be carried backward and forward. It was these that had first attracted the eye of Don Cornelio, who, on account of the elevation at which they were seen, fancied them to be moving among the tops of the trees!

There was something too unnatural in these blazing torches, agitated by the night breeze—but more especially in the strange lights that shone through the windows—now red, now blue, and then of a pale violet colour, and in an instant changing from one hue to another—something so fantastically singular, that Don Cornelio suddenly drew up, without daring to advance a pace further.

The superstitious ideas with which Costal had entertained him during their journey now came into his mind; and, despite his disbelief in them, he could not help conjuring up fancies almost as absurd. He remembered the bull fulminated against the insurgents by the Bishop of Oajaca—representing them as spirits of darkness—and he began to fancy there must be some truth in it, and that he was now within view of these very demons. The silence that reigned around tended to strengthen this fancy—which was now further confirmed by the sight of a phantom-like figure clothed in white, seen for a moment gliding among the trees, and then as suddenly vanishing out of sight. The phantom appeared to have come from the direction of the illuminated building—as if fleeing from some danger that there menaced it.

The Captain made the sign of the cross, and then sat motionless in his saddle—uncertain whether to remain where he was, or to gallop back to the ford.

While thus irresolute, and asking himself whether the phantom he had seen might have been a stray reflection of one of the torches, the lights all at once disappeared from the upper part of the building.

At the same moment four or five horsemen issued forth from the shadow of the walls, and galloped towards him, uttering loud yells. Don Cornelio perceived that his presence was discovered; but to put this beyond doubt, a light at the moment flashed up among the horsemen, followed by the report of a carbine, and the hissing of a bullet, which passed close to his ears.

He no longer hesitated as to whether he should stand or fly. The bullet was sufficient cue for flight; and, wheeling round, he set off in full gallop towards the river.

Trained by the misfortunes which had occurred to him, from the mistaken economy of his worthy father, Don Cornelio had ever since felt an aversion to second-rate horses, and on the present journey he had taken care to provide himself with a good one. Knowing the fact, he had fair hopes of being able to distance his pursuers. Driving his spurs deeply into the ribs of his horse, he permitted the animal to choose its own course—so long as it carried him in a direction opposite to that from which he was pursued.

Forgetting all about Costal and Clara, he rode away like the wind; and, in all likelihood, would have got clear beyond the reach of his pursuers, but for an unforeseen misfortune. In passing a gigantic cypress his horse stumbled upon its projecting roots, and came head foremost to the ground—flinging his rider out of the saddle with such force that, but for the softness of the spot on which he fell, some of his bones would undoubtedly have suffered fracture.

He was but little damaged by the fall, and, before he could get to his feet, and recover his horse, one of the pursuers had ridden up, and casting out a lazo, noosed him round the body.

To whom was the captain a prisoner?

Of this he was completely ignorant, still uncertain as to who were in possession of the hacienda. As soon as he had regained his feet, however, a voice cried out, interrogatively, "For Spain, or the Independence?"

Before making answer, Don Cornelio looked up. Half-a-dozen men had arrived upon the ground, and encircled him in their midst, forming a menacing cordon around him. Of one and all the aspect was sinister and doubtful.

"Spain, or the Independence?" repeated the voice, in a more threatening tone.

Thus brusquely called upon to proclaim his colours, the Captain, not knowing those of the party who surrounded him, hesitated to make answer.

"Very well, cavallero!" cried one of the men, "answer or not, as you please. No doubt of it," he continued, addressing himself to a comrade, "this fellow is in company with the other two. Bring him along to the hacienda!"

At these words one of his captors seized Don Cornelio by the arm, and commenced dragging him along toward the illuminated building.

"Hold!" cried the first speaker, as, under the glare of the distant lights, he saw that their prisoner was neither negro nor Indian. "*Por Dios*! this fellow is white."

"Red, black, and white!" added another. "We want only a *mestizo* to complete the collection."

From these speeches Don Cornelio conjectured that his comrades, Costal and Clara, had been already captured by the same party who were making him their prisoner.

He was still ignorant, however, as to whether his captors were royalists or insurgents; and, before proceeding further, he determined, if possible, to settle that question.

"What do you want with me?" he inquired, in the hope of obtaining some clue in the answer.

"Not much," replied the spokesman of the party. "Only to nail your head in the place of that of Lantejas."

"Lantejas!" exclaimed Don Cornelio, inspired with a fresh hope. "That is my name. It is I who am the insurgent Lantejas, sent here to Oajaca, by General Morelos."

The declaration was received with a burst of savage laughter.

"*Demonio*!" cried one of the guerilleros, coming up with the horse of Don Cornelio, "I have had trouble enough in catching this accursed brute. It is to be hoped he carries something to repay me for it."

Don Cornelio fancied he knew the tone of this voice, but he had no time to reflect upon where he had heard it, before its owner again cried out, "*Alabado sea Dios*! (Blessed be the Lord!) there is my cloak!"

Don Cornelio recognised the man who the day before had taken such a fancy to his cloak. In a word, the speaker was Gaspacho.

"What a lucky fellow I am to meet you again," continued the brigand; "that cloak is much too large for you. I told you so yesterday."

"Such as it is, it satisfies me," meekly responded the Captain.

"Oh! nonsense," rejoined Gaspacho, at the same time throwing off his own tattered scrape, and making a significant gesture to Don Cornelio to uncloak himself.

The latter hesitated to comply with this rude invitation; but almost on the instant Gaspacho snatched the garment from his shoulders, and coolly wrapped it round his own.

"Now, amigo," cried one of Gaspacho's confrères, "surely a man without a head has no need of a hat? Yours appears as if it would just fit me," and saying this, the bandit picked the hat from Don Cornelio's head, at the same time flinging his own battered sombrero to the ground.

As there was nothing more upon the person of the prisoner to tempt the cupidity of the brigands, the lazo was unloosened from around his arms, and he was ordered to accompany his captors to the hacienda. This he did willingly enough: for the presence of Gaspacho told him that he was in the hands of the guerilleros of Arroyo.

"Can I see the Captain?" he inquired.

"What Captain?"

"Arroyo."

"Ah! you wish to see him?" responded Gaspacho. "That rather surprises me. You shall have the pleasure of seeing him soon enough, I fancy. Come along!"

The guerilleros continued on to the house, conducting their prisoner along with them.

As they drew near to the walls, the attention of Don Cornelio was again attracted to the singular lights that seemed to be burning within the house. It could not be the flame of a conflagration, else the building would long since have been consumed.

A few minutes brought them up to the gate. It was shut, and one of the men knocked against it with the hilt of his sabre, at the same time giving utterance to a password, which Don Cornelio did not understand. What he did comprehend was, that the moment had come when, *bon gré mal gré*, he was called upon to acquit himself of the commission with which Morelos had entrusted him.

It often happens that danger in prospective is more dreaded than when it is present; and so was it in this instance: for, on his arrival at the gate, Don Cornelio felt less embarrassed with apprehensions than he had been ever since his departure from the camp at Huajapam.

The huge door turned upon its heavy hinges to admit the horsemen—in the midst of whom the prisoner was carried into a large, paved courtyard, illuminated by the flames of several fires that burned in the open air. Around these fires could be distinguished the forms of men—to the number of one hundred or more—grouped in different attitudes, or lying asleep upon the pavement. Along the walls stood as many horses, completely equipped for the road. The bridles only were off, and hanging suspended over the saddle-bow—in order that the animals might consume their rations of maize, served to them in wooden troughs. Here and there, stacks of carbines, lances, and sabres, glanced under the light of the fires, and Don Cornelio could not help shivering with terror as he looked upon these fierce bandits, in the midst of their picturesque accoutrements.

Most of them remained as they were, without offering to stir. The sight of a fresh prisoner was nothing new to them. One only coming forward, asked Gaspacho, in a tone of indifference, what had taken him out at that hour of the night.

"Well!" exclaimed the cloak-robber in reply. "They say that the mistress of the hacienda has escaped by a window. Her husband says she is absent. I don't care whether it's true or not. All I know is, that we can see nothing of her without; and we should have returned empty-handed, if good fortune hadn't thrown into our hands this gentleman here. I have no doubt he is a royalist spy, since he wanted to pass himself off for our old comrade—the Lieutenant Lantejas."

"Ah!" rejoined the other, "he would ill like to be Lantejas just now."

And as the man said this he returned to the fire, which he had for the moment forsaken.

The captors of Don Cornelio were soon lost amidst the groups of their associates—Gaspacho alone staying to guard him.

Only a few seconds did the cloak-robber remain in the courtyard; after which, making a sign to his prisoner to follow him, he commenced reascending the stone *escalera* that led to the second storey of the building.

Chapter Sixty Seven
The Colonel of Colonels

The day upon which these various events took place was anything but a happy one for Arroyo. It appeared to him as if the re-appearance in the neighbourhood of his deadliest foe—Don Rafael Tres-Villas—had been the signal for the series of disappointments which had occurred to him. Ten of his followers had fallen in a sortie of the besieged, besides two more killed by the hand of Don Rafael—who had himself escaped, as well as the prisoner Gaspar and the deserter Juan el Zapote.

The bloodthirsty disposition of the guerilla chief had been strengthened by these disappointments, and in order to give solace to his vexed spirit, he resolved to possess himself of the hacienda of San Carlos without further delay.

In addition to the wicked desires—which the promptings of Bocardo had excited within him—there was another reason urging him to carry out this design. The hacienda of San Carlos, with a little labour, could be converted into a fortress of considerable strength, and such as he might yet stand in need of.

He saw that he had miscalculated the power of resistance of the royalist garrison of Del Valle; and, still ignorant of its real strength, he deemed it better to call off the besieging force until after the taking of San Carlos. Then he could go back with his whole band, and make a determined assault against the place.

He had, for these reasons, ordered the besiegers to return to camp; and, striking his tent, had marched with all his followers to the capture of San Carlos. This will explain why Don Cornelio and his companions had been able to pass the hacienda Del Valle—and afterwards the ford of the Ostuta—without seeing anything of Arroyo or his band—Gaspacho alone excepted.

Numerous as were the servants of Don Fernando Lacarra—the proprietor of San Carlos—their master did not for a moment dream of making resistance. It would have been worse than useless against an experienced *guerilla* numbering in all above a hundred men. At the first summons, therefore, the gates of the hacienda were opened to Arroyo and his followers.

Having hitherto practised a strict neutrality, and being known to have a strong sympathy with the cause of the Independence, the young Spaniard believed that Arroyo only intended demanding from him a contribution in provisions—and perhaps money—for the support of his troops; and that with this he would be contented.

Although not suspecting the designs of the brigand in regard to his wife, he had deemed it prudent, before opening the gates, that she should conceal herself in one of the secret chambers of the mansion—where he was also in the habit of keeping his money and plate. There he fancied she would be safe enough—unless, indeed, the whole building should be ransacked and pillaged.

To strengthen this precaution, Don Fernando had informed the brigands on their entering the house, that his wife, Marianita, was not at home.

Unfortunately for him, it was not a mere levy of blackmail that was now to satisfy the partisan chieftains. One was determined upon robbing him of his wife—while the other coveted his money—and therefore the subterfuges of Don Fernando were not likely to avail him.

It was just at the time that the wretched husband was endeavouring to mislead his visitors as to the hiding-place of his wife and his treasure, that Don Cornelio Lantejas had come within view of the building, the lights of whose windows had so mystified him. That mystery was now to be cleared up, and the ex-student was to find the explanation of those bright coloured flames with their changing hues.

Following Gaspacho up the stone stairway, Don Cornelio reached a door upon the landing. It was closed; but inside, a tumult of voices could be heard, accompanied by cries as of some one in pain.

His conductor unceremoniously opened the door, and pushed Don Cornelio into a large room, the atmosphere of which almost suffocated him.

Several torches of resin, set in candelabras, were burning round the walls, but the reddish light which these produced was almost eclipsed under the glare that proceeded from a keg of brandy that stood near the middle of the floor, and which, having been set on fire, was completely enveloped in violet-coloured flames.

The heat, the smell of blood, and the effluvia of the burning alcohol, constituted an atmosphere horrid to endure; but even this was less painful to Don Cornelio than the sight which met his eyes as he entered the room. On one side was a group of guerilleros—clustered around some object which they were regarding with the most vivid interest—all seemingly pleased with the spectacle.

It was that of an unfortunate man, stripped almost naked, and tied with his face to the wall, while another man stood over him, grasping a strong cow-hide whip, with which, at intervals, he struck the wretched victim, apparently with all the strength that lay in his arms.

He who handled the whip was a man of the most sinister aspect; and the blue flames of the alcohol flashing over his countenance added to its demoniac expression. Gouts of blood, that had spurted from the back of the sufferer, spotted the wall on both sides of him; and the number of those spots showed that the punishment had been continued for some length of time.

By the side of the man who was inflicting the stripes—and whom Lantejas supposed to be some common executioner—stood a woman of a still more hideous aspect; who, by her gestures and words, kept exciting the wretch to still greater cruelty—as though he stood in need of such encouragement.

Gaspacho, perceiving that no one heeded his entrance, cried out, so as to be heard above the tumult—

"Señor Captain! we have captured the comrade of the negro and the Indian. Here he is."

To the astonishment of Don Cornelio, the person thus addressed as the captain was no other than the hideous individual who was handling the whip.

"Very well," responded the latter, without turning round. "I shall attend to him presently, as soon as I have made this *coyote* confess where he has hidden his wife and his money."

The whip again whistled through the air, and came down upon the back of the wretched sufferer, without producing any other manifestation than a deep groan.

It is scarcely necessary to say that the victim of this barbarous treatment was Don Fernando Lacarra. The words of Arroyo have already made this known to the reader.

Perfectly indifferent to the spectacle, Gaspacho, having introduced his prisoner to the presence of Arroyo, walked out of the room.

As regards Don Cornelio, he stood where the robber had left him, paralysed with horror. Independently of the compassion he felt for the sufferer, he was under the suspicion that both Costal and Clara had already perished, and that his own turn might come next.

While these fearful reflections were passing through his mind, a man whom he had not before noticed now came up to him. This was an individual with a jackal-like face, and the skulking mien of that animal, with all its ferocious aspect.

"My good friend," said this man, addressing himself to Don Cornelio, "you appear somewhat lightly clad for one who is about to present himself before people of distinction."

Lantejas, in reality—thanks to the bandits who had captured him—was almost naked: a torn shirt and drawers being all the clothing they had left him.

"Señor Captain,"—said he, addressing the jackal-like individual, and intending to account for the scantiness of his costume.

"Stop," interrupted the other, "not *captain*. Call me Colonel of Colonels, if you please. It is a title which I have adopted, and no one shall deprive me of it."

"Well then, Colonel of Colonels! if your people had not robbed me of my broad cloth cloak, my hat of Vicuña wool, and various other articles of clothing, you would not have seen me so lightly dressed. But it is not only that which grieves me. I have other serious complaints to make—"

"The devil!" exclaimed the Colonel of Colonels, without heeding the last remarks. "A broad cloth cloak and Vicuña hat, did you say? Two things of which I stand particularly in need. They must be recovered."

"I have to complain of violence offered to my person," continued Don Cornelio. "I am called Lantejas—Captain Lantejas. I serve the junta of Zitacuaro, under the orders of General Morelos; and I bear from him a commission, of which the proofs—"

A sudden thought interrupted the speech of Don Cornelio—a terrible thought, for it just now occurred to him that his despatches, his commission as captain, his letters of credence—in short, all the papers by which he could prove his identity—were in the pockets of the stolen cloak!

"Ho!" exclaimed the Colonel of Colonels, in a joyful tone, "you call yourself Lantejas, do you? I am delighted to hear it, and so will our captain be. It is the luckiest circumstance in the world for us, and for you, too, as you shall presently be convinced. Look here!"

The speaker raised the corner of a *serape* that was spread upon one of the tables standing near, and pointed to some objects lying underneath. Don Cornelio saw they were human heads.

There were three of them.

"Now, my good friend," continued the Colonel of Colonels, "there you see the head of our old comrade, Lieutenant Lantejas, which we have brought away from where it was nailed over the gate of the hacienda Del Valle. Conceive, then, what a lucky thing for us! What a splendid *revanche* we shall have when, in place of the head of the insurgent Lantejas, we shall nail up that of Lantejas the royalist spy!"

"But it is a mistake," cried Don Cornelio, rubbing the cold sweat from his forehead. "I am not a royalist nor a spy neither. I have the honour to serve the cause of the Independence—"

"Bah! everybody says the same. Besides, without any proofs—"

"But I have proofs. They are in the pocket of my cloak, of which I have been robbed."

"Who took your cloak?" inquired the Colonel of Colonels.

"Gaspacho," replied Don Cornelio, who had incidentally learnt the name of the brigand who had despoiled him.

"Ah! that is a terrible misfortune. Gaspacho has just received orders to go in all haste to Las Cruces. He is off by this time, and will not likely be back in less than ten days. You, by that time will have lost your head, and I my cloak and Vicuña hat. Both of them, I know, would have fitted me, since you and I are both of a size. What a damnable misfortune for both of us!"

A fearful cry interrupted the dialogue between Don Cornelio and the Colonel of Colonels. The cry came from the wretched sufferer, who fainted as soon as uttering it.

Almost at the same instant the alcohol shot up its last flickering flame—as the spirit itself was consumed; and in the reddish light of the torches Don Cornelio could perceive the men flitting about like shadows, or rather like demons assisting in the horrible drama that was being enacted.

Chapter Sixty Eight
The Commission Executed

While the Captain Lantejas stood in the midst of an atmosphere that nearly stifled his breathing, he saw one of these shadowy forms step out from among the rest and advance towards him. As the man came nearer, he recognised the ferocious captain of the bandits, who, licking his blood-stained lips like a jaguar after leaving its prey, cried out in a hoarse voice, "Bring me that spy! I can examine him while the coyote is coming to himself."

"Here he is," replied Bocardo, seizing Don Cornelio by the shoulder, and pushing him forward into the presence of his associate.

"My good friend," muttered Bocardo, addressing himself to Don Cornelio, "it's your turn now. Of course the lash will make you confess that you are a spy, and of course your head will be taken off immediately after. I would, therefore, advise you not to waste time about it but acknowledge your guilt at once."

While Bocardo was giving this fearful counsel, his associate stood regarding Don Cornelio with eyes that expressed a villainous pleasure, at the idea of having another victim to satisfy his bloodthirsty instincts.

"Confess quickly!" he cried, "and let that end it. I am tired, and shan't be kept waiting."

"Señor Arroyo!" replied Lantejas, "I am a captain in the insurgent army, and am sent by General Morelos to tell you—"

Don Cornelio paused. He was hesitating as to whether he dare proclaim his real errand.

"Your proofs?" demanded Arroyo.

"My papers have been taken from me," said Lantejas.

"A fig for your papers! Hola! wife!" continued Arroyo, turning to the hag who still stood by the fainting victim, "here's a little work for you, as I am somewhat fatigued. I charge you with making this spy confess who sent him here, and what design he had in coming. Make him speak out whatever way you please."

"By and by," answered the virago, "but not yet. This coyote has come round again, and better still, has come to his right senses at last: he is about to confess."

"Bring him here, then!" commanded Arroyo.

Several men hastened to execute the order, and, detaching the victim from the place where he had been bound, half dragged, half carried him across the floor. Don Cornelio saw that the unfortunate individual was a young man—of less than thirty, of noble aspect, though his features expressed at the moment the terrible agony he was enduring.

"Now, *Gachupino*!" exclaimed the woman, "where is your money hid?"

"Where is your wife?" cried Arroyo. On hearing this question so pointedly put, the hideous companion of Arroyo directed upon her husband a glance of concentrated rage and jealousy.

"I want the woman," muttered Arroyo, "in order that I may draw a good ransom out of her father."

The young Spaniard, his spirit tortured to a certain degree of feebleness, in a voice scarce audible, indicated to his persecutors where lay the secret chamber—the door of which, cunningly set in the wall, had escaped even the keen eyes of the robbers.

Both Bocardo and Arroyo immediately repaired to the spot. A keg of dollars, with a large quantity of plate, was found in the chamber, but the Señora Marianita had disappeared.

On hearing this news, a tremor of joy passed through the lacerated frame of the young Spaniard. Little cared he for his treasure, so long as his beloved wife had escaped from the outrages of the brigands. His emotion caused him to faint anew; and he lay once more senseless at the feet of his tormentors.

Don Cornelio now remembered the white phantom he had observed gliding among the trees, and he doubted not that what he had seen was she of whom they were in search.

Arroyo returned to examine his prisoner, but by this time the whole nature of Don Cornelio appeared to have become suddenly transformed. The perfumes of the alcohol, mixed with that of the resin torches, had mounted to his head; and as he had never in his life even tasted strong liquors, the effect was that of a partial but instant intoxication. He appeared to have become animated with a portion of that courage, with which in the field of battle the flaming eyes of Galeana had more than once inspired him—while combating under the aegis of the marshal's death-dealing lance.

"Señor Arroyo!" cried he in a voice whose thundering tones astonished even himself, "and you who call yourself the Colonel of Colonels! I command you both to respect the envoy of his Excellency the General Morelos—myself—who am charged to tell you, that if you continue, by your sanguinary cruelties, to disgrace the holy cause for which we fight—not as brigands but as Christians—you will both be *drawn and quartered!*"

At this unexpected and insulting menace the eyes of Arroyo sparkled with fury. Upon Bocardo the effect was somewhat different. He trembled and turned pale at the name of Morelos.

Lantejas, though somewhat alarmed at his own boldness, nevertheless continued in the same strain.

"Bring here the negro and Indian!" demanded he, "prisoners like myself—and see if both do not know me as Captain Don Cornelio Lantejas. If they do not I consent—"

At this point Arroyo interrupted the speaker, springing forward and crying out in a husky voice—

"Woe be to you if you are lying! I will pluck the tongue out of your head, and scourge with it the cheeks of an impostor."

Lantejas, now elevated in spite of himself to a point of haughty grandeur, replied to this menace only with a superb smile.

Clara being sent for, the moment after appeared within the room.

"Who is this man, dog of a negro?" interrogated the fierce brigand.

This time too punctual in executing the orders of his captain, the black displayed his ivory teeth in a smile of significant intelligence. "Don Lucas Alacuesta, of course!" he replied.

A cry of gratification issued from the lips of the bandit.

"But there is another name which I also bear, is there not?" inquired Don Cornelio, without losing countenance.

"Don Cornelio Lantejas," added Clara.

"The proofs—the proofs!" cried the guerillero, pacing rapidly backward and forward, like a caged tiger who sees the spectators outside the bars of his prison without being able to devour them, "the proofs!—I must have them at once."

At this moment confused and violent noises were heard outside the door, and rising above all the voice of Costal. The door was suddenly burst open, and the Indian rushed into the middle of the room, holding in one hand a bloody dagger, while the other was enveloped in a shapeless mass of what seemed to be cloth. The latter was serving him for a shield against the attack of several guerilleros, who were pressing him from behind.

Costal, on getting inside, turned abruptly and stood facing his adversaries.

These, finding themselves in the presence of their chief, desisted for a moment from the attack—one of them crying out to Arroyo, that the Indian had poniarded their comrade Gaspacho.

"I did it to get back my own property," replied Costal, "or rather that of Captain Lantejas; and here it is."

In saying these words, the Zapoteque unwound from his left arm what had served him as a buckler, and which was now seen to be the cloak so inopportunely missing.

Don Cornelio seized it from him with an exclamation of joy, and at once plunged his hands into the pockets.

"Here are my proofs!" cried he, drawing out a number of papers, so stained with blood, fresh from the veins of the slain robber, as to be scarce legible. Enough, however, could be read to establish the identity of Don Cornelio and the authority under which he was acting.

The names of Morelos and Galeana in the midst of this band of brigands were, for him, like the whisper of the Lord to Daniel in the den of lions. Even the two ferocious leaders lowered their tone at the mention of these names, so universally feared and respected.

"You may go, then!" cried Arroyo, yielding reluctantly to the authority that had awed him; "but if you ever boast of the arrogant language you have used to me, *Carajo!*" and the brigand hissed out the infamous oath. "As for General Morelos," he added, "you may say to him, that each of us fights according to his own way; and, notwithstanding his threats, I shall follow mine."

Saying this, an order was issued to let the three prisoners pass free, after delivering up to them their arms and horses.

"Let six horsemen get ready to pursue this runaway Señora!" cried the bandit chief, as Don Cornelio and his companions were leaving the room. "Some one bridle my horse, and quickly. I shall go along with them, and you too, Bocardo."

Bocardo made no reply, but not equally silent was Arroyo's female companion.

"What want you with the Señora?" she inquired, in a tone of angry jealousy. "Have you got the keg of dollars to satisfy you!"

"I have told you already," rejoined Arroyo, with a demoniac glance at his wife, "that I want her for the purpose of enabling me to extract a ransom from her father. I want her, and will have her. You stay here, and guard the treasure; and by all the devils if you don't behave yourself better—"

The bandit drew his dagger with such an air of resolution and menace, that the hag, cowed by the gesture, no longer offered opposition to his will. Shrinking to one side, she appeared to busy herself in looking after the keg of dollars.

Meanwhile Don Cornelio and his two acolytes, not caring to remain in such company longer than was absolutely necessary, hastened from the room; and, mounting their restored steeds, rode off into the darkness of the night.

Chapter Sixty Nine
The Catalan Lieutenant

It is already known how Don Rafael Tres-Villas had fortified his hacienda of Del Valle, and how, when called elsewhere by his military duties, he had left its garrison of nearly a hundred men, under the command of a Catalonian officer, Lieutenant Veraegui.

On the same day in which he had made a sortie from the hacienda, and succeeded in capturing ten of the besieging guerilleros, the Lieutenant received a despatch from the governor of the province, ordering him, without further delay, to attack the band of Arroyo, and annihilate it, if possible. Then, with his whole troop, to repair to Oajaca, which was now in danger of being besieged by Morelos. The despatch also conveyed to Veraegui the additional intelligence of the raising of the siege of Huajapam, and the total defeat of the besieging forces.

The news was anything but agreeable to the Catalonian Lieutenant. In the *alcavala*—which he had for the past two years been accustomed to levy on all the traffic between Puebla and Oajaca—he had found excellent pay for his soldiers; and being a man not over scrupulous, though brave as a lion, he felt greatly disinclined to change his comfortable quarters. A fierce royalist, moreover, the news from Huajapam excited his fury against the insurgents to the highest pitch; and he blamed himself for the clemency he had displayed that very morning in hanging four of the guerilleros he had taken, up by the neck, instead of by the heels—as he had done with three of their comrades.

About an hour after Don Cornelio Lantejas and his travelling companions had passed Del Valle—and only a few minutes from the time, when, thanks to the darkness of the night, two of Arroyo's followers had found an opportunity to carry off the heads of their three comrades—two men presented themselves in front of the fortified hacienda.

They were Gaspar and Juan de Zapote, who had hidden themselves during the day, and awaited the friendly darkness, to enable them to make their way through the lines of the besieging force.

"I see no one," muttered Zapote, as they glided into the avenue. "The place appears to be deserted! It's likely enough that my ex-comrades have abandoned the siege."

"So much the better—let us keep on then!" rejoined Gaspar.

"Gently, gently, compadre!" counselled Zapote. "You forget that my costume is of the military kind, and likely to make a sentinel suspicious of me. A carbine shot might be the only hail we should get from one of these Royalists."

"Your physiognomy, amigo, is more likely than your costume to beget suspicions."

"Ah! that comes of the bad company I have been keeping of late."

"Never mind that. I shall go forward alone, and make myself known to the sentries. I can then introduce you as a comrade, devoted to the service of Don Rafael Tres-Villas, and who offers to assist in delivering the Colonel from danger."

"Precisely so, that is, if the Colonel be still alive."

"*Quien viva!*" came the sonorous hail of a sentinel from the crenelled parapet.

"*Gente de paz!*" replied Gaspar, advancing alone, while Zapote, notwithstanding the obscurity of the night, instinctively placed himself behind the trunk of a tree.

"What is your wish?" demanded the guard.

"I am the bearer of important news from the Colonel Tres-Villas," answered Gaspar.

"And we wish to communicate them to Lieutenant Veraegui," added Zapote, from behind, but without leaving the shelter of the tree.

"How many of you are there?" asked the sentinel.

"Two."

"You may advance, then," said the soldier, dropping his carbine to the "order arms."

The gate was soon opened; and Gaspar and Zapote, entering within the fortress, were conducted by the corporal of the guard towards the quarters of his commander.

The Lieutenant Veraegui was, at the moment, within one of the chambers of the mansion, engaged over a game of cards with a young *alferez*. On the table before them stood a bottle of Catalan brandy—the product of his own native province—clear and strong as alcohol. A couple of glasses flanked the bottle, and beside them lay a pile of Havana cigars.

Zapote, on entering, could not help a slight tremor; which was increased as the Catalan Lieutenant bent upon him an inquisitorial look of his grey eyes, that glanced keenly under eyebrows long and grizzled like his moustaches.

Veraegui was a soldier of fortune, of rude unpolished speech, and with manners not very different from those which he had practised while wearing the chevrons of a Sergeant.

From the examination of Zapote, he passed unceremoniously to that of Gaspar, whose features he instantly recognised.

"Ah! it is you?" he said, addressing the messenger. "Well, you have seen the Colonel, and bring news from him? He has, I trust, escaped from the disaster of Huajapam."

"Señor Lieutenant," replied Gaspar, "I know not of what affair you are speaking. All I know is, that this morning the Colonel Tres-Villas was in the woods between here and the Ostuta—where the bandits of Arroyo were tracking him like a wild beast."

"Ho!" cried the Lieutenant, angrily, as he started up from his chair; "and it is only now you tell me of this, when you might have brought the news in an hour?"

"Pardon, Lieutenant: both my companion and myself were also hunted by the same brigands; and we were not able to escape from the woods one minute sooner than we have done."

"Ah! in that case, I ask your pardon, and that of your companion there," continued the Lieutenant, turning to Zapote, "whom I should certainly have taken for a friend of Arroyo, rather than an enemy to that worthy individual. Where the devil have I seen you, my good fellow?" he added, fancying he recognised the features of the deserter.

"Oh! your honour, I have travelled a great deal," replied Zapote, whose presence of mind did not forsake him. "It would not be strange if—"

"So the Colonel has sent you to apprise me of his situation?" said the Lieutenant, without waiting for Zapote's explanation.

"We met the Colonel without knowing him," blundered out Gaspar. "It was only afterwards we learnt it was he."

"Ha! that is very strange!" remarked the Catalan, again turning his eye upon the men with a suspicious glance.

Gaspar now related how, as he and his companion were flying from the bandits of Arroyo, Don Rafael had leaped down between them from the branches of a tree; and how they had parted from him without recognising him.

So far the story was well enough; but the narrator was treading on ground that was dangerous for Juan el Zapote. It remained to be explained how they had been informed, by the ex-comrades of the deserter, that the fugitive they had encountered was the Colonel Tres-Villas.

At this point Gaspar hesitated, while the suspicion glances of the Lieutenant flitted alternately from one to the other. Zapote, however, came resolutely to the aid of his companion.

"My compadre," said he, "does not wish to tell the whole truth, out of regard for me. I shall speak for him; and this it is. In going away from here on his message to the Colonel, my friend Gaspar was captured by the scouts of Arroyo, and taken to the camp of the guerilleros. There he stood a very fair chance of losing his life, when, out of regard for our *compadrazgo*, and old acquaintance' sake, I consented to assist him at the risk of losing my head."

"Oh! you are then from the camp of Arroyo?"

"Yes," muttered Zapote, in a tone of compunction, "the lamb is sometimes found in the company of wolves."

"Especially when the lamb so nearly resembles a wolf, that it is difficult to distinguish them," rejoined the lieutenant with a smile.

"I have always been an honest man," affirmed Zapote, with a demure look. "Virtue has been my motto through life; and I assure your honour, that I was forced to consort with these brigands very much against my will. I was only too glad, when, to save my old compadre here, I found an opportunity of making some amends for the wicked life I have been obliged to lead in their company."

"Hum!" said the Lieutenant, with a dubious shrug of the shoulders, "I suppose you expect your virtue to be well rewarded. But how did you ascertain that the man you encountered so unexpectedly was the Colonel?"

Zapote now recounted their subsequent interview with the brigands; and how he had learnt from them the object of their pursuit—as well as the adroit ruse he had practised to secure the escape of himself and his "compadre."

"It's all true as gospel!" affirmed Gaspar, when his companion had finished the relation.

Zapote also made known the advice he had given to Don Rafael: to conceal himself among the bamboos.

"At what place?" demanded the Lieutenant.

"Just below the ford," answered the deserter.

"But, Señor Lieutenant," added he, "I shall be most happy to conduct you to the spot myself."

"You shall do no such thing, my brave fellow. You and your worthy *compadre*, as you call him, shall remain here as hostages, till Don Rafael is found. I have no confidence in lambs that have been so long in the company of wolves. If the Colonel be living, so may you; but if I find it otherwise, then your prospects— Ho, there!" cried the Lieutenant, without finishing the threat, "take these two men to the guard-house, and keep them there, till I order them to be set free."

So saying, the Catalan poured out a glass of his favourite liquor, and commenced drinking it.

"What, and me, too?" inquired Gaspar, in a tone not very complimentary to his companion in misfortune.

"A fig for you! my worthy fellow!" rejoined the Lieutenant. "You should have remembered the proverb, *mas vale viajar in solo que mal acompanado.*" (Better travel alone than in bad company.)

"By the cross of Christ!" continued he, after quaffing off his glass, "I shall make short work of it with this bandit, Arroyo. To-night I shall finish with him and his band; and if I don't give the jackals and vultures a meal that will last them for a twelvemonth, my name's not Veraegui!"

At an order from his superior, the *alferez* flung down the cards, and hurried off to prepare the garrison troops for sallying out of the fort to the rescue of their Colonel; while the corporal of the guards conducted Gaspar and Zapote to the prison—the latter no little disconcerted at finding his first act of virtue so indifferently rewarded!

Chapter Seventy
News Sweet and Sad

From the middle of the cane-brake where Don Rafael had found shelter, he was able through the stems of the bamboos to see the camp of Arroyo and his bandits. He could note many of the movements passing within their lines; and at length perceived the guerilleros striking their tents, and riding off in a body from the banks of the river.

He still kept his place, however, until the night had fairly come on, and then wading back to the high bank where the bamboo thicket commenced, he looked out upon the open space between the river and the edge of the forest.

At first, all was silent along the bank of the stream; but shortly after three horsemen were seen riding past, and not far behind them two other men followed, also on horseback.

The first party were Don Cornelio and his companions, making for the ford of the river. The other horsemen were two of Arroyo's *guerilla*—who, by his orders, had remained near the hacienda Del Valle, for the purpose of taking down the heads of his three followers nailed over the gate—should an opportunity offer for their so doing. They had found the opportunity—as already known—and it was they who had passed Don Cornelio at the ford, and whose ambiguous speech had caused a difference of opinion, as to its meaning, between the Captain and Clara.

The first care of Don Rafael, as soon as he believed the road to be clear, was to recover his horse—which he had left tied in a thicket in the woods.

Like his master, Roncador had escaped the researches of the bandits; but so weak was he with thirst and hunger, that Don Rafael had doubts whether the poor animal would be able to carry him. It was necessary that he should take the horse to the river, in order to water him. This required to be done by stealth; for, although Don Rafael had witnessed the departure of the guerilleros from the ford, he did not know whether those who blockaded the hacienda had also gone away.

After giving Roncador his drink, just as he was leading the horse up the bank again, he perceived a man coming from the direction of the ford. As this man was on foot and alone, Don Rafael resolved to stop and question him. Sabre in hand, therefore, he placed himself in front of the pedestrian.

The latter, thus assailed by a man with a naked sword—and who was covered from head to foot with a coating of mud—was almost frightened out of his senses.

"Oh, Lord!" he cried, "help a poor servant who is seeking assistance for his master!"

"Who is your master?" demanded Don Rafael.

"Don Fernando Lacarra," answered the man.

"Of the hacienda San Carlos?"

"*Si, Señor*. You know him?"

"Yes: is he in any danger?"

"Alas!" replied this servant, "the hacienda is pillaged by guerilleros; and, just as I was leaving it, I heard the groans of my poor master under the lash of their Captain Arroyo—"

"Again this villain!" muttered Don Rafael, interrupting the narrator with his angry soliloquy.

"Ah! he is always committing some crime," rejoined the servant.

"And your mistress—the Doña Marianita—what of her?"

"It was to make him tell where she was concealed that Arroyo was flogging my master," replied the man. "Fortunately I was able to get her out of the way, by assisting her to descend from the window of the chamber where they had hidden her. Afterwards I got off myself, and am now on my way to the hacienda Del Valle, in hopes of getting assistance from its brave defenders, who themselves never violate the laws of war."

"But how will you get in there? Are not some of Arroyo's guerilleros still besieging the place?"

"No, Señor. The whole band is now at San Carlos."

"Good!" exclaimed the Colonel. "Come along with me, and I promise you a prompt and bloody vengeance."

Without further explaining himself, Don Rafael leaped upon his horse, directing the domestic to mount behind him, and then started off at a rapid trot in the direction of Del Valle.

"Where did you leave your mistress?" inquired Don Rafael, as they rode on.

"In truth, sir," replied the domestic, "I was so confused when she left me, that I did not think of reminding her to fly to Del Valle. I only told her to make into the woods near San Carlos. But the most important matter was for her to get out of the reach of Arroyo; and I hope she will be safe in the chapparal. Poor young creature! She was so happy this morning. She was expecting on this very night the arrival of her father and sister—neither of whom she has seen for a long time."

The Colonel could not hinder himself from shuddering.

"Are you sure that it is to-night that Don Mariano and Doña Gertrudis are expected at San Carlos?" he inquired, with a tone of anxiety in his voice.

"Yes; a letter had reached my master to say so. God forbid that they, too, should fall into the hands of these merciless men! They say, too, that Arroyo is an old servant of Don Mariano."

"Let us hope they may not come!" said the Colonel, with a choking effort.

"It may be," continued the domestic, "that the illness of Doña Gertrudis may detain them a day or two on the journey. That would be the luckiest thing that could happen."

"What say you? is Doña Gertrudis ill!"

"Señor!" exclaimed the domestic, "you, who appear to know the family, are you ignorant that Doña Gertrudis is only the shadow of her former self, and that some secret grief is wasting her away? But, Señor, why do you tremble?" inquired the man, who, with his arm round his waist, felt the nervous agitation of Don Rafael's body.

"Oh, nothing," replied the latter; "but tell me—does any one know the cause of her grief?"

"Rather say, who is there who don't know it, Señor? Doña Gertrudis was in love with a young officer; and so fondly, that it is said she cut off the whole of her beautiful hair, as a sacrifice to the Holy Virgin, for saving his life on an occasion when he was in danger! And yet for all this, he who was thus loved proved faithless, and deserted her!"

"Well?" mechanically interposed Don Rafael.

"Well," continued the servant, "the poor young lady is dying on account of being so deserted—dying by inches; but surely—why, Señor, you are certainly ill? I feel your heart beating against my hand as if it would leap out of your bosom!"

"It is true," answered Don Rafael, in a husky voice. "I am subject to severe palpitations; but presently—" The Colonel, for support, fell back against the domestic, his herculean strength having yielded to the powerful emotions which were passing within him. "Presently," he continued, "I shall get over it. I feel better already. Go on with your history. This man—this officer—did he ever tell Doña Gertrudis that he no longer loved her? Does he love any other?"

"I do not know," was the response of the domestic.

"Could she not have sent him word—say by some means agreed upon—which should bring him back to her from the farthest corner of the earth? Perhaps then—"

Don Rafael could not finish what he intended to have said. A bright hope, long time suppressed, began to spring up within his heart, and with such force, that he feared to know the truth—lest it should be crushed on the instant.

"Señor, you ask me more than I am able to answer," rejoined the domestic. "I have told you all I know of this sad story!"

Heaving a deep sigh, the Colonel remained for some moments silent. After a while, he resumed the conversation, by putting a question, the answer to which might terminate his doubts.

"Have you ever heard the name of this young officer?"

"No," replied the domestic; "but were I in his place, I should not leave this young lady to die, for one lovelier I never beheld in all my life."

These were the last words spoken on either side: for at that moment the voices of the sentinels, challenging from the walls of the hacienda, put an end to the conversation.

"Say to Lieutenant Veraegui," commanded Don Rafael, in reply to the challenge, "that it is Colonel Tres-Villas."

The sound of the trumpets inside soon after signalised the joy felt by the garrison at the return of their old commandant, while the domestic of Don Fernando flung himself promptly to the ground, asking a thousand pardons for not recognising the quality of his *compagnon de cheval*.

"It is I who have most reason to feel obliged," said Don Rafael. "Remain here till I see you again. I may, perhaps, need you for an important message."

The domestic bowed respectfully, taking hold of the bridle of Don Rafael's horse, while the Lieutenant Veraegui, the *alferez*, with several soldiers of the garrison, came forth with torches to congratulate their superior officer on his escape from the dangers that had so lately surrounded him.

As soon as their first greetings had been exchanged, Veraegui informed the Colonel that they were just about preparing to start upon an expedition against the banditti of Arroyo.

"You know where they are, then?" said Don Rafael.

"Not the precise spot. But it is not difficult to find the traces of these gentry," replied Catalan.

"True," rejoined the Colonel. "But I chance to know their whereabouts. They are just now at the hacienda of San Carlos. This faithful servant, who is holding my horse, has lately escaped from them, and come to beg your assistance to rescue his master from the brutal outrages they are at this moment inflicting upon him. Lieutenant Veraegui! see that your men are provided with a sufficient quantity of ropes. Let a piece of ordnance be mounted upon the back of a mule: we shall, no doubt, require it to force open the gate."

"But, Señor Colonel, what do you want with the ropes?" inquired the Lieutenant, with a significant smile.

"For the execution of these brigands. We shall hang them to the last man, my dear Veraegui."

"Good!" assented the Catalan, in a joyous accent, "and this time by the heels, I hope. I shall never forgive myself for my foolish indulgence—"

"What! you have spared some of them?" interrupted Don Rafael.

"I have been too merciful to four whom I captured yesterday—in hanging them by the necks. But, by the way, Colonel, now I think of it, two odd fellows came in a while ago, who say that they wish to speak with you."

"I cannot receive them now," answered Don Rafael, little suspecting the supreme happiness their message would have given him. "I shall see them on my return. We have already wasted too much time, while the worthy proprietor of San Carlos is no doubt counting the minutes in anguish. I shall not even stay to change my dress; so haste, and get your men upon horseback."

"Sound 'Boots and saddles!'" cried the Lieutenant, hurrying into the courtyard to give further orders; while Don Rafael, under the pretext of being alone for a few minutes, walked out into the garden, and directed his steps towards the spot where, two years before, he had deposited the remains of his father in the tomb.

His spirit once more excited by the revelations made by the domestic of Don Fernando, he felt he needed a moment of prayer to strengthen him for this final effort for the punishment of his father's assassins. The murder of his father had been for him a terrible blow, but, as time passed, even this grief, by little and little, had become appeased.

Far different was it with that other passion—which neither time, nor absence, nor the constant changing of scene, nor the duties of an active campaign, had been able to eradicate from his bosom.

He now knew that Gertrudis reciprocated his ardent love—that she was dying of it; and, in the midst of the mournful joy which this news had produced, he could have forgotten that his father's death was not yet avenged, as he had sworn it should be. One of the assassins was at no great distance from him, and yet he could scarcely restrain himself from yielding to the almost irresistible desire of galloping direct to Oajaca, where he supposed Gertrudis to be, and then, flinging himself at her feet, confessing that, without her, he could no longer live.

It was to steel his soul against this temptation, and enable him to keep the oath he had sworn, that Don Rafael now repaired to his father's grave.

Chapter Seventy One
The Capture of San Carlos

A few minutes sufficed for the performance of his sacred duty; and Don Rafael, returning to the courtyard, placed himself at the head of his troopers—already in their saddles. There were eighty in all ordered upon the expedition—only a small garrison of twenty men being left—just sufficient to defend the fortress. Two pack-mules accompanied the party— one carrying a small howitzer, while the other was laden with the necessary *caisson* of ammunition.

At a given signal the great gate of the hacienda was thrown open, and the troopers filing through, passed on down the avenue at a rapid trot, and in silence.

A dozen or so of light cavalry went in advance of the main body—for the purpose of reconnoitring the ground—and at the head of these was Don Rafael himself with the Lieutenant Veraegui.

On the way the Lieutenant, in brief language, rendered an account to his superior of the events that had happened since his last despatch to him—to all of which Don Rafael listened far from attentively. Absorbed in his thoughts, he sat abstractedly in his saddle until after they had forded the Ostuta.

On the other side of the river the advance guard halted to give the main body time to come up; and here Don Rafael ordered the domestic of Don Fernando to be brought into his presence.

"Do you know," said he, addressing the man, "if there be any road by which we can get round the hacienda, and approach it from the opposite side?"

The domestic replied in the affirmative. He knew a path by which he could conduct the troopers to the rear of the building, and by which they might advance up to the very walls without their approach being discovered.

"Go ahead then along with the scouts!" directed Don Rafael. "It is necessary we take these robbers by surprise, else they may get off from us as they have done before."

The guide obeyed the order, and placing himself at the head of the advance guard, the march was resumed.

The path by which the domestic conducted them made a détour round the foot of the hill, upon which the hacienda stood, and where, but a few hours earlier, Don Cornelio Lantejas had seen the flames shining so brightly through the windows. All was now silent as the tomb; and no sound of any kind announced that the approach of the assailing party was suspected.

A little further on the guide halted and pointed out to Don Rafael several paths that branched off from the one they were following, and by which the party, separating into several detachments, might completely encompass the hacienda. This was exactly what Don Rafael wanted.

Reserving to himself the command of the main body, he detached three smaller parties by these paths—one under the direction of Veraegui, the others each commanded by an alferez. These, at a given signal, were to attack on right, left, and in the rear; while Don Rafael himself with the howitzer would storm the building in front. Each party was provided with a supply of hand-grenades, to be thrown into the courtyard of the hacienda, or into such other places as the enemy might seek refuge in.

So long as the assailants were sheltered from view by the trees and shrubs that skirted the hill, they approached without being discovered: but the moment they became uncovered, on getting nearer to the walls, shouts of alarm and shots fired by the sentries summoned the garrison to the defence; and an irregular fusillade was commenced from the azotéa of the building.

The different parties of the attacking force, without heeding this, kept on throwing their grenades as they advanced; while the party of Don Rafael, on arriving in front of the building, at once mounted the howitzer upon its carriage, and opened fire upon the main gateway.

The first shot crushed through the heavy timbers, carrying away one of the posterns of the gate.

Meanwhile, the grenades, falling within the courtyard began to burst upon the pavement—frightening the horses of the guerilleros to such an extent, that the animals broke from their fastenings, and galloped about, causing the greatest confusion. The shouts of alarm, the groans of the wounded, and the furious imprecations of the bandits, was for a time the only answer made to the reports of the bursting grenades, which were making such havoc in their ranks.

The loud explosion of the howitzer proclaimed a second discharge; and this time the shot penetrated into the courtyard, and cut its way through a mass of insurgents crowded near the further end of it.

"Once more! once more!" cried Don Rafael. "Batter down the other wing of the gate, and then, sword in hand, let us enter!"

So quickly did the practised artillerists of Veraegui handle their piece, that almost on the instant it was loaded and discharged for the third time. The ball passed once more through the heavy door; the leaf gave way and fell back with a crash, leaving the entrance open.

Tres-Villas, sword in hand, rushed into the gateway, followed by his faithful adherents.

"Where is the dog Arroyo?" cried he, bounding forward among the thick of the brigands, and cutting down every one within reach of his sword before an answer could be given. "On, my men!" he continued, "neither prisoners nor quarter!"

"I shall hang by the feet all who surrender!" thundered the voice of the Catalan from behind.

But despite this moderate promise of mercy, not one of the bandits offered to deliver himself up; and very soon the courtyard contained only a pile of dead bodies of the insurgents—the few who still lived having betaken themselves to the upper rooms of the building, where they secured themselves from present death by barricading the doors.

"Where is the dog Arroyo? A thousand pesos to the man who can lead me to the presence of the monster!" cried Don Rafael, vainly searching for the guerilla leader.

But Arroyo and his associate Bocardo were sought for in vain: since it will be remembered that both had gone off from the hacienda in search of its fugitive mistress.

The dead bodies were examined one after the other, and with care, but no Arroyo—no Bocardo—could be found among them.

"Let us on, Veraegui!" said Don Rafael. "We must attack them in their stronghold. The chiefs must be hidden up yonder! There is no time to be lost."

"Alas!" rejoined the Catalan, with a sigh, as he stood regarding the dead bodies with an air of regret, "I fear, Colonel, our ropes will be useless after all. These fellows are all dead; and, as for their comrades up there, we shall have to set fire to their retreat, and burn them alive in it. If we attempt to dislodge them otherwise, it will cost us a goodly number of our people."

"Oh! do not set fire to the house, Señor Colonel!" interposed the faithful domestic, in an appealing tone; "my poor master is there, and would suffer with the rest. All his people, too, are with him, and in the power of the brigands."

"It is true, what he says," rejoined Don Rafael, moved by the appeal of the domestic; "and yet it will never do to let these fiends escape. If we attack them, entrenched as they are, and knowing that certain death await them, they may cost us, as you say, more men than they are worth. What is your advice, Lieutenant?"

"That we reduce them by a siege, and starve them into surrendering. For my part, I don't wish to be baulked about the hanging of them—especially after the trouble we have taken in bringing these ropes along with us."

"It will cost time; but I agree with you, it seems the best thing we can do. They must soon yield to hunger; and perhaps before that time we may find some opportunity of getting Don Fernando out of their power. At all events, let us wait for sunrise before renewing the attack. Meanwhile, I leave you to conduct the blockade. The poor lady, Marianita, is, no doubt, wandering about in the woods near at hand. I shall myself go in search of her."

Saying this, and giving orders for half a dozen chosen men to follow him, Don Rafael leaped into his saddle, and rode off through the gateway of the hacienda.

He had scarcely passed out of sight, when the sentinels placed by Veraegui were signalled by two men who wished to enter the courtyard. Both were afoot, and appeared to have come in such haste that they could scarce get breath enough to proclaim their errand.

"What do you want?" asked the Catalan, before looking at the men. "Eh! my droll fellows!" he continued, recognising Gaspar and Zapote, "it is you, is it? How the devil did you get out of my guard-house?"

"The sentry allowed us to go, your honour," answered Zapote. "He knew that you did not wish us to be detained, if the Colonel should be found alive; and as we have an important message to him—"

"The Colonel is gone away from here," interrupted Veraegui.

"Gone!" exclaimed Zapote, with an air of extreme chagrin. "Where is he gone to, your honour?"

The Lieutenant, after pointing out the direction in which Don Rafael had ridden away, turned his back upon the two adventurers—who, instead of being offended at this rudeness, were only too glad to terminate their interview with the dreaded Catalan. They lost no time, therefore, in making their exit from the courtyard; and, as fast as their legs could carry them, they started off in the direction taken by him whom they had so long unsuccessfully followed.

Chapter Seventy Two
The Enchanted Lake

It is ten o'clock at night, and a starry heaven is extended over a large expanse of level country—here clothed with virgin forests—there with broad, almost treeless savannas, now and then partaking of the character of marshes and covered with tall reeds. In the midst of this landscape a large lake opens to the view. Its aspect is sombre and sad—its dark, turbid waters scarce reflecting the stars that shine so brilliantly over it; while the waves beating against its sedge-encircled shores, utter only the most lugubrious sounds.

Near the centre of this lake rises a mountain of dark, greenish colour, resembling an immense cairn constructed by the hands of Titans. Upon its summit rests a cloud of white fog collected by evaporation from the surrounding water, which has been condensed by the freshness of the night. The numerous dark fissures distinguishable along the sides of this gigantic hill give it the appearance of being a mass of lava—the débris vomited forth by some extinct volcano—and at night, when the moon's rays fall obliquely upon its flanks, it presents a vague resemblance to the scales of an alligator. At the same time that this fancy is suggested, the huge saurian itself may be heard, plunging among the reeds at its foot, and causing their culms to rattle against the rhomboid protuberances of his hideous carapace.

The mournful and desolate aspect of this lake, as well as of the shores that surround it—the eternal silence that reigns over it—the bleak, lonely appearance of its island mountain—all combine to produce upon the spectator an irresistible impression of melancholy; and a spirit of superstitious inclinings cannot help giving way to thoughts of the supernatural. No wonder that in such a place the ancient Aztec priests should have erected an altar for their sanguinary sacrifices; and so strong is tradition, that even in modern times the lake of Ostuta and the mountain of Monopostiac, are invested with supernatural attributes, and regarded by the vulgar with feelings of awe.

It was to the shores of this lake that the domestic of Don Mariano de Silva had conducted his master, certain of finding there a secure resting-place for the night. He knew that the country surrounding the lake was entirely uninhabited; and the brigands of Arroyo would scarce extend their excursions to such an unprofitable foraging ground. The southern end of the lake was bordered by a strip of forest; and it was in this forest that Don Mariano had determined to make halt for the night.

A small glade surrounded by trees of many species was chosen by the travellers as a place of their bivouac. The ground was covered with a carpet of soft grass, and many flowering shrubs and blossoming llianas, supported by the trees that grew around, yielded to the night an odorous incense that was wafted over the glade. It was, in fact, a bower made by the hand of nature, over which was extended the dark blue canopy of the sky, studded with its millions of scintillating stars.

Don Mariano had selected this lovely spot with a design—that of distracting his daughter's spirit from the sad reflections which the more gloomy portions of the forest might otherwise have called up.

Shortly after halting, Doña Gertrudis had fallen asleep in her *litera*—through the curtains of which, only half closed, might be seen her soft cheek, white almost as the pillow upon which it lay.

Nature had almost repaired the outrage she had voluntarily committed on her long dark tresses; but the life within her seemed fast hastening to an end, and her breathing told how feeble was the spirit that now animated her bosom. She appeared like one of the white passion-flowers growing near, but more like one that had been plucked from the stem which had been the source of its life and sweetness.

Don Mariano stood near the *litera*—gazing upon the pale face of his child with feelings of sad tenderness. He could not help calling up this very comparison—although it was torture to his soul; for he knew that the flower once plucked must irrevocably wither and die.

At some distance from the *litera*, and nearer the edge of the lake, three of the attendants were seated together upon the grass. They were conversing, in low tones, for the purpose of passing the time. The fourth, who was the guide already mentioned, had gone forward through the woods—partly to search for the crossing, but also to reconnoitre the path, and find out whether the road to San Carlos was clear of the guerilleros.

Through a break in the forest that surrounded the glade, the enchanted mountain was visible—its sombre silhouette outlined against the blue background of the sky.

In all countries, every object that appears to vary from the ordinary laws of nature, possesses, for the vulgar imagination, a powerful interest; and the servants of Don Mariano were no exception to the rule.

"I have heard it said," whispered one of them, "that the waters of this lake now so muddy, were once as clear as crystal; and that it was only after they were consecrated to the devil, that they became as they are now."

"Bah!" rejoined another, "I don't believe what they say about the devil living up there upon the *Cerro encantado*. He would choose a more pleasant place for his residence, I should fancy."

"Well," said the first speaker, who was named Zefirino, and who was better acquainted with the locality than either of his companions, "whether the devil dwells there or not, some terrible things have taken place on that mountain; and it is said, still happen there. I have heard that the fog which you see upon its summit, and which always rests there at night, is extended over it by the god of the Indians—who is only the devil himself. He does that to hide what goes on up there. There's one strange story the Indians themselves tell."

"What is it? Let us hear it, Zefirino."

"Well, you've heard how in old times the Indian priests had an altar up yonder—upon which they used to sacrifice scores of human beings—so that the blood ran down the fissures of the rock like water after a shower of rain. Their plan was to cut open the breast of the victim, and tear out his heart while still alive. But why need I frighten you with a story that, by my faith, is fearful enough?"

"No—no—never mind! Go on, Zefirino."

"Stay!" cried the other domestic. "Did you not hear a noise—just down there by the edge of the lake?"

"Bah! it's only an alligator snapping his jaws together. Go on, Zefirino!"

"Well, comrades—the story is, that about five hundred years ago, one of the unfortunate victims was about to be sacrificed in this manner as usual. The cruel priest had opened his breast and taken out the heart; when, to the astonishment of all around, the Indian seized hold of his own heart, and endeavoured to put it back in its place. His hand, however, trembled, and the heart slipping from his grasp, rolled down the mountain side and into the lake. The Indian, uttering a terrible howl, plunged in after for the purpose of recovering his heart from the water, and was never seen again. Of course, a man like that could not possibly die; and for five hundred years the Indian has been wandering round the shores of the lake searching for his heart, and with his breast cut open, just as the priest had left it. It's not more than a year ago that some one saw this Indian, and just about here, too, on the southern shore of the lake."

As Zefirino finished his narration, his two companions involuntarily cast glances of terror towards the gloomy waters of the lake, as if in dread that the legendary Indian might suddenly show himself. Just at that moment, a rustling among the leaves caused all three of them to start to their feet, and stand trembling with fear.

Their alarm did not last long; for almost immediately after they perceived that the noise had been caused by Castrillo, the guide—who, in the next moment, stepped forward into the glade.

"Well, Castrillo! what have you seen?" demanded his fellow-servants.

"Enough to make it necessary that I should at once communicate with our master," and Castrillo passed on towards the *litera*, leaving his companions to form their conjectures about what he had seen as best they might.

Chapter Seventy Three
The Invalid

On perceiving the approach of the domestico, Don Mariano silently closed the curtains of the *litera*, in order that the slumbers of Gertrudis might not be disturbed.

"Speak softly!" said he to the man, "my daughter is asleep."

The domestic delivered his report in an undertone.

"I have been almost as far as the hacienda of San Carlos," said he. "The road to the house is clear; and I should have gone up to it, but for the strange sights which I saw there."

"Strange sight! what sights, Castrillo?"

"Oh, master! I can hardly tell you what I saw—at least I cannot explain it. The windows were all lit up, but with such lights! They were blue and red, and of a purple colour, and they appeared to be changing every instant, and moving about in the most mysterious manner. While I stood looking at them, and trying to think what it could mean, I saw a figure in white gliding past me in the darkness, like some one not of this world."

"My worthy Castrillo, fear was troubling your senses, I am afraid you only fancied these things?"

"Oh, my master! what I saw was but too real. If you had seen these lights as I, you could not have doubted it. May it please God that I may have been deceived!"

The tone of conviction in which the servant delivered his report produced its effect on Don Mariano; and he could not help feeling the unpleasant presentiment that some grand misfortune had happened to his daughter, Marianita, or her husband.

The information brought by Castrillo was only the reawakening of a doubt that had been already oppressing him.

A prey to afflicting thoughts, he remained for a while in that state of silent uncertainty which follows the receipt of calamitous news. The servant having finished his report had joined his three companions, and Don Mariano was alone.

Just then the curtains of the *litera* were drawn inside by a hand from within, and the voice of Gertrudis interrupted for the moment his gloomy reflections.

"My sleep has refreshed me," said the young girl; "do you intend soon to continue your journey, father? It is near daybreak, is it not?"

"It is not yet midnight, niña. It will be long before the day breaks."

"Then why do you not go to sleep, dear father? We are in safety here, I think; and there is no reason why you should keep awake."

"Dear Gertrudis, I do not desire to sleep until we are under the roof of Marianita, and I can see you both together."

"Ah! Marianita is so very happy," sighed the invalid. "Her life has been like one of the flowery paths we have been following through the forest."

"And so will yours be yet, Gertrudis," rejoined Don Mariano, with an effort to console her. "It will not be long before Don Rafael comes to see you."

"Oh, yes! I know he will come, since he has sworn it upon his word of honour. He will come, but what then?" murmured Gertrudis, with a melancholy smile.

"He will arrive to tell you that he still loves you," said Don Mariano, affecting a conviction which, in reality, he did not feel. "It is only a misunderstanding," he added.

"A misunderstanding that causes death, dear father," rejoined Gertrudis, as she turned her head upon the pillow to conceal her tears.

Don Mariano was unable to reply, and an interval of silence succeeded.

Then Gertrudis, by one of those sudden reactions common to invalids, seemed all at once inspired with a fresh hope, and raising her head, she inquired —

"Do you think the messenger has had time to reach Don Rafael?"

"He would be three days in getting from Oajaca to the hacienda Del Valle; and if Don Rafael, as we have since heard, is at Huajapam, in two days more the messenger should reach him. He has been gone four days; therefore, in four more, at the most, Don Rafael should arrive at San Carlos, where he will know we are awaiting him."

"Four days!" murmured Gertrudis. "Oh! it is a long, long time!"

Gertrudis did not dare to add, what she feared at the moment, that her life might not last so long.

After a moment of silence she continued—

"And besides, when, with a blush upon my cheeks, and my eyes turned away, I hear Don Rafael say to me, 'You have sent for me, Gertrudis, I have come,' what answer can I make? Oh, father! I shall die of grief and shame; for I shall then feel that he no longer loves me. He will see me as I am—a ruin—only the shadow of my former self, with my health gone, and my freshness faded. Likely enough, generosity will prompt him to feign a love which he does not feel, and which I could not believe in. What proof could he give that his words would only be spoken out of compassion for me?"

"Who can tell?" said Don Mariano. "Perhaps he may give you some proof that you cannot help believing in his sincerity."

"Do not wish it, father, if you love me; for if he should offer a proof I cannot refuse to believe in, I feel that I should die of joy. Poor father!" continued she, with a choking sigh, and throwing her arms round his neck, "in either case you are likely soon to have but one daughter."

At this mournful declaration Don Mariano could no longer restrain his grief; and returning the embrace of Gertrudis, he mingled his tears with hers. Both wept aloud, their voices being audible to the *centzontlé*, on a neighbouring tree—that catching up the mournful tones repeated them to the ear of night.

Just then the moon shot out from behind a thick mass of clouds, that had hitherto been shrouding her from the sight; and the landscape, illuminated by her silvery light, all at once assumed a less lugubrious aspect.

The lake, as well as the forest on its shores, appeared less sombre; and the corrugated flanks of the enchanted hill glanced with a vitreous reflection like the greenish waves of an agitated sea. Upon the surface of the water could be seen the dark, hideous forms of huge alligators moving along the edge of the reeds, and now and then giving utterance to their deep bellowing notes, as they disported themselves under the light of the moon.

The domestics of Don Mariano, seated close together, more than once fancied that they could distinguish the voices of human beings, and all shivered with fear as they recalled the legend which Zefirino had just related.

"I wish, comrades," said one of them, speaking in a tone of subdued terror, "I wish that this night was well over. From the noises we have heard, and those strange lights that Castrillo has seen, one might fancy some terrible misfortune was to happen to-night! It only wants the scream of an owl from one of the trees around here, and then we may pray for the soul of our poor young mistress."

At that moment a voice—this time certainly a human voice—proceeding from the direction of the lake, interrupted the speaker. It seemed to arise out of the bosom of the water.

The four domestics started, and sat regarding each other with looks of affright. There could be no doubt of its being a human voice which they had heard, as if intoning a song or chaunt, but uttered in some unknown tongue—such as that in which the ancient Indians used to converse with their divinities.

"Santissima madre!" muttered one of the domestics, "what if it should be the Indian who searches for his heart?"

His companions made no other answer than by nodding their heads to signify that such had been the thought of each.

At this moment another noise reached them. It was a rustling as of leaves, and almost simultaneously they saw the figure of a man making his way through the reeds that grew by the edge of the water.

In the clear light of the moon they could see that the man was completely naked, and that his skin was of a bronze or copper colour—in other words, that he was an Indian.

As he passed through the reeds he parted their stems with his outstretched arms—at the same time keeping his eyes bent downwards as if searching for something.

After reaching the edge of the open water, he plunged in; and, swimming vigorously out into the lake, appeared to direct himself towards the enchanted hill.

"God of heaven!" muttered Zefirino, in an accent of terror. "It is the Indian searching for his heart!"

Chapter Seventy Four
An Aerial Couch

After escaping from the company of Arroyo and his bandits, Don Cornelio mechanically followed the guidance of Costal—who was now aiming to reach the lake of Ostuta as soon as possible, in order that he might commence his incantations before the rising of the moon.

Don Cornelio knew that it would be breath thrown away to attempt persuading the Indian to abandon his absurd and superstitious design; and to propose accompanying him, and becoming either actor or spectator in the pagan ceremony, would be equally against the wishes of Costal.

After they had ridden for some distance towards the lake, the Captain admonished his companions of his intention to stay behind and wait for their return, after they should have accomplished their purpose, and had their interview with Tlaloc and his wife Matlacuezc. Costal was only too glad to agree to this proposition; and promised to find a proper halting-place for Don Cornelio at some distance from the shores of the lake. There was no house of any kind in the vicinity, not even the meanest hut. This, Costal, from his perfect knowledge of the locality, was aware of; but the night was a pleasant one, and a few hours might be passed in the open air without any great inconvenience.

Shortly after, the cool freshness of the breeze proclaimed that the lake was not far off; and a pleasant grove of shady palm-trees offered an inviting shelter to Don Cornelio. It was the spot which Costal had designed for his halting-place; and here, parting from the two acolytes, the Captain dismounted, and prepared to make himself as comfortable as possible during their absence. Meanwhile Costal and Clara kept on towards the lake, and were soon lost to view under the shadows of the forest.

Don Cornelio had not been long left to himself, ere he began to rue the disposition thus made of him. It now occurred to him, and not without reason, that the comrades of Gaspacho might fancy to avenge the brigand's death, and for that purpose follow him and his two attendants through the forest. Arroyo would now be absent from the hacienda; Don Cornelio had heard him proclaim his intention of going in search of its mistress; and his subalterns might pay less respect to the emissary of Morelos than their chief.

These considerations influencing the spirit of Don Cornelio, produced within him a certain degree of uneasiness—sufficient to make him discontented with the position he had chosen.

Determined to get nearer to Costal—whom he looked upon almost as his natural protector—he remounted his horse, and continued along the path that had been taken by the other two.

After riding a few hundred yards, he discerned rising up before his face a high hill crowned with mist; and shortly after, the woods becoming more open, he was enabled to perceive that this hill was surrounded by a large lake of dark, sombre aspect. Though he now looked upon both the lake and mountain for the first time, he had no difficulty in identifying them as the Lake Ostuta and the sacred mountain of Monopostiac.

A belt of forest still lay between him and the lake, extending around its southern end. Entering into the timber, he rode nearly across it, until the reedy shore of the lake came in view through the openings between the trees. Here he again halted, and after a moment's reflection, dismounted.

Although the change of locality might make it more difficult for the brigands of Arroyo to discover his retreat, he was still not so certain of being free from danger. To render his situation more secure, he determined upon climbing into a tree, and concealing himself among the branches.

He had another motive for freeing himself. At a short distance from the spot he saw the horses of Costal and Clara, standing tied to some bushes; and he knew that their owners could not be far off. No doubt it was there they intended to go through their absurd rites; and all at once Don Cornelio had become inspired with a curiosity to witness them. His Christian conscience slightly reproached him, for thus assisting, as it were, at a pagan ceremony; but he ended by persuading himself that there would be something meritorious in his being a witness to the confusion of the infidel.

A tree near at hand offered him a favourable point of observation. From its higher branches he could command a full view of the lake and its shores to a considerable distance on each side of him, and also the sacred mountain in its midst.

Securing his horse below, he ascended the tree, and seated himself among its topmost branches. He had taken the precaution to carry up his carbine along with him, which was hanging from his shoulders upon its sling.

He had just fixed himself commodiously upon his perch, when the full moon appeared, at once lighting up the waters of the lake with her most brilliant beams.

He looked to discover the whereabouts of Costal and the negro; but for some time he could see nothing of either. The enchanted hill, glistening with a vitreous translucence under the white moonbeams, presented a wild, weird aspect; and, from time to time, strange unearthly sounds appeared to proceed from it, as also from the woods around.

The nerves of the ex-student were at no time of the strongest; and he had not long occupied his elevated post before he began to rue his rashness, in having trusted himself alone in a place which seemed to be the abode of the supernatural.

All at once a sound reached him, proceeding from the margin of the lake; and, turning his eyes in that direction, he beheld the figure of a naked man moving among the reeds. It was the same apparition that had caused such alarm among the domestics of Don Mariano, who, although unseen by the Captain, were at that moment only fifty paces distant, screened behind the bushes that grew around the glade in which they had encamped.

The apparition, although it at first startled Don Cornelio, did not frighten him so much as it had the domestics; for, by the light of the moon, he was enabled to recognise the figure as that of his attendant, Costal. The Captain, moreover, saw—what, from their position, was invisible to the people in Don Mariano's camp—another human figure, naked like the first, but differing from it in the colour of the skin, which was black as ebony.

Both having passed through the reeds, plunged at once into the open water of the lake; and, swimming off towards the enchanted mountain, were soon lost to the eyes of Don Cornelio, as well as to those of the affrighted attendants of Don Mariano.

While the latter remained under the full conviction that they had seen the Indian who, for five hundred years, had been vainly searching for his heart, Don Cornelio knew that the two adventurers were his own followers, Costal and Clara.

From the direction they had taken through the water, he divined that it was their object to reach the mountain island, there, no doubt, to practise their superstitious ceremonial.

Although somewhat disappointed at being deprived of a spectacle he had felt curious to witness, he still remained on his perch upon the tree. His apprehension of being pursued by the bandits of Arroyo had not yet forsaken him; and in such a contingency, he believed that he would be safer among the branches than upon the ground. He could watch for Costal and Clara coming back through the water, and then rejoin them as they returned to take possession of their horses, which were still visible to him upon his elevated post.

For a short time he remained in his position without hearing any noise in particular, or seeing anything calculated to alarm him. Then a sound reached his ears that came from a direction opposite to that in which lay the lake. It was a booming sound, like the report of a cannon—shortly after followed by another and another of precisely similar intonation.

Don Cornelio had no suspicion that at that very moment the hacienda of San Carlos was being attacked by the garrison of Del Valle, and that the noise he heard was the report of the howitzer battering in the gates of the building.

Although at first rendered uneasy by these inexplicable sounds, as they soon after ceased to be repeated, Don Cornelio no longer troubled himself to explain them. He had heard so many others, as mysterious as they, that he despaired of finding an explanation. As time passed, however, and neither Costal nor Clara showed themselves, the Captain began to feel a strong desire to sleep, and his eyelids every moment grew heavier, until at length he felt that could no longer resist the desire. Like Colonel Tres-Villas, on the preceding night, he took the precaution, before committing himself to slumber, of making secure against a fall; and for this purpose he attached himself with his sash to one of the branches. In another minute he was in the land of dreams, unconscious of the singularity of the couch on which he was reclining.

Chapter Seventy Five
The Goddess of the Waters

For the first hour the sleep of Don Cornèlio was undisturbed, even by dreams. With the second it was very different; for, scarcely had he entered upon it, when a noise sounded in his ears, singular as it was terrible. He awoke with a start, on hearing what appeared to be the loud clanging of a bell rung at no great distance off.

At first he fancied he was dreaming, and that what he heard in his dreams was the bell of his native village; but a moment's reflection sufficed to convince him that he was awake, and couched in the fork of a tall tree.

The sounds that had ceased for a while, now recommenced; and Don Cornelio was able to count twelve strokes, clear and distinctly measured, as if some large clock was tolling the hour of midnight!

It was, in fact, just about that hour—as Don Cornelio could tell by the moon; but the observation did not hinder him from shuddering afresh at the mysterious sounds. From his elevated position he could see afar over both land and water; but no spire of village church or hacienda was visible— nothing but the sombre surface of the lake, the spray of the far-stretching forest, and the desert plains in the distance.

The tolling again vibrated upon the air; and Don Cornelio was now convinced that it was from the lake itself, or the enchanted mountain in its midst, that the sounds proceeded. It seemed as if it was a signal, to awaken the Indian divinities from their sleep of ages!

The moon was still rising higher in the heavens, and her brilliant beams broadly illuminated the lake, even penetrating through the thickly-set stems of the reeds that bordered it.

Certain vague noises that had from time to time fallen upon the ear of Don Cornelio, while half slumbering, now that he was awake, were heard more distinctly; and after a little while these sounds became converted into prolonged and dismal howlings, such as he had never before heard in his life.

Upon just such another night he had been sorely frightened by the howling of jaguars; but all the tigers in the world could not have produced such a frightful noise as that with which his ears were now assailed. It was a chorus of voices entirely new to him, and that seemed to proceed from the powerful lungs of some gigantic creature hitherto unknown.

As thoughts of the supernatural came into his mind, the Captain shivered through his whole frame; and had he not been tied to its branches, he would certainly have fallen from the tree.

His horse, standing below, appeared fully to partake of his terror; for after dancing about, and causing the branches to crackle, the animal at length broke away from its fastenings, and, galloping off, joined company with the horses of Costal and Clara that stood nearer the edge of the water.

The terrible howlings, combined with the mysterious tolling of the bell, produced upon the mind of Don Cornelio other impressions besides those of mere dread. He began to believe in a supernatural presence; and that the sounds he heard were the voices of those pagan divinities whom Costal had the boldness to invoke.

Captain Lantejas was not the only person whom these strange noises had inspired with fear. At little more than gunshot distance from him, and hidden behind the trees, could be seen a number of men closely grouped together, and whispering their fears to one another. It need scarcely be said that they were the domestics of Don Mariano, who had counted with equal terror and astonishment the twelve strokes of the mysterious midnight bell.

Their master, too, had heard the tolling, and was vainly endeavouring to account for the singular phenomenon.

Just then the frightful howlings came pealing from the woods behind, awaking Gertrudis, and causing her to raise her head with a cry of terror. The seven sleepers themselves would have been awakened by such a terrible fracas of noises.

At this moment one of the domestics—Castrillo—appeared by the *litera*, his face blanched with affright.

"What misfortune have you to announce?" inquired Don Mariano, struck with the expression upon the servant's countenance.

"Not any, Señor Don Mariano," replied the domestic, "unless to say that we are here in some accursed place, and the sooner we get out of it the better."

"Get your arms ready," rejoined Don Mariano, "it must be the jaguars that are howling near us."

"Ah! Señor master," replied the domestic, with a shake of his head, "never did jaguar howl after that fashion; and all our weapons will be useless where the spirit of darkness is against us. Listen, there—again!"

Once more a series of prolonged vociferations came echoing through the forest, which certainly had but little resemblance to the voices either of jaguars or any other known animals.

"There have been many strange things during this night," gravely continued Castrillo. "Everything in nature seems to be turned upside down. Dead men have been seen by us wandering about; bells have been heard tolling where there is neither church nor dwelling, and now the devil himself is howling in the depths of the forest. Oh, master, let us fly from this place while we may!"

"But where to? where can we go?" rejoined Don Mariano, casting an anxious glance towards the *litera*. "My poor child—she can scarce endure the fatigues of the journey."

"Oh, father," said Gertrudis, "do not think of me. I shall be able to go on; and I would rather go afoot, than remain longer in this frightful place."

"Señor Don Mariano," continued the domestic, "if you will pray God to protect us from the danger that threatens, I and the others will go after the mules, and we shall get ready for marching. Above all, we must leave this place at once; for if you stay I could not hinder the rest from running away."

"Very well, then," said Don Mariano, "be it as you wish. Harness the animals and let us start at once. We shall endeavour to reach San Carlos."

That which Don Mariano and his people were about to make—a movement from the place apparently haunted—the Captain Lantejas would not have attempted for all the gold in Mexico. Glued by fear to the summit of his tree, and cursing the evil fortune that had conducted him thither—regretting, moreover, his foolish curiosity—he continued to listen, though almost mechanically, to what he believed to be a dialogue between some Indian divinity and his fearless worshipper, Costal.

All at once the noises came to a termination; and a profound silence succeeded, which was equally fearful to endure.

This was of short duration, however; for in a few moments the stillness of the night was once more interrupted by other and different noises, that resembled human voices uttered at a considerable distance from the spot.

Gradually the voices were heard approaching nearer, and Don Cornelio was under the impression that it was Costal and Clara returning to where they had left their horses. He was mistaken about this, however, and soon perceived his error. The voices proceeded from the direction he had himself followed in approaching the lake. Costal and Clara could not be coming that way. Moreover, he now saw lights that appeared to be torches carried by those who were talking; and from the rapidity with which the lights flitted from point to point, they could only be borne by men on horseback. The Indian and negro could not be mounted, since their horses were still standing tied where they had left them, along with his own steed, that had just taken refuge by their side. It could not be Costal and Clara who carried the torches.

"Who then?" mentally demanded Don Cornelio; "might it be Arroyo and his bandits?"

He had scarce given thought to the conjecture, when a troop of horsemen rode out upon the open ground near the edge of the lake; and two of them at the head of the others were instantly recognised by Don Cornelio. They were, in truth, Arroyo and his associate, Bocardo.

The horsemen carrying the torches were seen riding from one point to another, quartering the ground by numerous crossings, and exploring the thickets on every side, as if in search of some person that had escaped them.

On approaching the border of the lake, the horsemen turned off along the margin of reeds, without having perceived the three horses that stood under the trees.

The torches were now thrown away; and, riding off under the pale moonlight, the horsemen disappeared from the eyes of Don Cornelio.

He was not without uneasiness as to the peril in which his two companions would be placed, should they chance to fall once more into the hands of the bandits; and he would gladly have warned them of their danger, had he known how. But ignorant of the locality in which Costal and Clara were at that exact moment, he could do nothing more than hope that they might perceive the horsemen first, and conceal themselves while the latter were passing. From Costal's habitual wariness, Don Cornelio felt confident, that the ex-tiger-hunter would be able to keep himself clear of this new danger.

The captain followed with anxious eyes the forms of the retreating horsemen; and his heart beat more tranquilly when he saw them turn round an angle of the lake, and disappear altogether from his sight.

The moon at this moment shining more brilliantly, enabled him to command a better view of the waters of the lake, and the selvage of reeds growing around it. Once more silence was reigning over the scene, when all at once Don Cornelio fancied he saw a movement among the sedge, as if some one was making his way through it. In another instant a form, at first shadowy and indistinct, appeared before his eyes. Presently it assumed the outlines of a human form, and what astonished Don Cornelio still more, it was the form of a woman! This he saw distinctly; and perceived also that the woman was dressed in a sort of white garment, with long dark hair hanging in disordered tresses over her shoulders.

A cold perspiration broke out upon the brow of Don Cornelio, as the female form was recognised; and his eyes became fixed upon it, without his having the power to take them off. He doubted not that he saw before him the companion of Tlaloc, the terrible Matlacuezc, who had just risen from her watery palace in the Lake Ostuta, whence she had been summoned by the invocations of Costal, the descendant of the ancient rulers of Tehuantepec!

Chapter Seventy Six
Tolling the Summons

We return to Costal. We have seen the Zapoteque making his way through the sedge, and boldly launching himself into the muddy waters of the lake—his blind fatalism rendering him regardless of the voracious alligators of the Ostuta, as he had already shown himself of the sharks of the Pacific. Could the eye of Don Cornelio have followed him under the gloomy shadow which the enchanted hill projected over the lake, it would have seen him emerge from the water upon the shore of the sacred Cerro itself, his black-skinned associate closely following at his heels.

The mountain Monopostiac is neither more nor less than a gigantic rock of obsidian, of a dark greenish hue, having its flanks irregularly furrowed by vertical fissures and ridges. This peculiar kind of rock, under the sun, or in a very bright moonlight, gives forth a sort of dull translucence, resembling the reflection of glass. The vitreous glistening of its sides, taken in conjunction with the mass of thick white fog which usually robes the summit of the mountain, offers to the eye an àspect at once fantastic and melancholy.

At certain places, of which Costal had a perfect knowledge, are huge boulders of obsidian, resting along the declivities of the Cerro, and which, when struck by a hard substance, gives forth a sonorous ring, having some resemblance to the sound of a bell.

After climbing some way up the steep declivity of the mountain, Costal and his neophyte halted by one of these boulders. Now apparently absorbed in profound meditation, now muttering in a low tone, and in the language of his fathers, certain prayers, the Zapoteque awaited that hour when the moon should reach its meridian, in order to come to the grand crisis of his invocation.

It would be a tedious detail were we to describe the many absurd ceremonials practised by Costal to induce the genius of the waters to appear before him, and make known the means by which he might restore the ancient splendours of his race. Certainly, if perseverance and courage could have any influence with the Indian divinities, Costal deserved all the favours they could lavish upon him.

Although up to this moment neither Tlaloc nor Matlacuezc had given the least sign of having heard his prayers, his countenance exhibited such hopeful confidence, that Clara, gazing upon it, felt fully convinced that upon this occasion there was not the slightest chance of a failure.

Up to the time of the moon reaching her meridian—the moment so eagerly expected—more than an hour was spent in every sort of preparation for the grand crisis. Up to that moment, moreover, Costal had preserved a grave and profound silence, enjoining the same upon Clara. This silence related only to conversation between them. Otherwise Costal had from time to time, as already stated, given utterance to prayers, spoken, however, in a low muttered voice.

The moment had now arrived when the dialogue of the two acolytes was to be resumed.

"Clara," said the Zapoteque, speaking in a grave tone, "when the gods of my ancestors, invoked by a descendant of the ancient Caciques of Tehuantepec, who has seen fifty seasons of rains—when they hear the sounds which I am now about to make, and for which they have listened in vain for more than three centuries, some one of them will appear beyond any doubt."

"I hope so," responded Clara.

"Certain they will appear," said Costal; "but which of them it may be, I know not; whether Tlaloc or his companion Matlacuezc."

"I suppose it makes no difference," suggested the negro.

"Matlacuezc," continued Costal, "would be easily known. She is a goddess; and, of course, a female. She always appears in a white robe—pure and white as the blossom of the *floripondio*. When her hair is not wound around her head, it floats loosely over her shoulders, like the mantilla of a señora of high degree. Her eyes shine like two stars, and her voice is sweeter than that of the mocking-bird. For all that, her glance is terrifying to a mortal, and there are few who could bear it."

"Oh, I can bear it," said the negro; "no fear of that."

"Tlaloc," continued Costal, "is tall as a giant. His head is encircled with a chaplet of living serpents, that, entwined among his hair, keep up a constant hissing. His eye is full of fire, like that of the jaguar; and his voice resembles the roaring of an angry bull. Reflect, then, while it is yet time, whether you can bear such a sight as that."

"I have told you," replied Clara, in a resolute tone, "that I wish for gold; and it matters little to me whether Tlaloc or his wife shows me the *placer* where it is to be found. By all the gods, Christian and pagan! I have not come thus far to be frightened back without better reason than that. No!"

"You are firmly resolved, comrade? I see you are. Now, then—I shall proceed to invoke my gods."

On saying these words, the Indian took up a large stone, and advancing to the boulder of obsidian, struck the stone against one of its angles with all his might. The collision produced a sound resembling that of a brazen instrument; in fact, like the stroke of a bell.

Twelve times did Costal repeat the stroke, each time with equal force. The sounds echoed over the waters of the lake, and through the aisles of the forest on its shores; but their distant murmurings had scarce died upon the air, when a response came from the woods. This was given in a series of the most frightful howlings—the same which had terrified Captain Lantejas upon his tree, and which Don Mariano had found himself unable to explain.

Clara partook of a terror almost equal to that of Don Cornelio, but it arose from a different cause. He had no other belief, but that the howling thus heard was the response vouchsafed by the pagan gods to the invocation of his companion. After a moment his confidence became restored, and he signed to Costal to continue.

"Sound again!" said he, in a low but firm voice, "it is Tlaloc who has responded. Sound again!"

The Indian cast a glance upon his companion, to assure himself that he was in earnest. The moon showed his face of a greyish tint; but the expression of his features told that he spoke seriously.

"Bah!" exclaimed Costal, with a sneer, "are you so little skilled in the ways of the woods, as to mistake the voice of a vile animal for that of the gods of the Zapoteque?"

"What an animal to make a noise like that?" interrogated Clara, in a tone of surprise.

"Of course it is an animal," rejoined Costal, "that howls so. Sufficiently frightful, I admit—to those who do not know what sort of creature it is; but to those who do, it is nothing."

"What kind of animal is it?" demanded Clara.

"Why, an ape; what else? A poor devil of a monkey, that you could knock over with a bit of a stick; as easily as you could kill an opossum. Ah, *hombre*! the voice of the great Tlaloc is more terrible than that. But see! what have we yonder?"

As Costal spoke, he pointed to the shore of the lake whence they had come, and near the point where they had left their horses. It was in this direction, moreover, the howlings of the ape had been heard.

Clara followed the pointing of his companion, and both now saw what gave a sudden turn to their thoughts—a party of horsemen carrying torches, and scouring the selvage of the woods, as if in search of something they had lost.

The two worshippers watched until the torches were put out, and the horsemen passing round the shore disappeared under the shadows of a strip of forest.

Costal was about to resume his invocations; when, with his eyes still turned towards the point where the horsemen had left the shore of the lake, he beheld an apparition that caused even his intrepid heart to tremble. By the thicket of reeds, and close to the water's edge, a white form appeared suddenly, as if it had risen out of the lake. It was the same which had been seen by Don Cornelio from his perch upon the tree.

It was not fear that caused the Zapoteque to tremble. It was an emotion of exulting triumph.

"The time is come at last!" cried he, seizing the arm of his companion. "The glory of the Caciques of Tehuantepec is now to be restored. Look yonder!"

And as he spoke he pointed to the form, which, in the clear moonlight, could be distinguished as that of a woman, dressed in a robe as white as the *floripondio*, with long dark tresses floating over her shoulders like the mantilla of some grand señora.

"It is Matlacuezc," muttered the negro, in a low, anxious tone, and scarce able to conceal the terror with which the apparition had inspired him.

"Beyond doubt," hurriedly replied Costal, gliding down towards the water, followed by the negro.

On arriving at the beach, both plunged into the lake, and commenced swimming back towards the shore. Although the white form was no longer visible to them from their low position in the water, Don Cornelio could still see it glancing through the green stems of the reeds, but no longer in motion.

Costal had taken the bearings of the place before committing himself to the water; and, swimming with vigorous stroke, he soon reached the shore several lengths in advance of his companion.

Don Cornelio could see both of the adventurers as they swam back, and perceived, moreover, that the white form had been seen by them, and it was towards this object that Costal was steering his course. He saw the Indian approach close to it; and was filled with surprise at beholding him stretch forth his arms, as if to grasp the goddess of the waters, when all at once a loud voice sounded in his ears, crying out the words—

"Death to the murderer of Gaspacho!"

Along with the voice a light suddenly flashed up among the bushes, and the report of a carbine reverberated along the shores of the lake.

Costal and Clara were both seen to dive at the shot; and for a time Don Cornelio could not see either of them.

The white form had also sunk out of sight, but near the spot which it had occupied, the long reeds were seen to shake in a confused manner, as if some one was struggling in their midst.

Don Cornelio could hear their stems crackle with the motion; and he fancied that a low cry of agony proceeded from the spot; but the moment after all was silent; and the lake lay glistening under the pale silvery moonbeam, with nothing visible in its waters, or upon its shores, to break the tranquil stillness of its repose.

Chapter Seventy Seven
The Pursuit

Only for a very short interval did the shores of the lake Ostuta preserve their tranquil silence. In a few moments after the white robe had disappeared from the eyes of Don Cornelio, he saw Costal and Clara rise to the surface of the water, and make their way rapidly through the reeds in the direction of the bank. Presently both appeared on dry land at less than a hundred yards distance from where he was perched.

The tragedy of real life which he was now witnessing, had so suddenly mingled its scenes with the fancies that had just passed through his mind, that for an instant his thoughts were thrown into confusion, and he could scarcely distinguish the true from the fantastic. Though he saw that his faithful followers were still alive and well, the words he had heard, and the shot that succeeded them, told him that they were in danger. That could be no fancy; and its reality was further confirmed on his perceiving two men, sabre in hand, rush forth out of the bushes and make after Costal and Clara, with threatening cries and gestures.

The latter ran towards their horses. The sight of his two followers in flight, completely restored Don Cornelio's senses; and almost mechanically he caught hold of his carbine, which he had by his side.

Resting the barrel over a fork of the branches, he sighted one of the pursuers, and fired. At the report a bandit fell forward on his face, who, after sprawling a while upon the ground, lay motionless. The other halted and bent over his comrade to see if he was dead.

The delay caused by this unexpected interruption of the pursuit enabled the Indian and negro to reach their horses, and both, naked as they were, their skins glistening with the water of the lake, at once leaped into their saddles, wheeled their horses round, and galloped back towards the pursuers.

It was now Costal's turn to pursue.

The bandit who still kept his feet had stopped only a moment over his fallen companion: but that moment proved fatal to him. Before he could reach his own horse—which, in order to effect his ambuscade, he had left behind him in the woods—the avenging Zapoteque was upon him, who, galloping over, trampled him under his horse's hoofs, and then riding back, ran his long rapier through the prostrate body without dismounting from his saddle.

Meanwhile Don Cornelio had made all haste to descend from the tree; and hurrying forward called his followers by name.

"Ah! Señor Capitan," cried Costal, seeing him advance, "I am glad you are still on your feet. Seeing your horse along with ours I had fears that some misfortune had happened to you. Quick!" continued he, addressing himself to Clara, and leaping out of the saddle, "we must back to the lake at once, else Matlacuezc—. Señor Don Cornelio, you will be good enough to wait for us here. We have important matters on hand, and need to be alone."

At this moment, however, a new incident arose to interrupt the designs of Costal. Five horsemen, and a *litera* carried by mules, appeared suddenly in the open ground by the edge of the wood. It was Don Mariano with his domestics.

Having heard Don Cornelio pronounce the well-known names of two of his old servitors, the haciendado had advanced in the direction whence the voice proceeded, full of hope in this unexpected succour which heaven seemed to have sent to him. He had seen the party of brigands as they rode past with the torches; and his people had easily recognised their old fellow-servants, Arroyo and Bocardo. It was a relief to know that two more faithful than they—Costal and Clara—were in the same neighbourhood. He advanced, therefore, calling them by name, while he also pronounced the name of Lantejas—asking if it were the Don Cornelio Lantejas who had once been his guest at the hacienda of Las Palmas.

"Yes; certainly I am the same," replied the Captain, agreeably surprised at thus finding himself among friends in a place which, up to that moment, had appeared to him so melancholy and desolate.

Before any conversation could take place between Don Cornelio and his former host, an incident of a still more thrilling character was to be enacted on the scene. From behind the belt of the cedrela forest—into which Arroyo and his followers had ridden but a few minutes before—six horsemen were seen debouching at full gallop, as if riding for their lives; while close upon their heels came six others, who appeared straining after them in eager pursuit!

For a moment the six in front seemed to waver in their course—as if undecided as to what direction they should take. Only for a moment, however, and then heading their horses along the shore of the lake, they pressed on in wildest flight. Galloping at such a rapid pace they appeared not to see either the party of Don Mariano or Don Cornelio and his two followers—who on their part had scarce time to draw back into the bushes, ere the horsemen went sweeping past the spot like a cloud of dust.

Despite the rapidity of their course, however, the keen eye of Costal enabled him to distinguish among the horsemen two of his old fellow-servants of Las Palmas—Arroyo and Bocardo.

"We are on dangerous ground here, comrade," said he in a whisper to Clara. "It is Arroyo and Bocardo, pursued, no doubt, by the royalists. Whichever wins it is no good for us."

He had scarce finished his speech, when the six horsemen in pursuit passed the group, going at a pace not less rapid and furious than the others. One of the pursuers, of commanding figure, was several lengths ahead of the other five. Bent down almost to the level of his horse's neck, he appeared to be straining every muscle in the pursuit; and although his horse seemed rather to fly than gallop, the rider still kept urging him with the spur.

Clutching convulsively his broad-brimmed sombrero—which the rapid course had lifted from his head—he crushed it down over his brows in such a manner that his face was almost hidden by it. His horse at the same instant, whether frightened by the *litera* of Gertrudis, or by some other object, shied suddenly to one side—as he did so giving utterance to a strange snorting sound, which was responded to by a feeble cry from behind the curtains of the *litera*.

The cry was not heard by the horseman, who, absorbed with the pursuit of his enemy, passed on without turning his head.

Gertrudis was not the only one who trembled with emotion on recognising the snort of the steed. It brought vividly to the remembrance of Captain Lantejas the chase he had sustained on the plain of Huajapam—just before the powerful arm of Colonel Tres-Villas had lifted him out of his stirrups.

Neither could Don Mariano fail to recognise the peculiarity of a steed that he had so long kept in his stables; and as for the rider, the figure appeared to answer for that of Don Rafael. Could it indeed be he whom they believed to be at the siege of Huajapam? Don Mariano could scarce doubt that it was Colonel Tres-Villas who had ridden past.

"By all the devils in hell!" cried Costal, swearing like a pagan, as he was; "what has set the world mad on this particular night? What sends everybody this way, to interrupt the worshippers of the great Tlaloc?"

"True, it is damnably vexatious," rejoined Clara, who was equally chagrined at this sudden and unexpected intrusion, upon what he regarded as the only chance they might ever have of an interview with the gold-finding goddess.

Putting off their invocations to a more favourable opportunity, both Indian and negro now hastened away to dress and arm themselves, in order that they might be in readiness for any untoward event; while Don Cornelio stayed beside the haciendado and his party.

As yet uncertain how to act, Don Mariano thought it better to remain where he was, and await the result of an action which he could not regard otherwise than with anxiety. It is needless to say that the occupant of the *litera* listened with still more vivid emotion, mingled with deep apprehension, to the sounds that rung back along the shores of the lake.

The chase was soon too distant to be witnessed by the eye, but upon the still night air could be heard confused cries of terror and vengeance—which indicated to all that the pursuers were closing rapidly upon the pursued.

Chapter Seventy Eight
Vengeance Forborne

By a lucky accident Don Rafael, after leaving the hacienda of San Carlos, had ascertained that the bandit chieftains were no longer within its walls. He had also learnt the object that had carried them out—the same which was influencing himself, only from a far different motive. A renegade guerillero had made known to him the intentions of Arroyo in regard to Doña Marianita; and it is needless to say that the noble spirit of Don Rafael was, on hearing this report, only the more stimulated to overtake and destroy the bandit chieftain.

Guided by numerous signs—which the bandits, unsuspicious of being pursued, had left along their track—Don Rafael and his party found no difficulty in following them, almost at full speed. In less than an hour after leaving the hacienda, they had arrived within sight of Arroyo and his followers—still continuing the search for Doña Marianita, along the borders of the lake. The impetuosity of Don Rafael's vengeance had hindered him from using caution in his approach—else he might at once have come hand to hand with the detested enemy. As it was, he had advanced towards them into the open ground; and going at full gallop, under the clear moonlight, his party had been discovered by the bandits long before they could get within shot range. Arroyo, from whose thoughts the terrible Colonel was never for a moment absent, at once recognised him at the head of the approaching troop, and, giving the alarm to Bocardo—who equally dreaded an encounter with Don Rafael—the two brigands put spurs to their horses and rode off in dastardly flight. Of course they were followed by their four comrades, who, recalling the fate of Panchita Jolas, had no desire to risk the reception of a similar treatment.

The sight of that hated enemy—for whom Don Rafael had so long fruitlessly searched—stirred within him all the angry energies of his nature, and, involuntarily uttering a wild cry, he charged forward in pursuit.

At each moment the space between pursuers and pursued appeared to be diminishing, and Arroyo—notwithstanding a certain brute courage which he possessed while combating with other enemies—now felt his heart beating convulsively against his ribs as he perceived the probability of being overtaken by his dreaded pursuer.

For a moment there appeared a chance of his being able to save himself. The troopers of Don Rafael, not so well mounted as their chief, had fallen behind him several lengths of his horse; and had Arroyo at this moment faced about with his followers, they might have surrounded the Colonel, and attacked him all at once.

Arroyo even saw the opportunity; but terror had chased away his habitual presence of mind; and he permitted this last chance to escape him. He was influenced, perhaps, by his knowledge of the terrible prowess of his enemy; and despaired of being able to crush him in so short a time as would pass before his troopers could come up to his assistance.

The pursued party had now reached the eastern extremity of the lake. Before them stretched a vast plain, entirely destitute of timber or other covering. Only to the left appeared the outlines of a tract of chapparal, or low forest.

The bandits, on looking forward, saw at a glance that the open ground would give them no advantage. Their horses might be swifter than those of their pursuers, but this was doubtful; and from the snorting heard at intervals behind them, they knew that one at least was capable of overtaking them. The bright moonlight enabled the pursuers to keep them in view — almost as if it had been noonday; and on the broad, treeless savanna, no hiding-place could be found. Their only hope then lay in being able to reach the timber, and finding concealment within the depths of the forest jungle.

To accomplish this, however, it would be necessary for them to swerve to the left, which would give the pursuers an advantage; but there was no help for it, and Arroyo — whom fear had now rendered irresolute — rather mechanically than otherwise, turned towards the left, and headed for the chapparal.

Despite the fiery passions that agitated him, Don Rafael still preserved his presence of mind. Watching with keen glance every gesture of the bandits, he had anticipated this movement on their parts; and, even before they had obliqued to the left, he had himself forged farther out into the plain, with a view of cutting them off from the woods. On perceiving them change the direction of their flight, he had also swerved to the left; and was now riding in a parallel line, almost head for head with Arroyo and Bocardo; while the shadow of himself and his horse, far projected by the declining moon, fell ominously across their track.

In a few seconds more the snorting steed was in the advance, and his shadow fell in front of Arroyo. A sudden turn to the right brought Roncador within a spear's length of the bandit's horse, and the pursuit was at an end.

"*Carajo!*" cried Arroyo, with a fierce emphasis, at the same time discharging his pistol at the approaching pursuer.

But the bullet, ill-aimed, passed the head of Don Rafael without hitting; and the instant after, his horse, going at full speed, was projected impetuously against the flanks of that of the bandit, bringing both horse and rider to the ground.

Bocardo, unable to restrain his animal, was carried forward against his will; and now became between Don Rafael and his prostrate foe.

"Out of the way, vile wretch!" exclaimed Don Rafael, while with one blow of his sabre hilt, he knocked Bocardo from his saddle.

Arroyo, chilled with terror, and rendered almost senseless by the fall, his spurs holding him fast to the saddle, vainly struggled to regain his feet. Before he could free himself from his struggling horse, the troopers of Don Rafael had ridden up, and with drawn sabres halted over him; while his four followers, no longer regarded, continued their wild flight towards the chapparal.

Don Rafael now dismounted, and with his dagger held between his teeth, seized in both his hands the wrists of the bandit. In vain Arroyo struggled to free himself from that iron grasp; and in another moment he lay upon his back, the knee of Don Rafael pressing upon his breast—heavy as a rock that might have fallen from Monopostiac. The bandit, with his arms drawn crosswise, saw that resistance was vain; and yielding himself to despair he lay motionless—rage and fear strangely mingling in the expression of his features.

"Here!" cried Don Rafael, "some one tie this wretch!"

In the twinkling of an eye, one of the troopers wound his lazo eight or ten times around the arms and legs of the prostrate guerillero, and firmly bound them together.

"Now, then!" continued Don Rafael, "let him be attached to the tail of my horse!"

Notwithstanding the terrible acts of retaliation, which the royalist soldiers were accustomed to witness, after each victory on one side or the other, this order was executed in the midst of the most profound silence. They knew the fearful nature of the punishment about to be inflicted.

In a few seconds' time the end of the lazo, which bound the limbs of the brigand, was tightly looped around the tail of the horse; and Don Rafael had leaped back into his saddle.

Before using the spur, he cast behind him one last look of hatred upon the murderer of his father; while a smile of contempt upon his lips was the only reply which he vouchsafed to the assassin's appeal for mercy.

"Craven! you need not ask for life!" he said, after a time. "Antonio Valdez met his death in the same fashion, like yourself meanly begging for mercy. You shall do as he did. I promised it when I met you at the hacienda Las Palmas, and I shall now keep my word."

As Don Rafael finished speaking, his spurs were heard striking against the flanks of his horse, that, apparently dismayed at the awful purpose for which he was to be used, reared violently upon his hind legs, and refused to advance! At the same instant the bandit uttered a wild cry of agony, which resounded far over the lake, till it rang in echoes from the sides of the enchanted mountain. Like an echo, too, came the strange snorting from the nostrils of Roncador, who, at a second pricking of the spur, made one vast bound forward, and then suddenly stopped trembling and affrighted. The body of the bandit, suddenly jerked forward, had fallen back heavily to the earth, while groans of agony escaped from his quivering lips.

Just at this moment—this fearful crisis for the guerilla leader—two men were seen running towards the spot, and with all the speed that their legs were capable of making. It was evident that they were in search of Don Rafael with some message of great importance.

"A word with you, Colonel, in the name of God!" cried one of them, as soon as they were near enough to be heard. "For Heaven's sake do not ride off till we have spoken to you. My companion and I have had the worst of luck in trying to find you."

The man who spoke, and who had exhausted his last breath in the words, was no other than the veritable Juan el Zapote, while his companion was the honest Gaspar.

"Who are these men?" indignantly inquired Don Rafael. "Ah! it is you, my brave fellows?" continued he, softening down, as he recognised the two adventurers whom he had met in the forest, and whose advice had proved so advantageous to him. "What do you want with me? You see I am engaged at present, and have no time to attend to you?"

"True!" replied Juan el Zapote. "We see your honour is occupied; and that we have arrived at an inconvenient time! Ah! it is the Señor Arroyo with whom you are engaged! But your honour must know that we have a message for you, and have been running after you for twenty-four hours, without being able to deliver it. It is one of life and death."

"Mercy! mercy!" shrieked Arroyo, in a tone of piteous appeal.

"Hold your tongue, you stupid!" cried Juan el Zapote, reproachfully addressing his former chief. "Don't you see that the Colonel has business with us? You are hindering him from attending to it."

"A message of life and death!" repeated Don Rafael, his heart suddenly bounding with a triumphant hope. "From whom do you come?"

"Will your honour direct your people to step aside?" whispered Zapote. "It is a confidential mission with which we are charged—a love message," added he, in a still lower tone.

By a commanding gesture of the Colonel—for the communications of Zapote had deprived him of the power of speech—the troopers moved off to one side, and he was left alone with the messengers—to whom he now bent downwards from his saddle, in order that their words might not be heard.

What they said to him need not be repeated: enough to know that when their message was finally delivered it appeared to produce a magical effect upon the Colonel, who was heard to give utterance to a stifled cry of joy.

Holding by one hand the withers of his horse—which he appeared to need as a support to hinder him from falling out of his saddle—with the other he was observed to conceal something in the breast of his coat, apparently a packet which the messengers had handed to him. They, in their turn, were seen to bound joyfully over the ground at some word which Don Rafael had spoken to them, and which seemed to have produced on Zapote an effect resembling the dance of Saint Vitus.

In another moment the Colonel drew his dagger from its sheath, and called out in a voice loud enough to be heard by all:—"God does not will that this man should die. He has sent these men as the saviours of his life. I acknowledge the hand of God!"

And forgetting that he held in his power his most mortal foe, the murderer of his father—forgetting his oath, no more to be remembered amidst the delicious emotions that filled his heart—remembering only the promise of mercy he had made to Gertrudis, herself—he leant back over the croup of his saddle, and cut the lazo by which the brigand was attached to the tail of his horse.

Disdaining to listen to the outpouring of thanks which the craven wretch now lavished upon him, he turned once more towards the messengers.

"Where is she who sent you?" inquired he in a low voice.

"There!" answered Zapote, pointing to a group of horsemen who at that moment were seen advancing along the shore as the escort to a *litera* which appeared in their midst.

Roncador, freed from the human body, which attached to his tail had so frightened him, no longer refused to obey the spur; and in another moment he was bounding in the direction where the curtains of the *litera* of Gertrudis were seen undulating under the last rays of the waning moon.

Chapter Seventy Nine
A Brace of Crafty Couriers

It is necessary to explain the cause of Don Mariano's advance towards the spot.

From the place in which he and his party had taken their stand, they could witness most part of the pursuit, as well as the events that followed it; but so confusedly, that it was impossible to tell by the eye who were the victors, and who the vanquished. The ear gave them a better clue as to how the strife was turning; for the chase had not been carried on in silence.

So long as the shores of the lake at that especial point were cleared of people, it mattered little to Costal and Clara who should have the advantage. With Don Mariano the case was difficult.

Convinced by what he had seen, that the leader of the sanguinary pursuit could be no other than the Colonel Tres-Villas, whose life was now almost as precious to him as that of his own daughter—since hers depended upon it—he stood for a while absorbed in the most painful uncertainty. From the commencement of the drama he had, in fact, preserved a solemn silence—feeling that words could in no way relieve the anxiety of Gertrudis.

A vivid sentiment of curiosity had equally kept in silence Don Cornelio and his two followers, who at some paces from the *litera* stood listening.

Don Mariano was still ignorant of the fact that the hacienda of San Carlos had been captured and pillaged by the band of Arroyo. Had he known of this, and other events of a yet more horrid nature, his soul might have been harrowed by a far more agonising emotion than that of mere uncertainty; and perhaps he might have become an actor instead of spectator in the strife that was accruing.

As for Doña Gertrudis, she had easily distinguished that strange sound that issued from the nostrils of the well-known steed; and with her ear eagerly bent, she listened with mortal anguish to every breath that was borne back from the scene of the struggle.

Costal, who was impatient to return with Clara towards the spot where he had been so near capturing the white-robed Matlacuezc, was the first to break the prolonged silence.

"Whatever may be the result," said he, in hopes of inducing Don Mariano and his party to move away from the place, "the path is now clear for you, Señor Don Mariano. If it is to the hacienda of Las Palmas you are going, you will find the road both open and safe."

"We are not going to Las Palmas," answered Don Mariano, with an air of abstraction, at the same time advancing a few paces in order to have a better view of what was passing.

"If I were in your place," persisted Costal, in a significant tone, "I should go there. It is the safest route you can take, and let me assure you the moments are precious—Carrambo!" continued he, in an angry tone, and suddenly facing round, as the crackling of branches announced that some one was passing near through the thicket. "By all the serpents in the hair of Tlaloc, there are some more people in the woods. In the name of—"

The invoked deity was not mentioned, as just at that moment voices were heard where the bushes were in motion, and Costal interrupted his speech to listen. The words were—

"This way, *compadre*—this way! I hear over yonder the voice of the man we are in search of. Listen! that's the Colonel's voice to a certainty. Quick, by all the devils! Let us run at full speed, or we shall miss him, again."

The voice of this speaker was not known to any of those who had heard it, and he who was addressed as "*compadre*" appeared not to have made any reply. But the sound of their footsteps, and the swish of the recoiling branches, each moment became more indistinct, till at length the noises were lost in the distance.

It is scarcely necessary to say that the two men, who had thus passed so near, were the messengers so often disappointed, Gaspar and Juan el Zapote. As already known, they had been to the hacienda San Carlos, where they had learnt the direction taken by Don Rafael on leaving it. They had followed his tracks, which to Juan el Zapote, a skilled *rastreador*, was easy enough—especially in such a moonlight. They had even recognised Don Mariano and his party, on coming near the spot where the haciendado had halted; and for a moment Gaspar hesitated about going up to the group and reporting himself to his master, as he ought to have done.

From the performance of his duty he was dissuaded by his astute associate, who represented to him, that, in case of his reporting himself, Don Mariano might countermand the message he had sent to the Colonel, now that the latter was known to be on the ground. He might prefer delivering the precious talisman in *propria personâ*, and then where would be the bounty they had long expected, and for which they had more than once risked their necks?

These arguments prevailed even with the honest Gaspar; and to such an extent, that from this very motive he had declined to answer the speeches of Zapote, lest his voice might be recognised by Don Mariano, or some of his fellow-servants! Cautiously did the two make a détour through the trees, and so rapidly, that no one was likely to be able to intercept them, before they could reach the place to which the voice of the Colonel was guiding them.

As soon as the men had passed out of hearing, Costal and Clara, who saw that Don Mariano showed no sign of following their advice, exchanged glances of vexatious disappointment. The haciendado still kept his ground; and with his ear catching every sound, was vainly endeavouring to obtain a solution to the painful uncertainty that surrounded him.

The moon, about to sink behind the summit of the enchanted hill, cast oblique rays along the level shore of the lake. There he could make out a confused group of men and horses, some of the former dismounted and flinging long shadows over the plain. What was passing in the middle of this group? Some terrible scene, no doubt, was there being enacted—to judge from the hurried movements of the men, and the angry intonation of their voices.

At that moment a frightful cry rose upon the air, and, borne upon the still breeze, was distinctly heard by Don Mariano and the people around him. It was the agonised cry of a wretch begging for mercy. The voice even could be distinguished by Don Mariano, by Costal, by Clara, and the domestics. All knew it was the voice of Arroyo.

The cry was significant. Beyond doubt Don Rafael was the victor, and was now executing upon the murderer of his father the act of merciless justice he had promised before the walls of Las Palmas.

Don Mariano hesitated no longer; but, giving the order to his attendants, advanced towards the scene of vengeance.

Chapter Eighty
Matlacuezc a Mortal

The shores of the Lake Ostuta, hitherto so solitary and silent, appeared upon this night to have become a general rendezvous for all the world. The *litera* of Gertrudis had scarce moved from the spot which Don Mariano had chosen for his bivouac, when another *litera* was seen entering the glade, and moving onward through it. This, however, was borne by men, and preceded by some half-dozen Indian peons with blazing torches of *ocote* wood carried in their hands.

On reaching the shore of the lake, the second *litera* with its escort made halt, while the Indians bearing the torches commenced searching for something among the reeds.

Costal and Clara, instead of accompanying the party of Don Mariano, had remained upon the ground, in hopes that they would now be left free to continue their pagan incantations, and once more behold the Syren of the dishevelled hair. Don Cornelio also lingered behind, not caring just then to encounter the victorious royalists.

As soon as Costal perceived the approach of this new party—once more interrupting his designs—his fury became uncontrollable; and, making towards it on horseback, he snatched a torch from the hands of one of the Indians who were in advance, and then rode straight up to the *litera*. The apparition of a gaunt horseman with a torch in one hand, and a bloody sword in the other, his countenance expressing extreme rage, produced an instantaneous effect on the bearers of the *litera*. Without waiting to exchange a word, they dropped their burden to the ground, and ran back into the woods as fast as their legs could carry them.

A stifled cry came from the interior of the *litera*; while Don Cornelio, who had followed Costal, hastened to open the curtains. By the light of the torch which the Zapoteque still carried, they now saw stretched inside the body of a man, with a face wan, pallid, and stained with blood. Don Cornelio at once recognised the young Spaniard—the proprietor of the hacienda San Carlos—the victim of Arroyo's ferocity, and of the cupidity of his associate.

The dying man, on seeing Costal, cried out—

"Oh! do not harm me—I have not long to live."

Lantejas made signs for this Zapoteque to step aside; and bending over the *litera*, with kind and affectionate speeches endeavoured to calm the apprehensions of the unfortunate sufferer.

"Thanks! thanks!" murmured the latter, turning to Don Cornelio with a look of gratitude. "Ah, Señor!" continued he, in a supplicating tone, "perhaps you can tell me—have you seen anything of her?"

The interrogatory caused a new light to break upon him to whom it was addressed. He at once remembered the phantom which he had seen while approaching the hacienda; the white form that had vanished into the woods, and again the same apparition just seen among the reeds. Both, no doubt, were one and the same unfortunate creature. Twice, then, had he seen living, one whom the young Spaniard was never likely to see again, except as a corpse.

"I have seen no one," replied Don Cornelio, hesitating in his speech, and unwilling to make known his dread suspicions, "no one, except two brigands, who had hidden themselves in the thicket, and who are now—"

"Oh! Señor, for the love of God, search for her! She cannot be far from this place. I am speaking of my wife. We have found just now her silk scarf, and not far off this slipper. Both I know to be hers. She must have dropped, them in her flight. Oh! if I could only once more see her—embrace her—before I die!"

And so speaking the young man bent a look of suppliant anguish upon Don Cornelio, while exhibiting the two objects which his attendants had found upon the path, and which had served to guide them in their search.

Don Cornelio, unable longer to endure the painful interview, allowed the curtains of the *litera* to close over the wretched husband; and, stepping aside, rejoined the Zapoteque—who was still giving vent to his anger in strong and emphatic phraseology.

"Costal," said the Captain, "I fear very much that the wife of this young Spaniard is no longer alive. I saw a woman robed in white down there among the reeds, just as the brigand fired his carbine; and from what I saw afterwards, I am afraid that she must have been hit by the bullet. Surely it must have been her that they are now searching for."

"You are a fool!" cried Costal, in his ill-humour forgetting the respect due to his superior. "The woman you saw in white robes was no other than Matlacuezc, and I should have had her in my arms in another second of time but for that accursed coyote, who, by firing his carbine, caused her suddenly to disappear. Well! he has paid for his indiscretion: that's some comfort, but, for all that—"

"It is you who are a fool, you miserable heathen," said Don Cornelio, interrupting Costal in his turn. "The poor creature, who has no doubt been struck with the bullet, is no other than the wife of this young Spaniard! Do you hear that?"

This last interrogatory had relation to a cry that came up from the reeds, where the Indians with their torches were still continuing their search.

"Look yonder!" continued Don Cornelio, pointing to them, "they have stopped over the very spot, and that wail—that is significant."

As Don Cornelio spoke a chorus of lamentations came back upon the breeze, uttered by the Indian searchers. It was heard by the dying man in his *litera*, and apprised him of that which Don Cornelio would otherwise have attempted to conceal from him. It was now too late, however, and the Captain ran towards the *litera*, in hopes of offering some words of consolation.

"Dead! dead!" cried the young Spaniard, wringing his hands in mortal anguish. "Oh God! she is dead!"

"Let us hope not," faltered Don Cornelio; "these people may be mistaken."

"Oh! no, no! she is dead! I knew it; I had a presentiment of it! O merciful Saviour! dead, my Marianita dead!"

After a moment, becoming more calm, the dying man continued:—

"What better fate could I have wished for her? She has escaped dishonour at the hands of these pitiless brigands, and I am about to die myself. Yes, friend! death is now sweeter to me than life: for it will bring me to her whom I love more than myself."

And like those who, calmly dying, arrange everything as if for some ordinary ceremonial, the young man laid his head upon the pillow; and then stretching out his hands, composed the coverlet around him—leaving it open at one side, as if for the funereal couch of her whom he would never see more.

Don Cornelio, turning away from the painful spectacle, advanced towards the lake, making signs for Costal to follow him.

"Come this way," he said, "and you shall see how much truth there is in your pagan superstitions."

Costal made no objection: for he had already begun to mistrust the evidence of his own senses; and both proceeded together towards the spot where the torch-bearers had halted.

A white robe, torn by the thorns of the thicket, stained with blood, and bedraggled by the greenish scum of the water, enveloped the lifeless form of the young wife, whom the Indians had already deposited upon a couch of reeds. Some green leaves that hung over her head appeared to compose her last *parure*.

"She is beautiful as the Syren of the dishevelled hair," said Costal, as he stood gazing upon the prostrate form, "beautiful as Matlacuezc! Poor Don Mariano!" continued he, recognising the daughter of his old master, "he is far from suspecting that he has now only one child!"

Saying this the Indian walked away from the spot, his head drooping forward over his breast, and apparently absorbed in painful meditation.

"Well," said Don Cornelio, who had followed him, "do you still believe that you saw the spouse of your god Tlaloc?"

"I believe what my fathers have taught me to believe," replied Costal, in a tone of discouragement. "I believe that the descendant of the Caciques of Tehuantepec is not destined to restore the ancient glories of his race. Tlaloc, who dwells here, has forbidden it."

And saying this the Zapoteque relapsed into silence, and walked on with an air of gloomy abstraction that seemed to forbid all further conversation on the subject of his mythological creed.

Chapter Eighty One
Two Happy Hearts

We have arrived at the final scene of our drama. The shores of the Lake Ostuta, which in so short a space of time had witnessed so many stirring events, are once more to relapse into their gloomy and mournful silence.

Already Don Cornelio and his two companions have disappeared from the spot, and taken the road for Oajaca.

The funeral cortège is moving off towards the hacienda of San Carlos—the Indians who carry the bier marching in solemn silence. On that bier two corpses are laid side by side—the Spaniard Don Fernando de Lacarra by the side of his youthful wife.

Don Mariano, accompanied by his attendants—to whom have been added Caspar and Zapote—follows at a short distance; and still further behind, the troopers of Don Rafael form a rearguard closing up the procession. The most profound and solemn silence is observed by all: as if all were alike absorbed by one common sorrow.

This, however, is only apparent; for there are two individuals in that procession whose hearts are not a prey to grief. On the contrary, both are at this moment in the enjoyment of the most perfect felicity which it is permitted for mortals to experience upon earth. Both are now assured of a mutual love, tried by long tortures, and scarce too dearly bought, since the past anguish has resulted in such delicious ecstasy.

At nearly equal distances from the escort of Don Mariano and the troopers forming the rearguard, these two personages appear: one borne in her *litera*, the other mounted upon horseback, and riding alongside. It need not be told who is the occupant of the *litera*, nor who the tall horseman who, bending down from his saddle, whispers so softly and gently, that no one may hear his words, save her for whom they are intended.

Absorbed with this interchange of exquisite emotions, both are still strangers to the sad event that has occurred within the hour. Don Mariano, devouring his grief in silence, has left them ignorant of the terrible misfortune. God has been merciful to him in thus fortifying his soul against sorrow at the loss of one child, by permitting him to behold the unspeakable happiness of the other, who is thus preserved to him as an angel of consolation. He well knows the strong affection of Gertrudis for her sister, and fearing in her feeble state to announce the melancholy event, lest the shock would be too much for her, he has carefully concealed the sad news, until some opportunity may arise of preparing her to receive it. A few hours of the happiness she is now enjoying may strengthen her long-tortured spirit, and enable her to bear up against this new and unexpected sorrow.

Still riding by the side of the *litera*, his eyes fervently glancing through the half-open curtains, his ear close to them lest he might lose a single word that falls from the lips of Gertrudis, Don Rafael devours the sweet speeches addressed to him, with the avidity of the thirsty traveller who has reached the pure and limpid fountain, so eagerly yearned for on his long and weary route.

As the moon is now low in the sky, and gleams with an uncertain light through the curtains of the *litera*, Don Rafael can only trace indistinctly the features of Gertrudis. This half-obscurity, however, favours the young girl, concealing at the same time her happiness and confusion, both of which are betraying themselves in full blush upon her cheeks, hitherto so wan and pale.

Impelled by the strength of her love, from time to time she casts a furtive glance upon the face of her lover. It is a glance of strange significance; its object being to discover whether upon his features the tortures of long absence have not also left their imprint.

But the passion which Don Rafael has suffered under, although as incurable as her own, has left no other trace upon his countenance than that of a profound melancholy, and at the moment, his heart filled with exquisite happiness, all traces of this melancholy have disappeared. Gertrudis only looks upon a countenance that shows not a souvenir of suffering.

Don Rafael no longer doubts the love of Gertrudis. She has given him proofs no more to be questioned. But of his? What proof has he offered in return? Gertrudis cannot yet hinder herself from doubting!

The young girl endeavours to conceal the sigh which these thoughts have summoned up, and though the moon is still bright enough for her to perceive upon the countenance of Don Rafael an expression of the most loyal love, she cannot rest satisfied. Unable to restrain herself, again and again she repeats the interrogatory, "Do you still love me, Rafael?" Again and again she receives the same affirmative answer without being assured!

"Oh, it is too much happiness!" cries she, suddenly raising her head from the pillow, "I cannot believe it, Rafael. As for the sincerity of my words, you could not doubt them. The messenger has told you—plainly, has he not?—that I could not live without you? Then you came to me—yes, you have come," continues she, with a sigh that betokens the mingling of sorrow with her new-sprung joy; "but for all that, oh! Rafael, what can you say to me that will convince me you still love me?"

"What shall I say?" rejoins Don Rafael, repeating her words. "Only this, Gertrudis. I vowed to you that whenever I should receive this sacred message," at this drawing the tress from his bosom, and pressing it proudly to his lips, "I vowed that though my arm at the moment might be raised to strike my deadliest enemy, it should fall without inflicting the blow. I have come, Gertrudis—I am here!"

"You are generous, Rafael. I know that. You swore it! and—oh! my God; what do I hear?"

The interruption was caused by a wild cry that seemed to rise out of the earth close to the path which the procession was following. It seemed like the voice of some one in pain, and calling for deliverance or mercy. Gertrudis trembled with affright as she nestled closer within the curtains of the *litera*.

"Do not be alarmed," said Don Rafael; "it is nothing you need fear; only the voice of the monster Arroyo praying to be set free. He is lying over yonder upon the sand, bound hand and foot. He is still living; and to you, Gertrudis, does he owe his life. This assassin of my father—whom for two years I have pursued in vain—but a moment ago was about to receive death at my hands when your messenger arrived. I hesitated not, Gertrudis. It was but too much happiness to keep my oath. I cut the cords that attached him to the tail of my horse—in order that I should come to you the sooner."

Gertrudis, almost fainting, allowed her head to fall back upon the pillow; and as Don Rafael, frightened at the effect of his communication, bent closer to the *litera*, he heard murmured in a low voice, the sweet words—

"Your hand, Rafael! Oh! let me thank you for the happiness you have given me, a happiness that no words can describe."

And Don Rafael, his frame quivering with exquisite emotion, felt the soft pressure of her lips upon the hand which he had hastened to offer.

Then, as if abashed by this ardent avowal of her passion, the young girl suddenly closed the curtains of the *litera*, to enjoy in secret, and under the eye of God alone, that supreme felicity of knowing that she was beloved as she herself loved—a felicity that had, as it were, restored her life.

Like phantoms which have been called up by the imagination—like the unreal shadows in a dream, which one after another vanish out of sight—so the different personages in our drama, whose sufferings, whose loves, and whose combats we have witnessed, are all gradually disappearing from the scene where we have viewed them for the last time—Don Fernando and Marianita on their funereal bier; Gertrudis, in her *litera*, restored to new life; Don Rafael, Don Mariano, and his followers.

Don Cornelio, Costal, and Clara had already gone far from the spot; and soon the last horseman of the Colonel's escort, forming the rearguard of the procession, had filed through the belt of cedrela trees—leaving the Lake Ostuta apparently as deserted as if human footsteps had never strayed along its shores.

And yet this desertion was only apparent. Upon the edge of the lake at that point where the chase of the bandits had terminated, two human bodies might, be seen lying along the ground. One was dead; and the other, though still living, was equally motionless. The former was the corpse of Bocardo, who in the *mêlée* had been despatched by the troopers of Don Rafael. The living body was that of Arroyo, who, still bound hand and foot with the lazo, was unable to stir from the spot. There lay he with no one to pity—no one to lend a helping hand; destined at no distant time to make a meal for the vultures, to perish by the poignard of some royalist, or to excite the compassion of an insurgent.

The moon had disappeared below the horizon, and the vitreous transparence which her light had lent to the enchanted hill, giving it a semblance of life, was no more to be observed. The lake no longer glittered under the silvery beam. Both Ostuta and Monopostiac had resumed the sombre aspect that usually distinguished them, with that mournful tranquillity that habitually reigned over the spot—interrupted only by the cry of the coyote, or the shrill maniac scream of the eagle preparing to descend to the banquet of human flesh!